Precious Stones

 W9-ATG-436

Precious Stones

Darrien Lee

No Longer the Property of
New Castle County

www.urbanbooks.net

Urban Books, LLC
78 East Industry Court
Deer Park, NY 11729

Precious Stones Copyright © 2012 Darrien Lee

All rights reserved. No part of this book may be reproduced in any form or by any means without prior consent of the Publisher, except brief quotes used in reviews.

ISBN 13: 978-1-60162-349-2
ISBN 10: 1-60162-349-6

First Trade Paperback Printing June 2012
Printed in the United States of America

10 9 8 7 6 5 4 3 2 1

This is a work of fiction. Any references or similarities to actual events, real people, living, or dead, or to real locales are intended to give the novel a sense of reality. Any similarity in other names, characters, places, and incidents is entirely coincidental.

Distributed by Kensington Publishing Corp.
Submit Wholesale Orders to:
Kensington Publishing Corp.
C/O Penguin Group (USA) Inc.
Attention: Order Processing
405 Murray Hill Parkway
East Rutherford, NJ 07073-2316
Phone: 1-800-526-0275
Fax: 1-800-227-9604

Precious Stones

Darrien Lee

Prologue

Keilah woke up in a panic, gasping for air, which startled their German shepherd, Target, out of his sleep. He quickly came to her bedside and whimpered upon seeing her in distress.

She gently patted his head and said, "I'm okay, boy. It's just another bad dream."

Her sleep hadn't been disturbed by nightmares of her ex in a long time, but for some reason he had seeped into her subconscious tonight. Her husband, Ramsey, was in Atlanta on a business trip and wouldn't be returning until tomorrow, and their one-year old daughter, Neariah, was sleeping peacefully across the hallway. She glanced over at the clock, which read 1:45 A.M., and sighed. Needing to regroup, she slowly climbed out of bed, and with Target following close behind, she made her nightly routine trip across the hall to check on her daughter. Neariah was sound asleep but had kicked her blanket off her tiny body. Keilah pulled the blanket back over her sleeping child and quietly exited the room.

With a dry throat she descended the stairs and made her way into the kitchen to quench her thirst. Target decided to seize the opportunity for a cool drink of water as well while standing guard over his owner. Keilah walked over to the French doors and look out over their perfectly manicured yard and large pool. They lived in a gated community in an upscale section of D.C.

Being in the personal security business, Keilah and her husband took their privacy and security seriously. Their property was equipped with special sensors and cameras, but having Target around was an added bonus and he was a great companion, especially when Ramsey was out of town.

"Are you ready to go back to bed, boy?" Keilah whispered to Target before turning out the light.

That was when a perimeter alarm siren went off, startling her. Out the window she could see the strobe light flicker, indicating a breach of their property. She immediately picked up the telephone and called the neighborhood security officer who patrolled a couple of neighborhoods in the area. The officer made his way over to the Stones' residence, where he surveyed the property for possible intruders. After about thirty minutes he met Keilah at the front door and gave her the all clear.

"Mrs. Stone, I didn't find any evidence of a break-in or anything disturbed on your property. If anyone tried to get over your gate, they're long gone now. More than likely it was an animal. If you have any more problems, feel free to call me and I'll come right over."

"Thank you, Officer Blake. I really appreciate you getting over here so fast."

He smiled and said, "You're welcome."

Keilah waited until the officer exited her gate before reactivating her perimeter alarm. Feeling uneasy, she made her way back upstairs and moved Neariah's crib into her bedroom just as a precaution. It wasn't like her to be shaken from the alarm going off, but since she had become a wife and mother, a lot of things had changed.

Family had always been important to her since she grew up in California with four older brothers, who were more like fathers than brothers. They showered her with love and affection, and while she knew they meant well, their attentiveness sometimes turned into overprotectiveness. Now that she was grown and living in D.C., she didn't get to see them as often. That was why she had convinced her husband to volunteer their home for Thanksgiving dinner this year. She knew it was going to be an exhausting weekend, and she had only a week to prepare, but it would be worth it having everyone together under one roof.

Before climbing into bed, she pulled her 9 mm handgun out of the nightstand and slid it under Ramsey's pillow and prayed that sleep would come easily for her. As she closed her eyes, a vehicle slowly drove past the entrance to her driveway and then sped toward the expressway.

Chapter One

It was a cool fall morning as Keilah kissed her daughter good-bye. Camille, the Stones' nanny/housekeeper/chef/friend, had arrived, and after having a short conversation with Keilah, she had quickly taken the baby out of her mother's arms and placed her in the high chair so she could start her breakfast.

"Don't worry about a thing, Mrs. Stone. Neariah and I have a big day planned," Camille said as she kissed the baby's forehead. "We're going to the market to get some fresh vegetables and some other goodies so we can make a delicious dinner for you and Mr. Stone tonight."

Keilah picked her purse up off the countertop and said, "Camille, I told you to call us by our first names."

Camille waved her off and said, "It's difficult to do that, Mrs. Stone. As you young people say, I'm old school, but I'll try."

"Great," Keilah replied with a smile. "Besides, you're practically family, anyway."

Camille Harrison was an African American lady in her midsixties who was a retired schoolteacher. She'd come highly recommended by their friend Kyle Bradford, who worked in a high-level government office at the Pentagon. Camille had kept the small children of a high-ranking military officer for a few years, until he was relocated.

"Call me if you need anything," Keilah stated as she gave her daughter one more kiss. "Ramsey should be back in town this afternoon, so whatever you decide to cook for dinner, we'll love."

Camille followed her over to the door leading to the garage and basically pushed her out to door. "Okay. Now, get out of here, before you're late to work. You're in our way. Neariah and I have a lot to do today."

Keilah opened the garage door and then turned back to her nanny and said, "Before I leave, I don't want to alarm you and it's probably nothing, but the perimeter alarm went off early this morning. The security guard didn't find anything or anybody, but I wanted to mention it to you as a precaution."

Camille listened attentively and said, "I'm sure it was nothing, but I'll be extra attentive, anyway."

Keilah hugged her nanny's neck and said, "I knew you would. I'll see you this evening." She blew her daughter one more kiss before picking up her coffee cup and climbing into her car.

Driving in rush-hour traffic was never fun, and for some reason, this morning was worse than others. If it wasn't for her satellite radio playing smooth jazz, Keilah didn't know how she would make it. Then she thought about her unsettling night, and it angered her. Her child's safety came first, and she would die before she would let anyone or anything harm her.

At that moment, her cell phone rang. "Hello?"

"Keilah, this is Patrick Welch. I have a problem."

Keilah listened as one of her employees explained to her that his vehicle would not start and he was late meeting a client for an assignment. She looked at her watch and realized she didn't have time to replace him with another employee on such short notice, so she had to make a decision that her husband wasn't going to be happy about.

"I don't have my itinerary in front of me, Patrick. What is your assignment today?"

Patrick explained to his boss that his assignment was to accompany a model to New York on a day trip for some appointments. He was supposed to meet her at the airport and fly on a private jet owned by her modeling agency.

"Forward the itinerary to my phone so I can cover you until you can get to New York to relieve me."

"I will," he answered before apologizing again for the mishap.

Keilah and Ramsey told their agents to always make sure their private vehicles were in pristine condition, and if for some reason they had a situation like this, they had to have a backup plan in order to make sure they made it to their assignments. On this day, Patrick didn't, and he would have to be reprimanded for it later.

At the airport Keilah parked her car, texted the client that she would be there shortly, then hurried into the terminal building. She didn't get a response, which didn't surprise her. She wasn't dressed for running in her tailored navy suit and three-inch heels, and she hadn't planned to, anyway. If the client wasn't there when she arrived, she wouldn't be upset about it, but something told her the model would be there and would probably have an attitude because she was late. Most of them were like that.

"It's about time!" the model yelled at Keilah. "You're forty-five minutes late! What kind of business are you running?"

Keilah calmed herself before speaking, because the businesswoman in her was telling her to say one thing, but the hood in her was telling her to say something else.

"I'm sorry I'm late, but the agent assigned to you had some unexpected personal issues to attend to this morning, so I'll be accompanying you on your trip."

The model looked Keilah up and down and asked, "What kind of protection could you possibly be? You look like you weigh a hundred pounds wet!"

At that moment a male voice from behind Keilah interrupted them, and it was a voice she had never expected to hear.

"Chill out, baby," the man said as he walked over to the model and gave her a kiss. "You're in the best hands possible with Keilah Chance."

"Hello, Trenton," Keilah greeted as she held out her hand.

He walked over to her and gave her a hug instead. "It's been a while, huh?"

Trenton was Keilah's ex-boyfriend and a professor at Howard University. Since they had broken up, he had had several books hit the national best-sellers list. He had basically become an overnight sensation in the lit world and had recently got a part-time gig on BET, leaving him to teach at Howard on a part-time basis.

"You two know each other?" Chrisette asked with a scowl on her face.

"Yeah, we go way back," Trenton answered without offering Chrisette any more details.

"How do you two know each other?"

He clapped his hands together and said, "Let's just say we used to hang out in the same circle."

"Is that so? I thought maybe she was one of your students," Chrisette replied sarcastically.

He laughed and said, "She sure does look the part, but I can attest to you that she is definitely an adult."

Chrisette gave Keilah a nasty look and asked, "Can we please leave now? The Big Apple's waiting on me."

Keilah couldn't move for a moment, but once she got her legs to move, she followed them down the tunnel to a private jet. She hadn't seen Trenton in almost two years. Their breakup had left her bitter because he couldn't accept her career choice. What he wanted was to be the breadwinner and for her to be a housewife, but that wasn't who Keilah was and she wasn't going to change and live a miserable life. In the end it was Keilah's good fortune that Trenton ended their relationship, sending her right into Ramsey's arms and life.

On the plane Chrisette immediately entered the bathroom as Trenton took his seat across from Keilah.

"So, how have you been? How's your family?"

Keilah reluctantly answered, "Everyone's fine. Thanks for asking."

He smiled and then whispered, "I think about you all the time. I really hate how things ended between us."

"I really didn't have a say in the matter, now did I?" Keilah reminded him.

"Wow! I guess I deserve that," he admitted. "Keilah, you have to understand where I was then. I loved you dearly, but I wasn't used to a woman like you. I couldn't handle that life."

Keilah put her hand up to stop him from talking. "Trenton, I'm here on business, not to talk about our past. It's over and done with. Okay?"

He leaned forward and took her hands in his and said, "I don't mean to upset you by bringing this up, but I need to know if you're happy, Keilah. I mean, are you really happy?"

She pulled her hands away from him and said, "I've never been happier in my entire life."

He leaned back in his seat and was about to speak when Chrisette exited the restroom, interrupting his thought.

"What do you think about this dress, Trent? I'm thinking about wearing it to the first appointment."

"The dress is fine, babe," he answered, barely looking at her.

"I kind of like the red one better," she replied as she twirled around in the dress.

He ran his hands over his face with frustration and said, "Then wear the red one, Chrisette. You look great in everything you own. Just pick one."

Just then the pilot came over the intercom and instructed the passengers to buckle up and prepare for takeoff.

Chrisette leaned down and gave him a peck on the lips and said, "Thank you, sweetheart. I'll be right back."

Trenton grabbed Chrisette's wrist and pulled her down in the seat. "Sit down so we can take off."

"But I have another dress to try on," she told him, pouting.

"It'll have to wait," he replied as he discreetly stared at Keilah's shapely legs as they all sat back and prepared for takeoff.

In Atlanta, Ramsey tried calling his wife again as he finished up breakfast with some business acquaintances at the Omni Hotel. He had one more meeting to attend before finally catching a flight home to his family. Keilah's voice mail came on again, so this time he left her a loving message. It wasn't abnormal not to reach her on her cell, so he decided to call his office.

"The Stone-Chance Protection Agency. How may I direct your call?"

Ramsey recognized the voice of the receptionist on duty and spoke personally to her.

"Good morning, Tia. It's Ramsey. Transfer me to Keilah's office, please."

With a jubilant tone of voice, the receptionist said, "I would love to transfer you to Keilah's office, but she's not in yet."

Ramsey glanced down at his watch and tried not to get worried. "Okay, then transfer me to Cameron, please," he said.

Within seconds, Keilah's assistant, Cameron, picked up the line. "Good morning, Ramsey. Are you on your way back?"

"I will be shortly," he revealed. "Listen, Tia said Keilah wasn't in the office yet. I tried to reach her on her cell, but she's not answering. Is everything okay?"

Cameron could hear the tension in his voice. He had been Keilah's assistant for a long time and had witnessed the progression of their relationship. He knew when he had a fire to put out.

"Calm down, Ramsey. Keilah called me before Tia made it into the office. She's just fine," Cameron said to reassure him. "Unfortunately, she's on her way to New York."

"New York? What's in New York?"

Cameron hesitated before answering because he knew Ramsey was going to blow a gasket. "Patrick was supposed to escort a client there this morning, but he had car problems, so Keilah went in his place."

"Car problems?" Ramsey asked angrily. "Has he forgotten what our company guidelines are?"

"I'm sure he hasn't, but I don't know the details of his problem. For all I know, his car could've been vandalized or stolen."

"Call him and tell him he'd better be in my office by the time my plane hits the tarmac so we can have a one-on-one."

"I would if I could, but Keilah told him to fly to New York ASAP to relieve her as soon as he was able to get to the airport. The client she's with might decide to make it an overnight trip."

Ramsey's blood pressure went up a few more degrees, because he had made it clear to his wife that they were not field agents anymore, especially to Neariah. While he knew she wouldn't put herself in immediate danger, she was in a high-risk position anytime she was guarding a client.

"Did you clear Keilah's appointments for today?" he asked.

"Yes, she made sure everything was rescheduled or taken care of. Don't worry, Ramsey. I got this."

He laughed because Cameron was right. He and Keilah had two of the best assistants in the business, and they compensated them well for their efficiency and expertise.

"Okay. I'm getting ready to go to my last meeting, and then I'll be heading to the airport. If you talk to Keilah before I do, tell her to call me as soon as she can."

"I will," Cameron replied. "And don't worry. She'll be fine. Have a safe flight."

Ramsey hung up his cell and hurried off to his meeting.

The flight to New York seemed to be taking longer than Keilah had anticipated. It didn't help that Trenton kept staring at her seductively. Chrisette returned to the restroom to try on yet another outfit as soon as the pilot gave the all clear for them to relax.

Trenton started laughing, obviously irritating Keilah. "What's so funny?" she asked.

"I'm sorry. It's just that I never expected to have this type of emotional reaction upon seeing you again."

Keilah shifted in her seat and said, "You're full of it, Trenton."

He put his hand on her knee and, gently stroking it, said, "Have you forgotten how explosive we were together?"

With lightning speed, Keilah grabbed his wrist and twisted it, doing her best to break every bone possible.

"Damn, Keilah! That shit hurt!"

She pointed her finger at him and angrily said, "I meant for it to hurt. Don't you ever touch me! You lost that privilege a long time ago, so whatever fantasy you're sitting over there and having about us, forget about it."

"Just hear me out," he requested. "I know I was a fool for putting my male pride over my heart. You have a strong personality, and I now understand just how important your career is to you. I wasn't ready for your type of independence. I guess you could say I felt like my manhood was threatened, but I'm ready now," he revealed. "I still love you, Keilah, and I would love it if you would give us another chance."

Clearly pissed off, Keilah pointed toward the restroom and said, "You're a damn fool! How dare you step to me like this and your woman is in the next room?"

He chuckled and said, "Oh, you don't have to worry about Chrisette. We're just good friends."

"I don't care who the hell she is. I've moved on with my life, so I'm good. You need to do the same."

"Are you sure you won't . . ."

Keilah raised her left hand to display her wedding ring and said, "I'm married, Trenton, happily married, to be exact. I'm over you and have been for a long time."

"Married?" he whispered to himself in disappointment and disbelief as he laid his head against the back of his seat. He had been so busy looking at her legs and into her eyes, he hadn't noticed the huge diamond on her finger.

Chrisette exited the bathroom in a red Donna Karan dress that accentuated her long, magnificent legs and struck a model pose.

"Ta-da!" she yelled. "So what do you think?"

"It's nice, babe. You look great," Trenton replied with little enthusiasm.

Chrisette sat down next to him and gave him a seductive kiss on the lips. "Do you really like it?" she purred as she snuggled up to him.

He smiled and said, "Of course I do. You make the dress. The dress don't make you."

Pleased, Chrisette hugged his neck and gave him a longer, passionate kiss. "That's my baby," she whispered as she reached up and lovingly wiped her lipstick off his lips. She looked over at Keilah and asked, "Do you like my dress?"

"Yes, it's very pretty," Keilah answered as she stared at Trenton.

Chrisette laid her head on Trenton's shoulder and said, "I don't know why people like you risk your life doing the kind of work you do. You know you could be a model too, don't you?"

Keilah laughed.

"No, seriously," Chrisette responded. "You're very beautiful, and you have a fabulous figure. My agency would sign you in a heartbeat. You have that exotic look that a lot of the designers are looking for."

"Thanks, but I'm not interested. I'm happy just being a wife and mother."

"Okay, but I don't think you realize what you're turning down. You could travel all over the world, wear beautiful couture clothes, and make a lot of money."

"Like I said, I'm not interested," Keilah repeated before asking if she could get a bottle of water from the refrigerator.

"Leave it alone, Chrisette. Keilah's happy with her life, and money's the last thing she has to worry about. Her business and family are very successful," Trenton explained.

"Wow! Rich, brains, and beauty," Chrisette replied. "You can't go wrong with that."

"Passengers, we have been cleared for landing. Buckle your seat belts, and I'll have you on the ground very shortly," the pilot said over the intercom.

Keilah buckled her seat belt and prayed that Patrick was en route to New York to get her away from these clients. In the meantime she hoped that she had shut Trenton up for the remainder of the day.

Chapter Two

Ramsey entered the office around three in the after-noon, and his expression amplified his mood. It was obvious that he wasn't very happy with the events of the day and some heads would roll because of it.

He'd finally spoken with Keilah just before she boarded a plane back to D.C. Patrick had got a royal chewing out by Ramsey, who demanded that he report to the office first thing in the morning.

Making his way down the hallway to his office, he stopped at his assistant's desk.

"Hey, Sherrie. Do I have any messages?"

"Well, hello to you too," she replied as she passed a handful of messages to him. "I also sent them to you electronically, because you and I both know you're go-ing to misplace some of them."

He smiled and slowly made his way into his office. "You think you know me, don't you?"

"I do know you," she replied as she stood and fol-lowed him into his office. "Are you hungry? I can go out and pick something up for you if you'd like, or I can have something delivered to you."

He removed his jacket and sat down at his desk. "Thanks, but I'm only going to be here for a second. Ca-mille's cooking a big dinner tonight, and I don't want to ruin my appetite. You can go ahead and head out if you like. I shouldn't need you for anything else."

She watered his plants and asked, "Are you sure?"

He glanced up at her and smiled. "Yes. I'm sure your family would love for you to get home at a decent time for a change."

"You don't have to tell me twice," she replied before exiting the room. "Have a great evening, and go easy on Keilah when she comes home. She didn't do anything you wouldn't have done."

"Good night, Sherrie," he answered without commenting on her statement.

Giggling, she answered, "Good night, boss."

Finally alone with his thoughts, he leaned back in his chair and stared out over the beautiful skyline, anxiously waiting for his wife's plane to land. He would try to go easy on her, but he had to make her understand once and for all that their business was not worth her life.

At that moment his cell phone rang. "Hello?"

"Hey, sweetheart," Keilah said, greeting her husband. "Are you home?"

"Not yet. I stopped by the office first. Where are you?"

"I just landed, and I'm headed to the garage to get my car."

He let out a sigh of relief and said, "Good. I'll meet you at home. Drive safely."

"I will. I love you," she told him.

"I love you more. See you shortly," Ramsey said as he slid into his jacket and headed home.

Keilah couldn't be happier to finally be home. Traffic was terrible as usual, so it had taken her longer than normal to get home. She lowered the garage door and climbed out of her car. Inside, Target met her at the door, wagging his tail. She patted him on the head and entered the kitchen, where she found Camille putting the finishing touches on dinner.

"It smells wonderful in here!" Keilah said as she looked into a steaming pot.

Camille put her hands on Keilah's shoulders and directed her toward the hallway. "You can eat after you greet your husband."

"He beat me home?"

"Yes, he got here about fifteen minutes ago. He's up-stairs with his little princess."

"That figures," Keilah answered. "Thanks for cook-ing dinner for us."

"Oh, Keilah, you know I don't mind cooking for you and Ramsey. You're like my children."

Keilah gave her a kiss on the cheek and said, "You're the best. I'm going to run upstairs for a second. We'll be back down in a second."

"You haven't seen that man in a few days . . . Take your time, baby."

"If you insist," Keilah joked as she exited the kitchen.

Upstairs, Keilah found Neariah stretched out on the bed with her sippy cup. Target was in his usual spot, lying beside the bed, keeping a watchful eye over her. Keilah kicked off her shoes and climbed up on the bed next to Neariah and gave her a kiss.

"Hey, baby girl. Where's your daddy?"

Ramsey stepped out of their large walk-in closet and said, "I'm right here." Then he walked back into the closet.

Keilah's heart thumped in her chest. Seeing him standing there in his jeans and white T-shirt over-whelmed her and sent shivers down her body.

She gave Neariah another kiss before climbing off the bed. She walked into the closet, wrapped her arms around Ramsey's waist, and whispered, "Welcome home, baby."

He hugged her tight to his body and leaned down and gave her a long sultry kiss on the lips. "You taste good," he said as he showered her lips and neck with kisses.

"So do you," she replied as she nuzzled his neck.

"You do know you're in trouble for what you did this morning, don't you?"

She looked up into his eyes and batted her eyelashes. "I know. I'll let you spank me after dinner."

His large hands slowly eased under her skirt and gave her hips a sexy squeeze. Keilah's lower region immediately started aching from his touch.

"I don't think I can wait that long," he answered as he started unbuttoning her blouse.

She stepped out of his embrace and said, "Ramsey! Camille's downstairs, and our daughter is in our bedroom."

Ramsey took Keilah by the hand and walked back into their bedroom, where they found Neariah fast asleep.

Ramsey smiled, as it seemed that luck was on his side. He patted Keilah on her backside and said, "Put Neariah in her crib while I go say good-bye to Camille. We can reheat dinner later if we have to, but right now I want some loving."

Keilah picked Neariah up into her arms and whispered, "You think you're slick, Stone," as she quietly made her way across the hallway to the nursery.

"Stop tripping. You know you want it as much as I do," he said before disappearing downstairs.

After putting Neariah down in her crib, Keilah hurried into her bathroom for a quick shower so she could wash the scent of New York off her body. After quickly rubbing suds over her body, she felt a breeze of cool air and turned to find Ramsey entering their large shower. Before she could say a word, he covered her mouth with his and pushed her wet body against the wall. She moaned as she savored the warmth of his hands and mouth all over her body. Seconds later, they were on the tile floor of the shower and Ramsey's tongue and lips were electrifying sensitive spots she was unaware of as the hot water rained down on their bodies. Keilah was trying her best to stay composed, but her husband was making it difficult.

She lost all resolve when he dipped his head between her thighs, causing her to cry out in ecstasy. His sensual assault sent electrifying chills over her body as his tongue toyed with her feminine nub. Her body felt like it was on fire and was paralyzed under his spell. The echo of her sighs and soft moans sent shock waves through his body, making him unable to resist the main course any longer. He eased his throbbing maleness into her heated cavity and gently ground his hips against hers.

"Ramsey," she purred in his ear.

"You feel so good, baby. I missed you so much," he whispered back to her.

"I missed you too," she replied as they held on to each other for what seemed like an eternity. Their bodies moved in complete unison as they became one. She never wanted to leave his arms and couldn't imagine herself with anyone else. At that moment Ramsey felt his body peaking, which caused him to intensify his pace. With each thrust, Keilah let out a soft whimper or a loud moan, and a short time later, Ramsey's release erupted long and hard, causing him to groan and call out her name.

Exhausted, he collapsed on top of her, softly kissing her lips and breasts and stomach. Her man had given her undeniable love, and she savored it as the hot water continued to shower down on them.

"I can't move," she said after minutes had passed.

He smiled and slowly stood, pulling her up into his arms. He picked up the shower gel and slowly caressed her body, generating a handful of suds. Keilah returned the favor, and they bathed each other in silence before finally exiting the shower. Once dressed, they looked in on Neariah, who was lying quietly in her crib, playing with her feet. When she looked up and saw her parents, she started to cry.

Keilah picked her up and said, "Don't start, li'l lady. You were fine until you realized we were in the room."

"Do you want me to take her?" Ramsey asked as he hugged Keilah from behind and kissed her shoulder.

"No, I got it," she answered as she laid Neariah on the changing table. "You can go warm up dinner while I change her diaper. We'll be right down."

"Okay. Don't be long."

Keilah quickly put a dry diaper on Neariah and carried her downstairs to the dining room.

Dinner was delicious, as expected. Camille was an excellent cook, and the steak was so tender, they didn't have to use a knife. The steamed asparagus was seasoned to perfection, and the potatoes were fluffy and buttery. While they prepared their plates, Keilah told Ramsey about the perimeter alarm going off the night before and how uneasy she'd felt afterward. He assured her that he'd made sure they had the best security system on the market and that if someone was stupid enough to try and invade their home, he welcomed them, because he would put a couple of shotgun blasts in them by way of greeting.

Feeling safer already, she gave his hand a squeeze to thank him for the reassurance. Neariah began to whine, so Keilah gave her a spoonful of potatoes.

"Now, tell me about New York," Ramsey said.

Keilah gave Neariah another spoonful of potatoes and said, "It was crazy. You're not going to believe who was on the plane."

"Who?" Ramsey asked before eating a piece of steak.

"Trenton."

Ramsey looked at her in disbelief and asked, "Your ex?"

She rolled her eyes and nodded.

"Why was *he* on the plane? Was he the client?" Ramsey asked.

"No, he was with his supermodel girlfriend. Her agency sent a private plane to pick her up for some appointments in New York."

"Interesting."

"Torture was more like it!" she replied.

"I'm sure he had something suave to say, huh?" Ramsey asked.

"Every chance he could," she answered as she jabbed her fork into her steamed asparagus. "He had the nerve to ask me to give him a second chance while his girl was in the restroom."

"Does he know about us?"

Being honest, she said, "He knows I'm married and have a daughter, but he doesn't know I'm married to you. I nearly broke his damn wrist when he touched my leg."

"Touched your leg?" Ramsey yelled as a vein in his neck started to pulsate. "What do you mean, touched your leg? He put his hands on you?"

Keilah noticed the bulging vein and smiled. "Sweetheart, you don't have anything to worry about. Believe me, I handled him. His wrist will be bruised and sore for a few days."

Ramsey smiled and relaxed. It surprised him sometimes just how physically strong his wife was for her size. She was definitely all woman, and she was his woman. What he liked most was that she was soft in all the right places and firm exactly where she needed to be. Having a child hadn't stolen any of her feminine assets, and her muscles and strength were concealed by her beauty, making her a perfect agent and the reason they became business partners in the first place.

"He's not going to sue us, is he?" Ramsey joked.

She looked at her husband with seriousness in her eyes and said, "He knows better. Had that flight been any longer, I would've thrown his ass right out of the plane."

"I can't believe he was coming on to you with his girl right there."

"Her Royal Highness was in the bathroom most of the time, trying on dresses. I couldn't wait for Patrick to get to New York to relieve me."

"Do you think you're going to have any more problems out of him?"

She looked at her husband's concerned face and said, "No, sweetheart. I made my stance very clear to him. That's why he's probably wearing a brace on his wrist as a reminder."

He took a sip of wine and said, "Good, because I would hate to put that pretty boy in the hospital for disrespecting my wife."

Keilah laughed because Ramsey had always called Trenton a pretty boy when she was dating him. He had a light complexion, light brown eyes, and wavy hair. Not to mention a nice physique, and a debonair personality to go along with it.

Seconds later the doorbell rang, causing Target to run to the front door, barking viciously.

"Are you expecting anyone?" Ramsey asked with a frown as he got up from the table.

"No. You know how I hate people popping in."

Ramsey made his way down the hallway to the front door. Target continued to bark and jumped at the door as Ramsey opened it to find his brother-in-law Malachi standing on the porch.

"Happy Thanksgiving!" he yelled out as Ramsey opened the door wider to let him in.

Ramsey gave him a brotherly hug and asked, "What the hell are you doing here? Thanksgiving's next week."

"I know, but I needed a break from California and I missed my two favorite girls, so I decided to come early," Malachi replied as he started rough playing with Target.

"Who is it?" Keilah asked as she rounded the corner with Neariah on her hip.

"Hey, sis," Malachi said, greeting her with a loving hug and a kiss before taking Neariah out of her arms. "Why is your hair wet?"

"Don't worry about my hair. What are you doing here?" she asked, clearly agitated. "And why didn't you call to let us know you were coming?"

After kissing Neariah again, Malachi asked, "Since when do I have to call to visit you guys?"

"Do you show up at everyone's house unannounced?" she asked.

Malachi ignored her and continued to love on his niece.

"I'm not a little girl anymore, Malachi. Respect my house!" Keilah said as she rolled her eyes and disappeared down the hallway.

"Well, damn. I'm happy to see you too, sis!" he yelled out to her.

Ramsey scratched his chin and then grabbed Malachi's suitcase. As they headed for the grand staircase, he turned to his brother-in-law and said, "You know she's right. It's just common courtesy to call people before you show up on their doorstep. We travel a lot, which means you never know when we're going to be here. I've been in Atlanta the past few days and just got home today."

Malachi stopped on the landing and said, "I can leave if this is going to be a problem."

"Don't be an idiot," Ramsey answered as they entered the guess bedroom. He sat the suitcase on the floor and turned on the lamp. "You're family, so it's cool . . . this time."

"My sister's not acting like she's cool," Malachi replied as he sat down and bounced Neariah on his knee.

"She'll be fine. Keilah loves you. Just make sure you call next time."

Neariah giggled loudly as she grabbed a fistful of Malachi's dreadlocks. He gently pulled his hair out of her grasp and said, "I will, and I'm sorry if I ruined your homecoming."

With a sly grin on his face, Ramsey said, "You can't ruin my homecoming, bro, but I do accept your apology. Now, hand me my daughter. After you wash up, bring your ass downstairs so you can get some dinner."

"Sounds good," Malachi answered as he opened his suitcase. "Save me a chicken leg or whatever you have down there."

After washing his hands and freshening up a bit, Malachi joined his sister and Ramsey at the table. He took a seat across from Keilah and poured himself a glass of wine. He took a sip and said, "This is good. What is it?"

Ramsey said, "You're the connoisseur of wine. You tell me."

Malachi turned the bottle around and saw that it was a three-hundred-dollar bottle of 2008 Far Niente Estate Cabernet Sauvignon.

"Not bad, brother-in-law. It's a good pick."

Ramsey proudly pointed at Keilah. "Praise my wife. She picked it out, not me."

With a huge grin on his face, Malachi looked over at his sister and said, "I see I taught you well."

Malachi was a serious wine collector, even though he didn't look the part. He looked more like a hip-hop artist with his dreadlocks and flashy attire. He had a very impressive wine cellar, which consisted of several types of wine in a wide price range. He even had some bottles that cost thousands of dollars. Over the years, his love of wine had rubbed off on Keilah, and she had become somewhat of a collector herself.

Keilah gave Neariah a piece of steak and said, "Whether you believe it or not, I do listen to you when you're try to teach me things, especially about wine."

"That's good," Malachi said with smile of admiration. "By the way, this food looks delicious. Did you cook it?"

"No, Camille did," she answered as she added more vegetables to her plate.

Malachi took a bite of the steak and said, "Damn! She grills almost as good as I do. It's tender and seasoned just right."

"She's a great cook," Keilah said before changing the subject. "What's going on, Malachi? I mean, seriously, why are you here a week earlier than everyone else? Is there something you're not telling me? Is everything okay back home?"

Malachi put his fork down and smiled. "Everything's cool. I needed a break, that's all. You know it can be hard sometimes being around family all the time. I love my brothers, but damn! They can get on my last nerve. Besides, I wanted to spend some time with you guys before everybody else got here. You do know it's going to be crazy, right?"

"It's not going to be crazy, because if you and Keytone start tripping, I'm going to shut it down with the quickness," Keilah retorted.

"Why are you singling us out?" Malachi asked.

"Because it's always you two, that's why. Everyone else gets along just fine."

Keilah was the only girl and the baby in her family. Her brothers, Luke, Roman, Malachi, and Genesis, had basically raised her after their parents died. Her half brother, Keytone, was the same age as her oldest brother, Luke. He had a shady past, and it had been difficult for the brothers to accept him into the family dynasty, but he had changed his ways and had been a great manager at one of the family-owned casinos.

Ramsey laughed and asked, "Babe, how are you going to shut down Thanksgiving?"

She looked at her husband in disbelief. He had seen her family in action and was well aware of how quickly things could get out of hand with them.

"Ramsey, I know you're not going to sit there and act like you don't know how stupid they get," Keilah said.

Ramsey laughed again. "I know they can get a little passionate about things—hell, I can too—but you can't cancel Thanksgiving, so this is how it's going to go down. . . . We're going to fellowship as a family, give thanks to God, and enjoy some of Sabrinia's delicious cooking."

Sabrinia was Luke's wife and a well-known professional chef who owned her own catering business. She often volunteered to cook for family functions, including Thanksgiving.

"Okay, if you say so," she replied. "By the way, when are your parents and the rest of the family coming?"

"They'll be here Tuesday, and my brother and sister will be here Wednesday."

She rubbed her eyes and asked, "Where are we going to put everyone?"

"You don't have to worry about me. I've already booked my room at the St. Regis, because I might hook up with somebody," Malachi revealed.

Ramsey gave Malachi a high five and said, "I ain't mad at you, bro. A man needs his privacy when he's entertaining the ladies."

"Please! Can we get back to the sleeping arrangements?" Keilah asked as she rolled her eyes. It didn't take much to get Malachi talking about hooking up with women.

With a huge smile on his face, Ramsey said, "Okay, we have six bedrooms, so we can move Neariah's crib into our room and my parents can sleep in Neariah's room."

"Your mom is not going to let us take Neariah out of her room. They have some spoiling to catch up on," Keilah reminded him.

"Well, whatever they want to do is fine with me," said Ramsey. "Then Aunt Judy can have a guest room, and so can Luke and Sabrinia. Their kids are going to spend all their time in the theater and game rooms, anyway, so they will sleep wherever. That leaves two more rooms. I say let Roman and his wife have one and let my sister, Xenia, and her husband, Keith, have the other. Roman's kids will camp out with the teenagers downstairs. The rest can get rooms at the St. Regis with

Malachi. What do y'all think about that?"

"Sounds good to me," Malachi replied.

Keilah nodded in agreement and informed her brother that he had the task of reserving rooms at the hotel and calling everyone to let them know about the arrangements.

"Me? Why me?"

She picked up Neariah's cup. As she headed toward the kitchen, she said, "You show up a week early, you're going to have to work, and that's your first task."

Malachi looked over at Ramsey, hoping to find an ally, but he was mistaken. Ramsey threw up his hands and said, "Sorry, bro. I can't help you. The boss has spoken."

Keilah returned to the table with the cup refilled for her daughter, who quickly turned it up. "How's business?" she asked as she sat down.

Malachi finished off his second glass of wine and said, "The casinos are doing great, especially the Special K, but it's hard working with Keytone."

The Special K was the family's second casino, named in honor of Keilah since she was the brothers' only sister. Their other casino, the Lucky Chance, had been a huge success for the family as well, but it had experienced its ups and downs as the Chance men worked hard to continue running their late father's legacy.

"I know it can be hard working with family, but Keytone is our brother, whether you like it or not. You're going to have to figure out a way to get his past out of your system. He did save your life, remember?"

Malachi lowered his head and remembered when the head of a gang kidnapped him and his brothers—with the help of their trusted attorney, who had betrayed them—and held them hostage until they signed over their rights to their casino. They were freed only after

Keilah, Ramsey, and Keytone rescued them in a huge shoot-out that left the gang leader and his entourage dead and the brothers free.

"You don't have to remind me. I know he had a little bit to do with that, but you guys were there too."

Keilah yelled, "Just face it, Malachi! He's our brother. Accept it and respect him."

Ramsey interrupted the pair, trying to bring peace to his household. "Listen, Malachi, I know it's hard working with family sometimes, but Keilah's right on this one."

Keilah turned to Ramsey and asked, "Babe, are you saying I'm difficult to work with?"

Ramsey reached over to his wife and took her hand and kissed it. "No, sweetheart, I love working with you. I'm just saying it can be stressful. You're my wife, so if anyone disrespects you, the husband in me will come out a lot faster than the business partner."

Neariah squealed to get some attention. Malachi reached over and gave Neariah a tender piece steak.

"With my situation it's a little different. It's harder to run a business with family when all we seem to do is agree to disagree," Malachi said.

"You must be doing something right," Ramsey replied. "You guys have two very successful businesses. To keep your sanity, take more vacations. Otherwise, you'll burn out."

Keilah stood and picked up her empty plate. As she walked toward the kitchen, she said, "Yes, Malachi, take more vacations. Just make sure it's far away from D.C."

Malachi leaned back in his chair and yelled, "Why you got to be so damn mean, Keilah?"

She walked back into the room and said, "I'm not being mean. I'm keeping it real."

Feeling he needed to put the subject to rest once and for all, Ramsey jumped into the conversation. "That's enough, Keilah. Cut Malachi some slack. He's your brother, and family is always welcome here. Stop giving him a hard time, because you know you miss them as much as they miss you."

Ramsey then turned to Malachi. "Now for you, Keilah just wants to be treated as an adult and with respect. You're welcome here anytime as long as you call first. Are we clear on the rules of visiting?"

Malachi held his wineglass out to his brother-in-law and his sister and said, "Crystal clear and, sis, I'm sorry if I overstepped my boundaries. It's hard for me to accept you being all grown up, but I'm going to work on it. Okay?"

Keilah climbed out of her chair and walked around the table and hugged her brother's neck. She gave him a kiss on the cheek and said, "That's all I want. Thank you."

The three of them touched their wineglasses together, and with that, the issue was resolved.

Major Michael Monroe stepped off the plane at Andrews Air Force Base in full dress uniform. He stopped to take in a breath of fresh air and said, "It's good to be home."

The two military personnel accompanying him said, "I'm sure it is, sir."

Major Monroe had been missing in action in Iraq for over a year, with his fate unknown to his family and his unit, until he was found in a house by patrolling units in Baghdad . He also happened to be the main character in Keilah's nightmares ever since they'd broken up a little over a year ago. Being in Iraq had given him a lot of time to think things over. Now he was back, and he had some unfinished business that he needed to take care of, but first things first. Michael and his entourage entered a government vehicle, which quickly drove them in the direction of the Pentagon.

Inside the shiny halls of the Department of Defense, Major Monroe took a seat in an office and prepared himself for his debriefing and his recounting of what was a remarkable story of survival.

Chapter Three

It was nearly eight o'clock in the evening when the doorbell rang once again at the Stone residence. Malachi and Ramsey were watching a football game in the theater room. Keilah was upstairs giving Neariah her bedtime bath, unaware that their friend Kyle Bradford had called, needing to speak with them, and had conversed briefly with Ramsey. Ramsey had picked up on the urgency in Kyle's tone of voice, so he invited him over and decided to keep the phone call to himself until he found out what was really going on. Kyle worked at the Pentagon, and not only did he hold a prestigious position, but he was also one of D.C's most eligible bachelors.

Shaking Kyle's hand after letting him in the house, Ramsey said, "I thought you were out of town."

Following Ramsey into his office, Kyle said, "I got back this morning."

Ramsey closed the door to his office to give them some privacy.

Kyle sat down across from Ramsey's desk and asked, "Where's Keilah?"

"Upstairs, giving Neariah a bath," Ramsey answered. "What's going on? Because this doesn't feel like a social visit."

Kyle leaned forward and said, "I wanted to talk to you guys before this hits the media."

"What?" Ramsey asked with concern.

"Some of what I'm about to tell you is classified, so you know you can't repeat it outside the house."

"You know I understand the rules," Ramsey assured him.

Kyle took a deep breath and then said, "Major Michael Monroe has resurfaced. A unit found him in a house with an Iraqi family. According to him, his Humvee was ambushed by insurgents and he was the only one who survived. He was held prisoner for the past year. He said they moved him around from house to house to try and stay ahead of the American troops."

"You're kidding, right?" Ramsey asked, even though he knew Kyle would not kid about something of this magnitude.

"No, I'm not kidding. I saw him with my own eyes. He looked remarkable well, considering what he's gone through. He still has a lot more debriefing to go through, and he has to have a psych exam too. I'm sure he went through hell over there. Sources said he'll probably need therapy for a while. I don't know what state of mind he's in, but I'll see what I can find out."

Ramsey rubbed his chin in silence. "Do you think he's still fixated on Keilah?"

"I have no way of knowing. You know the doctor-patient confidentiality guidelines."

"What happens next?" Ramsey asked.

"You know the drill," Kyle reminded his friend. "If everything checks out, he'll probably retain his rank and maybe even get a promotion. If he's smart, he'll go ahead and retire. Whatever he does, Homeland Security is going to be interested in his story. Who knows what kind of intelligence he brought back with him."

"That's some bullshit," Ramsey mumbled.

"I agree, but you know how this works. There will probably be some interviews with the national media, so Keilah needs to know he's back. I remember you talking about those bad dreams she had after he disappeared."

Ramsey walked over to the window and looked out over the lawn and said, "Yeah, for some reason she had it in her mind that he was going to try and take Neariah from us."

Ramsey stood there in deep thought as he recalled how Keilah had dated Michael Monroe for a short period of time. He had even asked her to marry him. Fortunately, she was able to see him for what he really was when she caught him in bed with his male lover. Hurt and angry, she couldn't understand why he had taken her down that dangerous path, so she interrogated him to get the reason behind his actions. He admitted to honestly loving her, but he was bisexual, and eventually he revealed that he wanted to marry her only to have a child. His plan was to marry her, ultimately file for divorce, and sue her for custody of the child. This admission sent Keilah over the edge. With every fiber in her body she wanted to kill him, but she shot him in the foot instead, leaving him begging for forgiveness, something she couldn't do at the time.

"Bro, I can't tell you that Monroe won't try to contact Keilah. In his debriefing he made a statement regarding making amends with people he had wronged and being thankful for a second chance at life. Personally, I don't think he's being truthful," Kyle said.

"What do you mean?" Ramsey asked.

"It's a gut feeling, and it was something in his eyes. You had to be there to know what I'm talking about," Kyle said as he stood. "You're going to tell Keilah, right?"

"I have to. It's been too hard convincing her that Neariah is safe. Besides, I can't have her blindsided by him if he decides to approach her on the street," Ramsey replied just before opening his office door and escorting Kyle to the front door.

When Kyle reached the front door, he turned and said, "You know I'll do what I can to keep you informed on his movements. Give Keilah and Neariah my love."

Ramsey opened the door for him and said, "I will. Call me tomorrow so we can talk more about this."

Kyle shook Ramsey's hand and said, "Will do."

Ramsey closed the door behind him and rejoined Malachi in the theater room.

"What was that all about?" Malachi asked.

"Michael Monroe is no longer MIA," Ramsey said as he took a swallow of his beer. "He's back in D.C., and he's alive and well."

"No shit!" Malachi yelled out, causing Target to bark. He patted the dog's head to let him know everything was okay.

"It's the truth, but I haven't told Keilah yet, so keep it to yourself for now. I'll tell her between tonight and tomorrow, because it's going to hit the media any day now."

Malachi turned the sound down on the football game and looked his brother-in-law in the eyes. "Ramsey, I'm going to say this as plain as a brother can say it. If his punk ass comes anywhere near my sister or my niece, I'm not going to be responsible for my actions. His drama shook her up."

"I'm right there with you," Ramsey replied as he stood and finished off his beer. "I'm going upstairs to check on them."

"Cool," Malachi answered as he picked up the remote and started scanning the channels for other games.

Ramsey exited the room with Target following close behind. Upstairs he instructed his canine to lie down in the hallway outside their bedroom. He entered the room and found Keilah in bed, reading softly to their daughter. Her eyes were barely opened—that was, until she saw her father. Her eyes immediately lit up, and she started wiggling in her mother's arms to get over to him. It warmed Ramsey's heart to see his daughter's strong reaction to his presence. He climbed onto the bed and kissed both of them on the cheek.

"Thanks a lot, Ramsey Stone," Keilah said softly as Neariah crawled over her to get to her father. "She was almost asleep."

He placed his daughter on his chest and said, "I'm sorry. I thought she was asleep."

"It's okay," Keilah replied as she gathered up Neariah's lotion and brush. "Where's Malachi?"

"Downstairs, watching the game," he whispered as he cuddled his daughter in his arms. "I'm going back down there, but I wanted to talk to you first."

"About what?" she asked as Neariah cuddled with her father.

"Let me get her to sleep first," he said before taking his daughter across the hallway to her room.

When he returned thirty minutes later, he found Keilah sitting on the small sofa at the foot of their bed, putting lotion on her arms and legs. She looked heavenly in her gold satin nightgown, and the sight of her caused his body to stir. He pulled her up into his arms and hugged her tightly to his body. He leaned down and gave her a seductive kiss on the lips.

"Mmmm, that was nice."

He kissed her again and whispered, "I love you."

She noticed the seriousness in his eyes and said, "I love you too. What's wrong? What do you want to talk to me about?"

He sat down on the sofa and pulled her into his lap. As he held on to her, he searched for an easy way to tell her about her ex-boyfriend, and then he realized the only way to tell her was straight-out.

"Bradford came by tonight while you were giving Neariah a bath."

"What did he want?" she asked as she massaged the back of his neck.

"He wanted to let us know that Michael Monroe was found alive in Iraq a few days ago and now he's back in D.C."

"I knew he wasn't dead, and I knew he would come back," she revealed. "Do you think he's going to try and come after Neariah?"

"Babe, he has no reason to come after her, and if he does, he'll have me to deal with, and you and I both know he don't want that," Ramsey said to reassure her.

"What if he's delusional and thinks Neariah is his daughter—"

"She's not," he said, interrupting her. "Those were bad dreams, babe. You have nothing to worry about, and Kyle's going to keep us informed on his where-abouts. He wanted us to know about it before the news media broke the story."

Keilah buried her face in her husband's warm neck and said, "Thanks for the heads-up."

He lovingly patted her backside and said, "You're welcome. Can I get you anything before you turn in?"

She climbed out of his lap and said, "No, I'm okay. You're not going to be up too late, are you?"

He leaned down and gave her another kiss. "No, I'm tired too. It's been a long day. I'll be back up as soon as the game is over."

"Okay," she said as she got in bed and pulled the comforter over her body.

Ramsey dimmed the lights and walked toward the door.

"Ramsey, does Malachi know Michael's back?"

He turned back to her and admitted that he had filled Malachi in on Michael Monroe's surprising return.

"I'm sure he wasn't happy to hear it, was he?"

He shoved his hands in his pockets and leaned against the door frame. "You know your brother."

"I know, and that's the problem. I don't want anyone to get hurt. Tell him I said good night and that I'll talk to him in the morning."

"I will," he answered as he started to pull the door closed. "Sweet dreams, babe."

Ramsey knew in his heart that the only way he could give his wife peace was to get Michael Monroe out of their lives once and for all. An hour or so later Ramsey returned to his bedroom and climbed into bed and cuddled with his sleeping wife.

At the medical facility, Michael lay in bed, staring up at the ceiling. It had been a grueling day, and he was glad it was over. It was after midnight, and he had a hard time closing his eyes because of the images he would see. Images of blood, death, poverty, sorrow. It was a lot to take in, especially when you were in distress and didn't know if you were going to live or die. As he lay there, he thought of Kevin, his lover, and what he'd probably gone through over the past year, not knowing if he was dead or alive. He turned over in bed, and images of Keilah flashed in his head. Tears started running out of his eyes as his emotions overtook him. He'd hurt her unimaginably, and he wanted—no, needed—to see her as soon as possible. He needed to make amends with her for all the pain and suffering he'd caused her so he could finally get on with his life.

***

A few days later, after more debriefings and a psych exam, Major Michael Monroe was finally allowed to leave the base. His uncle, Malcolm Randolph, a Supreme Court justice, picked up his nephew in a waiting limo.

The judge hugged him and said, "Welcome home, son."

"Thank you, Uncle Malcolm. Where are Aunt Teresa and Arhmelia?"

The limo driver put Michael's bag in the trunk and then opened one of the back doors for the pair to climb in.

Once inside the limo, Malcolm said, "They're making sure your homecoming dinner is perfect. You know my daughter has been tweeting about your homecoming ever since we got the great news that you were rescued."

"Technology at its best and worst," Michael softly replied.

The judge laughed and said, "Everybody's tweeting now. You know, she'll be graduating from high school next year."

"I can't believe she's grown up so fast."

"Indeed," Malcolm replied.

"Listen, Uncle Malcolm, I told Aunt Teresa not to make a big deal out of me coming home. I'm just glad to finally be back on American soil," Michael revealed. "I know she means well, but I still have a lot on my mind. I'm just looking for some peace and quiet for a while. I'm not ready for a lot of people to be in my face, asking me a lot of questions about what went on over there. Everything is still too fresh, you know?"

"Of course I understand," Malcolm replied as he patted Michael on the knee. "If it's going to be too much for you, we can cancel and do this another time, when you're feeling up to it."

Michael sighed and said, "I'm sorry, Unc."

Malcolm pulled out his cell phone and said, "Don't you worry about a thing, because the last thing we want to do is to make your homecoming unbearable."

Michael sat back and listened as his uncle called his wife to talk to her about their dinner plans.

"Teresa, I have Michael, but he's not ready to face a room full of people right now, so you have two choices, sweetheart. Clear everyone out so Michael can come home and relax, or you can go ahead with the party, and Michael and I can check into the Ritz-Carlton for the night and see you tomorrow."

"Tomorrow? Let me speak to him," Teresa demanded.

Malcolm covered the telephone with his hand and whispered, "Don't let her bully you."

Michael smiled and said, "Hello, Aunt Teresa."

"Michael, we're so glad you're home safe. Malcolm tells me you're a little apprehensive about coming to the house. Sweetheart, if you need time to yourself, I will tell everyone to leave. You've been through so much. You need to be around your family right now."

"It's okay. Go ahead with your dinner party. I'll be fine at the hotel, and I'll send Uncle Malcolm home to you so he can help you entertain. Okay?"

"Darling, I don't think you need to be alone right now," Teresa replied.

"To be honest, Auntie, that's exactly what I need," he answered. "Don't worry. I'll be fine. I just need some time to readjust. I'll see you tomorrow. Okay?"

"Only if you assure me that you'll call us to come get you if you have a change of heart. I love you, Michael, and my heart is heavy that you had to go through that horrible ordeal."

"So do I, Auntie. I love you."

Tears welled up in his aunt's eyes. Michael was her deceased sister's only child, and she loved him like he was her own son.

"If you need anything, and I mean anything, you give me or your uncle a call. Do you hear me?"

Michael ran his hand across the medals on his military jacket and said, "Yes, ma'am."

He handed the cell phone back to his uncle, who tucked it back into his pocket.

"The Ritz-Carlton it is," Michael announced with a smile.

The limo pulled up to entrance of the Ritz-Carlton, and Malcolm and Michael exited the vehicle and entered the lobby.

At the counter, Malcolm asked, "Do you want a suite?"

Michael looked at the beautiful young woman behind the counter and said, "No, sir. I just want a room, nothing fancy."

The desk clerk said, "All of our rooms are upscale, sir, but if you like, I can assign you to our least expensive room."

"Are you sure?" the judge asked. "I want you to be comfortable."

Michael wrapped his arm around his uncle's shoulders and said, "I know, but I don't need a suite, just a hot bath and a soft bed."

Malcolm handed the desk clerk his credit card and told her that his nephew was welcome to charge whatever he needed to the room.

The clerk handed Michael the key to his room and said, "Enjoy your stay, sir."

Michael and his uncle headed toward the elevator.

"Unc, you don't have to come upstairs with me. I'm sure Aunt Teresa is anxious for you to join her and your guests."

"Are you sure you don't want me to stay with you?" Malcolm asked one more time, just to be sure he wasn't abandoning his nephew in a time of need.

"I'm sure," Michael reassured his uncle as he pushed the button for the elevator and stepped inside it.

The judge was still a little apprehensive about leaving Michael alone, so he said a short prayer of peace for him, returned to the limo, and left it in God's hands.

Chapter Four

Keilah and Ramsey had gotten comfortable with Malachi at the house. To keep him occupied, they made sure they gave him more tasks to do for them. His task for this day was to supervise the carpet cleaners and go purchase everything on Sabrinia's shopping list for Thanksgiving dinner.

Keilah walked into Ramsey's office with a handful of files and said, "If Malachi calls me one more time, I'm going to lose it."

Ramsey leaned back in his chair and laughed. "He just wants to make sure he doesn't screw up anything."

She set the files on the edge of his desk and leaned against it. Ramsey's eyes immediately fixated on her legs as the short skirt she wore rose slightly, exposing her thighs.

"How hard is it to watch over some people cleaning the carpet? I didn't ask him to do the job, just oversee it."

He picked up one of the files and opened it. "Don't you think you're being a little hard on him?"

She crossed her legs and said, "I'm not being any harder on him than he's been on me. I told him I was going to work him while he was here. That's what he gets for coming out here so early—" Keilah stopped talking mid-sentence and looked over at him.

Ramsey's eyes were on her legs again. This time he couldn't resist running his hand up her thigh and under her skirt.

"What are you doing?" she finally said.

"I'm sorry, sweetheart, but I can't help myself," he answered in a low, seductive tone of voice as his hand moved even higher.

She closed her eyes and bit down on her bottom lip. Breathlessly she whispered, "If you don't stop right now, we're going to miss our conference call."

He stood over her and kissed the curve of her neck.

Lock the door, baby," he whispered as he pulled her into his arms, kissing her.

A wave of heat consumed her body as he eased his hand inside the waistband of her undergarment and began to slowly stroke her.

"We can't," she replied with bated breath as her body quickly heated up. "We have a conference call in twenty minutes."

"All I need is ten," he answered while deeply caressing her feminine core and showering her with sizzling kisses.

If he couldn't have her the way he wanted to, he was going to make sure he gave her a moment of sheer pleasure. Ramsey was in control now, and she knew there was no way she could resist him now. She closed her eyes and enjoyed his sensual massage and hot, wet kisses. Seconds later she felt her skin become enflamed. Ramsey smiled, realizing she was close to her release. He leaned down to her ear, nibbled on her earlobe.

"Ramsey!" she called out in an elevated tone as her body shuddered hard and then went limp against him. Her eyes were filled with tears when she finally looked up at him.

He gave her a tender kiss on the forehead and asked, "Are you okay?"

Silent, she shook her head and then laid it against his chest.

He hugged her tightly and said, "You make me lose control of all my senses."

"I ditto that," she answered with her voice barely above a whisper. "Now, let me go so I can get my notes for the conference call."

After freshening up in their private restroom, the couple made it to their conference call with their Atlanta real estate agent on time; however, Keilah was clearly distracted during the call. Her body was still full of electricity from the tender contact with her husband.

"Keilah, what do you think?" Ramsey asked.

Caught off guard, she sat up in her chair and said, "I'm sorry. Can you repeat the question."

Ramsey smiled and asked, "Barry, do you mind repeating what you just said?"

"Not at all," he answered. "The owner of the building you're interested in is willing to accept our offer if we sign a five-year contract."

Keilah shook her head and said, "No, I disagree with that. Five years is too long. I say no more than two years for starters, and if the location works out and the business does well, then we can look at a longer lease or possibly a purchase."

Ramsey looked over at his two office managers, who nodded in agreement, and then he said, "We're all in agreement with Keilah. Run that by the owner and let us know what he says. If he can't meet those terms, we need to keep searching. Okay?"

"Whatever you say," Barry replied.

"We want to try and have this settled by the first of the year, so do whatever you have to do to make it happen, but make sure he understands that we have no problem walking away from this deal."

"You got it. Consider it done."

Keilah stood, picked up her leather planner, and said, "Thank you, Barry. Keep us posted."

"Will do."

Ramsey disconnected the call and turned to his office managers, who were taking notes from the meeting. "We're really going to need you guys to help us as we go through this transition. Things are going to start moving fast around here, and there's going to be some days that you have to fly to Atlanta to assist with the staffing. Are you up for the challenge?"

Both of them happily accepted their bosses' offer.

"Great!" he replied as they all stood and exited the conference room.

As they walked down the hallway together, Ramsey took Keilah by the arm and guided her toward his office. "I need to see you for a second."

She entered his office and waited for him to close the door behind them. She sat her planner on his desk and turned to him. "What's up?"

He walked over to her, then stared into her beautiful brown eyes. "Answer me truthfully. Are you okay?"

She covered her face with her hands and said, "Not really. I was so distracted in the meeting. I'm sorry."

He hugged her and asked, "It's my fault, isn't it?"

"It's just that you drive me crazy when you touch me like you did earlier."

He smiled and said, "You're so damn irresistible, you make it hard for me to keep my hands to myself no matter where we are."

Keilah looked up into his eyes and said, "The feeling's mutual."

He released her and walked around his desk and sat down. "Why don't you cut out early? It'll give you the chance to spend some one-on-one time with your brother."

She picked up her planner and said, "I think I will. Maybe I was a little hard on him for showing up without calling. I just feel like all my brothers have moments where they treat me like I'm still sixteen."

Ramsey picked up the telephone and dialed a number and said, "If that's how you feel, then fix it. You're their only sister, and they love you. Go ahead. Get out of here. I'll see you when I get home."

She blew him a kiss and said, "Thank you, baby."

"You're welcome. Just give me a courtesy call when you get home so I'll know you made it home safely."

"I will," she said before exiting his office.

Keilah felt a little guilty about leaving the office early. Then again, she was the boss and had that luxury, especially when husband practically ordered her to leave. After all, it was his fault she was in this emotional state, anyway, so she made her way to her office, gave her assistant a few instructions, and then grabbed her purse and left. Once she got in her car, she picked up the phone and dialed her brother's number.

"Hello?"

"Malachi, I'm headed home. What kind of progress have you made today with your assignments?"

"I see you have jokes."

Keilah giggled.

Malachi looked around and said, "Since you asked, I have completed everything, so I'm good. Why are you checking up on me?"

"I'm not checking on you, Malachi. I got off work early and wanted to know if you wanted to hang out."

He opened the door so the carpet cleaners could load up their equipment.

"What do you have in mind? I'm up for anything."

"Do you want to grab some lunch?"

"Sounds good," he answered as he rubbed his growling stomach. "I am starving."

"Great. I'll be there in fifteen minutes. What do you have a taste for?"

"It doesn't matter to me, but I am leaning toward Caribbean food. I haven't had that in a while."

She smiled and said, "Caribbean it is. I'll see you shortly."

About fifteen minutes later, Keilah arrived home and changed into a pair of jeans, a casual top, a leather jacket, and boots. Before leaving with her brother, she looked in on Neariah, who was taking a nap, and had a short conversation with Camille about their dinner menu. When she joined Malachi in the driveway, she tossed him the keys to her Land Rover, and they drove off to an appetizing lunch.

At the restaurant Keilah chose *arroz con camarones,* shrimp with yellow rice, which was served with beans and a salad. Malachi ordered a *burrito cubano,* a burrito filled with roast pork, *sofrito,* beans, and cheese, and served with rice, beans, and a salad. Keilah enjoy her afternoon with her brother. After treating him to lunch, they stopped by a local market to purchase a few items for Thanksgiving. Malachi had been a big help getting everything ready for Thanksgiving, and she apologized to him for overreacting to his unannounced arrival. Now she couldn't wait to see the rest of her family.

It had been a fun-filled day with her brother, but she was tired now and ready to crash. Once they returned home, she headed upstairs, started her bath, and went into the bedroom to get her slippers. As she made her way back into the bathroom, her cell phone rang. She didn't recognize the number, so she answered it.

"Hello?"

"Keilah, it's Trenton. Don't hang up. We need to talk."

Stunned, she sat down on the side of the bed without speaking for a moment. Once she gathered her senses, she said, "We have nothing to talk about, and how did you get my number?"

"That's not important right now. What *is* important is that I can't get you out of my head. I know you're married, but I have to see you. You have to still have feelings for me. We almost got married, for God's sake."

Angry, Keilah said, "You know what, Trenton? I did love you at one time, but now all I feel for you is disgust. Feelings of disgust that you would have the nerve to approach me like you did on the plane. I told you I was happily married, so please, just leave me alone."

"The only shame I have is that I let you get away from me. I'm not afraid to fight for you, Keilah. You mean that much to me."

"The best advice I can give you is to lose my number and forget we ever ran into each other. Do you understand where I'm coming from?"

Trenton held the telephone in silence for a moment, and then, before hanging up, he said, "I'm sorry, but I can't let go. Not yet, so what happens, happens. Goodbye, Keilah."

She hung up the telephone, not understanding what Trenton meant or where his head was. It was her hope that this was the last time she would hear from him, but she couldn't be sure. She didn't want to ruin Thanksgiving, but on the flip side she didn't want to keep secrets from Ramsey, either. She returned to the bathroom, and to the hot bath awaiting her, so she could think about her next move.

Chapter Five

It was two days before Thanksgiving, and Luke and his family had arrived, and so had Ramsey's parents, Valeria and Marion, and Ramsey's aunt Judy. Since Camille had been given time off to spend time with her own family for the holidays, Malachi had stepped in to help around the house, which included watching over Neariah while the Stones went to work. Sabrinia went straight to the kitchen when she arrived, with Valeria and Aunt Judy right behind her. She wanted to prepare as much food as possible ahead of time so she would have the opportunity to enjoy the holiday. It helped that Keilah had a refrigerator that was capable of storing large amounts of food. However, when Sabrinia entered the kitchen, Keilah had a surprise for her.

"What is this?" Sabrinia called out to her sister-in-law as they gathered around the large island. The smell of garlic and other spices was in the air, and when Sabrinia looked in the oven, she saw a large tray of baked chicken. On the stove top she found a huge pot of pasta, Alfredo sauce, delicious vegetables, and homemade rolls.

"Calm down, Sabrinia," Keilah instructed her sister-in-law as she popped opened a bottle of wine and started filling their glasses. "I knew you would come in here like a tornado and start slinging pots and pans, but not today, sis. You're going to relax and enjoy yourself, because dinner is taken care of for tonight. We have plenty of food, drinks, appetizers, and snacks. Tomorrow we can get serious about preparing for Thanksgiving dinner, and you're not going to do it alone."

"Keilah's right," Valeria added. "There are enough of us here to put dinner together in no time. Besides, I plan on making my famous corn-bread dressing and stuffed bell peppers."

Sabrinia smiled as she picked up her wineglass and took a sip. "Okay, you twisted my arm, because I have no problem relaxing and drinking Keilah's wine."

Aunt Judy had already finished her first glass and was holding it out for a refill. She belched and said, "You don't have to tell me twice. Fill 'er up."

The ladies laughed together as Luke and Sabrinia's children, eighteen-year-old Lucas, sixteen-year-old Danielle, and twelve-year-old Paris, headed downstairs to the game room. The men quickly grabbed their beer and headed to the theater room to watch football.

"I can't believe our granddaughter has gotten so big," Valeria stated. "What are you feeding her? Steroids?"

Keilah laughed.

"She's not big, but then again, your son is her father, so the apple doesn't fall far from the tree." Keilah replied.

About that time they heard a loud cheer coming from the theater room.

Aunt Judy drank up her second glass of wine and said, "I guess somebody scored."

Valeria rolled her eyes at her sister and said, "Stop drinking so fast, Judy, before you pass out before dinner. Come help set the table, because I'm starving."

"Me too," Sabrinia replied as she opened the oven and pulled out the steaming tray of baked chicken.

Aunt Judy reached into the cabinet and handed Sabrinia a platter for the chicken before she started buttering the rolls. Neariah noticed all the food preparation and started squealing with excitement. Keilah walked over to the high chair and gave her a buttered roll. Neariah immediately stopped squealing and stuffed the roll into her mouth. Once everything was set, Sabrinia called the family to the dinner table, where they joined hands in prayer and finally enjoyed a delicious dinner.

An hour or so later, the family continued to sit around the table, laughing and reminiscing. It was only after Keilah yawned that Valeria suggested they clear the table.

Keilah stood and said, "If anyone wants dessert and coffee, it'll be in the kitchen."

"No coffee for me," Aunt Judy answered. "It'll have me up all night, but I will take some dessert."

A few others also wanted dessert, so everyone pitched in clearing the table while Ramsey and Luke took Target out into the backyard for a short walk. Luke was like a father to Keilah, and Ramsey not only admired him but also respected him.

Sabrinia pointed to her two teenagers and said, "I want you two to clean up the kitchen before going back downstairs."

Lucas let out a loud sigh and rolled his eyes.

"Lucas, I know you're not giving me attitude."

"No, ma'am."

Danielle tossed her brother a dish towel and said, "I'll wash. You dry."

Keilah cut a slice of red velvet cake and said, "You guys can use the dishwasher if you want to."

"Thanks, Auntie," Danielle replied.

Valeria walked into the kitchen with Neariah, who was lying against her chest. "Keilah, I think Neariah's ready for bed. Do you mind if I take her upstairs and give her a bath?"

"I don't mind at all," Keilah replied as she leaned down to give her daughter a kiss. Neariah immediately reached for her. "You want your mommy?" Keilah asked her baby girl as she briefly took her into her arms. "Your grandmother is going to get you ready for bed, okay?" Keilah kissed her daughter's cheek and quickly handed her back to her mother-in-law. "I'll be up to check on you two shortly. Have fun."

Valeria headed down the hallway with her grand-daughter and said, "Take your time, sweetie. Neariah and I are going to spend some girl time together and have a spa night."

Keilah finished off her piece of cake and handed the saucer to Danielle before going into the theater room. The men were watching the last quarter of the football game when Keilah crawled into Ramsey's lap and laid her head on his shoulder.

He immediately ran his hand over her thigh and said, "You look sleepy."

"I am."

"Is Neariah in bed?"

She kissed his neck and said, "Her grandmother is giving her a bath."

Malachi glanced over at the couple and sarcastically said, "You two need to get a room."

"Mind your business," Luke replied, defending his sister's public display of affection. "You're just jealous."

"Please! I'm not jealous! I have women," Malachi announced.

"That's your problem. You're not eighteen any-more. You need to get your house in order and settle down and stop sleeping around with a bunch of loose women," Luke reminded him.

Malachi drank some of his beer and said, "I will when I'm ready, and I'm not ready yet."

Keilah took her husband's hand as she stood. She looked at Malachi and said, "I understand where you're coming from, Malachi, because not many women can handle your strong personality or antics, so you're going to have to take your time to find Mrs. Right. You need to let me pick your future wife. I'll pick someone good for you."

"You done lost your damn mind," Malachi replied with a laugh, and he watched Ramsey lead Keilah out of the room by the hand. "Where are you two going?"

Ramsey turned to his brothers-in-law and said, "I'll be back. I want to tuck my wife in bed and check on Neariah."

Luke smiled at the couple as he took a sip of his beer. He couldn't be happier that Ramsey had married their sister. He was the ideal man to handle her. They were a perfect fit, and there was no doubt that Ramsey was in love with her.

"Take your time, bro," Luke called out to him.

In the game room the couple found Lucas concentrating on a video game, while Danielle was painting her younger sister, Paris's nails. Target had been hanging out with the teenagers, but as soon as his owners entered the room, he stood and started wagging his tail. Keilah and Ramsey had a short conversation with the teens about sleeping arrangements. Danielle and Paris would share a small bedroom off the game room, while Lucas would camp out on the sectional's hide-a-bed. Before going upstairs, they stepped out on the patio, where they found Marion enjoying one of his large cigars.

"Dad, I thought you were going to quit smoking."

Marion turned to his son and raised his hand and said, "My New Year's resolution is to cut back a little bit, Scouts' honor."

Keilah gave him a kiss on the cheek and said, "Good night, Pops."

"Good night, sweetheart."

Upstairs they looked in on Aunt Judy, who had just bedded down with a book and a glass of wine. Sabrinia was relaxing in the jetted tub, while down the hallway Valeria was singing a soft lullaby to Neariah as she rocked her to sleep. She waved them off, not wanting her granddaughter to be awakened by the presence of her parents. The last stop was their master bedroom, which was their private room of relaxation. Decorated in ivory and gold, it was fully equipped, with a fireplace and an intimate sitting area near a large window overlooking the pool, the fountain, and a perfectly manicured backyard.

Ramsey pulled Keilah's sweater over her head, exposing her bra and full chest. He kissed her neck and the cleavage of her breasts, causing her to let out a soft whimper.

"Do you want me to finish undressing you?" he asked with a mischievous expression on his face.

"Baby, if you undress me now, I don't think you'll be rejoining my brothers downstairs."

He unbuttoned her jeans and pulled them down over her hips and said, "I think they'll understand if I don't come back."

Ramsey stood back and admired his wife's beautiful body as she stood before him in her pink lace undergarments.

"Damn," he whispered as he felt himself about to lose control of his body.

She cuddled up to him and ran her hand over his broad chest and said, "Thank you. I feel the same way when I look at you."

He gave her a sultry kiss on the lips and then patted her on the backside. "Get some rest. I'll be back after watching a few highlights."

"That's fine," she said as she turned and walked toward the bathroom so she could get ready for bed.

Ramsey closed the door behind him and headed back downstairs to join his father and brothers-in-law. He spent the next hour or so enjoying their company. When he checked the time, he realized how late it was and called it a night. He made his way upstairs after securing the house and eased into bed with his wife, who had drifted off the sleep, but he had no problem waking her up with his soft kisses and gentle tongue.

It wasn't until she lay in her husband's arms after making love to him that Keilah decided to tell him about Trenton's phone call.

"Ramsey?"

He pulled her closer and answered, "Yes, dear?"

"You know I love you, right?"

He kissed her and said, "Of course I do."

"You also know that I would never do anything to disrespect or hurt you."

He opened his eyes and said, "Yeah, baby, I know. What's up?"

"Trenton called my cell phone the other day."

"What?"

She sighed and said, "He was talking crazy, saying he was still in love with me and that he wasn't able to let go after seeing me on the plane. He said he was willing to fight for me, and before he hung up, he said what happens . . . happens."

Ramsey sat up in bed and rubbed his eyes. "What did he mean by that?"

"I don't know, babe."

"That bastard is just asking for me to break his damn neck."

Keilah lovingly wrapped her arms around her husband's neck and gave him a kiss on the cheek. "Baby, I don't want you to get into any trouble over this. He's arrogant, not stupid."

Ramsey stood and walked over to the window and looked out into the night. He turned to her and said, "You're my wife, and nobody's going to disrespect our marriage."

Keilah climbed out of bed and joined her husband at the window. It was a clear night, and the moonlight shining through the window seemed to illuminate their bodies, especially Ramsey's and his military tattoos. She sat on the window seat and looked up into her husband's distressed face.

"You have nothing to worry about. You know where my heart is."

He looked down at her and said, "That's never been in question. I know you would never cheat on me. I trust you, but not him or what he might do."

She took his hand and kissed the back of it and said, "He won't do anything."

Ramsey leaned down, kissed her soft lips, and said, "I know he won't. Let's go back to bed. I'll take care of this tomorrow."

He took her by the hand and led her over to the bed, but before crawling under the covers, she said, "You're not going to do anything stupid, are you?"

He fluffed his pillow and said, "Of course not."

In the middle of the night, Ramsey made his way down to his office and Googled Trenton's book-signing schedule. He found out he was holding an early morning signing at an upscale café in the downtown area.

The next morning, Ramsey got up bright and early, while everyone else was still asleep. He drove downtown; entered the café; bought a newspaper, a cup of coffee, and some oatmeal; took a seat at a table in the corner; and waited for the guest of honor. Fortunately for him, his wait wasn't long. Trenton, along with his big ego and a female assistant, walked into a crowd of fans anxiously waiting to get their books signed. Ramsey felt like jumping over the table and smashing Trenton's head, but he decided to be patient. He watched as Trenton worked the early morning crowd of people, who had to work the day before Thanksgiving. This was D.C., which meant the government had work to do even around the holidays. It was only a matter time, and Ramsey couldn't wait.

Chapter Six

Two hours had passed, and the crowd had slowly diminished. While employees packed up Trenton's remaining books, the guest of honor headed toward the restroom. Ramsey slowly rose from his chair and entered the restroom, where he found Trenton at the sink, washing his hands. Trenton looked into the mirror and recognized a familiar face. He pulled some paper towels out of the holder and dried his hands.

Trenton held his hand out to shake Ramsey's hand. "Ramsey Stone, what a nice surprise. It's been a while."

Instead of shaking his hand, Ramsey walked up to him and punched him square in the face, knocking him on the floor.

"What the hell is wrong with you?" Trenton asked as he touched his lip and saw that it was bleeding.

Before he could say another word, Ramsey grabbed him by the neck and pulled him off the floor and slammed him hard against the wall. Trenton eyes bulged in disbelief, making it obvious that he'd been caught by surprise. Ramsey's grip on his neck was tight as he got right in his face and spoke.

"If I hear of you calling, touching, or even breathing in the same space as my wife, I will kill you. Do you understand?" Ramsey released his grip slightly on Trenton's neck so he could speak.

With his voice nearly ripped from his throat, he whispered, "I don't know what you're talking about, man."

Ramsey slammed his head into the wall again and said, "I'm talking about Keilah."

Trenton's eyes widened with surprise.

"What?" Ramsey asked. "You didn't think she would tell me, huh? She told me about the telephone call you made to her and what happened on the plane to New York."

"I didn't know Keilah was married to you," he replied in sheer terror.

"She didn't have to tell you!" Ramsey yelled. "Once she said she was married, that should've been the end of it. You will not disrespect my wife or our marriage. You had your chance with her, and you blew it. Move on."

Trenton now had tears in his eyes as his oxygen supply was slowly being cut off. He could tell by the grip on his neck that Ramsey could actually kill him if he wanted to.

"I'm sorry, Ramsey. Please, you have to—"

Ramsey punched him hard in the stomach, causing Trenton to grimace in pain. "Shut your damn mouth! I don't have to do anything."

"Okay, okay, I'm sorry."

Ramsey released his grip on Trenton's neck and asked, "Do we have an understanding?"

Trenton nodded in agreement.

Ramsey smacked him on the side of the head and said, "I can't hear you. Do we have an understanding?"

Still trying to catch his breath, Trenton leaned over with his hands on his knees and said, "I understand. You don't have to worry about me bothering or contacting Keilah."

Ramsey reached for the door, but before opening it, he turned to Trenton one more time and said, "Oh, and if you decide to get a brain and think you can sue me for assaulting you, think again, unless you want Keilah to charge you with sexual harassment. I'm sure Howard University, your publishing company, or BET wouldn't want their golden boy involved in a scandal."

And with that comment, he was gone. Alone in the restroom, Trenton got himself together as best he could. He made his way over to the sink and doused his face with cold water so he could wash the blood from his lip. When he looked in the mirror, he grimaced at the sight of himself. His shirt was wrinkled and smeared with blood droplets, so he grabbed a wet paper towel and tried to clean it, and then he pulled his sunglasses out of his pocket and put them on before leaving the restroom.

When Ramsey returned home, he hoped everyone was still asleep after being up so late the night before. He entered the kitchen, and to his surprise, he found his father reading the paper and drinking coffee.

"Good morning, son."

"Good morning, Daddy," Ramsey answered as he patted Target on the head.

Marion closed the newspaper and said, "What's got you up and out so early this morning?"

Ramsey turned away from his father to get a cup out of the cabinet. "Nothing much. I just had to run an errand."

Marion took the cup, poured his son a cup of coffee, and handed it to him. "Does it have anything to do with that blood on your shirt?"

Ramsey looked down at the droplets of blood on his shirt. He'd been so angry when he left the café, he didn't think to check his attire. "It's nothing. I cut myself shaving."

"I'm no fool, Ramsey Stone," Marion replied. "I'm your father, and I know trouble when I see it."

"Everything's fine, Dad. You don't have anything to worry about."

Marion took another sip of his coffee and closed the newspaper and said, "I hope not, and you'd better change your shirt before your mother or Keilah sees it, and believe me, they won't accept your explanation as easily as I did."

Ramsey poured a little cream in his coffee and politely answered, "Yes, sir."

He disappeared into the laundry room to remove his shirt. When he returned to the kitchen, he found Valeria holding Neariah.

"Good morning, son."

"Good morning, Mom.

As soon as Neariah heard her father's voice, she immediately reached out for him and started to whine.

Valeria handed her granddaughter over to her son and said, "She's too spoiled."

Ramsey held his daughter high above his head and smiled up at her, ignoring his mother's comment. Neariah looked down at her dad and let out a loud giggle. It was obvious that she was quite comfortable with what he was doing. She was beautiful with her light complexion matching his, her dark brown eyes, and a head full of curly hair. There was no doubt she was his daughter. She looked so much like him, except that she had her mother's eyes.

"Ramsey, be careful. You're going to drop her," his mother warned him as she tightened the belt on her bathrobe.

He lowered Neariah and held her close to his heart. "Mom, I would never drop my daughter. She loves it when I hold her up in the air."

Marion picked up his cup of coffee and headed toward the patio doors.

"Where are you going?" Valeria asked as she prepared breakfast for her granddaughter.

"I'll let you two have a moment. I'm going to take Target out for a little walk around the backyard."

Valeria turned her attention back to her son, looking him up and down. "Why are you fully dressed so early in the morning? Where are you going?"

Marion laughed as he closed the door behind him, knowing his wife was going to give their son the third degree.

Ramsey placed Neariah in her high chair, sat down in the chair next to her, and said, "I had to run an errand."

His mother sat down across from him and set his cup of coffee in front of him. She stirred the bowl of cereal for Neariah and asked, "What kind of errand did you have so early in the morning?"

Ramsey looked over at his mother and gave her a look to let her know that she was prying a little too much for his taste.

"Well, excuse me for asking," she said as she held the spoon of cereal out to Neariah. "You and Keilah need to let Neariah stay with us more often so she'll get used to us."

He leaned back in the chair and took a sip of coffee and said, "When she gets a little older, we will. Right now neither one of us can stand being away from her for too long."

Valeria pointed at him and said, "I'm going to hold you to it."

Ramsey finished off his coffee and asked, "Is Keilah up?"

"Not really," she answered. "She brought Neariah into the room to change her, but I told her to go back to bed and I would take care of her."

He stood and said, "I'd better go check on her. I'm sure Sabrinia and Aunt Judy will be getting up shortly to start cooking. Do you want me to take Neariah back upstairs with me?"

"She's still eating. I'll bring her up to you if I have a problem."

Across town, Michael felt like he had lost track of time after being held in captivity for so long. He had had a comfortable night at the hotel, but he was anxious to get his life back and sleep in his own bed. He needed time to readjust to his military and personal world. He would start with his personal life by staying at his town house. The hotel was nice, but there was nothing like home. He asked the taxi cab driver to take the scenic route home to drive him by some of his favorite landmarks of D.C.

When he finally arrived home and entered the foyer, it smelled clean and like fresh flowers. He knew his aunt and uncle had spruced up the place before his arrival, and he was thankful they had maintained it and had handled all his bills and business in his absence. In the kitchen he opened the refrigerator to find it fully stocked with all his favorite foods. As he made his way into the family room, he noticed a slight chill in the air and turned on the gas fireplace before heading upstairs. He propped his bag against the wall, sat down on the side of the bed, and hung his head. It felt strange to be sitting in the room, which held so many memories, some good and some very bad. A lot of people had been hurt in that room physically and emotionally, and he wanted to make amends since he knew firsthand how short life was after nearly losing his own. He picked up the telephone and dialed his uncle's number. As he waited for him to answer, a sense of calmness overtook him and he was immediately energized.

"Hello, Unc. It's Michael."

"Michael, I'm glad you called. Are you settling in okay?"

"Yes, and I appreciate you guys cleaning the place for me and stocking the fridge with food, but I need a huge favor."

With concern in his voice, Malcolm said, "Sure, nephew. What do you need?"

"I need the name and number of your friend that's a real estate agent. I want to sell my town house."

"Sell it?" Malcolm asked. "Michael, you love that place. Why do you want to sell it?"

Michael sighed and said, "After everything's that's happened, I need a fresh start. I don't know if D.C. is the place for me anymore."

"Wait a second, Michael. You've been through a very traumatic event, and you don't want to make any major decisions without thinking them through. Son, you just got back. Give yourself time to exhale. Besides, your aunt would be devastated if you moved away."

"I don't know, Unc. I don't feel comfortable here anymore."

"All I'm asking you is to give yourself time to think things over," Malcolm suggested. "Now, I'll give your number to my friend in a few days, and if you still feel the same way, then do what you feel you need to do. We'll support you no matter what."

"Thank you, Uncle Malcolm."

"Great! Now, your aunt is preparing a nice Thanksgiving dinner for the family, and she expects to see you. She's driving me crazy, so you'd better show up."

Michael chuckled and said, "I'll be there."

"Perfect. In the meantime relax and enjoy being back in your home."

"I will. Talk to you soon."

Michael hung up the telephone and walked over to his desk and turned on his laptop. He sat down and Googled the Stone-Chance Protection Agency and entered the Web site. He wanted—no, needed—to see Keilah, even though he knew she hated what he did to her. He had deceived her in the worst way. He never got a chance to apologize to her for his deception, not that she wanted to hear anything he had to say, anyway. He should be thankful for the fact that she had allowed him to live after what he did to her. It was the ultimate betrayal, but everyone deserved forgiveness . . . right? He jotted down the telephone number to the agency and tucked it into his pocket and then began to unpack his bag. In every room he went into, he had vivid memories of heartbreak.

The town house was in an ideal location, close to downtown, near restaurants and shops, and was now worth double what he had paid for it a few years ago. It also helped that he had upgraded his kitchen and master bathroom and all the landscaping. He had also finished the basement and had turned it into a great entertaining space, fully equipped with a bar, a big-screen TV, and a pool table. He needed a fresh start and something to keep his mind off his past. He also had some other decisions to make, one that included possibly retiring from the military and settling down once and for all. His desire for a family was stronger than ever now. He'd messed up once, but he vowed never to do it again. In fact, his therapist had encouraged him to move forward with his life and not get stagnate, so as soon as Thanksgiving was over, he would put his *new* life into motion.

Chapter Seven

Thanksgiving Day had finally arrived, and Michael had a lot to be thankful for as he stepped up on his aunt and uncle's porch and rang the doorbell.

Malcolm opened the door and greeted him with a hug. "Michael, you're right on time! What do you have there?"

Michael handed his uncle the large bag, which contained a delicious chess pie and two bottles of their favorite wine.

As they walked toward the dining room, Malcolm looked into the bag and said, "This pie smells delicious. You know you didn't have to bring anything."

"I know, but I wanted to. You and Aunt Teresa have really supported me through all my drama. I'm mostly thankful for you guys this Thanksgiving."

Malcolm patted him on the back and said, "We only do what families are supposed to do, son."

"Michael!" Arhmelia yelled as she entered the dining room with a tray of utensils.

Michael's uncle smiled and said, "I'll put the dessert in the kitchen for now. We should be eating shortly."

Michael smiled and gave his teenage cousin a loving hug. "You look all grown up now. Have I been gone that long?"

Arhmelia twirled around and said, "I do look good, don't I?"

"You do, and if I catch any knuckleheaded boys talking to you, there's going to be hell to pay."

Arhmelia giggled.

"I bet you're anxious about leaving for college next year, huh?"

"Yes, and I can't wait," she answered as she put the wine bottles on ice and began placing the utensils on the table.

"Is Spelman still your first choice?" Michael asked.

"Of course," she answered. "Momma would freak if I didn't at least have it as one of my top choices."

He laughed and said, "Well, it is her alma mater."

"I know but an all girls' college? I don't know about that."

Michael gave her a kiss on the forehead and said, "I understand, but you'll be fine. Besides, Morehouse is right down the street, and there's Georgia Tech, Emory, and so many more colleges in the area. Spelman has a rich history, and it's an excellent school."

Arhmelia finished setting the table and said, "I guess, but enough about me. How are you doing?"

Michael took a deep breath and picked up the tray, and together they walked toward the kitchen.

"I'm good," he answered as he sat the tray on the countertop.

"You look good, considering everything you've been through. I was so worried about you," she admitted, her voice cracking as she held back her tears.

He hugged her and said, "That's so sweet, Arhmelia. I thought about you guys all the time. That's the only thing that got me through it."

Arhmelia stepped out of his embrace and wiped away a stray tear.

"What is that look for?" he asked as he sampled the icing on a red velvet cake.

"Did the thought of anyone else help you with your ordeal?" she asked.

"Okay, who are you talking about?"

"Listen, Michael, I know things with you and Keilah ended kind of crazy. I felt bad for both of you, because I love you and I really like her, so I went to see her."

"You saw Keilah? When?"

"A few months ago. I wanted to see how she was and if she had forgiven you."

He folded his arms and asked, "Is that so?"

"I hope you're not mad."

"I could never be mad at you, Arhmelia, even though I don't agree with you going to see Keilah. I really hurt her. What I did was unforgivable."

Arhmelia took Michael by the hands and said, "I know you hurt her, but everyone deserves a chance for forgiveness."

He thought about how mature his cousin had become. He picked up the centerpiece of red, orange and yellow flowers and made his way into the dining room where he placed it in the center of the table.

"Well, are you going to tell me what you guys talked about?"

"She really didn't want to talk about you or what happened between you guys, but she does seem very happy. She showed me a picture of her daughter."

That comment immediately got Michael's attention. "Daughter? She has a daughter?"

"Yes, and she's so pretty, Michael," Arhmelia admitted.

Michael turned and looked out the window at the Randolphs' backyard. "How old is she?" he asked curiously.

"I think she said she's a year old. She sure is cute. She looks like a Gerber baby," Arhmelia told him, referring to the babies used in the Gerber baby food commercials.

Michael quickly went into deep thought and did the math in his head. There was a strong possibility that he could be the father of Keilah's child. Yes, they had used protection, but nothing was 100 percent effective. Now that he knew she had given birth to a daughter, he wouldn't be able to rest until he knew the truth.

"Michael! Michael! Are you listening to me?" Arhmelia asked.

"Yes, I'm listening," he lied as he snapped back to reality.

"Are you still friends with that guy?"

He laughed nervously and asked, "What guy?"

Placing the wineglasses she'd brought from the kitchen on the table, she rolled her eyes and said, "I've known you are bisexual for a long time."

"And just how do you know, young lady?" he asked inquisitively as he followed her back into the kitchen.

"I watched you with Keilah. You were attentive, but you weren't passionate. She was beautiful and hot. It would've been hard for most guys to keep their hands off her. And then there was that time I came by your house unexpectedly and that guy was there with you. You two had this weird way of looking at each other, even though you were only chilling and watch football. Then I heard you on the phone once. I knew you were talking to a guy, but some of the things you said weren't what a man would say to another guy. I knew, but it never made me love you any less."

He stared at his cousin. She was young, and so he'd never realized she was so in tuned with his behavior and lifestyle, and he'd thought he was being careful around her. When it came to Keilah, he really loved her, which had made it difficult for him to deceive her like he had by having a secret relationship with a man.

"Michael!" Teresa said with affection as she entered the kitchen and hugged her nephew. "What are you two doing holed up in here? All the family is gathered in the family room."

"I was helping Arhmelia with setting the table."

His aunt cupped his face and asked, "Sweetheart, is this going to be too much for you?"

"No, ma'am," he replied with a smile. "I am starving, and I'm anxious to see the family. It's been a while."

"Great, because we were just about to come into the dining room to eat. Arhmelia, help me bring the food in."

Arhmelia winked at Michael and then opened the double oven so she could retrieve a couple of platters of food.

Teresa rubbed Michael's arms and said, "If any of this gets to be too much for you, just step away and go upstairs, but I do not want you to leave. Agreed?"

He kissed her cheek and said, "Agreed."

With tears in her eyes, she said, "You look so handsome, Michael. A little thin, but that's under-standable . . . but still handsome."

"I'm sure you'll fatten me up in no time, Auntie," he joked before picking up the large turkey and carrying it into the dining room.

Michael and his family enjoyed a wonderful Thanksgiving dinner together. At the suggestion of the Randolphs, they made sure no one brought up Michael's recent ordeal overseas. The trauma of it was still fresh, and all they wanted to do was be thankful for his return and look forward to more family gatherings like this one. It touched Teresa's heart to see her nephew laughing at stories being told by various family members.

Malcolm held his wineglass up and said, "I would like to propose a toast if everyone would hold their glasses up."

Once he had everyone's attention and their glasses were held high, he began his toast.

"First of all, I want to thank God for allowing our family to be able to gather together for another Thanksgiving. Secondly, I'm thankful for my lovely wife and daughter, who are the reason I get up every morning. Ladies, I love you, and you are my life."

Teresa blew a kiss to her husband in reply.

"Lastly, I'm thankful for God for watching over Michael and bringing him home safely, and that's all that needs to be said about that. So I ask all of you to lift your glasses high in thanksgiving and love, and I pray that we're all able to do this all over again next year."

"Amen," Teresa said before taking a sip of wine, along with the other family members.

Across town, Keilah and her family were also sitting down to a large Thanksgiving meal courtesy of Sabrinia, Ramsey's mom, Valeria, and Aunt Judy. Since Keilah was the hostess, she was given a pass from kitchen duty. Instead, she was allowed to enjoy family time with all her brothers, including her half brother, Keytone.

"Baby sis, you're looking more mature every time I see you. You're filling out in the hips and everything," Keytone announced.

Keilah rolled her eyes and said, "Leave it to you to say something ignorant."

"Ignore him, Keilah. You look fine," his wife answered. She padded his stomach and said, "He's the one who could stand to lose a few pounds."

"Whatever," Keytone mumbled as he took a sip of wine.

"Thanks for having my back, but I'm not listening to him. As long as my husband is happy with my figure, that's all that matters," Keilah responded.

"And I'm definitely happy with your figure, baby," Ramsey proudly announced as he leaned over and kissed his wife.

"Can we change the subject please? There are children at the table," Luke suggested before turning to Keytone. "Come on, bro. You don't go there with any woman, let alone your sister. It's Thanksgiving."

Keytone put his hands up in defense and said, "You're right. My bad. Keilah, I'm sorry if I offended you. You look beautiful, as always, and you don't need to change a thing."

"Apology accepted," Keilah replied.

The family continued to enjoy the delicious dinner, complete with a deep fried turkey.

After dinner Keilah enjoyed quiet time with her brother Roman, who loved the written word like she did. He was also like a father to her and was always the voice of reason when there seemed to be some type of disagreement within the family. He was also the peacemaker in the family. Keilah owned an extensive book collection in her private library, and they often read books together so they could discuss them later. Upstairs in her library for nearly an hour they discussed the latest book, a memoir by a well-known journalist, over Aunt Judy's pecan pie and coffee.

Genesis walked in carrying a teary-eyed Neariah and said, "I think somebody is missing her mom."

Keilah took her daughter into her arms and said, "I think there's been too much commotion for her in one day."

"Probably so," Genesis replied. "I gave her to Ramsey, but she kept whining, so he told me to bring her to you."

She gently patted her daughter on the back to comfort her as she lay against her chest. "Yeah, when she gets like this, she only wants me. It's a momma thang."

Roman stood and gave his sister a kiss on the cheek. "Go ahead and take care of her. I think we were done here, anyway. I'll take the plates back downstairs."

"Thanks, Roman. Genesis, do you want to come hang out with me and Neariah for a bit?" she asked.

Keilah and Genesis were extremely close, and he was the one she confided in the most growing up. Even as an adult, she shared things with him that she couldn't share with her other brothers.

"Are you sure?" he asked. "I don't want to upset her any more than she is."

Keilah walked out into the hallway and said, "She's fine as long as I'm close by. Come on to the nursery with me. I'm going to rock her a little bit. She'll probably take a nap."

Genesis followed his sister down the hallway to the nursery and took a seat while Keilah changed her daughter's diaper.

"You're a good mother, Keilah."

She smiled and said, "I appreciate that, Genesis. We had a good mom, and you guys were great until I turned sixteen."

Genesis laughed, knowing exactly what his sister was referencing. "What did you expect? You are our only sister."

Keilah sat down in the rocking chair and started rocking Neariah. "Looking back, it's funny now, but you guys made it hard for me to have a boyfriend. All the boys were afraid of you, so they were afraid to talk to me."

He smiled and said, "That's not what we wanted, but we wanted them to know that we weren't going to allow them to take advantage of you."

"I understand what you were trying to do now that I'm older, but when I was sixteen, it all seemed wrong."

"Well, we don't have to worry about that anymore," he replied softly so he wouldn't startle his niece. "You have a good man. I just wish you hadn't wasted your time with that punk Trenton and that other guy."

"Speaking of Trenton, guess what?"

"What?" Genesis asked.

Keilah went on to tell her brother about the incident on the airplane with Trenton and the phone call. Neither one of them knew that Ramsey had paid Trenton a visit and had roughed him up, and if they did know, they wouldn't have a problem with it. Then there was Michael Monroe, a guy Genesis had never really warmed up to. He was glad that Keilah had seen Michael for what he was before she made a huge mistake.

"Well, we're glad you have a husband like Ramsey, who is capable of handling any man who's stupid enough to act crazy with you. You still have to be careful, because he can't be with you twenty-four-seven, but you're a tough sista. We taught you well."

Keilah looked down at her daughter, who was now fast asleep. She stood so she could place her in her crib. Once Neariah was in her crib, Keilah turned to Genesis and said, "I want my daughter to have a normal life with no fear or drama. I want more for my children. Life was difficult growing up without Momma."

Genesis hugged his sister and said, "We all miss Momma, but she'll always be with us in some way, even when you least expect it."

"You're right," Keilah replied as she wiped away a few stray tears and then turned on the baby monitor.

"Come on. Let's go downstairs. I think I saw some banana pudding with my name on it."

"I just had pecan pie. I don't know if I can eat any more," Keilah admitted.

Chapter Eight

Trenton was still sore from his altercation with Ramsey, but it wasn't going to stop him from promoting his book and making money. He mingled with fans in a small bookstore in an affluent area of town, and when asked about his injuries, he lied and said he tripped over his dog and fell down the stairs. His story seemed to intrigue fans even more and make him even more popular. He was charming, handsome, and knew how to work a crowd, especially the women, and when one particular woman walked through the door, he immediately made his way over to her.

"Andria Rockwell, what a nice surprise," he said as he greeted her with a kiss on the cheek. Andria was the spoiled daughter of Thomas Kirkland Rockwell, the U.S. secretary of defense, and she was Ramsey's ex.

She smiled and said, "Well, you're a sight for sore eyes yourself. I never thought our paths would cross again. It's great seeing you."

"You too."

"You're blowing up with this book and your spot on BET. What next?"

"Who knows? Maybe I'll run for mayor," he joked before whispering to his assistant that he was taking a break. "Can I buy you a cup of coffee?"

"Sure," Andrea answered, and he escorted her over to a table, where they sat down.

The waitress came over to take their orders. After she left, Trenton said, "You look stunning, Andria. I see life is still treating you well."

"I do okay, but I want to talk about you and what happened to your face."

He touched his jaw and told the same lie he had told everyone that had asked.

"You're lucky you didn't break your neck," she responded. "So tell me, how did you turn your ordinary life into this?"

He leaned back in his chair and crossed his legs and proudly said, "It was being at the right place at the right time, meeting the right people."

The waitress returned with their coffee and complimentary pastries. Trenton pulled out a twenty and handed it to the waitress, but she refused to take it. She reminded him that his coffee was also on the house. Trenton insisted that the waitress take the twenty as a tip for good customer service, which she happily accepted.

Andria took a sip of her coffee and asked, "So since you've become so successful, is there anyone special in your life?"

He sighed and said, "I don't know how to answer that. I am with someone. Are they special? Good question. The jury's still out on that one."

Andria giggled.

He took a sip of his hot beverage and asked, "What about you? Have you been able to get over the almighty Ramsey Stone?"

She covered her face with her hands and said, "Not really. I don't know what's wrong with me. I know I wasn't the only woman he was dating. Looking back now, I know I was just a booty call and I made myself available for him anytime he wanted me. I fell in love with him. I still can't believe he married that woman."

"I'll have to say I was shocked as well," he replied.

"What about you? Does your lady friend compare to Keilah?"

"My situation is a little different. I broke up with her, remember?"

"Oh yeah, I had forgotten about that. You basically left her at the altar. Ramsey told me she had her dress and everything. I hate her guts, but I don't know how you could do her like that."

He sighed and said, "I just couldn't go into a marriage with her doing what she did for a living. She wouldn't quit and I wouldn't bend, either, so I said to hell with it. Do I regret it? Hell yeah! Do I want her back? It would be nice. Do I think it'll happen? The chances are pretty slim."

"I still don't see how you dumped her so close to your wedding. Didn't you love her?" Andria asked.

"Yeah, but I had to stand my ground. It was my job to be the man of the house, but she was acting like she wanted the position. She had more balls than I could deal with."

Trenton was beginning to get angrier by the second about the demise of his relationship with Keilah. He'd thought he was over her, but he realized he wasn't. She was supposed to be heartbroken over him, not the other way around. He was upset that she had moved on and found happiness with not just any man. She'd married Ramsey Stone.

"Anyway, that's enough about me," he added. "What about you? Is love in the air?"

She smiled and said, "Well, there is this one guy I'm seeing now. He's no Ramsey, but he's sweet. He's a little older than me, but he has a great job where he gets to travel, and he adores me. I can see making a life with him."

Trenton laughed and said, "I can already tell there's no love connection, but I understand how you feel. You're looking for security and stability, and it don't help that the brother's got a fat bank account, huh?"

She stirred her coffee and said, "Who says he's a brother?"

"Don't tell me you've crossed over," he joked. "What about the sex? Because I remember hearing that you were practically a freak."

She threw a napkin at him and exclaimed, "I'm not! Who told you that?"

They laughed together, and she admitted that he was, in fact, African American and the son of an acquaintance of her father's.

They talked a little while longer, and then Andria touched Trenton's hand and said, "I don't want to keep you from your fans any longer. I know you have to get back over there and work the crowd. I need to go to the ladies' room. Do you mind watching my purse?"

"I'm in no hurry. Take your time.," he answered. "My time here is almost over, anyway. It's been nice catching up with you."

They stood, and she said, "The same here, Trenton. I know we didn't always get along when we were with those other people, but I'm glad we've grown since then."

"Me too," he answered as he watched her make her way to the ladies' room.

With Thanksgiving behind them, the Stones could finally exhale. It had been a long holiday weekend, but it had also been special because they had had their entire family present to give thanks. They had so much to be thankful for and looked forward to seeing one another for Christmas in a few weeks.

Keilah was busy going over records, preparing for year-end reports, while Ramsey took off early for a weekend trip with his two best friends, Neil Jackson, an ex-military officer like Ramsey and now a D.C. police officer, and Kyle. Keilah's eyes were tired and she needed a break, so she called her best friend and asked her to meet her for lunch.

Keilah met her dear friend Tori Giles for lunch at a restaurant that specialized in healthy Southern cooking. Tori was an attractive woman, slender with long, muscular legs. She wore a Halle Berry–style haircut, and being from Jackson, Mississippi, she took her Southern heritage seriously, especially when it came to cooking. After graduating from Howard, she moved to New York, where for several years she worked in a public relations firm. She had moved back to D.C a few months ago and was now working as a lobbyist in the gas and oil industry. She had done very well for herself financially, and presently she was single and waiting for Mr. Right so she could settle down.

Keilah hugged her and said, "Tori, you look fabulous."

Tori sat down and said, "So do you. You're wearing that suit. You look so professional."

"So do you. I know you're a pit bull on Capitol Hill."

"Something like that," Tori replied as the two women laughed. "Marriage and motherhood agree with you, Keilah. You're glowing, and you haven't aged a bit. You still have that same majorette figure that you had in college."

Keilah took a sip of her water and said, "Thank you, Tori, but I am a little heavier in the hips."

"That's baby and marriage weight, and so what? The extra weight looks great on you."

Keilah smiled and said, "You sound like my husband. Seriously, though, I never thought I could ever be this happy. I'm so glad my eyes were opened and I saw Ramsey for who he was. We were friends for so long, I never thought of him in any other way."

"That's funny," Tori said as she buttered a hot croissant.

"Hello, ladies," a baritone voice interrupted. "What a nice surprise."

Keilah made eye contact with him and asked, "Are you stalking me, Trenton?"

Trenton put his hands up and said, "Whoa, calm down, Mrs. Stone. I saw you guys from my table across the room, and I only came over to say hello."

"Hello, Trenton," Tori replied. "You look good."

He didn't remove his sunglasses, because if he did, they would see the black eye he had courtesy of Ramsey Stone.

"Thank you, Tori. You're looking rather hot yourself," he said in response.

"Congratulations on the book," Tori stated. "I see you with your bling."

He looked down at his diamond-encrusted watch and said, "I appreciate that. I can tell life is treating you well too."

Tori held her glass up to him and said, "It is. Thank you."

He glanced back over his shoulder and said, "I would ask you ladies to join me, but Keilah's husband don't take kindly to me being in her personal space. God forbid he walks in and finds me talking to you."

Tori giggled.

"What the hell are you talking about?" Keilah asked.

Trenton smiled, realizing that Keilah didn't know that Ramsey had paid him an unfriendly visit. He rubbed his chin and with a frown said, "I guess he didn't tell you, huh?"

"Tell me what?" Keilah asked, clearly agitated.

He leaned down close to her and sniffed her perfume, and then he whispered, "Damn, you smell good."

Keilah leaned away from him and said, "Get the hell away from me, Trenton."

He laughed, and then his expression went from warm to cold in an instant. "Tell Ramsey my memory is long, and if he's not careful, something or someone will remind him that he's not invincible."

Keilah stood and threw her napkin on the table and said, "Get the hell out of here before I shove my Jimmy Choo shoes up your ass. Don't you ever threaten my husband, you bastard. Everything that happened to you was brought on by you."

He laughed, then reached into her glass of water, pulled out a cube of ice, stuck it in his mouth, and said, "Hmmm, I can still taste you. See you around, babe."

Tori gasped in shock.

Keilah sat down and said, "Ain't that a bitch? He has lost his damn mind."

"What do you think he was talking about?"

Keilah motioned for the waiter to come remove her glass and said, "Who knows? He's delusional and sad."

"I can't believe he did that," Tori said as she placed her napkin in her lap. "You are going to tell Ramsey, right?"

"If I do, I'm afraid he might kill him," she answered just as the waiter brought her another glass of water. She was furious and couldn't believe that Trenton would approach her like he did. She had every right to kick his ass across the room, but exercising restraint, she decided not to feed into his arrogance and ignorance. This was something her husband definitely needed to know about. Who knew what he would do next? In the meantime she would try her best to enjoy lunch with her best friend.

"Okay, enough about Trenton. I want to know what's been going on with you. How's work?"

"Work is great. I love spending time on Capitol Hill, around all that power."

Keilah opened her menu and said, "And you love spending all that money you're making too, huh?"

"I do like the finer things in life," she replied as she scanned her menu. "Like these shoes, which I had to have."

Keilah looked down at her friend's feet and said, "Those are nice. I don't blame you. You only live once."

"Ditto! But I'm not stupid. I am investing and saving too. A girl's got to have a nest egg. Everyone can't be a millionaire like you."

"May I take your order?" the waitress said, interrupting the pair.

"Yes, I'll have the crispy crab cakes, collard greens, and triple corn grits with a lemonade," Keilah recited to the waitress.

"Okay. What about you, ma'am?"

Tori said, "I'll have the honey-soy broiled salmon with the zucchini-rice casserole, a small house salad, and an iced tea."

The waitress smiled and said, "I'll be right back with your drinks and more honey buttered croissants."

When the waitress left, Keilah stared Tori in the eyes and asked, "How's the dating scene going for you?"

"I go out to dinner from time to time. You know I don't have a lot of time to date."

"You're not getting any younger," Keilah reminded her just as the waitress returned with their drinks and croissants.

"Your entrées will be out shortly," the waitress informed them.

"Thank you," Keilah replied.

The two friends continued to talk over the next ten minutes about their lives and occasionally reminisced about their joyous college days before returning back to the subject of dating.

"So when are you going to take the time to date?" Keilah asked. "You're a beautiful, intelligent woman, and I know your mom has been asking the same question."

About that time the waitress arrived with their entrées. As soon as she left, Tori said, "Well, I do have something to tell you, but you can't freak out."

Keilah bit into her crab cake and said, "I promise."

"Well, I did meet someone, but I don't want to say any more, because I don't want to jinx it."

"Who is it? What does he do for a living? Where is he from?" Keilah asked, bombarding her friend with questions.

"See, this is exactly why I haven't said anything. You're freaking out, and you said you wouldn't."

Keilah put her fork down and said, "I'm sorry, Tori, I'm just so happy for you."

"Don't count him in too soon. He's fine and he's sweet, but I need to get to know him a little more."

Keilah took a bite of her collard greens and said, "I understand, but hurry up, because Neariah needs someone to play with."

"Don't hold your breath. It's hard to find a good man these days, especially one who's worth marrying."

Keilah gave her friend's hand a squeeze and said, "Good men are still out there, sis, so don't throw in the towel yet."

"I won't. I'll give him a chance," Tori answered before she took a bite of her salmon. "He has the most handsome eyes and smile, and he smells so good."

"Really?" Keilah asked with a smile.

Tori closed her eyes and said, "Yeah, and he has the softest lips. Hmmm, he's a great kisser."

Keilah threw up her hands and said, "Now, that's what I'm talking about. You do the damn thang, girl."

Tori giggled and said, "I'll keep you posted."

"You'd better, and you had better bring him over for dinner. I can't believe I haven't been able to get you over to our new house since you moved back from New York. You're either out of town or you're working. Life is too short, and you need to relax and have fun."

"I promise I'll make the next one."

Keilah wiped her mouth with the napkin and said, "Good, because I want to meet this guy, but I'll wait until you feel comfortable bringing him over. I don't want him to feel pressured."

"Thanks, Keilah. Now, do you have any new pictures of Neariah? I know she's growing."

"Of course," Keilah said as she proudly pulled out her wallet and handed it to her best friend.

"Oh, Keilah, she's beautiful. She looks just like you."

"You think? I think she looks like Ramsey, but I see myself in some of her expressions," she answered as she slid her wallet back inside her purse.

"Are you planning on having any more?"

Keilah finished off her lunch and said, "I would love to have at least two more. It'll limit my time in the office, but that's okay. I'm ready to cut my hours, anyway."

"You do know that you really don't have to work, right?"

Keilah leaned back in her chair and said, "I know, but the business is our creation. I never dreamed we would be this successful with our business."

"But you love being a wife and mother, don't you?" Tori asked.

"Without a doubt," Keilah admitted. "I'm doing okay juggling both right now, but if I have two more, there's no way I can work."

"I can understand you wanting to be in your office every day, but seriously, Keilah, if you don't have to, don't push yourself unnecessarily. Hell, you could probably be just as productive working from home. You do that sometimes, anyway, don't you?"

"Yes," Keilah answered.

At that time the waitress came over to see if they wanted any dessert. Both ladies declined and continued to enjoy each other's company for a little while longer before finally asking for the check. When the waitress sat their checks on the table, Keilah quickly snatched Tori's out of her hand.

"I got it!"

Tori grabbed both checks out of Keilah's hand. "You got the check all the time when we were in college. I have some paying back to do, so it's my treat." Tori handed both checks to the waitress along with her credit card. After the waitress walked away, Tori said, "I'm so glad we got together. We're going to have to do it more often."

"We will," Keilah replied as she pulled her lipstick out of her purse and reapplied it. "And keep me posted on that new man."

The waitress returned to the table with Tori's receipt and credit card.

Tori signed the slip and said, "I'll definitely keep you posted." She handed the receipt back to the waitress and said, "Thank you."

The two ladies grabbed their purses and headed toward the exit, where they hugged before the valet returned with their vehicles.

Chapter Nine

Ramsey and his friends started out their day with brunch at their hotel, during which they enjoyed an abundance of smoked salmon, eggs Benedict, strawberry and banana waffles, gourmet scrambled eggs, home fries, bacon, and a multitude of omelets and other delicious breakfast items. As Ramsey waited for the chef to finish making his steak and veggie omelet, he felt someone slide their arm around his waist. Startled, he quickly turned and found his old flame, Andria, smiling up at him.

"My, my, my. Ramsey Stone, you have gotten finer and sexier since the last time I saw you."

He eased out of her embrace, and without making eye contact, he said, "Are you stalking me, Andria?"

"Don't flatter yourself. I'm here on business. What about you?"

He looked her in the eye and said, "Pleasure."

"Oooh, I like the way that sounds," she replied as she scanned his body up and down.

Anxious to get his omelet so he could put some distance between himself and Andria, he said, "Well, it was nice to see you. I hope all is well."

She licked her lips, and with a seductive glare she said, "I've been better, but seeing you has made my day."

The chef handed him the plated omelet, and Ramsey said, "That's great. Well, enjoy your trip."

Andria grabbed his arm as he turned to walk away.

"Ramsey, is there somewhere we can go talk? I would really like to catch up with you."

He pointed over at Neil and Kyle and said, "It's really not a good time. I'm here with my friends, and it wouldn't be appropriate."

She walked closer to him and asked, "In that case, aren't you going to invite me to join you? I haven't seen Kyle and Neil in a while."

Ramsey looked her in the eyes and politely said, "No. Sorry. This is a guys' weekend."

She frowned upon seeing that she wasn't getting her way.

"*No?* What do you mean, no? Have you forgotten that you used to be all up in this?" Andria asked as she grabbed her crotch. "I haven't forgotten how you dissed me over that bitch—"

He put his finger in her face and yelled, "Don't you say one more word, Andria, or I swear to God, I'll—"

"You'll what?" she yelled, drawing attention to their argument. "Hit me!"

"I don't hit women," he announced as he turned and walked away.

Andria followed him over to his table and continued to cause a scene.

Ramsey sat his plate on the table and calmly said, "You need to leave, Andria. I don't know why you're acting like this, but no matter the reason, you need to go on about your business before I have your crazy ass arrested."

She put her hands on her hips and said, "You can't have me arrested. Do you know who I am?"

Neil smiled and then discreetly showed her his badge.

"We all know who you are, Andria. In fact we could never forget it, but if you don't leave, I'll call the police myself." Neil announced.

"Negro, please! You don't scare me."

It wasn't long before a hotel security guard approached their table and asked, "Is there a problem here?"

Ramsey stared at Andria and said, "Miss Rockwell was just leaving."

The security guard, who had been observing the altercation from afar, turned to Andria and said, "Ma'am, the gentlemen would like you to leave. Are you going to leave on your own, or will I need to escort you out of the building?"

Andria looked at him and said, "I wish you would put your hands on me, you rent-a-cop."

"Ma'am, I'm not going to ask you again," the security guard replied.

Andria pulled her purse strap up on her shoulder, pointed at Ramsey, and said, "You haven't seen the last of me. You'll answer to me one day." As she angrily walked off, she pulled out her cell phone and dialed a number and said, "Rico, you're not going to believe who I ran into."

Ramsey sat down, picked up his fork, and started eating without responding. There wasn't a day that went by that he didn't regret getting involved with her intimately.

Once she was gone, Kyle said, "Damn! You said she was crazy, but I didn't know she was that crazy."

Ramsey smiled and said, "I would never hit her, but I started to shake the shit out of her."

Laughing, Kyle said, "Bro, I was sitting here thinking I was going to have to get some bail money ready for you. I could see it in your eyes. She really knows how to push your buttons."

"That's what pisses me off," Ramsey replied.

"I wish I would've had my cuffs with me," Neil said with a big grin on his face. "She sure is fine, though."

Ramsey looked over his shoulder and said, "Yeah, fine and crazy. I'm just glad she's gone."

"Yeah, but you better watch your back," Neil replied as he picked up his cup of coffee and took a sip.

The gentlemen finished their brunch on a light note, talking about sports, and then it was on to Richmond, Virginia, to a car show and auction. When they got outside to Ramsey's car, they were stunned to see that the finish was severely scratched. It was obvious that the car had been keyed.

"Damn!" Neil yelled as he inspected the car. "I bet Andria did this. She jacked you up."

Ramsey was so livid, he just shook his head in disbelief.

"This is going to cost you a pretty penny, bro," Kyle said as he also inspected the damage.

"Come on, so I can call the cops," Ramsey said as he headed back into the hotel. "I hope they have her on tape keying my car. There's no reason to believe anyone else did it."

"That's true," Kyle answered as he and Neil followed Ramsey into the hotel to report the incident. Unfortunately, one camera's view of Ramsey's car was obstructed by a van. The other camera showed the incident as it took place, but it happened too far away for security to say without a doubt that it was a woman, let alone Andria. But Ramsey knew it was her, and that was all that mattered.

They were like any other men when it came to cars. They liked them shiny and fast, but not damaged.

Ramsey came prepared to place a bid on one, especially since his prized Mercedes was now scarred. He had always wanted a classic car, and he was leaning toward a Mustang, but if something else caught his eye, he could easily be swayed if the price was right.

"Damn, Kyle, did you come here to look at cars or not?" Ramsey asked as he noticed Kyle continuously texting on his phone.

Neil laughed and said, "Give him a break, Ramsey. He has a girlfriend. I'm sure he's checking in with her."

Ramsey stopped in his tracks and asked, "Since when?"

Kyle looked over at Neil and gave him a look that indicated he wasn't ready to tell Ramsey about his new lady friend.

"He met her in the vegetable aisle at one of those organic food markets," Neil volunteered.

Ramsey turned to Kyle and asked, "Bro, why didn't you tell me?"

Kyle tucked his cell phone in his pocket and opened the car show program. "I wanted to wait to see if she would hang around longer than a week after she found out I worked for the Department of Defense. You know how women are. They like to ask, 'How was your day? Did anything good happen at work?' Shit like that. You know I can't talk about my job."

Ramsey and Neil laughed together because they knew they were probably the only people Kyle could talk to about his job and know that what he said would be kept in the strictest confidence.

"How long have you been dating her?" Ramsey asked.

Kyle stuck a piece of gum in his mouth and said, "About a month and a half."

Ramsey looked over at Neil and asked, "Have you met her?"

"No, he keeps her under lock and key."

"Is she ugly or something?" Ramsey asked his best friend.

Kyle shook his head and said, "No, she's not ugly."

"Have you hit it yet?" Neil asked with a sly grin on his face.

"No! And if I had, I wouldn't tell you!" Kyle answered, clearly irritated. "Are we going to look at cars or not?"

"Oh, now you want to look at cars," Ramsey replied with a chuckle as they started walking toward the showroom full of cars. "We can look at cars, but this conversation is not over. We will continue this at dinner, because I can't believe you hid her from me. I want to know all about her."

Kyle stopped walking again and said, "Okay! Damn! You two are acting worse than my mom."

"I still can't believe he hasn't hit it after six weeks," Neil added. "Something must be wrong with her."

"Shut up, Neil," Kyle said. "Nothing's wrong with her."

"Then something's wrong with you. Do you need some Viagra to help you out?" Neil joked.

"Go to hell," Kyle replied as they walked over to a classic Corvette. "I'm not like you. I don't jump in bed with a woman just because she has a pulse. I like a woman who's attractive, educated, and classy. So far she has met all my expectations."

Neil opened the Corvette's door and eased into the leather seat and pretended he was driving. "What's her name?" he asked.

"I'd rather not say right now," Kyle replied.

"Why not? Are you afraid I might've already tapped that ass?" Neil asked and then laughed.

Intervening, Ramsey said, "Leave him alone. It's obvious he likes the woman. Why don't you bring her over for dinner so we can meet her?"

Kyle rubbed his chin and said, "I don't know. You guys can be a tough audience. I'm not ready to put her through all the questions, especially from Keilah."

The threesome moved over to a Porsche and started inspecting it.

"That's not fair. We care about you, bro, and you know Keilah loves you. She has a sixth sense when it comes to women. If this woman is not right for you, she'll know."

"This is nice!" Neil announced loudly to his friends. "Ramsey, you need to buy this for your boy."

"What kind of Porsche is it?" Ramsey asked as he admired the sleek design.

"It's called a Cayman," Kyle answered after glancing at the listing of cars.

"It's sweet, but I've never been a Porsche fan," Ramsey replied.

"I know. That's why I told you to buy it for me," Neil told him.

Ramsey laughed. He often gave his friends and family lavish gifts, but he knew Neil really didn't expect him to buy him such an expensive car, even though he could easily afford to.

"If anybody's getting a car, it'll be my baby."

Neil closed the door of the Porsche and said, "You are so whipped."

"Don't hate. I love my wife. She deserves this and more," Ramsey declared.

"No, you're just afraid of her," Neil joked. "Keilah could gut you in your sleep if she wanted to, and she might just do that after she finds out about Andria and what she did to your car."

Ramsey ignored his remark as they moved on to some classic 1950-style Chevrolet cars.

"You're ignorant, Neil," Kyle pointed out. "Ramsey would never give his wife a reason to gut him, unlike you, and he can handle Andria without getting Keilah involved."

"You know Keilah's not the average woman," Neil replied. "She's vicious, but sexy as hell. I've seen her handiwork. She's accurate with a nine-millimeter and not a woman you would want to cross. Personally, I think it's a turn-on when you know your woman's capable of killing you."

Ramsey laughed out loud after this particular remark. He turned to Neil and said, "You're only saying that because your second wife threatened to cut your throat, and for good reason, after she caught you kissing that legal secretary. You don't know how to keep your pants up."

All three of them laughed because Neil had had a few close calls with some of the women in his life. Now he was single and on the prowl once again.

"You keep up that kind of behavior and one of them will take you out for real. You're too old for games like that. Be honest with the women," Ramsey stated.

"Yes, and stop dating the ones with mug shots," Kyle added before laughing.

"Enough about women. This is supposed to be a guys' weekend," Neil announced.

"Oh, now you want to shut the conversation down," Ramsey pointed out.

Neil was always teasing everyone else, but when the table was turned on him, he was ready to change the subject.

"Bro, you're a work in progress," Ramsey informed Neil. "We won't give up on you, though." Ramsey then turned to his buddy Kyle and patted him on the shoulder. "Kyle, don't listen to Neil. He's an idiot. Bring your lady over for dinner next weekend. I'm sure we'll love her."

"Thanks, Ramsey. I'll talk to her and let you know."

"What about me?" Neil asked. "Am I invited too?"

"No!" the pair said in unison.

Neil turned away from them and said, "That's all right. I see how you guys treat me."

"If you come, you'll scare the woman away for sure," Ramsey explained. "You'll start cracking your ignorant jokes, and then you'll ask the woman a million questions. I want the evening to be relaxing."

"That's cool," Neil answered. "Kyle, I joke around with you and give you a hard time, but I'm just bullshitting with you. You're a cool dude, and on the real I hope things work out between you and this woman."

Kyle shook Neil's hand and said, "Thanks, bro."

Chapter Ten

Back in D.C., at the Stone-Chance Protection Agency, the receptionist greeted the tall, handsome visitor standing in front of her. She smiled and asked, "May I help you, sir?"

With a bouquet of beautiful flowers in hand, he smiled back at her and said, "I'm here to see Keilah Chance, and I apologize, but I don't have an appointment."

"Your name, sir?"

"Michael Monroe."

"I'm sorry, Mr. Monroe, but Mrs. Stone is not available at the moment, but I'll be happy to make you an appointment."

Confused, he frowned and then asked, "Did you say Mrs. Stone?"

The receptionist smiled and said, "Yes, sir."

He smiled back and said, "I'm sorry. I didn't know Keilah had gotten married. It's been a while since we've spoken, and I've been out of town for a while."

"I understand, sir. So would you like me to make you an appointment?"

Michael handed the receptionist the flowers and said, "No, that's okay. These are for her, if you would be so kind as to give them to her."

As he turned to walk away, the receptionist said, "I'll make sure she gets them."

With a smile he answered, "Thank you."

"Are you sure you don't want to make an appointment?"

Still smiling, he said, "I'll call later. I have somewhere I have to be."

After the elevator doors closed, the receptionist placed the flowers on her own desk so that Keilah would see them as soon as she returned.

On the elevator ride down, Michael rubbed his head in despair. He had hoped to meet with Keilah and apologize for all the pain he had caused her. He had had no idea she had gotten married, because all Arhmelia had said was that she had a daughter, but since she was Mrs. Stone, it was obvious she had married Ramsey. They were close, but he had never seen any kind of attraction between the two of them. Perhaps she'd married one of his family members or something, he thought. One thing he knew for sure was that he needed to get home so he could do some research to find out exactly what he'd missed while he was overseas during the past year and to determine if there was a chance that he was the father of Keilah's daughter. If he was, he wanted all his rights as her father, whether Keilah wanted him to exercise them or not.

When he arrived home, Michael entered his house and threw his keys on the table. He made his way into his office and opened his laptop. As soon as it powered up, he logged on to Google Keilah's name. Almost immediately, several links popped up, and he began selecting each one. The first was a local newspaper article, in the society section, confirming that Keilah had married Ramsey. Michael felt like the wind had been knocked out of him as he read the paragraph line by line telling the fairy-tale love story of how the young couple met. The article went on to highlight the success of their business. There was no mention of children in this article or in any others. Whether it was on purpose or not, he didn't know, but he had to find out, and the best way to do that was to go to the source, so maybe, he thought, making an appointment to see Keilah was the best plan of action at this point to get to the truth about everything.

Keilah stepped off the elevator and entered the office, only to be stopped by the receptionist.

"Mrs. Stone, a friend of yours dropped off these beautiful flowers for you this morning."

Keilah walked over to the receptionist's desk and asked, "Who?"

The receptionist picked up a piece of paper and said, "He said his name was Michael Monroe and that he's been out of touch with you for a while. He didn't want to make an appointment."

Keilah turned to walk away and said, "If he calls or comes back, let me know."

"Yes, Mrs. Stone," she answered.

Keilah stopped, turned back to the young receptionist, and said, "It's Keilah. You don't have to call me Mrs. Stone."

"Yes, ma'am."

The hallway to her office seemed longer than usual. She had known the possibility was always there that Michael would show his face, but she hadn't been sure if he was going to have the nerve after what he did to her. She was curious to find out what the nature of his visit was, but she wasn't going to panic and would wait to see if he decided to make a return visit. At that point she would meet him head-on and would settle their differences once and for all.

***

The next afternoon, Ramsey returned home, and like usual, he was met at the door by his beloved German shepherd, Target. After rewarding his pet with some treats for guarding his loved ones over the past few days, he made his way into the family room, where he found his wife, dressed in sweatpants and a snug T-shirt, on the sofa, going through the Sunday paper. Neariah was sitting next to her mother, playing with toys. When Neariah saw her father walking toward her, her eyes immediately lit up and she started calling out to him.

"How are my two favorite girls?" he asked as he picked Neariah up and gave her a big kiss on the cheek before sitting down next to his wife.

She admired the loving interaction between father and daughter and said, "We're fine. How was your trip?"

"I'll tell you after you give me a taste of those luscious lips."

Keilah blushed and then leaned over and gave him a loving kiss on the lips and lingered there, inhaling his manly scent.

He looked in her eyes and whispered, "I missed you guys."

"We missed you too," she replied as she laid her head on his chest and caressed his face.

Ramsey didn't want to tell Keilah about his altercation with Andria, but he did tell her his car was keyed. There had been no love lost between the two women when he was dating Keilah. When Andria found out Ramsey had married Keilah, she claimed she was devastated by it, even though their relationship had been mostly based on physical intimacy and not on emotions, at least not on his end.

Target tried to jump on the sofa to get some attention from his owner, but Ramsey stopped him and ordered him to lie down on the floor. Target knew he wasn't allowed on the furniture, but he tried it, anyway.

"Neariah looks like she's grown since I've been gone."

"She probably has. She eats like a six-year-old."

Ramsey chuckled and bounced his daughter on his knee and then held her high over his head. She giggled loudly, and he continued to play with her. After a few moments he looked over at his sexy wife and put his hand on her inner thigh and massaged it seductively.

"Stay home with me tomorrow," he said.

"Are you serious?" she asked with a giggle.

"Hell, yeah, I'm serious. I have some catching up to do."

Keilah stood in front of him to give him a full view of her body and said, "If you help me with dinner and put Neariah to bed, I'm all yours."

He stood with Neariah in his arms and said, "Sounds like a plan to me. I'm starving. What are we having?"

"Glazed pork chops, rice, and steamed vegetables," she replied as she led him into the kitchen.

Ramsey sat Neariah in her high chair and then washed his hands. "Do you want me to do the meat or the vegetables?" he asked.

"Whatever you want to do," she answered.

When he looked at Keilah, he noticed she was bent over in the refrigerator. He picked up a dish towel and dried his hands while admiring the view of her backside. When she turned around with an armful of vegetables, she noticed the sultry look on his face.

"I dare to ask what you're thinking," she said as she placed the vegetables on the countertop.

"You don't have to ask, because you already know," he said with a chuckle.

"Are you that bad, Stone?"

He washed the vegetables and then started chopping them. "I'm not going to lie to you, babe . . . hell yeah! I haven't seen you in three days. I'm aching."

Neariah giggled loudly, as if she knew what her parents were talking about.

Keilah washed the pork chops and the seasoned them with salt, pepper, garlic, and a few spices. She loved working side by side with her husband in the kitchen.

"I'll have to admit, I'm no different. I hate sleeping alone."

At that moment he pulled Keilah into his arms and gave her a deep, sizzling kiss. This went on for several seconds, until the couple found themselves almost at the point of no return.

"Baby, you're killing me," he said softly after breaking their kiss.

Keilah ran her tongue along his lips and then gave him another kiss and whispered, "Why don't we hurry up with dinner so we can take this upstairs?"

Ramsey turned on the gas stove, poured a little extra virgin olive oil in the pan, and began sautéing the vegetables. "That's a date. Give me twenty minutes and I'll be done," he said.

"Me too," she replied with a smile as she placed the tray of pork chops in the oven.

Ramsey knew he needed to change the subject before they found themselves on the kitchen floor, so he pulled a bottle of wine out of the wine cooler and popped the cork. As he poured the pinot grigio into crystal glasses, he said, "I almost bought you a Porsche this weekend."

She looked into his eyes to see if he was joking. When she saw that he wasn't, she answered, "A Porsche? Are you crazy? Besides, I'm perfectly happy with my Land Rover. I don't need a Porsche."

"I know, but I let Neil get into my head and he almost talked me into it."

Keilah hugged her husband and said, "You should know not to listen to Neil. He can be an idiot sometimes. I'm glad you resisted the urge. If you want to buy me something, think about a vacation home in the Caribbean."

He took a sip of wine and said, "We do need somewhere to go to unwind. As a matter of fact, I wish I had you down there right now, buck naked on the sand, with the waves crashing all around us."

"I'll drink to that."

Neariah called out to her mother and reached for her.

"Somebody's hungry," Ramsey said as he scooped a small amount of the sautéed vegetables onto a saucer.

Keilah mashed up the vegetables and blew on the mixture to cool it before giving Neariah a spoonful. Neariah squealed, wanting more food.

"Check the chops, babe, because Neariah's hungry. They should be ready by now."

Ramsey opened the oven and pulled out the chops. As Keilah watched him arrange the food on their plates, she saw the perfect opportunity to ask him about Trenton.

"Hey, babe, did something happen between you and Trenton?"

He glanced up at her and said, "I just reminded him that you were my wife and not to ever disrespect you or call you again."

She put her hands on her hips and asked, "And just how did you remind him?"

He smiled and said, "In a manly way. That's all you need to know. Why are you asking, anyway? Did he call you again?"

"No, I ran into him when I was having lunch with Tori the other day."

He frowned and asked, "Are you sure it was a coincidence?"

She could see her husband's jaw quivering. She wasn't sure what had taken place between him and Trenton, but if she had to guess, it was physical. "I'm pretty sure it was a coincidence, but I will say that he's not happy over what happened between you two. He said to tell you his memory is long and that you're not invincible."

He sat their plates on the table and said, "I'm not the least bit worried about pretty boy Trenton. He knows I'm not going to tolerate him disrespecting you."

She wrapped her arms around his waist, gave him a kiss on the cheek, and said, "I'm sure he does. Maybe that's why he was wearing sunglasses, huh?"

Ramsey laughed and said, "Maybe."

"Come on. Let's eat," Keilah said as she sat down across from her husband.

Conversation over dinner was light and loving, while inside, Ramsey's blood was boiling. Trenton was asking for another beat down, and he would be happy to oblige him as soon as he could find him. Keilah couldn't feed Neariah fast enough. She didn't have a lot of teeth, but she had enough to eat table food.

"I can't believe the appetite she has," Ramsey remarked.

Keilah laughed and said, "She's your daughter."

He smiled and said, "You got that right. Oh, before I forget, I invited Kyle over for dinner next weekend.

He has this new, mysterious girlfriend, and I told him I wanted to meet her."

"Kyle has a girlfriend?" she asked as she put their empty plates into the sink. "I thought he said he was too busy for a relationship."

Ramsey pulled Neariah out of her high chair and said, "Obviously, this one must've made an impression on him. He's been dating her for a couple of weeks now."

Keilah washed their plates and said, "Well, I hope she's not a gold digger. He's a good man, and he deserves a good woman who's not with him because of his money, and she has to understand his job."

"That's true," he replied as he held Neariah high above his head, causing her to giggle. "Let me finish the kitchen while you give Neariah her bath."

She took her daughter into her arms and said, "Okay, and when I'm done, I'll have a hot bath waiting for you too."

"Now, that's what I'm talking about," he said before giving her a kiss on the neck and a loving pat on her backside.

Thirty minutes later, Ramsey made his way upstairs, with Target following close behind. When he peeped into the nursery, he found Neariah wide awake as Keilah gently rocked her.

"She's still up?" he asked.

"I'm sorry, babe."

He walked farther into the room and asked, "Why is she so wired?"

"I don't know. She's acting like she's had some Red Bull or something."

Ramsey reached out for his daughter and took her out of Keilah's arms. "Go run that bath you were talking about. I got this."

She stood and asked, "Are you sure?"

He held Neariah high about his head and smiled up at his beautiful daughter and said, "Yeah. I'm sure."

"If you say so," Keilah replied as she sat her cup of milk on the table.

Twenty minutes later, Ramsey laid his sleeping daughter in her crib and turned out the light. He had a special touch when it came to putting his daughter to sleep when she wasn't sleepy. Keilah was a great mother, and her bond with her daughter was unlike any he'd ever seen, even with his sister. Maybe it was the fact that Keilah had been without her mother most of her life or that she was raised by four brothers. Either way, he wouldn't trade her for anything or anyone. She was his match and the love of his life.

When he entered the bedroom, it was dark except for a few candles that had been lit in the center of the fireplace.

"Keilah?" he called out.

"In here," she answered from the bathroom.

He entered the bathroom and found candles illuminating that room too, and his wife in their large tub, covered in suds.

"I hope you didn't start without me," he joked as he kneeled down and slid his hand into the warm water and caressed her thigh.

"No, I didn't, but you need to get in before the water cools off."

Ramsey stood and quickly stripped out of his clothes. He eased into the water and pulled Keilah into his arms. "I don't know what you're talking about. The water is still hot."

She nuzzled her face against his warm neck and said, "So are you."

He gave her a tender kiss on the cheek and said, "I love you, Keilah."

She straddled his lap, wrapped her arms around his neck, and said, "I love you too, Ramsey. I don't think I can be any happier than I am right now here with you and Neariah."

He covered her breasts with his mouth and pulled her hips closer to his body. The temperature of the water immediately went up several degrees, especially when Keilah started to let out loud sighs. The attention he was giving her sensitive nipples was amplified with each flick of his tongue.

"Ramsey," she whispered.

"I know, baby," he whispered back before kissing her hard on the lips.

Shivers radiated over her body when she felt his manhood swell between her thighs. She looked him in his eyes and saw love staring back at her.

"I think we're ready to get out of here," she murmured. Before he could respond, she nibbled on his neck, in a spot that was one of his erotic zones and never failed to send him over the edge.

He sucked in a breath and then said, "I agree."

The couple wrapped their bodies in plush towels and blew out all the candles before returning to the bedroom. Once there, they dropped their towels on the floor and climbed into the warm bed. Ramsey pulled Keilah into his arms and showered her with kisses, starting at her lips and working his way down to her manicured toes. On his way back up, he stopped at a spot he was very familiar with and buried his face between her thighs. She writhed, moaned, and cried out in ecstasy as he deepened the oral pleasure he bestowed upon her.

"Ramsey!" she screamed, causing Target to bark from the hallway. Keilah could feel her legs trembling uncontrollably as her husband showed no signs of stopping his sensual assault. "Baby, please!" she cried out just before she shuddered hard, sending a hot wave of pleasure through her entire body.

"Did you like that?" he whispered softly in her ear.

She needed to catch her breath, so all she could do was nod. Ramsey's warm, wet kisses on her body made it difficult to move, especially after he placed her legs over his shoulders and eased his throbbing manhood inside her and began to thrust his hips against hers, first slow and deep and then fast and precise. In either case Keilah was in sheer bliss, and so was her husband. Wanting to get the best angle to give the most sensitive pleasure, he flipped her over on her stomach and made love to her from behind. Hearing her soft sighs and moans let him know she was enjoying his loving, and when her breathing got even deeper, he knew the end was near. Therefore, he flipped her back over on her back and quickly reentered her body.

He covered her lips with his tongue against hers as he quickened his pace. His body felt like it was on fire, and he was covered with perspiration. With each thrust of his hips, Keilah let out a moan, especially when he covered her brown peaks with his mouth and sucked hard on her nipples. Ramsey's body finally stiffened as he had a massive orgasm, causing him to cry out and groan. Keilah kissed him hard on the lips and proclaimed her love for him once again. He buried his face against her warm neck and tried to bring his breathing under control, but he was hit with another orgasm when Keilah ran her tongue over his ear and neck. He was completely exhausted and could barely move.

"Baby, are you okay?" she asked as she rolled him over onto his back and cuddled up to him.

"Couldn't be better," he mumbled as he caressed her curvy backside.

She ran her hands across his broad chest and kissed his luscious lips and then asked, "How much time do you need before we do it again?"

He opened his eyes and asked, "Are you serious?"

"Of course I am, babe. That was amazing, but I'm still a little hungry," she revealed. Ramsey took her hand into his and placed it over his groin and said, "You tell me, babe."

Keilah gently stroked him and said, "If you ask me, things are looking pretty promising right now."

Ramsey looked into her eyes and uttered, "Make me a believer, sweetheart."

At that moment she lowered her head and covered his shaft with her soft, warm lips. Ramsey allowed his wife to take his mind and body to a very special place, and he loved watching her as she pleasured him. She was extremely skillful and had him fully involved and spouting his appreciation in a matter of seconds.

"Are you ready for me, baby?" she asked as she straddled his body and eased down on his massive, throbbing rod.

"Always," he responded as he gripped her round backside and assisted her as she started a slow grind that would soon intensify when he began to thrust his hips up against her body.

This session didn't last as long as the first one, because after a few taps against her hypersensitive core, her release came quickly, as did his, putting both of them in a deep, coma-like sleep for the rest of the night.

The next morning, before Neariah woke up, Ramsey mounted his wife once more and made love to her with so much intensity, it brought her to tears. He had never been with a woman with so much love, sex appeal, courage, and beauty, and he craved her every minute of every day. Controlling his appetite wasn't easy, and he was glad his wife understood and welcomed his affection with open arms.

As they lay in each other's arms, they could hear Neariah begin to cry.

"Neariah's up," he whispered. "Do you want me to get her?"

She gave him a kiss on the lips before climbing out of bed and said, "No, you rest. You put in a hard night's work."

Ramsey smiled and watched her slide into her robe and then exit their bedroom.

Chapter Eleven

Michael couldn't believe someone was ringing his doorbell so early in the morning. He angrily stormed to the door, yanked it open, and yelled, "What!"

To his surprise, his former boyfriend, Kevin, was standing on the porch with a bewildered look on his face.

"Damn! Well, good morning to you too," he replied.

Michael sighed and asked, "What are you doing here, Kevin?"

Kevin slid his hands into his pockets and asked, "Aren't you going to invite me in?"

Michael ran his hands over his head and slowly stepped to the side, and against his better judgment he allowed Kevin to enter. Kevin stepped into the foyer and turned to look at Michael.

"You look good."

Without responding, Michael made his way into the kitchen, with Kevin following close behind. He pulled a cup out of the cabinet and made himself a cup of coffee on his Keurig coffeemaker.

"Do you want any coffee?" he asked.

"No."

Michael grabbed his cup of coffee and sat down at the bar. He put cream and sugar in his cup and asked, "Why are you here, Kevin?"

Kevin sat down next to him. "I'm here because I thought you would've called by now. Since you haven't, I thought I would come by to see what's up."

Michael took a sip of coffee and said, "Nothing's up."

"You have got to be kidding me. Nothing's up?" Kevin retorted. "So, what about us?"

"There is no *us,* Kevin. In fact there never was. I made a mistake. *We* were a mistake."

Kevin looked at him, clearly confused by his sudden change of heart. When Michael was deployed, Kevin felt that their relationship was solid. It was definitely strained when Keilah found out about their love affair, but it was solid nevertheless. Kevin played with the salt and pepper shakers on the table and asked, "Where is all this coming from? I thought we were cool."

Michael looked at his friend and said, "I've been confused about a lot of things, Kevin, including you. This is not me."

"Don't start with that bullshit. I know you, remember?" Kevin replied with a sly grin on his face.

"You think you know me, but you have no idea. There are some things in my past that you don't know about, things that caused me some confusion. I should've told you the truth a long time ago. Maybe if I had, we wouldn't be sitting here."

Kevin reached across the table and touched Michael's hand and said, "I don't believe you. Something happened to you over in Iraq that has you confused. What we have between us is no mistake. I know you love me, and I know you still want to have a child."

Michael removed his hand from Kevin's reach without answering.

Kevin leaned back in his chair and asked, "Does this have something to do with that bitch that shot you?"

"This has nothing to do with her, and you watch your damn mouth when you speak about her. She was the best thing that ever happened to me, and I blew it."

"I can't believe my ears. That psycho bitch shot you, or have you forgotten?"

Michael sighed and said, "Leave Keilah out of it. This has everything to do with me doing the right thing. Everybody makes mistakes. I'm sorry this is hurting you, Kevin, but I'm trying to be as honest about it as possible, and you deserve to find the right person for you. I'm not that person."

Kevin pointed his finger at Michael and said, "Don't think I'm going to let you get away with this. You owe me."

Michael jumped out of his chair, causing it to the fall to the floor. He pulled Kevin out of his chair by the collar and said, "Get the hell out of my house! I told you it never should've happened. I'm not gay!"

Kevin tried to reach up and touch Michael's face, but Michael threw him across the room and yelled, "Don't make me hurt you, Kevin. I said get the hell out of my house, and don't come back."

Pulling himself off the floor, Kevin said, "You must have that post-traumatic stress syndrome, because you're not the person I knew last year."

"You're right! Now, leave and don't ever come back," Michael yelled as he opened the front door.

Kevin looked him in the eyes and said, "You said we were going to have a child. You're going to pay for this."

"I told you it was a mistake, and I don't take kindly to threats. If you think someone is going to give you a child, you're dreaming. Give it up, Kevin!"

Kevin stared into Michael's eyes and gave him an evil look for a few seconds, before finally walking out the door and out to his car.

Michael slammed the door and made his way back upstairs. Once there, he sat down on the side of the bed and covered his face with his hands. He felt somewhat liberated, as if a weight had been lifted off his shoulders. His plan hadn't been to hurt Kevin, but he knew he wasn't being true to himself living the lifestyle he had been living. He was confused, and he needed forgiveness for his trysts with Kevin, and the only way he could redeem himself was to pray for forgiveness and then face his fears. It wasn't going to be easy confronting the man who had molested him years earlier. This had caused him to question his sexuality. This man was responsible for catapulting his career, and while Michael was thankful, he didn't want anyone to think he had been shown favoritism with his career moves. This man had screwed up his head, and it was time for him be held accountable.

Michael pulled himself off the bed and went into the bathroom to take a shower. He had a lot to do today, and if he was going to get his life back, he needed to start at the source of all his misery and ultimate shame. An awakening had happened to Michael in Iraq, and it was long overdue.

Across town, Kevin was still fuming over his argument with Michael. He was hurt, and he wanted Michael to hurt more. He'd taken off work today with plans of spending it with someone he loved, but those plans had changed. So he called his friend Jeremy at the *Washington Signal* newspaper to see if he was interested in running an updated story on the military's latest hero and POW. His friend didn't seem interested until Kevin mentioned Michael's connection to mogul Keilah Chance Stone. Kevin told his friend the whole story of how Michael had been his lover and how he had planned to impregnate Keilah so they could fight for custody of the child and raise it together as a couple. He even told his friend that Keilah had caught them in bed and had shot Michael.

"I don't know, Kevin," Jeremy said. "I mean, it all sounds like a great story for a soap opera or a reality show, but to put this in print could put my reputation and job in jeopardy. I mean, the Stones are a high-powered couple in D.C. and they have some friends in high places."

Kevin let out a breath and said, "Don't tell me you're scared. I thought you were a journalist."

"I am a journalist. I just have to make sure I verify the information if I decide to go with it."

"What other verification do you need?" Kevin asked.

"We're cool and all, but we're talking about my career. I would have to interview Michael or Keilah to get their side of the story before going forward," Jeremy asserted.

Kevin was silent on the other end of the telephone. Then he said, "What if I can get you verification on tape?"

"That might work, as long as I can authenticate the voices. Videotape would be so much better, but have you really thought this through? Are you sure you want to do this? The Stones could make your punk ass disappear if they wanted to, and that fine Michael Monroe could snap your damn neck like a twig," Jeremy stated with a laugh. "If you're going to do this, you'd better understand the consequences."

"I understand them clearly. Michael and that bitch Keilah are going to pay dearly for what they did to me. We had plans for a life together, but Keilah took away any hope of that and Michael let her."

"Hold up! You're not talking about blackmail, are you? 'Cause if you are, I can't be a party to that. That kind of shit will get you put in prison, and prison is

124 Darrien Lee

no place for a guy like me or you. You'd better reconsider—"

Kevin cut him off and said, "There's nothing for me to reconsider. I'll get back at them one way or the other. You let me work out all the details. I just need to know if you're interested in doing the story, because a story like this could reward you with all types of journalism awards."

"That remains to be seen," Jeremy answered. "Look, I have to go. I have a meeting in ten minutes. You have the number. Call me when you have something I can use."

"That's a bet," Kevin replied before hanging up the phone.

Michael got dressed and tucked his cell phone in his pocket. He had a long drive ahead of him, and he wanted to hit the road as soon as possible, before he lost his nerve. It was a cold December morning with clear skies, but he was on a mission. A mission that could release him from his demons so he could get back to living.

Three hours later he pulled up to the secure gates of a prestigious institution and showed the guards his credentials. Being an alumnus, he had more freedom to visit the facility than outsiders. He'd even been a guest speaker at events on various occasions. After being waved through, he parked his car in a visitor's parking space and exited the vehicle with a gift box in hand. He quickly entered the administration building and made his way to retired lieutenant colonel Cornelius Biggs's office. When he opened the door, he found the lieutenant colonel on the telephone. With a smile on his face, Biggs continued to talk on the telephone, but he waved Michael into the office. He quickly ended his telephone call and walked over to Michael and gave him a friendly handshake.

"What a nice surprise. Why didn't you call to let me know you were coming?"

Michael stepped back from the lieutenant colonel and said, "I wanted to surprise you. This is for you."

"You didn't have to bring me anything," Biggs announced. "I should be giving you a gift for surviving in that godforsaken country. I'm glad you made it back safely. Not many of our soldiers do."

"I don't want to talk about what happened over there. Open your gift," Michael instructed him.

"Sure, son. Have a seat. Do you want some coffee, juice, or anything?" the lieutenant colonel asked as he ripped open the wrapping paper and pulled out a beautiful crystal hourglass with the inscription of Matthew 24:36. "This is beautiful," he said as he sat it on the shelf, next to his gold and crystal awards. He made his way back over to his desk and asked, "Are you sure you don't want any bagels or juice or anything?"

Michael waved him off and said, "No, I'm good. I'm not here to take up your time, but there's some things we need to talk about."

The lieutenant colonel poured himself a glass of orange juice before sitting down and said, "Of course. What's on your mind?"

Michael closed his eyes briefly and then opened them to look directly into Biggs's eyes. "I need to know why you felt it was okay to molest me when I was one of your cadets."

The lieutenant colonel's body stiffened, and then he slowly lowered his glass to his desk. With a frown on his face he asked, "What the hell are you talking about?"

"Don't insult my intelligence, Lieutenant Colonel. I'm not delusional, and I'm not fourteen anymore. I know what you did to me and so do you, you son of bitch."

Biggs jumped up from his desk and said, "How dare you come into my office with these accusations? The only thing I ever did was to mentor you boys and helped you gain the illustrious military careers you're enjoying now!"

"I didn't make this up!" Michael shouted back. "You molested me and ruined my goddamn life!"

Biggs's assistant knocked on the door, interrupting them.

The lieutenant colonel, who was clearly distressed, gathered his composure and said, "Come in."

"Lieutenant Colonel, is everything okay?" she asked as she studied the pair. "I thought I heard shouting."

"Yes, Juanita, we're fine. I was just having a spirited conversation with one of my former students. You can go ahead and take your lunch now if you like."

"If you insist," she replied before closing the door.

Once the assistant left the outer office, Biggs turned back to Michael and said, "I don't know what your agenda is for coming here, but I'll be damned if I let you ruin the reputation I've worked so hard to build."

"You screwed up my life!" Michael yelled. "I trusted you, and so did a lot of other boys. You're going to pay for what you did."

"Is this what I think it is? A shakedown?" Biggs asked. "Are you here to try and blackmail me for money?"

"I don't want your damn money. I want you to resign and get treatment before you hurt any more boys, or so help me God, I'll press charges against you," Michael roared. "I'm sure you don't want your wife and family to know what kind of pervert you really are."

The lieutenant colonel started laughing in disbelief. He walked across the room, over to a wall that was full of awards and certificates. He was a huge man in stature, very fit, and even though he was in his early sixties, he had the physique of a man in his early forties. "I hate to be the bearer of bad news, Michael, but no one will believe you. These awards and honors speak for themselves."

Michael walked over to the lieutenant colonel and stood toe-to-toe with him. Being so close to him made him feel nauseated and enraged. He wanted to punch his ass right through the wall, but he controlled himself. With his finger pointed in Biggs's face, he said, "All I need is one person to believe me and your reign here over these boys will be over, you sick bastard. I won't allow you to scar another child like you scarred me."

"Get the hell out of my office before I call security," Biggs firmly ordered Michael.

"I'm not going anywhere until you tell me why you felt it was okay to molest me."

The lieutenant colonel smiled and then tore open Michael's shirt in a fit of rage. "Are you wired? Did the police send you here to get some kind of illegal confession on tape?"

Michael punched Biggs hard on the jaw, knocking him against the wall and onto the floor.

"Don't you ever touch me! You're going to jail or to your grave, old man! I'll see to it up until I take my last breath."

The lieutenant colonel pulled himself off the floor and into his chair, where he pulled out a handkerchief to wipe the blood off his lip. Breathless, he finished off his orange juice, and with his head lowered and fingers interlocked, he said, "Michael, if somewhere in your mind you think I did something to hurt you, I'm sorry.

All I ever wanted was to see young black men like myself succeed in the military like I did. If along the way you think something inappropriate happened between us, I'm sorry you misunderstood my actions."

"Go to hell!" Michael snapped at him. "You know exactly what you did to me! I was fourteen years old, goddamn it!"

"I just wanted to make you happy, Michael. You seemed so angry, lost, and you hated the world. You needed that anger redirected, so I redirected it for you."

With tears streaming down his face, Michael asked, "How does giving me oral sex redirect my anger? Because of you, I haven't been able to have a healthy sexual relationship."

"Why don't you stop playing games with me, Michael? You liked it, didn't you?" the lieutenant colonel said with a smug expression on his face. "There were times I think you looked forward to our little study sessions. You know you were my favorite. As a matter of fact, if you play your cards right, I might consider giving you a welcome home gift, if you know what I mean."

Michael's hands were shaking, and he was sweating profusely. He was ready to choke the life out of his abuser, but he somehow gathered the strength to fight the urge, even though his comment sickened him.

"I should kill you after that remark, but I've given you power over me for too long. I'm confident that you'll get the punishment you deserve."

The lieutenant colonel leaned back in his chair and said, "Don't hold your breath. I'm Lieutenant Colonel Cornelius Biggs. It's going to take more than your word against mine to stop an old jarhead like me. Now, get the hell out of my office before I have you arrested for assault."

Michael smiled, and before walking out of the office, he said, "This isn't over, Lieutenant Colonel."

Biggs pulled a file out of his desk and, without making eye contact with him, replied, "I think it is."

Michael made his way to his car and closed the door. He quickly started the vehicle and turned on the heat. As he waited for the car to warm up, he pulled out his cell phone and selected a new app on it and gazed at the image that appeared.

"Perfect," he mumbled to himself as he put the car in reverse. He pulled out of the parking space and headed off campus for the long drive back to Washington. Little did Lieutenant Colonel Biggs know that Michael's little gift was equipped with a hidden camera to hopefully record him committing more illicit acts against minors. He thought the hourglass was perfect, because it showed the lieutenant colonel that his time was running out and he would be brought to justice soon.

Chapter Twelve

The gold and red leaves covering the trees had been replaced with snow. Christmas was two weeks away, and the Stones' house was finally decorated from roof to basement. A large Fraser fir stood in the foyer of their home, decorated with plenty of lights and ornaments. The rest of the house was decorated with red and gold wreaths and garland and candles, making it look and feel festive. It took three days for Keilah and Ramsey to get everything exactly like they wanted it, but the hard work had paid off. Their house stood out as one of the most admired houses in the neighborhood.

"Sweetheart, Kyle and his date will be here any minute. Is dinner ready?" Ramsey asked as he walked into the bathroom.

Keilah put the finishing touches on her makeup as she sat at the mirror and said, "Relax, Ramsey. I have everything under control. Are you okay? You seem a little nervous."

"I'm not nervous, just anxious to meet this woman. Kyle's my boy. It's going to take a special woman to be compatible with him and his career."

She twirled around in her chair and said, "Well, your wait won't be long. How do I look?"

He took her hand into his and twirled her around so he could get a 360-degree view of her sexy body. "Stunning," he said as he kissed the curve of her neck.

"This outfit isn't too much, is it?" she asked, referring to her maroon velvet skirt with matching leather boots and an ivory cashmere sweater.

"No, it's fine. You look very sexy and festive."

Keilah checked her appearance one more time before walking hand in hand with her husband downstairs to wait for their guests. Luckily, their wait wasn't long, because when they reached the bottom of the stairs, the doorbell rang.

"Sweetheart, answer the door while I get dinner plated."

Keilah made her way into the kitchen, while Ramsey greeted their guests. However, when he opened the door, he got a surprise he wasn't expecting.

"What are you doing here? Keilah didn't tell me you were coming."

Tori stepped into the foyer and said, "Ramsey? Wait a minute. This is your house?"

"Yeah. Hold up. Did you come by yourself or with Kyle?" Ramsey asked, clearly confused.

"How do you know, Kyle?" Tori asked.

Ramsey started laughing just as Kyle stepped into the foyer. "Sorry about that, Victoria. I had to take that call. I see you two have already met, but I'll introduce you, anyway. Victoria, this is my best friend, Ramsey Stone. Ramsey, this is Miss Victoria Giles, my date."

Ramsey shook Tori's hand and continued to laugh as he looked at her first and then over at Kyle.

"What's so funny?" Kyle asked as he helped Tori out of her coat.

Keilah rounded the corner and said, "Okay, it's about time you—" She stopped mid-sentence when she saw the couple standing in the foyer. She put her hands on her hips and asked, "Tori, why didn't you call to tell me you were coming?"

Kyle gave Keilah a confused look and asked, "How do you know Victoria?"

Keilah walked closer. "Victoria is one of my best friends. We went to college together. How do you know her?"

"She's my date," Kyle answered.

"Wait a second!" Tori interjected with an elevated tone. "I need a drink, because I'm confused as hell."

"I'll get the wine," Ramsey said as he continued to laugh.

Keilah escorted Kyle and Tori into the family room and said, "I can't believe this."

Ramsey returned right away with wine and four glasses. Once the wine was poured, Tori quickly drained her glass and held it out for a refill.

"Will somebody please explain to me what's going on?" Kyle requested.

Ramsey laughed and said, "Well, my friend, Tori, whom you know as Victoria, is Keilah's college room-mate."

"Seriously?" Kyle asked.

Tori nodded in agreement as she sipped on her second glass of wine.

"How is it that you didn't know where we were when I pulled up to the house?" Kyle asked.

"I've only been back in town for a few months," Tori explained, "and I've been so busy that I haven't had a chance to visit them, and you never mentioned their names. You just said dinner with some friends."

Keilah stared at Tori and said, "This is the guy you were talking about at lunch the other week?"

"Yes," Tori admitted. "I had no idea you knew him."

"Well, you never mentioned his name, either, so I had no idea," Keilah replied. "You were guarding the relationship so carefully."

Ramsey sat down and said, "Let's all agree that this is a Kodak moment."

"Agreed," they all said in unison.

"I have to admit that I'm angry at myself for not introducing you two to each other before," Ramsey told them. "To be honest, I'm glad you two met. Kyle is a good man, and he'll treat you right."

"As weird as this night has started out, I have to agree with Ramsey," Keilah remarked as she stood. "I say let us go into the dining room, because dinner is hot and ready to serve. We can continue this conversation there, because I want to hear all about how you guys met."

As Keilah led the way into the dining room, Tori asked, "Where's Neariah?"

"She's asleep right now. She normally sleeps through the night, but she's an early bird," Keilah explained.

"I can't wait to see her," Tori replied as Kyle held out her chair for her. She looked around the room and said, "Your house is beautiful. I can't wait to see the rest of it, and dinner smells wonderful. What are we having?"

Keilah put her napkin in her lap and said, "Porterhouse lamb chops, baby spinach, and buttermilk and chive potatoes, and for dessert I have a sour cream cake to die for."

"You cooked all this?" Kyle asked.

"Of course, with some help from the man of the house."

"You guys did a great job. It smells delicious."

"Why, thank you, Tori," Ramsey replied.

The four of them joined hands to bless the food before partaking in the delicious meal.

After dinner, Keilah gave Tori a tour of the house. As they walked upstairs, Keilah said, "I can't believe you two met in a supermarket."

Tori giggled. "I know. He was inspecting the organic tomatoes, and he looked so serious. I politely walked over to him and eased his mind by telling him he was making a good selection. When he smiled and thanked me, something inside me clicked. He was so clean cut and handsome."

"He is handsome," Keilah replied as they entered one of the guest bedrooms. "Kyle has had trouble dating because of his work schedule and the confidentiality of his job. He's a classified government official, and a lot of women couldn't handle it. They wanted more time from him than he had available."

"Well, I like him, and he's been nothing but a gentleman to me. I know what it's like to have a strenuous schedule."

Keilah turned to Tori and stared at her for a second.

"What?" Tori asked.

"Have you slept with him?"

Tori blushed. "No, but we've come close a couple of times. I was ready, but he pulled back."

"I'm not surprised. Kyle is old school. He's not going to put the full-court press on you and risk messing up the relationship. You're going to have to let him know it's okay so he won't be so uptight about it."

They continued to walk down the hallway toward Neariah's room. Outside her door Tori said, "I don't want him to think I'm horny, even though I am."

Keilah laughed and said, "Girl, rip that man's clothes off and ride him like a cowgirl."

"You're stupid, Keilah, but I understand what you're saying. I am extremely curious, because everything else seems so right about him. If he's good in bed, I'm sold."

Keilah gave Tori a sisterly hug and said, "Well, I hope it works out between you two. I love you both, and I want you to be happy."

"Me too," Tori whispered as Keilah opened the door to Neariah's room. "Where's my goddaughter?"

They walked over to Neariah's crib and found her lying wide awake in the dimly lit room. When she saw her mother, she started smiling.

"What are you doing up, young lady?" Keilah asked as she picked her up.

"I can't believe she wasn't crying for you."

Keilah laid Neariah on the changing table and said, "She would've eventually. She's a good baby, though."

Tori looked around the room and said, "Her room is so cute. I love the pink and cream colors with the angels. It's the perfect room for a little girl."

"Thank you, Tori. My mother-in-law helped me decorate her room."

Tori kissed Neariah's hand and asked, "Can I help?"

"Sure," Keilah replied as she took the wet diaper off her daughter. "Look in that small fridge and get a cup of milk and put it in the warmer. I'll let you give it to her."

Tori did as she was told and anxiously waited to hold her sweet little goddaughter. When the milk was ready, Keilah handed her daughter to Tori and then sat down. Tori sat down in the rocking chair and gave Neariah the cup.

"You're a natural," Keilah whispered.

"She's so beautiful, Keilah. She looks like you."

"Everybody says that, but I think she looks like her dad."

"Maybe it's because she has your eyes," Tori replied as she hugged Neariah close to her heart. "I could hold her all night."

"You're hired," Keilah joked. "On a serious note, I'm glad you're back in D.C."

At that moment, Ramsey slowly opened the door and whispered, "Are you guys going to be in here all night?"

"No, we'll be right down."

After he closed the door, Keilah took Neariah out of Tori's arms and said, "Go on back downstairs with your date. I'll be down after I get her back to sleep."

"Thanks, Keilah."

Tori exited the room, and then Keilah looked into her daughter's eyes and said, "Okay, young lady. It's time for you to go back to sleep. Momma and Daddy have friends over."

Keilah placed her daughter on her shoulder and patted her back. Seconds later she burped. Keilah rocked her for about ten minutes, until she was fast asleep.

It didn't take her long to rejoin her guests for some delicious sour cream cake and hot buttered rum to take the chill off of the cold December evening.

"This is so good, I might need a designated driver to get us home," Kyle joked.

"You guys are welcome to spend the night if you feel like you may have had one too many," Ramsey suggested. "I don't want to see your face plastered on CNN in the morning for getting pulled over with a DUI."

"He's right," Keilah added. "We have plenty of room and we would love to have you."

"It's a sweet offer, but I don't want to impose on Victoria," Kyle stated.

Ramsey made eye contact with his buddy and read his mind. He knew exactly why he didn't want to stay overnight, and he couldn't blame him.

It was nearly eleven o'clock when Kyle saw his date yawn and decided it was time to call it a night. They thanked their gracious hosts and friends and headed out into the cold, dark, night.

***

On the drive back to her house, Tori thanked Kyle for a wonderful evening. He smiled and took her hand into his and kissed the back of it.

"Thanks for making it so wonderful," he replied.

She gave his hand an assuring squeeze.

Kyle pulled into her driveway and shut off the engine. He immediately hopped out and made his way around to the passenger side of the vehicle and opened the door for his beautiful date. He took her hand into his once again and escorted her to the front of the house, where she took out her keys and unlocked the door.

"Do you have time to come inside for some coffee?" she asked as she wrapped her arms around his waist and snuggled against his body in the cold night air.

He pulled her closer into his arms and gave her a subtle kiss on the lips and said, "I'd love to."

The couple entered her modest home, which was neat, with a classic feminine touch. They took off their coats and hung them in the hall closet.

"Make yourself at home while I brew the coffee. It won't take but a second," she announced. "Oh, and if you don't mind, can you make a fire? It's chilly in here."

"Sure," he answered as he made his way into her family room and over to the fireplace. Kyle was a pro at making cozy fires. He had done it as a young boy growing up in Chicago, and by the time Tori made it back into the family room, he had the fireplace roaring.

"Wow! I've never been able to get it going like that," she said with praise.

He smiled and said, "I'm a Northern boy, so I know all about building fires."

Tori sat the tray of coffee down on the coffee table and said, "That's right. You're from Chi-town."

He smiled as he poured two cups of coffee and handed one to her before sitting.

She crossed her legs and said, "Thanks, Chi-town."

He nodded and asked, "Sugar and cream?"

"I can't wait," she mischievously replied as she held her cup out to him.

Kyle chuckled and added two scoops of sugar and some cream to her coffee and then to his own. He leaned back against the sofa and took a sip of the steaming hot beverage. "This is delicious."

"I thought it would be a nice nightcap after all that liquor the Stones poured down our throats," she said with a giggle. "Besides, I would worry about you driving home if you didn't get some caffeine in your system."

Now it was his time to blush, and when he did, it revealed two sexy dimples.

"Where is that music coming from?" he asked.

"It's my satellite radio. I turned it on before I brought the coffee in."

"You like jazz, huh?"

"Smooth jazz. My dad was in a jazz band when I was growing up. He plays the sax. I've been in love with it ever since."

"That's cool. Is he still playing?"

"Just for my mom," she answered.

"He sounds like a romantic."

"He is. I learned a lot by watching my mom and dad interact."

Kyle couldn't take it any longer. Sitting next to her, looking into her sultry eyes, seeing her sexy legs, and watching her luscious lips, was driving him crazy. Tori was a beautiful, sexy woman, and it was obvious that she was nurturing as well, which was one of the traits he desired in his woman. He sat his cup on the coffee table and then took her cup out of her hand, placing it down as well. Then, without hesitation, he put his arm around her shoulders and covered her lips with his, giving her a long, slow heated kiss.

What pleased him even more was that Tori welcomed his kiss, molding her body into his, and when the couple finally came up for air, Tori gazed into his handsome eyes and whispered, "Wow."

He caressed her face and said, "I second that."

Tori showered his face, neck, and lips with tender, soft kisses. He smelled wonderful, and his hands were so soft, yet manly.

"Kyle?" she whispered.

"Yes?" he answered as he hugged her tight against his chest.

"Spend the night with me," she whispered as she nibbled on his lips.

"Are you serious?" he asked as his heart pounded in his chest.

She laid her head on his chest and listened to the rapid beating of his heart. "I've never been more serious than I am right now."

Kyle caressed Tori's back and gave her a tender kiss on the forehead. Seconds later she stood and took his hand in hers.

"Let's go upstairs, where we can get more comfortable."

"I'd love to, but we can't leave the fire burning like this. It's not safe."

She put her hands on her hips and said, "Okay. What do you suggest?"

"Well, we could camp out here until the fire burns itself out."

Tori smiled and said, "I haven't done this since I was a little girl at my granny's house in Mississippi, but it could be fun. I'll go get the linens, if you don't mind moving the coffee table over by the bookcase."

"I don't mind at all," he answered as he watched Tori disappear upstairs. After moving the table and a chair, he found himself in a predicament. He was at a disadvantage not knowing for sure if she wanted sex or just a sleeping companion for the evening. Then again, she did invite him upstairs and she had been very flirty, welcoming his advances, but he still didn't know if he should strip. That was until Tori yelled down the stairs.

"Kyle, I'll be there in a second. Make yourself comfortable, and I'll bring you a hanger for your clothes."

Bingo! There it was. She wanted him out of his clothes, but he still didn't want to be too presumptuous, so he stripped down only to his T-shirt and boxer briefs.

She reappeared with her arms full with two comforters. She tossed them on the floor and stared at Kyle's well-toned physique. He had large, muscular thighs; a round, firm backside; and strong, broad shoulders. She swallowed hard and asked, "How's your back, Chitown?"

"My back is fine, Mississippi," he answered with a chuckle as he spread the comforters on the floor.

Tori giggled and said, "Good, because I don't want this little camping trip to have you in pain in the morning. Oh! I forgot the pillows. I'll be right back."

Kyle watched as she sprinted back up the stairs. Tori was shapely in her pink pajama pants and matching tank top. She had a runner's body, and he couldn't wait to enjoy it. Her midsection was exposed, and he noticed she had a pierced belly button, which instantly turned him on. Her toned body showed that she obviously worked out, but she was still feminine.

"Down, boy. Not yet," he whispered to himself as his lower region began to stir.

"Heads up!" she yelled as she tossed two pillows across the room to Kyle. She brought two more for herself and dropped them on the floor. She hugged his waist, then gave him a kiss and said, "Kyle, I hope you don't think I'm being too aggressive with you."

He smiled and said, "No, I think you're fine. To be honest, I love receiving all this affection, and just for the record, I've been struggling to restrain myself with you."

She nuzzled her face against his warm neck and said, "You don't have to restrain yourself, Kyle. I want to be with you. I really do."

Kyle cupped her face and covered her lips with his as they eased down on the soft comforters without breaking contact. As she lay before him, he was still reluctant to make any sexual advances, so Tori did it for him. She pulled her tank top over her head, exposing her full breasts. Needing no more confirmation, he reached over and covered them with his large hands and gently caressed her. Her breathing became slow and deep with his caress, and when he slowly covered her brown peaks with his mouth, she let out a soft, breathy moan. Her moans become louder as he tenderly feasted upon her.

"Kyle?" she softly called out to him.

He looked her in the eyes and answered, "Yes, baby?"

She opened her mouth to speak, but nothing came out. Her eyes told him everything he needed to know, and he wasn't going to let her down. With the fire crackling beside them and the warm flames kissing their skin, Kyle grabbed the waistband of her pajamas and pulled them down over her hips, leaving her totally exposed before him. She was stunning. He pulled his T-shirt over his head and removed his briefs, giving her a bird's-eye view of his throbbing manhood. She gasped and then closed her eyes with anxious anticipation, but he didn't want to rush the moment. He applied protection and then moved between her thighs. He gazed into her beautiful, teary brown eyes.

"This is your last chance to back out. Are you sure about this?"

She wrapped her arms around his neck and said, "I let you undress me, didn't I?"

He chuckled and said, "That's true. I guess I'm a little nervous. It's been a while for me."

"Kyle, I have to tell you that it's been a while for me too, so I'm a little nervous too, but I never wanted to be with a man as much as I want to be with you. I know we haven't known each other long, but I've never felt closer to any man before you," she revealed before kissing him.

That was all he needed to hear as he proceeded to kiss her lips and neck. He lingered at her breasts, her belly button, and then finally found the prize he was looking for. He flicked his tongue a few times against her pulsating nub, causing her to wither and moan loudly. His sensual torture went on for several seconds, until he completely devoured her.

"Kyle, please," she begged.

He immediately mounted her and took them both on a heart-stopping, extremely explosive, yet sensual journey, causing them to lose control of their senses and inhibitions. Their erotic lovemaking went on for what seemed like hours. It was Tori who screamed first as her body shuddered hard beneath him. Her screams of satisfaction set off a chain reaction, causing him to grind his body into hers even harder, until his body stiffened, causing him to call out her name in complete fulfillment.

Her body was fully charged by her new lover, and she hungered for more. She ran her tongue over his ear and whispered, "That was awesome, Kyle. Can we do it again?"

With a huge smile on his face, he kissed her hard on the lips and said, "Your wish is my command. Just give me a minute to catch my breath."

Tori and Kyle shared intimate conversations between making passionate love. It was nearly four in the morning when the fire died down, and they eventually fell asleep in each other's arms, completely exhausted.

Chapter Thirteen

It was a few days before Christmas, and the office was functioning with a skeleton crew. They had been able to reduce their staff because a lot of their clients were out of town visiting family. Ramsey and Keilah chose to throw a Christmas party for the staff and present them with well-deserved bonuses and gifts as the party wound down before leaving to go to the Stones' family farm in North Carolina for Christmas.

The security guard entered the break room and pulled Keilah to the side.

"Excuse me, Keilah. You have a visitor at the front desk."

"Who is it?"

"He said his name is Michael Monroe," the security guard replied.

Keilah immediately experienced an overwhelming feeling of anxiety. She had had no doubt that Michael would eventually return to see her. She hadn't expected it to be during the holidays. She followed the security guard out to the reception area and greeted Michael.

"What are you doing here, Michael?"

"I didn't mean to show up unannounced, but I felt like if I didn't, you wouldn't see me."

She folded her arms and said, "You could've called. What's so important that you had to see me and talk face-to-face?"

He glanced over at the security guard and said, "It's personal."

Keilah gazed into Michael's eyes and decided he looked like a wounded puppy. She never thought she would ever give him the time of day again, but for some reason, she felt like she needed to hear what he had to say so she could get some closure once and for all. She didn't feel threatened by him, because she could take him down in an instant.

"Okay, Michael, you have ten minutes," she answered. She turned to the security guard and looked at her watch and said, "Trevor, log Mr. Monroe in on your sign-in sheet. Trevor, we won't be long."

"Will do," Trevor said before returning to his post.

Michael followed Keilah down the hallway to her office. She was stunning in her designer jeans and waist-length brown leather jacket with matching boots. She escorted Michael to her office and invited him to have a seat.

She sat down at her desk and gave him the floor. "Okay, Michael, what's so important that you had to see me?"

Michael let out a breath and said, "First, I want to apologize for everything that happened between us. I never meant to hurt you, and whether you want to believe it or not, I did love you."

"Apology accepted. What else?" she asked with urgency to move their conversation along.

"Keilah, I did a lot of things with my life that I'm not happy with, especially when it came to my relationships. It was a mistake that I got into a relationship with a man, and I'm trying to right all the wrongs that I caused—"

She sat up in her chair and interrupted him. "Why are you telling me all of this, Michael? I've moved on with my life, and you should move on as well."

"I couldn't go on with my life knowing you hated me."

"I wasn't raised to hate, Michael. I despised you, but I didn't hate you, even though you had intentions to ruin my life."

He lowered his head and said, "I deserve that. I just wanted to let you know that I'm happy for you. Arhmelia told me you have a daughter too."

"We do," she answered.

"May I see a picture of her?" he asked.

Keilah showed him the family picture she had on her desk and watched his expression.

"She's not yours, Michael, if that's what you're trying to insinuate. As you can see, she looks just like Ramsey."

He smiled and said, "You're right, but you can't hate a guy for holding out hope."

Keilah stood and said, "Well, you're wasting your breath, and your ten minutes are up. I'm at peace over what happened between us. I'm happy now, and I would appreciate it if you wouldn't come around here anymore."

Michael stood and said, "That's understandable. I just needed some peace of mind in knowing that you forgive me. I won't take up any more of your time."

She walked him back out to the reception area and said, "Good luck, Michael."

He turned to her and said, "One more thing."

"What is it?" she asked.

"Some of the things that I'm trying to rectify might stir up some unfavorable attention. It could hit the media, and there's a possibility that it could get ugly if it's not settled quietly. If it comes down to an investigation, it could lead back to my relationship with you."

"What exactly are you talking about, Michael?"

"I can't say right now, but if you're approached by any investigators I don't want you to be caught off guard. I trust you to handle it any way you see fit."

At that moment Keilah felt a small amount of compassion for her ex-lover. He obviously had gone through some type of awakening while he was being held hostage, and she commended him for making amends in order to redeem himself.

"Listen, Michael, however things turns out with whatever you're dealing with, I'll do what I can to help you."

He smiled and then leaned down and gave her a subtle kiss on the cheek just as Ramsey rounded the corner. "Thank you, Keilah. I appreciate that. I'll get out of your hair now. Good-bye."

"Good-bye," she answered as she watched him climb onto the elevator and the doors close.

"What the hell is he doing here?" Ramsey asked with a frown on his face.

She hugged his waist and said, "He came to apologize for everything that went down between us. I forgave him."

"I don't want him around here anymore," Ramsey proclaimed.

She looked up at her husband and said, "Okay, boss. He won't be back. Now kiss me."

Ramsey kissed his wife lovingly on the lips and said, "Let's get out of here. We have a long drive ahead of us, and it's supposed to snow. We need to pick up Neariah and Target from Camille's house and then hit the road before we get snowed in."

"Okay, let's tell the team good-bye so we can leave," she replied.

***

Ramsey and Keilah were enjoying their wonderful white Christmas with the Stones in their two-story ranch-style house, which sat on ten acres of prime farmland. Neariah was getting super spoiled by her grandparents and other relatives, and it was a welcomed change of pace from the couple's busy schedule. They had been treated to some wonderful Southern food, and Target enjoyed running around on the Stones' spacious farm. While there, Keilah spoke with all her brothers, sisters-in-law, and nieces and nephews on speaker-phone Christmas Day because they were all together at her brother Roman's house. She missed them but was thankful they had had a chance to be together on Thanksgiving.

It was only eight o'clock, but Keilah was exhausted. She walked into the theatre room and found Ramsey, his dad, and his brother-in-law watching a football game.

She wrapped her arms around Ramsey's neck and gave him a kiss on the cheek. "Babe, I'm going to bed. I feel a little queasy."

He pulled her into his lap and felt her forehead. "You're not coming down with anything, are you?"

"I don't think so. Maybe I just ate too much."

"Where's the rug rat?"

"She's upstairs with her auntie Xenia."

Ramsey massaged her thighs and said, "I should've known. Keith, you'd better watch out. I think my sister's ready to start a family."

His brother-in-law laughed and said, "I already know, bro."

Keith and Xenia had been married for about three years, and it was obvious that she was ready to have children of her own. Their careers were on track; Keith was an investment banker, and Xenia was a middle school principal.

"Well, I think it's time. Neariah needs someone to play with," Keilah said as she crawled out of her husband's lap.

"Get some rest. I'll be up later to check on you."

"Enjoy the game, boys. And, Pops, no more cigars tonight. You said you were cutting back," Keilah said.

Marion tucked the cigar back inside his humidor without responding.

"Before I go upstairs, can I get you guys anything?" Keilah said.

"Keilah, do you mind handing me another Corona?" Keith asked.

"Sure. Pops, do you need anything?"

Marion adjusted his recliner and said, "Yeah, my cigar."

"Well, because I love you and it's Christmas, you can have one more, but that's it for tonight."

With a smile of victory on his face, Marion pulled the cigar out of the humidor, ran it under his nose. "Keilah, I love you, but you're getting worse than Valeria. Go to bed," he said jokingly.

Keilah giggled as she made her way into the kitchen and quickly returned with two Coronas. She handed one to Keith and then leaned down and gave Ramsey a good-night kiss before handing him the other beer.

"Good night, babe."

"Good night."

Upstairs, the nauseous feeling hit Keilah's stomach once again, which caused her to run into the bathroom. Whatever ailment she had, she didn't want to pass it on to her family, so she hoped whatever it was that was making her sick would soon pass and she could get some sleep. After she had two glasses of club soda and some crackers, the sick feeling finally subsided.

***

A couple of days later Ramsey packed up his family and said his good-byes to his parents, his sister, and his brother-in-law. Valeria had tears in her eyes when she handed Neariah over to her son. Marion gave his granddaughter a loving kiss before watching his son secure her in the car seat, while Keilah said her good-byes to Keith, Valeria, and her sister-in-law, Xenia.

Valeria gave her daughter-in-law a hug and said, "You guys come back soon. Okay?"

"You and Ramsey need to come to Tampa soon too. We don't get to see you guys enough," Xenia pointed out.

Keilah hugged Xenia and promised they would visit them soon. "You and Keith have a safe flight back to Florida."

"We will and take care of my niece."

Marion loaded the last suitcase in the back of the Range Rover, along with Target, and closed the door. "Ramsey, you take your time driving back. The roads might still have some slick spots," he instructed. "Call when you get back, and take care of your girls."

"Yes, sir," Ramsey answered as he gave his dad a big hug. "I love you, Dad."

"I love you too, son."

Ramsey kissed his mother and gave her a loving hug as well.

Ramsey and Keilah waved good-bye to their family once more and then drove down the long driveway to begin their long drive back home.

An hour and a half into the trip Ramsey had to pull over because Keilah was feeling sick once again. Neariah needed to be changed, and he had planned to stop, anyway, so it didn't hurt their traveling time at all. After walking Target and giving him some water, Ramsey went into the convenience store and returned with two bottles of 7Up and some potato chips for his wife.

As he changed Neariah, he said, "When we get back to D.C., you need to see a doctor."

"I'll be okay," she replied as she took a sip of the soda. "I hope it's not a touch of the flu."

He tossed the dirty diaper into a plastic bag and then into the trash and said, "Until we know for sure, I'll handle the rug rat. I can't have both of you sick."

Keilah watched her husband's tender interaction with their daughter. Neariah's eyes were bright and full of love as she smiled up at her dad.

"I can handle this, but I agree with you about not wanting to make Neariah sick."

He put his daughter back into her car seat and handed her a cup of juice. He climbed back behind the driver seat and asked, "Is everybody set?"

With juice running down her chin, Neariah pulled the cup out of her mouth and said, "Da-dee!"

He looked in the rearview mirror and said, "That's my girl." He patted Keilah on the thigh and asked, "What about you, babe?"

She closed her eyes and slightly reclined her seat. "I'm good. I'm just ready to get home so I can lie down."

He turned on the ignition and said, "Hang on a little bit longer and I'll have you home in no time."

Two and a half hours later, the Stones pulled into their garage.

"I've never been so happy to see my house," Keilah said as she unlocked the door and stepped into the kitchen. "I'll let Target out if you can get the luggage."

He followed her into the house and placed Neariah in her high chair. Keilah escorted Target out into the backyard so he could relieve himself. When she came back in, she sat down at the kitchen table and held her head in her hands as her husband finished bringing in the luggage.

Ramsey pulled his wife out of her chair and held her in his arms.

"I'm worried about you."

"I've never felt like this before."

Ramsey smiled down at her to try and lighten the mood. "You're sick, and I haven't even given you my Christmas gift yet," he replied.

She laid her head against his chest and said, "I haven't given you my gift, either."

He kissed her forehead and said, "We can do it later, when you're up to it. For now I want you to go upstairs and relax while Neariah and I make you some soup. It's chilly in here, so I'll be up to build you a fire."

"I'm not hungry right now," she replied. "Go ahead and feed Neariah first, and maybe then I'll fell like eating."

"Regardless, you have to put something on your stomach. Now go," he ordered her.

Keilah made her way up the stairs, with Target following close behind. Ramsey called his parents to let them know they were home and then made dinner for Neariah and soup for his wife.

Upstairs, Keilah couldn't believe how fast she had got sick. It was definitely flu season, but she'd made sure she got the flu shot a few months ago. Now her concern was Neariah's health. She wanted to rule some other things out before going through the hassle of making a doctor's appointment. In the meantime she would take a shower and let her husband pamper her until she felt better.

Thirty minutes later Ramsey entered the room with Neariah in one arm and a bowl of hot chicken soup in his other hand.

"Soup's on," he joked as he walked in the room. "How's my patient?"

"I'm pregnant," Keilah blurted out with a dazed look on her face.

Stunned, Ramsey sat Neariah on the bed and the soup on the nightstand.

"Pregnant?" he repeated. "How do you know? When did that happen?"

She held the results out to him and said, "I took the home test, and it came back positive."

He stared at the stick in disbelief. They wanted more kids, but he hadn't planned to have another one so soon. Neariah was only one year old.

Silence surrounded the couple. Neariah crawled over to her mother's lap and started playing with her earrings.

"Are you going to be okay with this? I know it's not what we planned," Keilah said.

He wrapped his arm around her shoulders and said, "Of course, I didn't expect us to have another baby so soon, but we'll deal with it."

Tears spilled out of her eyes as she whispered, "I'm sorry."

"Sorry for what?" he asked, recognizing that his comment had hurt his wife's feelings. "I'm not blaming you. You're my wife. I love you, and I did have a part in this."

Keilah sat next to her husband in silence while Neariah continued to play with her earrings.

Ramsey put his hand over her abdomen and said, "I'm the one who should apologize. I didn't mean it the way it sounded. You and Neariah are my life, and now I'm going to have another little person to love."

She turned to him and looked into his concerned eyes. "I didn't plan this, Ramsey. I take my pill every day. . . ."

He put his finger over her lips to silence her. "Sweetheart, I'm cool. Stop trying to explain, because there's nothing to explain. It's cool. Okay?"

She smiled and said, "Okay. I guess I'm just a little emotional and shocked. Maybe my hormones are already kicking in. I don't know."

He picked up the bowl of soup and held a spoonful up to her lips. "Don't worry. My soup will fix you right up. Now, open wide, li'l momma."

Keilah giggled and opened her mouth so her husband could feed her his hot chicken soup.

Chapter Fourteen

Keilah visited her doctor's office the next day, which confirmed her pregnancy. However, she and Ramsey decided to wait a while before breaking the news to their family members. In the meantime it was business as usual around the Stone household. Keilah's morning sickness had diminished with the help of some peppermint tea, suggested to her by her doctor.

With New Year's Eve a day away, the agency had increased its staff for upcoming parties and celebrations. It was a prime time of year for bad things to happen to their clients, so they wanted to make sure their agents were prepped and focused on their responsibilities

While Keilah was going over the schedule in her office, the receptionist called her line and announced that she had a visitor.

"A journalist?" Keilah asked the receptionist. "Why does he want to interview me?"

"He didn't say, Keilah. Do you want me to have him make an appointment to come back another time?"

She closed her laptop and said, "No, take him into the conference room. I'll be right there."

Keilah walked into Ramsey's office and said, "There's a reporter in the conference room, waiting to interview me."

"A reporter from what source?" he asked as he stood and slid into his jacket.

"I'm not sure."

He took her by the arm and led her down the hallway and said, "Well, we're about to find out."

When they entered the conference room, the journalist greeted the couple and gave them his business card.

Ramsey tucked the business card into his pocket and asked, "What can we do for you, Mr. Wayman of the *Washington Press?*"

The journalist ignored Ramsey and immediately turned to Keilah. "Mrs. Stone, I'm here to get your side of the story on your relationship with recent POW and war hero Michael Monroe. Sources tell me that he is bisexual and that you had a love child as a result of the relationship. Do you care to comment?"

Before Keilah could respond, Ramsey stepped in front of his wife and angrily said, "Have you lost your goddamn mind? This is my wife you're talking to! Why the hell would you come in here with that bullshit?"

Startled, the journalist took a step back and said, "I'm sorry, Mr. Stone. I don't mean to upset you or Mrs. Stone. Michael Monroe is a national hero, and people want to know all about him and his life."

Ramsey poked him in the chest with his finger, pushing him hard against the wall. "There is no story here, and if I see one damn word implicating my wife in a relationship with Michael Monroe, I will snap your neck."

"You don't have to get hostile, Mr. Stone," the journalist said as he backed away from him.

Keilah could see the vein in Ramsey's neck pulsating, so she knew he could lose it at any second and seriously hurt the man. Thus, she gave his hand a loving squeeze to try to calm him down.

"Mr. Wayman, I'm sorry you came all the way down here with this nonsense. I keep my private life private, and I think the story you need to write should honor our military, not exploit them," Keilah calmly suggested.

"Does that mean you're denying the accusations that you were involved with a man in a bisexual love triangle?" The journalist was doing what newshounds were known for doing best: aggravating the hell out of people.

Ramsey tried to calm himself and still remain professional, but his eyes were glazed over and they were as red as fire. He took a breath and said, "Listen, bro. I don't give a damn what you print about Monroe. That's between you and him, but I swear to God, if print anything linking my wife and child to the story, it'll be the last story you ever write. Do you understand where I'm coming from?"

The journalist was used to threats, so he took a chance and turned to Keilah one more time. "Mrs. Stone, is it true that you shot Mr. Monroe in a jealous rage after catching him in bed with another man?"

Ramsey had heard enough. He grabbed the journalist by the neck and threw him out of the conference room into the hallway, slamming his body against the wall.

"Get the hell out of my office!" Ramsey yelled at him as he charged him.

Two agents walking down the hallway heard the commotion and quickly ran over to back up their boss. They took the journalist by the arms and quickly dragged him toward the lobby, handing him over to the security guards.

"Mr. Stone, is there a problem?" Trevor asked.

"Yes. Get this man off the premises, and if he shows up again, you have my permission to beat his ass before calling the police."

With a smirk on his face the journalist breathlessly stated, "I guess this interview is over, huh?"

Ramsey looked at his two agents and the security guards and said, "Escort his ass to his car and make sure he vacates the property."

"Yes, sir," one of the security guards replied with a smile as he and one of the agents escorted the journalist onto the elevator and off the property.

Ramsey turned and marched back into his office, with Keilah following close behind. She closed the door behind them as he sat down at his desk.

"Find Michael Monroe and get his ass down here right now. I want to know who he's been talking to and why he's running his damn mouth about his private life."

Keilah massaged her husband's shoulders and said, "When Michael was here apologizing, he said he was working on trying to right all the wrong he's done to people. He mentioned that some things might hit the media and if investigators came around to handle it however I wanted to."

"Investigators? Are you sure he said investigators and not journalists?" Ramsey asked.

"I'm positive."

"This doesn't make sense. Why would investigators come around here, and why didn't you tell me?"

She continued to massage his shoulders and said, "I had no idea he was talking about something like this."

Ramsey covered his face with his hands. Keilah turned his chair and removed his hands so she could look into his weary eyes.

"Sweetheart, don't stress over this. You're going to give yourself a heart attack."

He frowned and said, "How can I *not* stress? I'm not going to sit back and let that clown or anybody like him disrespect my family and get you stressed out. You're carrying my child."

"Your baby is and will be just fine. I was pregnant with Neariah through that shoot-out back home, and she turned out just fine, remember?"

"I don't know. We might need to check her diaper for a nine-millimeter," he joked. "I want to know why that reporter showed up, asking all those bullshit questions."

Keilah headed toward the door and said, "I'll call Teresa Randolph and see if she will tell me where he is or give me his number."

Ramsey picked up the telephone and said, "I'm serious, Keilah. I want him in here today."

"I'm working on it, boss," she replied before closing the door.

Ramsey dialed Kyle's number and got his voice mail, so he left a message. "Kyle, I need to talk to you as soon as possible. It's about Michael Monroe, and I need to know everything you can find on a Jeremy Wayman at the *Washington Press*."

After leaving the message, he twirled around in the chair and looked out over the city below and thought about the storm brewing in the distance.

Keilah returned to her office and dialed Teresa Randolph's number and waited for her to answer.

"Hello?"

"Mrs. Randolph, this is Keilah Stone. How are you?"

With a smile in her voice, she answered, "Keilah! What a nice surprise. How are you, dear?"

"I'm fine, Mrs. Randolph."

"Keilah, how many times do I have to tell you to call me Teresa?"

Keilah hesitated and then said, "Okay, Teresa. I need to get in touch with Michael. It's urgent. Do you have his number?"

"Of course I do, Keilah," she replied. "Is everything okay? You sound a little tense."

"Everything is fine," Keilah lied. "I just need to talk to Michael."

She didn't want to worry her unnecessarily, until she found out why Michael would be so careless with their private life, but she needed answers . . . now.

Teresa gave Keilah the number and then said, "Keilah, I would love to do lunch one day soon. I'll always hold you near and dear to my heart, even though your relationship with my nephew didn't work out."

"That's sweet and I appreciate you not taking it personally."

"You're welcome, "Teresa replied. "Call me after the holidays and let me know when will be a good time."

"I'll do that, Teresa, and thanks for giving me Michael's number."

The two ladies chatted a few more minutes before hanging up.

Keilah stared down at the number, contemplating dialing it. She had hoped that Michael was finally out of her life, but the incident today had shown her otherwise. Now all she wanted was to get to the bottom of this reporter's inquiry before Ramsey killed someone, so she dialed the number. After two rings it went into his voice mail. As soon as she got the beep to leave a message, she spoke with a firm tone of voice.

"Michael, this is Keilah. I need to see you as soon as possible. It's urgent, so please call me back when you get this message. I don't care what time it is. Just make sure you call me back," she instructed before leaving her number on the voice mail. After hanging up the telephone, she returned to Ramsey's office, sat down in the chair in front of his desk, and crossed her legs. He was on the telephone, and as soon as he ended the call, he rubbed his eyes.

"Did you get in touch with Michael?"

"No, I got his voice mail, but I left a message."

He looked at his watch and then said, "It's getting late. I'm tired, you're tired, and we both need some peace and quiet."

"I know, baby. Sometimes I feel like we're spinning our wheels in the sand."

He smiled and said, "You know, we still haven't exchanged Christmas gifts."

She blushed and softly replied, "I know. With the shock of the pregnancy, preparing for New Year's Eve, I guess we both got sidetracked."

"I agree, but not anymore," he said as he stood and turned off his computer. "Let's go. I've had enough for one day. We have the team set and ready to go, and I want to take you out to dinner. Are you up to it?"

She also stood, and as she was walking out, she looked back over her shoulder and said, "I'm always ready to eat, and I'm craving a big, juicy steak."

"Steak?" he asked as he opened the door to let her walk out ahead of him. "That's different. I thought you were watching your intake of red meat."

"I am, but tonight I want a steak and it better be good."

As they walked down the hallway, Ramsey pulled out his cell phone and tried to call Kyle again, but this time for pleasure, not business. He wanted to invite him and Tori to join them for dinner. They hadn't seen them since that surprise dinner at their home, and the couple was anxious to catch up with them to see how their relationship was going. Little did the Stones know that Tori and Kyle had been inseparable since their intimate encounter. In fact, unbeknownst to the Stones, the new lovers were presently tangled up together in the soft sheets of Kyle's bed.

***

"Someone's really trying to get in touch with you," Tori stated breathlessly as Kyle covered her mouth with hot kisses.

Frustrated, Kyle looked at the phone and said, "It's just Ramsey. I'll call him back later. I'm busy right now."

Tori giggled and wrapped her arms around his neck. "And I like the way you work."

He winked at her and said, "Then you're going to love this presentation," just before disappearing under the sheets.

Tori let out a sensual moan as Kyle's soft lips came in contact with her center.

Ramsey put his cell back inside his jacket.

"No answer?" Keilah asked.

"His voice mail came on. I guess he's busy. If he calls back, I'll just invite them over for New Year's Eve, if they don't already have plans."

She stepped into the elevator ahead of him and said, "Sure. I'm glad they're dating. Oh, and make sure you invite Neil too, since he didn't get to come the last time."

Ramsey laughed and asked, "Are you sure about that?"

"Neil's okay. He just needs to settle down and stop being a dog with women."

They walked to their vehicle, and Ramsey opened the door for her and said, "He will eventually. Where do you want to get your steak?"

"You know J&G Steakhouse has the best, and I can't wait."

He closed the door and said, "J&G it is."

***

Across town, a very satisfied Kyle checked his voice messages while Tori showered.

When she returned to the room, wrapped in a plush towel, she lay across the bed and asked, "Is everything okay?"

He hung up the phone and said, "Yeah, it was just Ramsey calling to invite us out to dinner with them."

"Ah, that was nice. Is it too late?"

While massaging her foot, he answered, "Yeah, I'm sure they already have their entrées. Maybe we can do something with them on New Year's Eve. Is that okay with you?"

She sat up and kissed his neck and said, "I'll go anywhere with you, Kyle."

He looked into her eyes and asked, "Are you serious?"

Tori crawled on top of him and wrapped her arms around his neck and kissed his chest and whispered, "Anywhere."

"In that case, I have the perfect place if you're up to it."

She kissed his neck and said, "Just tell me when and where, and I'm there."

He pulled her hips closer to him and said, "In that case, pack a bag, because there's somewhere we have to go . . . tonight."

"Tonight?"

He smiled and repeated, "Tonight."

Chapter Fifteen

In Virginia, Michael sat alone at the hotel bar and finished off his rum and Coke. He had spent a long day in the commandant's office, filing his complaint against Lieutenant Colonel Biggs, and was due to go back in the morning to finish the interview and sign off on the official complaint to kick off the investigation. He hadn't been able to get any video of Biggs assaulting any more cadets, because as soon as he left his office, the lieutenant colonel threw the gift he had given him and smashed it on the floor. Michael knew he was at the point of no return, but he also knew it was something he should've done years ago, and that was the only regret he had.

He pulled out his cell phone to make a call, and that was when he realized he had forgotten to turn it back on after his deposition. Once he pushed the power button, the phone lit up, alerting him to several messages. One was from his aunt, another was from one of his military buddies, and the last one was from Keilah and it quickly caught his attention. As he listened to her message, he couldn't imagine why she was calling. Once he finished reviewing all the messages, he looked at the time and contemplating calling Keilah. Her voice had a sense of urgency in it, so he dialed her number and hoped he wasn't disturbing her.

"Hello?" she answered softly.

"Keilah, it's Michael. I apologize for my delay in calling you back. I'm just getting a chance to check my messages. Is everything okay?"

"No, Michael, everything is not okay," she answered as she exited the restaurant's bathroom. "We need to talk as soon as possible."

Michael asked the bartender for another drink as he tried to figure out why Keilah wanted to talk to him after making it clear that she didn't want to see him again.

"Sure, Keilah, whatever you need. I'm out of town right now, but I should be back in a couple of days. What is this about?"

"You told me investigators might come asking questions about us. Well, they came."

"You mean someone came to see you today?"

"Yes, today! Some fool from the *Washington Press*. Why would you do that?"

"I didn't do anything, Keilah. I'm just as confused as you are."

"Then what the hell were you talking about? You said investigators might come see me. Ramsey almost killed that guy."

Michael twirled the ice around in his glass and tried to figure out who could've approached his ex.

"I wish I had answers for you, but I don't. This doesn't make sense. What I was referring to hasn't even been put in motion, but I'll do my best to get back to you soon once I look into this a little more, but it won't be until after New Year's. If I can find out what's going on before I return, I'll call you back."

"Do whatever the hell you need to do to get to the bottom of this nonsense, and call me as soon as you hit the city limits," she answered before hanging up the cell phone.

Michael hung up his cell and whispered, "One crisis at a time," before downing his third rum and Coke. He was starting to feel the effects of the rum, and at that moment it soothed his anxiety. He knew there was no way that the press could've gotten wind of his allegations against Lieutenant Colonel Biggs, because the military was just beginning their investigation. He had no idea why the *Washington Press* would've approached Keilah about their past. Then a lightbulb went off, and a wave of anger swept over his body. This was a matter that needed to be handled in person, so he ordered one more drink and returned to his hotel room and called it a night.

It looked like the Stones night ended full of frustration, but at least they were able to get in touch with Michael, who assured Keilah he would get back to her as soon as he returned to town. In the meantime, Ramsey wanted to lighten the mood. So after saying good night to Camille, they headed upstairs to look in on Neariah. She was sound asleep, but Ramsey couldn't help but pick her up and give her a kiss.

"Don't wake her," Keilah whispered. "That's why she's spoiled rotten now."

He gave his sleeping daughter one more kiss before placing her back in the crib.

"Stop hating. That's my daughter, so I'm going to love on her anytime I feel like it," he said as they exited the nursery and he pulled Neariah's door closed. "Come. Let me give you your Christmas gift."

"I can't wait," she replied as she rubbed her hands together.

In the privacy of their bedroom the couple sat on the sofa, and Ramsey presented her with a box the size of a jewelry box, placing it in her lap. He had very good taste in diamonds, and there was no telling what sparkling gem he was presenting her with this year.

"I love you, Keilah. I just wish it could be more."

She kissed him gently on the lips and said, "I love you too, baby, and whatever it is, I know I'll love it."

He watched as his wife ripped open the box and pulled out a set of shiny gold keys. She held them up and asked, "What is this?"

"Open the card, baby."

Keilah opened the card and read it aloud.

To my beautiful wife, who happens to be the love of my life, Keilah, I wish I could give you the world. Since I can't, this is just a small token of my love.

Merry Christmas, sweetheart.

                                    Love,
                        Your Devoted Husband

Tears welled up in Keilah's eyes as she clutched the card to her chest. "This is beautiful, babe, but what are the keys to?"

With a big smile on his face he said, "They're the keys to your new beachfront vacation house in Clearwater, Florida."

Her eyes widened with excitement as she asked, "Are you serious? That's not far from Keith and Xenia."

"You're right. It's only about a half hour away from them. You're going to love it, Keilah. It's has Key West–style characteristics, and it's located on an exclusive, gated, private island. It has a boat dock, a heated pool and spa, and water views that you wouldn't believe."

"How many bedrooms does it have?" she asked.

He kissed her neck and said, "It has five bedrooms, with three bedrooms downstairs, plus it has a separate guesthouse, all with private entrances. You know we have a big family. The guesthouse is equipped with a half kitchen, a full bath, and an elevator to its own garage, and it has complete privacy as it's separate from the main house. You're going to love the master suite, because it has a sitting area and a huge bathroom."

"I'm ready to go now," she admitted. "What about a pool?"

"It has one of those infinity pools that you've been talking about."

The tears fell out of Keilah's eyes onto her blouse. She couldn't love Ramsey any more than she already did. She had been sort of joking when she told him she wanted a vacation home in the Caribbean, but he'd been listening and he did what he could to make her happy.

"You didn't have to—"

He put his finger up to her lips and said, "I did this for us. I'm planning on retiring early so I can enjoy you and our children. We've established our businesses to the point where we can do it. We have a great management team that we trust, so we should take more time off to relax, and this house is exactly what we needed."

Keilah hugged his neck and said, "I wish we could pack up and go tonight."

"Don't tempt me," he answered. "You can look at the picture gallery of the house on my laptop. On a serious note, after the New Year, and once we get this mess settled with Michael, we're out of here. Agreed?"

She stood and said, "Agreed. Now, are you ready for my gift?"

He pulled her body close to his and said, "All I need is right here in front of me."

She giggled and wiggled out of his grasp and said, "Later, Stone. I want to give you my gift first."

He watched as Keilah disappeared into their closet. She returned with her hand behind her back.

"I don't know what I was thinking when I bought this, but I know it's something you've been talking about for several years."

Keilah handed him a black velvet box, and when he opened it, he jumped up and let out a loud scream before picking his wife up in his arms and twirling her around.

"Yeah, baby! Now, that's what I'm talking about!"

She hugged his waist and said, "I know you're happy, but I have some ground rules, Stone."

He gave her a long kiss on the lips, and when he came up for air, he said, "Anything you say, babe. Damn! I love you!"

Ramsey was excited to get the keys to a 2011 Harley-Davidson Softail Heritage Classic motorcycle, which cost Keilah only seventeen thousand dollars and change.

"Where is it, babe?"

Keilah sat down on the side of the bed and crossed her legs and said, "Kyle has it in his garage, but, Ramsey, seriously, I was apprehensive about buying that bike for you because they're so dangerous, and then I thought about what we do for a living. You work very hard and you deserve a toy, but you have to promise me that you'll be careful when you ride it."

He laid her down on the bed and hovered over her, his eyes beaming with love. "I promise you I will be on my best behavior when I ride, especially when you're on the back with me."

She rolled over and scooted off the bed and said, "I don't know about that."

"Come on, Keilah. You have to be my biker babe."

She started undressing and said, "I'm your babe, but I don't know about getting on the back of that bike."

Within seconds she was down to her lacy undergarments. Ramsey stared at her in silence, in a trancelike state.

"What I wouldn't give to have you on the back of my bike just like you are right now."

She seductively walked over to him and leaned over him to give him a bird's-eye view of her full breasts. She nibbled on his ear and whispered, "I'll make you a deal. You take me for a ride tonight and I'll think about being your little biker babe tomorrow."

He flipped her onto her back on the bed, and while towering over her, he kissed her cleavage and said, "You got yourself a deal."

On New Year's Eve Ramsey and Keilah once again hosted dinner for their friends. First to arrive was Neil and his date, a dispatcher at the 911 center.

"Keilah, Ramsey, this is Olivia King. Olivia, this is Keilah and Ramsey Stone."

Olivia held out her hand and said, "It's nice to meet you. I've heard nothing but great things about you, and your home is very beautiful."

"Thank you," Keilah answered as she led them into the family room and offered them champagne and hors d'oeuvres in front of a roaring fire.

Ten minutes later the doorbell rang again. Ramsey answered the door and found Tori and Kyle in a passionate kiss when he opened the door.

"Damn! It's not midnight yet," Ramsey joked, interrupting the couple.

"Stop hating, Ramsey," Tori said as she stepped into the foyer and gave him a hug.

Ramsey gave his best friend a brotherly handshake and said, "Y'all are acting like a couple of sixteen-year-olds."

Kyle blushed and then hugged Tori's waist after helping her out of her coat. "We're no different than how you are with Keilah."

Ramsey bumped fists with him and with a smile said, "You're right about that. Come on, you two. We're in the family room."

Neil introduced his date to Kyle and Tori, and they all continued to enjoy the champagne, the soft music, and the hors d'oeuvres until Kyle got everyone's attention.

"I know we've been sort of MIA for a while, but for good reason," Kyle explained. "One, we've been extremely busy, and two, we've been spending a lot of time together."

When Tori picked up her champagne glass, Keilah screamed, startling everyone.

"What the hell, Keilah?" Ramsey asked.

Speechless, Keilah pointed to Tori's hand. She'd spotted the huge diamond resting on her best friend's ring finger.

"Are you serious? You're engaged?" Ramsey asked.

With tears of joy in her eyes, Tori smiled and said, "No, we're not engaged. We're married."

"Married?" Keilah, Neil, and Ramsey asked in unison.

Tori held Kyle's hand and said, "Yes, and I couldn't be happier. We had hoped to tell you all during dinner. I didn't expect Keilah to spot the ring so quickly."

"How could I not see that huge rock blinding me?" Keilah replied as she held Tori's hand to get a closer look. "I'm speechless."

Kyle held his hands up to calm everyone. "Listen, guys, I know this might seem like a whirlwind romance to you, but I'd never been so sure about anything in my life until I met Victoria." Kyle looked into his new wife's eyes and said, "I knew she was the one for me the moment I laid eyes on her."

Neil took a sip of champagne and said, "You mean to tell me you got married after only dating a few weeks?"

Kyle looked at Neil and said, "That's all the time I needed with a beautiful, intelligent, and classy woman like Victoria."

Ramsey hugged Kyle and said, "Well, I'm happy for you, bro. You both made a great choice."

"Thanks, Ramsey."

Ramsey kissed Tori on the cheek and said, "Congratulations, Tori. He'll make you the perfect husband."

"Thank you, Ramsey," Tori answered as she looked over at her best friend, who had her hand over her heart.

"I'm sorry, but I'm still stunned," Keilah said as stared down at the large diamond on Tori's finger again.

Ramsey shook his head and said, "Babe, congratulate them."

Keilah hugged Tori and said, "I'm sorry, Tori. I'm happy for you and Kyle, but I'm just shocked."

Tori held Keilah's hands and said, "I know, Keilah. We haven't even told our families yet."

Neil's date held up her glass and said, "It seems like they deserve a toast."

"I agree," Ramsey replied as he held up his glass. "Kyle, you're like a brother to me, and I couldn't be happier for you. Tori, you're a beautiful, smart, sassy, and nurturing woman. You're all the things Kyle needs, and I have no doubt that the two of you will live long,

love hard, and have a wonderful life together. Congratulations. We love you guys."

After hugs and kisses were exchanged, Tori joined
Keilah in the kitchen as she helped set the dinner table.

Keilah smiled at her friend, with tears in her eyes.
"I'm so happy for you, Tori. I still can't believe you guys
are married."

Tori leaned against the kitchen island and stared
down at her wedding ring. "I know, right?"

"You're in love and happy. That's all that matters."

Tori picked up her champagne glass and said, "I was
beginning to think I wouldn't find a good man, and
along came Kyle."

Keilah closed the oven and said, "Well, you hit the
jackpot. He really is a great guy."

Tori took a sip of Keilah's champagne and frowned.
"This is not champagne. What is this?"

"Oh, don't worry about it. It's only juice," Keilah said
as she took the glass out of Tori's hand.

"Why are you drinking juice?"

"Because it's healthy."

"It's New Year's Eve, and you're drinking juice and
not champagne?"

Keilah ignored Tori's question for a few seconds as
she took a couple of platters into the dining room. Then
she turned to her friend and said, "I'm trying to cut
back on my alcohol intake."

Tori burst into laughter. "You, the wine connoisseur,
cut back on wine and champagne, and you chose New
Year's Eve to do it? Yeah, that will be the day," she said
as she arranged more food items on the table. "That
doesn't even sound right."

"Don't worry. I'll have some champagne at the stroke
of midnight."

Keilah hoped she was able to get Tori off the subject, because if she gave her enough time to think about it, she would definitely put two and two together. The last thing she wanted to do was reveal her pregnancy to their friends before telling their families.

"Dinner's ready!" Keilah called out to her guests from the dining room, and it was just in the nick of time.

Neil held out the chair for his date and said, "It smells good in there. What's cooking, Keilah?"

"Well, I have prime rib, garlic potatoes, black-eyed peas, salad, and a few other goodies."

Neil patted his stomach. "That's why I love coming over here. You're a California girl, but you can cook like you're a Southern girl."

Keilah put her napkin in her lap and said, "Thank you, Neil. Ramsey, will you bless the food please?"

Ramsey took her hand in his, kissed the back of it, and said, "Yeah, because I'm ready to get my grub on."

During dinner the friends talked about their plans for the coming year, Tori and Kyle's marriage, and the happenings around D.C. Before they knew it, midnight was upon them, and as a group they counted down to a brand-new year and began to shower their spouses and lovers with kisses. Ramsey couldn't stop himself from placing his hand over Keilah's abdomen.

He leaned down to her ear and whispered, "Happy New Year, Mrs. Stone. I love you."

She nuzzled his neck and then looked up into his dark brown eyes and said, "I love you too, Ramsey."

Chapter Sixteen

Michael brought the New Year in with strangers in a D.C. bar. As he drank the complimentary champagne and watched the celebration in Times Square on the TV, a beautiful woman in a red dress, who looked like she was Creole, walked over to him and asked, "Is anyone sitting here?"

He looked into her mesmerizing green eyes and said, "No, it's all yours."

The woman took a seat and quickly ordered a *mojito*. She turned to Michael and said, "Happy New Year."

Michael raised his glass to her without responding.

"Are you here with anyone?" she asked as she glanced at his full lips.

"No, just enjoying the festivities," he replied.

She crossed her legs, giving him a full view. "I came with my girlfriends, but it looks like they have all abandoned me and hooked up," she said as she pointed to a nearby table.

Michael could care less about her friends. It was her shapely legs that caught his eye.

"A woman as beautiful as you shouldn't have any problem finding a date, either."

She giggled and gave his bicep a flirty squeeze. "You're sweet, and you look very familiar. Have we ever met before?"

"Not that I remember," he answered casually as he took another sip of champagne.

She took a sip of her *mojito* and shook her head and said, "No, I never forget a face. This bar is usually a hangout for journalists and people in the political arena, but I must say you don't look like either, and I have to admit . . . I love a good mystery."

Michael laughed before finishing off his drink and said, "That will make you a journalist, huh?"

She smiled and said, "Touché. Well, actually, I'm a freelance writer for a local magazine, so I wouldn't call myself a journalist."

Michael pulled out a fifty-dollar bill, handed it to the bartender, and said, "Thanks for the drink. This should be enough to take care of her drink and whatever else she wants."

"Thanks," she said seductively as she took his hand in hers. "You're not leaving, are you?"

He smiled and said, "I would love to stick around, but it's been a long day."

"But the night is young, and the party's just beginning. I wish you would stay a while longer."

He gave her a kiss on the cheek and said, "Happy New Year . . ."

"Madeline," she said, to finish his sentence. "Madeline Savoi."

He gave her hand a gentle shake and said, "Well, Madeline, my name is Michael Monroe, and it was nice meeting you. I hope you have a great rest of the night."

Madeline watched as he disappeared in the crowd of inebriated revelers.

As he walked through the crowded room, he thought about Keilah and the special place she held in his heart. He really did care deeply for her and wished he could turn back the hands of time and do things differently when he was dating her. After stepping outside the bar, he closed his coat tighter as the cold night air swirled around him.

"Sir, do you need a cab?" the valet asked.

Before he could answer, he was interrupted by a soft voice.

"I'll split a cab with you, Michael."

He turned to find the exotic beauty he had just met standing behind him. He turned around and smiled.

"Where are you headed?" she asked.

"Spring Valley. What about you?"

"I live in Bethesda," she revealed as she linked her arm with his. "We're practically neighbors."

"In that case, maybe we can split a cab," Michael replied as he motioned to the valet to hail a cab. "Aren't your friends going to miss you?"

She snuggled closer to him in the chilly night air as they waited for the valet to wave over a cab.

"They're too preoccupied with their hookups. I sent them a text and told them I was leaving."

"Then I guess we should get out of here," Michael replied.

Twenty minutes later, Michael and Madeline found themselves intertwined in the sheets in his bed, throwing caution to the wind. Michael knew he was long overdue for some sexual healing, so if making love to a gorgeous stranger was going to satisfy his needs, so be it. He couldn't believe how limber and acrobatic Madeline was. She was doing things he'd seen only on TV, and it turned him on like he'd never been turned on before. He wondered how he could get so lucky to meet a woman with no inhibitions. Her hands, mouth, and body were all over him, and she had his heart pounding in his chest as he did his best to keep up with her.

"Michael, you taste so good," she whispered as she ran her tongue across his chest.

He grabbed fistfuls of her dark, wavy auburn hair and playfully smacked her on her beautiful bronzed backside. "You're an amazing woman, Madeline."

She winked at him, then softly replied, "Baby, you haven't begun to enjoy what I'm capable of. Hold on, Michael. I'm getting ready to take you on the ride of your life."

He kissed her hard on her rosy lips and said, "Go for it, baby."

Madeline licked her lips and slowly made her way down the length of his long, lean body until she found exactly what she was looking for, and ever so slowly engulfed his thick, pulsating manhood. The sounds coming out of Michael surprised even him. He didn't know who this woman was, but whoever she was, she was an expert in sexual pleasure. Never in his life had he felt the type of sensations she was able to give him, and just maybe this was the type of healing he needed to overcome his dreary past. She seemed happy to give Michael all her attention, but he was a gentleman, and a woman with these types of skills needed to be rewarded, so he decided it was time to return the favor.

"Madeline, come here, baby."

Michael flipped her over onto her back and parted her thighs. She closed her eyes and caressed her breasts as he flicked his tongue against her flesh and partook of her sweet nectar. She squirmed against him as her sighs and moans got louder and louder. Breathlessly she called out his name, praising him on his performance, and guided him to her most sensitive spots.

Michael's body was on fire and ready for the luscious main course lying before him. He kissed his way up her trembling body and lowered his hips into her hot, moist abyss and made love to her vigorously and methodically. Michael could see the strain on Madeline's face with each thrust. He was out of control now and began to release all his frustration, anger, and pent-up lust on her firm, curvaceous body. Madeline's fingernails clawed Michael's back and hips as he hit a very potent G-spot, which caused Madeline to let out a loud scream just as her body exploded with her sensual release. Michael followed, letting out a loud baritone groan before collapsing on top of her.

The next morning Michael eased out of bed and slipped into his briefs and T-shirt. He couldn't help but stare at the sleeping beauty lying in his bed. He noticed a fleur-de-lis symbol tattooed on her ankle. That all but confirmed to him that she was Creole and was probably born and raised in the New Orleans area. Nonetheless, she was beautiful and had a fiery personality and sexuality to go along with it.

Michael carefully closed the bedroom door so as not to wake his guest, then made his way downstairs to the kitchen. He had no idea if this was going to be a one-night stand or something meaningful, but now he wanted to treat her to a delicious breakfast of crisp bacon, sausage links, fresh fruit, eggs, and homemade waffles, along with coffee and orange juice. It wasn't long afterward that Madeline followed the mouth-watering aroma downstairs. When she entered the kitchen, she was barefoot and was dressed in Michael's dress shirt, and her wavy hair was slightly tousled.

She climbed into a seat at the bar and said, "This smells delicious. Do you need any help?"

"No, I got everything under control," he said as he washed his hands. "Did you sleep well?"

She blushed and said, "Like a baby, thanks to you."

"Would you like coffee or orange juice?" he asked as he held up a glass and a coffee cup.

"Coffee for now, thank you," she replied as she looked around the room and admired his decor. It was clear he had an eclectic sense of style with a masculine touch.

Michael poured coffee into two cups and gave her the creamer and sugar. As she stirred her coffee, their eyes met.

She smiled. "I appreciate you helping me bring in the New Year. It was the most amazing night of my life."

He took a sip of his coffee, and with a huge smile on his face, he answered, "I would have to agree with you on that one. You are an amazing woman."

She crossed her legs and said, "You brought it out in me, Michael. I don't know what it is about you, but I feel like I've known you for years, and I want you to know that I've never spent the night with a stranger before, but for some reason, I feel extremely safe and comfortable with you. I like you, Michael."

Michael sat their plates on the kitchen table and said, "This was out of character for me as well, but I'm glad we met, and I hope I get to see you again."

She opened his shirt and gave him a full view of her shapely nude body and asked, "You mean like this?"

He nearly dropped the carafe of orange juice when he laid eyes on her fabulous body. She giggled and then buttoned the shirt back up.

"Your reaction was priceless, Michael."

Michael held Madeline's chair out for her so she could sit down. "You never cease to amaze me. I almost swallowed my damn tongue."

Before sitting, she wrapped her arms around his neck and gave him a long, passionate kiss on the lips. Michael's hands gripped her backside and pulled her flush against his body. Once they broke their kiss, Michael blew out a breath of satisfaction.

He took his seat across from her and said, "You have soft lips. I could kiss you all day."

She giggled again. Madeline's actions and comments had made it perfectly clear that she was smitten with him and was ready to take their relationship forward.

After breakfast, she helped him with the dishes, and then the couple headed back upstairs, where they spent the rest of the afternoon in bed, getting to know each other and making love. It was nearly five in the afternoon when they finally showered and got dressed. Before driving Madeline home, Michael took her out for a romantic dinner, during which they continued to get to know each other. At the end of dinner they exchanged numbers and agreed to see each other again soon. Michael dropped Madeline off at her modest home and walked her to the door.

He pulled her into his arms and said, "I hope I haven't taken up too much of your time."

She snuggled up to him and said, "My time with you was well spent, and I'd do it again in a heartbeat. I can't wait to see you again."

He tilted her chin upward and gave her a firm, sultry kiss on the lips.

She pressed her hips against his and asked, "Do you want to come in?"

"I'd love to, Madeline, but I have a meeting first thing in the morning that I can't miss," he revealed. "I'll call you when I finish and maybe we can get together then. Okay?"

She took his hand and placed it between her legs and said, "I'll be waiting."

He chuckled and gave her one more kiss before returning to his car. The entire drive home he couldn't get Madeline off his mind. That was until he pulled into his driveway and found the words *You're Going To Pay! Fake-Ass Bitch* spray painted in large black letters on his driveway.

Chapter Seventeen

Ramsey paced the floor as he and Keilah waited for Michael to arrive.

"He's late."

"No, he's not," she responded as she went over various reports on her laptop. "He said he would be here. He'll be here."

"Am I the only one upset about this?"

She looked up at him and said, "No, but you're the only one who's going to have a stroke over it."

Ramsey sat down behind his desk and exhaled. "I'm telling you now, if he says one thing to piss me off, I'm going to be on his ass quicker than lightning."

Keilah closed the lid of her laptop and said, "No, you're not. He was really surprised by this, and I think we need to hear him out before drawing any conclusions."

Just as Ramsey opened his mouth to speak, the receptionist called to alert them to their guest's arrival. Ramsey hung up the telephone, then hurried down the hallway to meet Michael. When Michael glimpsed Ramsey's face, he could see the stress, but he held out his hand, anyway, to greet him.

"Hello, Ramsey. I'm sorry we have to meet under these circumstances."

Ramsey frowned. "So am I. Therefore, you have to understand why I don't want to shake your hand. What I really want to do is throw your ass through the wall for causing us all the drama. I'm still pissed over the things you did to Keilah, but since she's forgiven you, I'm trying to exercise restraint."

"I understand," Michael replied. "And I don't blame you. However, I hope at some point you'll learn to forgive me too."

Ramsey motioned for him to follow him down the hallway. "Keilah's waiting in my office."

Michael followed Ramsey down the hallway to his office. After greeting Keilah, he took a seat while Ramsey instructed his assistant to hold all calls. Ramsey closed the door, sat down at his desk, and immediately started drilling him about the journalist. Keilah put her hands up to interrupt him.

"Wait a second, baby. Let me do this. You're way too emotional."

Michael crossed his leg over his knee and said, "It's okay, Keilah, I understand why Ramsey's so upset. I would be, too, if I was in his shoes."

"You don't know the half of it, Michael," she replied. "Listen, all we want to know is why that journalist would show up with all these questions about our relationship. He knew a lot of intimate details about us, especially about me catching you in bed with that man. Who have you been talking to, Michael?"

With a scowl on his face, Michael answered, "I haven't been talking to anyone. I don't discuss my personal business with anyone."

"Then why did you warn me about investigators?" Keilah asked.

"I don't know where this is coming from. I was warning you about the *possibility* of military investigators approaching you."

"Why would military investigators want to talk to Keilah?" Ramsey asked.

"Because I've filed sexual abuse charges against the commander of my military academy for molesting me when I was fourteen," Michael revealed, his face in his hands.

Keilah and Ramsey were both stunned. They had no idea Michael had suffered through such a horrible ordeal. While no one deserved to be taken advantage of, especially a child, they were still upset that they could be dragged into all his drama.

"I'm sorry that happened to you, Michael, but why now?" Keilah asked.

Michael looked into her eyes and said, "While I was being held hostage in Iraq, I had a lot of time to think about my life. That man is the source of my troubled relationships and the main reason I've been so confused about my sexuality, and I want my life back, so I started at the source."

"That still doesn't explain why military investigators will come here," Ramsey pointed out.

"And they probably won't," Michael explained. "I only mentioned it so you and Keilah would be prepared just in case they did show up. Listen, this lieutenant colonel is going to do anything to fight for his reputation, and he'll try to discredit me because his career is at stake. Investigators from the academy might want to talk to anyone I've been involved with. The strange thing is that I had just finished up my deposition when you called me the other day. The investigation is in the beginning stages, so I don't believe that journalist is related to my complaint at the academy."

"Then who could've sent a journalist here?" Keilah asked as she handed Michael the business card the journalist had left with them.

Michael read the card and shook his head. "I don't have a clue. Since I've come back from Iraq, I've been approached by a lot of reporters wanting to write a story about my ordeal, but I declined. It was hell over there, and it's not something I'm ready to talk about."

Ramsey nodded. "I understand that Michael, but there's only four people who knew about Keilah catching you in bed with that guy, and three of us are sitting here. What about your boyfriend?"

Michael chuckled and said, "I don't have a boyfriend. That lifestyle is behind me now."

"He wasn't there when I shot you," Keilah added. "Did you tell him about it?"

Michael shrugged. "So much has happened since then. I really don't remember."

Ramsey leaned back in his chair and said, "I don't care who he is or where he came from. I'm not going to allow him or you to pull my wife into any of this mess that you created, so you need to do whatever it takes to get rid of him and make sure no military investigators approach us, because if they do, it's not going to be a pleasant situation for you."

Michael stood and said, "I understand, Ramsey. I'm so sorry for all of this, and I'll do what I can to get to the bottom of this. Again, I only told you about the military investigator as a precaution. It's not a sure thing. But the story will probably hit the news. The lieutenant colonel is highly decorated and respected, but that's how he's been able to gain power over young boys."

"That's sad, Michael, and I appreciate your warning us," Keilah said as she tenderly touched his arm to console him. "I hope everything works out for you."

"I'm sure it will. One way or the other," Michael answered as he reached for the door. Before exiting, he turned his attention to Ramsey, who was also standing. "Ramsey, for what it's worth, I would never allow Keilah to be embarrassed or disrespected if I can help it."

"I'm going to hold you to that. In the meantime I have a friend looking into this journalist's background and his credentials. If I have to slap him with a slander lawsuit, I will."

"Sounds good," Michael said as he opened the door. "If there's nothing else we need to discuss, I'll get out of your way."

Ramsey slid his hands in his pockets and said, "No, that's it for now."

"I'll keep you informed of any progress I make," Michael replied.

"I'll walk you out," Keilah said as they exited the room together.

Remaining in the office, Ramsey picked up the telephone and called Kyle. On the third ring he answered.

"Ramsey, I'm glad you called. I have some information for you."

"Good," Ramsey answered as he sat down and leaned back in his chair. "I want to know everything you found out on that journalist."

"Cool," Kyle replied. "Do you want to meet for lunch and go over it?"

Ramsey twirled around in his chair and said, "I wish I could, but my schedule's tight today. Fax it over so I can see what you got."

"I can do that, but don't get into any trouble. This dude has a scandalous reputation in the industry," Kyle revealed. "I'm surprised he's working for a reputable newspaper."

"All they want is the latest scandal to sell papers and make money," Ramsey answered. "If he comes anywhere near here again, I'm going to end his career and maybe his life."

"I hear you, bro. Oh, there will be two reports. Mine and one Neil was able to get."

"Great. I'll have to shoot him a text and thank him."

"Cool," Kyle replied. "Let me know if you need any-thing else."

Ramsey hung up the telephone just as Keilah re-turned to the office. She sat down and said, "That was interesting and sad. I hope Michael can get his life to-gether."

"Forget him. My only concern is protecting my fam-ily. I say Michael gets everything he deserves."

She stood and walked toward the door without re-sponding. She put her hand on the doorknob, but in-stead of leaving, she turned back to her husband and said, "You know, I love you and I love the fact that you want to protect me from all this drama, but what hap-pened between me and Michael was almost two years ago. He deserves forgiveness, and he deserves the op-portunity to turn his life around. If you keep holding on to this grudge, it's going to eat away at you. He said he would get to the bottom of it, and I believe him. I for-gave Michael for what he tried to do to me. I just hope you can find it in your heart to forgive him too."

Without waiting for a response, she closed the door behind her, leaving Ramsey to think about her state-ment. He knew she was right, but it wasn't easy for him to forgive a man who had put his wife's life at risk and had betrayed her in a way that he thought was unfor-givable.

Across town, Michael pulled up to the complex of newly built town houses. He shut off the engine and made his way up to the front door of number 742. He braced himself against the door frame and rang the doorbell. As soon as the door opened, he grabbed Kevin by the throat and shoved him back inside the house and onto the floor. Kevin dropped the bottle of Heineken he was drinking, causing it to shatter on his hardwood floor

"What the hell is wrong with you?" Kevin yelled as he tried to pull himself off the floor.

Michael walked over to him and grabbed him by the collar, pulling him off the floor. He slammed him against the wall and said, "You know exactly why I'm here, you son of a bitch! You've gone too far with this fantasy of yours."

"Come on, Mike. You don't have to do this. You know how I feel about you. I would never—"

Michael tightened his grip on Kevin's throat, interrupting him. "Shut the hell up! I know you spray painted my driveway! I should have your ass arrested."

Kevin had never seen Michael as enraged as he was right now. His eyes were red, and he could see the veins in his neck.

"Get your damn hands off me!"

Michael loosened his grip briefly and said, "If you come near my house again, I'm going to blow a hole in your ass."

"I don't know what you're talking about," Kevin gasped.

Michael tightened his grip again on Kevin's throat. Through gritted teeth he said, "I'm going to tell you this one time and one time only. If you don't back off, and I mean right now, I will kill you. Do you understand?"

"You are a fake bitch, so yeah, I spray painted your driveway. I don't know who that whore was, but she's not your type," Kevin whispered, straining for a breath.

Kevin's eyes were now watering, and he was beginning to get lightheaded. Michael's military training had taught him how to kill with his bare hands, and he knew just how far to go before taking a life. He was angry and he wanted Kevin to know what being close to death felt like before he released him, causing him to fall to the floor. As he lay on the floor, gasping for air, Michael leaned over him and smacked his face a couple of times.

"Hurry up and catch your damn breath, because I know you've been talking to a reporter about my relationship with Keilah, so this is what you're going to do. You're going call him and tell him to kill the story. Are you listening to me?"

Kevin continued to gasp for air, and when he looked up, Michael's finger was pointed directly in his face. He still hadn't admitted to being involved with the reporter, but now he was afraid that if he tried to deny it, Michael just might kill him for real.

Michael looked around the room and spotted a cell phone sitting on an end table. He looked at his watch and then tossed the cell over to Kevin. "You have thirty seconds to get your ass on the phone."

Kevin stood up, picked up a bottle of beer he had on the table, and gulped it down. His throat was raw and swollen, and the coolness of the beer soothed it momentarily.

"Call him, now! I don't have all day!" Michael yelled.

Kevin slowly touched a series of buttons on the phone.

Clearly agitated, Michael sat down and said, "Put it on speaker. I want to hear everything."

Kevin pushed the speaker button and drank more beer as he waited for the person to answer. Luckily, it didn't take long.

"Kevin, I'm glad you called. You must be psychic or something. Listen, I was just getting ready to call you. You were right. This story is going to win me all kinds of awards. . . ."

"Jeremy," Kevin said, trying to interrupt him, "we need to talk."

"I know, because I need more details," Jeremy answered. "This story is golden. I stayed up most of the night researching the Stones. Did you know all of them come from money? And your boyfriend has a Supreme Court judge as an uncle. This is too sweet! I don't know why you held back on me. I can't wait to write this story."

Kevin noticed the scowl on Michael's face and yelled, "Jeremy! Shut up for a second and listen to me. I've changed my mind. Cancel the story. I don't want to do it anymore."

"Kill the story?" Jeremy asked with a chuckle. "Have you lost your damn mind? I'm not killing this story. You got me salivating all over it, and now you want to pull the plug? You must be smoking crack."

"I'm serious, Jeremy. I've had time to think about it, and I've decided not to pursue this."

Jeremy started laughing even more. "I can't believe this. What happened? You and your boyfriend get back together or something?"

Becoming frustrated, Kevin yelled, "No, we're not together. Just kill the story."

"And what if I don't?" Jeremy asked.

"I'll deny everything, and you'll be setting yourself up for a lawsuit. Your career in journalism will be dead, and you'll never get another job in the industry. You'll be finished."

"You son of a bitch! You'd do that to me after all I've done for you? You came to me, remember?"

"I'm sorry it has to go out like this," Kevin explained. "I'm willing to pay you for your time if it'll help."

"I don't want your damn money!" he yelled back at Kevin. "This story could finally get me a corner office, and now you want snatch it all away from me? I don't think so. Go to hell! Delete my number, and don't you ever call me again."

The phone went dead, and Kevin looked over at Michael and asked, "Are you satisfied?"

Michael stood and said, "Time will tell. He could still run the story if he wanted to."

Kevin massaged his throat and said, "He won't do that."

Michael open the front door and, before walking out, said, "You'd better pray he don't, because if he does, I'll be back and next time I won't be so gentle."

When Michael slammed the door, it sounded like a bomb going off. Kevin let out a sigh of relief. He felt like he'd been holding his breath the whole time. He slid down to the floor as tears fell out of his eyes. He had never expected Michael to treat him this way. They used to be so close. Now it seemed as if Keilah was in his head more than ever before, and because of her, he had lost someone he really cared about, leaving him angry, brokenhearted, and feeling abandoned.

Traffic was unusually heavy on the Capital Beltway. Michael's hands were trembling as he drove toward the base. He needed to talk to someone quick, and a conversation with one of the army therapists was exactly what he needed to help him release his uncontrollable urge to hurt someone. Since his ordeal in Iraq, he'd had nightmares, reliving what was done to him. The therapists hadn't been able to make any progress with him, mostly because of the wall he had built up, and in most cases it took months, sometime years, to help a soldier recover from traumatic ordeals. Michael was no different.

Chapter Eighteen

Ramsey entered the kitchen and found Keilah feeding their daughter while Target rested comfortably under her feet. The protective German shepherd raised his head briefly but laid it back down as his owner approached.

"Hey, babe." He greeted her with a kiss on the cheek.

"Hey," she answered as she spooned mashed peas into her daughter's mouth.

Ramsey put his leather briefcase on a chair after kissing the top of Neariah's curly head. He studied his wife and asked, "Are you still mad at me?"

She looked up at him and frowned. "I was never mad at you."

He sat down next to her and took over feeding Neariah. "It sure felt like it."

Keilah wiped some the peas off her stained blouse as she made her way over to the sink. "I'm sorry if I made you feel that way. I know you're only looking out for me."

He looked into her beautiful eyes and softly replied, "Exactly."

"You do know you can be a little intense at times. Then again, that's one of the reasons why I love you."

He smiled and then scanned her lovely body as he watched her refill Neariah's cup with apple juice. She handed her daughter the cup and yawned.

Ramsey put a piece of chicken in Neariah's mouth and said, "Why don't you go on upstairs and chill? I'll finish this."

Keilah yawned again and asked, "Are you sure?"

He tickled Neariah and said, "Yeah, go ahead."

She massaged his shoulders and said, "Thank you, babe."

Ramsey and Neariah watched her as she exited the room. Seconds later Neariah looked up at her daddy with her bottom lip poked out and started to cry.

"No, no. I don't want to see any tears. Your mother just went upstairs," he explained as he removed his necktie. "This is daddy-daughter time, and we're going to have some fun. Okay?"

Neariah glanced back over to the door and waited for her mother to return. When she didn't reappear, she looked at her father with tears in her eyes and apple juice running down her chin and said, "Da-dee."

"Yeah, Da-dee," he repeated as he wiped her mouth and disposed of her leftover food. After removing her bib, he picked her up in his arms and grabbed his brief-case. "Daddy's getting ready to give you a nice warm bath, and then we're going to watch a movie together. How does that sound?"

Neariah laid her head against her father's chest and started singing as he slowly climbed the stairs with Target on his heels.

In the bedroom Keilah lay across the bed in deep thought over the events of the day. It had been an emotional twenty-four hours, and it had taken a toll on her physically. Since she was pregnant, she wanted keep herself surrounded by peace and harmony as much as possible. Instead of her normal sexy lingerie, she was dressed down in one of her husband's T-shirts and nothing else. As she lay there, she could hear Ramsey singing to their daughter as he gave her a bath. It brought a smile to her face and warmed her heart. Ramsey was an excellent father and a perfect husband. Yes, they often butted heads over things, but they always found a way to work through their disagreements. Her thoughts were interrupted when her cell phone chimed. She glanced down at her phone and opened the text message.

The situation with the reporter has been taken care of.

With best regards,
Michael.

She immediately felt as if a weight had been lifted. She just prayed it was really over, but before she could give it more thought, her cell phone rang. She looked at the caller ID and saw that it was her brother Luke.

"Hey, Luke," she answered.

"Hey, baby girl," he greeted her. "You sound terrible. Are you okay?"

She rolled over onto her back and let out a loud sigh. "I'm good. How are Sabrinia and the kids?" she asked.

"Everyone's fine. Now back to you. Are you putting in long hours again?"

Her eyes were stinging with tears. They always did when she talked to Luke. He was like a father to her, and his concern for her well-being made her emotional. She felt vulnerable and came really close to telling him she was pregnant, but she wanted to break the news to their entire families with her husband by her side. It had been almost three months since she'd seen her brothers, and she missed her family terribly.

"No, I'm not keeping long hours anymore. Camille is a great caretaker, but I make sure I'm home to spend time with Neariah and put her to bed."

"Good, because there's no reason for you or Ramsey to work like that anymore. You guys have to take the time to enjoy each other."

"We do," she replied with a solemn tone.

"Is Ramsey home?"

"Yes, he's giving Neariah a bath."

Luke had seen this behavior in his sister before, and he knew she was homesick. He didn't want to make it obvious that he was on to her, so he decided to gradually ease into a conversation about home to feel her out.

"Do you guys have any plans for Super Bowl weekend?" he asked.

"We haven't talked about it yet. What are you going to do?" she asked.

With a smile in his voice he said, "Well, Roman was talking about having a party, but it wouldn't be complete without you guys here."

"I'd love to come, but we have to check our schedule. You know that's a busy time for us, she answered.

Luke let out a frustrated breath and said, "Keilah, every day is a busy time for you. When are you guys going to relinquish some of your duties to your managers?"

"Soon," she replied.

"When?" he asked. "You're trying to run the D.C. location and open the office in Atlanta too. You and Ramsey can't keep going at this pace."

"You work just as hard," she pointed out.

"That's where you're wrong, sis. I work hard when I'm there, but we split the responsibilities among each other. I work two days a week, and the other days belong to my family. That's how it's supposed to be, sweetheart. You're successful, and you've done your job. Now it's time for you and Ramsey to back the hell up and enjoy the benefits you worked so hard to build."

Tears spilled out of her eyes. She softly replied, "I know."

"What you gon' do?" Luke asked with a firm tone of voice.

She swallowed the lump in her throat and said, "I'll let you know what we decide."

"Okay. I'm going to hold you to that. I miss you and want to see you, especially my niece."

She laughed and said, "She's grown so much. Her personality is really coming out. I can't wait to see you guys too. I love you, Luke."

"I love you too," he assured her with tenderness in his tone. "Tell Ramsey hello, and kiss Neariah for me. I'll call you in a couple of days."

"Okay. Good night, Luke."

"Good night, Keilah."

She hung up the phone and pulled her comforter over her body. Establishing a normal life had become even more important to her now. Family should always come first, and having another baby on the way made her long for a carefree life more than ever. Her mind was made up as she slowly drifted off the sleep.

It was nearly midnight when she woke up and noticed that Ramsey wasn't in bed. She slowly climbed out of bed and made her way across the hall to Neariah's nursery. Her crib was empty as well, so she headed downstairs to get a drink of water. Target met her at the bottom of the stairs, alerting her that he needed to go out. She went into the kitchen and pulled a bottle of water out of the refrigerator. She deactivated the alarm, and as soon as she opened the door, Target sprinted into the backyard. She sipped her water as she waited for him to finish his business. Minutes later he returned to the back door so she could let him in.

Keilah reset the alarm and made her way into the family room, where she found the TV on and Ramsey asleep on the sofa, with Neariah lying across his chest, securely wrapped in his arms. It was a Kodak moment, and she couldn't resist taking a picture with the camera they kept in the kitchen. Then she knelt down beside him and started gently caressing his arm to wake him. He slowly opened his eyes and smiled.

"What time is it?" he murmured.

She ran her hand over her sleeping daughter's back and said, "Late."

"I didn't realize how tired I was," he said as she cuddled his daughter as he sat up.

Keilah stood and said, "Give her to me so I can put her in bed."

Ramsey handed Neariah to his wife and yawned. She kissed her daughter's cheek and said, "I might as well change her diaper before putting her down."

He picked up the remote and turned off the TV and then stretched. Target whined for attention, so Ramsey patted him on the head and said, "Not now, boy."

"I just let him out, so he's good," Keilah said as she walked ahead of him.

Upstairs Keilah quietly changed the baby's diaper. She was able to do it so gently and methodically that Neariah stayed asleep the whole time. When Keilah re-entered the bedroom, she found Ramsey in the shower. She crawled back into bed and waited for her husband to join her. Minutes later he crawled under the covers and pulled her close to his body, and minutes later they fell asleep in each other's arms.

Michael was up nursing a glass of rum and Coke as he watched a late-night segment on CNN. He felt calmer after his session with the therapist. The therapist's main concern was Michael's enraged state of mind during his assault on Kevin and the trigger that set him off. If Kevin hadn't complied or if he had fought back, the outcome could've gone from bad to worse in an instant. The therapist had advised Michael to refrain from alcohol if he could; however, most soldiers who returned from the war zone drank to try and relax. Many of them also turned to recreational drugs to try and rid their minds and dreams of the horrible things they saw overseas.

Michael's kidnapping was something he wasn't ready to talk about, but in time he knew he would have to with his therapist. He wanted to wait until he settled his complaint against Lieutenant Colonel Biggs before opening his soul. He had admired Biggs for so long and hated that he hadn't told authorities about his molestation when it happened. Now it was going to be an uphill battle to get justice. *There's only so much a man can bear mentally, emotionally, and physically,* he thought. His ordeal with Lieutenant Colonel Biggs was horrific, as was his stint as a prisoner of war. He had felt like he was dying a slow death ever since he'd been molested, but it wasn't until he was kidnapped that he felt that he would take his last breath on foreign soil. He poured himself another glass of rum and Coke just as he received a text from Madeline.

Bored. Wish you were here.

He picked up his cell and sent a text back.

Would love to, but I've had a few. Don't want to get a DUI.

The couple sent flirty text messages back and forth for a few minutes, until Madeline sent one last text.

Can't take it anymore. See you in ten minutes. Save some rum for me.

Michael smiled and turned on the porch light and waited for his lovely guest to arrive. While he waited, he decided to spruce up the living room, wash the dirty dishes in the sink, and turn on a scented warmer to send a relaxing fragrance throughout the house. The doorbell rang, announcing Madeline's arrival, just as he finished up his chores. Michael wanted to have her drink cold and ready for her, so he held it in his hand as he headed to the front door. He opened the door and found his gorgeous date smiling back at him. She was as stunning as expected, with her beautiful hair blown straight and light makeup on her face. He took the small overnight bag out of her hand as he pulled her inside.

"Thanks for coming over," he greeted before giving her a sizzling kiss on the lips.

She wrapped her arms around his neck and said, "I'm glad I'm here too. Why don't you help me out of my coat?"

Michael sat the drink on the table in the hallway and untied the belt of her coat. When he opened her coat, he was stunned to find her completely nude underneath.

"Damn, girl! Where are your clothes?"

Without answering, she allowed the coat to slide off her shoulders onto the floor. She picked up the glass and gulped down the rum and Coke.

"Thirsty?" he asked, with an admiring grin on his face, as he scanned her body.

She burped and then took him by the hand and said, "I want you upstairs now."

Michael turned out the lights and then followed her up the stairs to his bedroom with two glasses and a bottle of rum. He sat the glasses and bottles on the table and turned. Madeline immediately started undressing him, but he stopped her after she unbuttoned his shirt.

"Is everything okay, Michael?"

He caressed her cheek and said, "Everything is fine, but we do need to talk."

Michael was really starting to like Madeline, and even though they hadn't known each other for very long, he could see himself having a future with her. He felt that now was a better time than any for him to be honest with her about his past. If she never called or wanted to see him again, he would understand, but if she stayed, he would know she cared about him as much as he cared about her. Needing her undivided attention, he picked up his robe and helped Madeline into it so he wouldn't be distracted by her sexy body. Then he walked her over to a small love seat, where they sat down in the moonlight.

He kissed her hands and said, "Madeline, I really, really like you, and I've found myself falling hard for you, but before we take this relationship any further, I think there's some things I need to be honest with you about."

She cupped his face and said, "Michael, I'm into you as well. I'm an astrology fanatic, and all the stars point to you being a wonderful man."

"We'll see how you feel after I tell you about my life."

Madeline crossed her legs and said, "I'm a big girl. Give it to me, and I mean everything."

Michael had planned on being honest, but he wasn't ready to tell her his life story. Still, he felt compelled to share all and just started talking. He took a deep breath and started by telling her about his molestation at the military academy and the charges he had filed against Lieutenant Colonel Biggs. From there he revealed the details of his relationship with Kevin and how Kevin hadn't been able to accept that their affair was a mistake, and the results of the abuse he had suffered at the hands of the lieutenant colonel. He mentioned his short relationship with Keilah and how he had planned to get her pregnant and fight her for custody of their child.

Once he was finished, Madeline stared at him and said, "Wow! You've been a busy boy, huh?"

"I'm sorry to drop all that in your lap, but I didn't want you to get to know the man I am without knowing the man I was. I also want you to know that I'm not that person anymore, and to be honest, that wasn't me in the first place. Being held in captivity in Iraq for all those months was an awakening for me. I truly am a changed man, and I'm tired of being hurt and hurting others."

She snapped her finger and said, "That's where I know you from. I knew I'd seen you somewhere before. One of the magazines I freelance for did a short story on your rescue. You look different than you do in uniform, but handsome nonetheless. I'm so proud of you, Michael, and I admire you. You're a brave man. Not just for what you did in Iraq, but also for being honest with me. I'm sure that wasn't easy to do."

He swirled the ice around in his glass and said, "I didn't want any fanfare with my homecoming, and what I told you about my past is only right for me to do, and I did the magazine interview at the urging of my superiors. They want the public to know what our guys are going through over there."

She put her hand on his leg and said, "Babe, there are a lot of people who don't have a clue about what the soldiers experience over there. I'm glad you did the article. It was well written. I wish I had done the interview."

Without making eye contact with her, he said, "Thanks for the reassurance."

"Can I ask you something, Michael?"

"Sure," he answered as he finished off his drink.

"Did you love that girl?" she asked.

"I did, but I wasn't in love with her. She's a very nice woman, and I hurt her very bad. She was so pissed, she shot me in the foot when she caught me in bed with Kevin. She's married now, and it gives me peace that she's forgiven me for what I did to her."

Madeline sat there, her eyes wide with amazement, holding on to every word. She felt his sadness and his feeling of repentance. She kissed his hands, then held them over her heart.

"I'm sure she was in shock and hurt. She could've killed you, huh?"

"Without a doubt."

"Michael, who among us hasn't had a sexual experience with someone of the same sex? I tried it in college, and while it was cool, it wasn't me, and to be honest, I can't picture you being with another man."

He got up and poured himself another drink and said, "Me either. Do you want a drink?"

"No, but I do have one more important question."

"Yes?" he asked softly as he rejoined her on the love seat.

"Did you practice safety in your relationships?"

He took a sip of his drink and looked her in the eyes and answered, "Always. I would never jeopardize my health or another person's health, either."

She studied his expression and saw the sincerity in his eyes. "I appreciate your honesty, but I want us to do something together that I do every year, anyway."

"What's that?" he asked as he hung his head with shame.

She tilted his chin upward so she could look into his handsome brown eyes. "I want us to take the HIV test together. I took one three months ago, but I'll do it again for you. It will be nice to do it together."

Michael pulled Madeline into his lap and caressed her shapely bronze thighs. "Of course I'll take the test with you. If you're willing to hang with me after I told you about all my drama, I'll do anything for you, Madeline."

She looked up at the full moon and tenderly said, "Michael, I have a feeling that you've been carrying that burden for a long time. I want you to know that I'm here for you. I don't judge, and what that colonel did to you was evil. I hope you get your day in court and they put his ass under the jail."

"So do I, Madeline. So do I," he repeated. "Let's go to bed, sweetheart."

The couple climbed into bed and held each other in silence for a moment.

Madeline caressed Michael face lovingly and said, "Babe?"

He opened his eyes and stared into her angelic face. "Yes, dear?"

She kissed him and said, "Let me write your story. It might be liberating for you. I've always wanted to write a book, but I never found a story that I had enough passion for until now."

Michael closed his eyes and pulled her closer to his body. "Maybe later. I don't think that would be a good idea right now, especially since my business with the lieutenant colonel is not settled. I don't want to draw any unfavorable attention to my family and the people I care about until it's behind me. Okay?"

She nuzzled her face against his warm neck and said, "You're right. The only thing that's important right now is me helping you get past all the hurt and pain that you've suffered so we can get on with our lives."

He kissed her lips and neck and jokingly said, "You're hired."

Madeline giggled and gave him a fiery kiss. "Seriously Michael, if you don't already have one, you need to get an attorney to help you with your complaint against that colonel. I've been around enough brass to know that they fight hard and dirty, especially if it looks like they could lose everything they've worked for."

Michael listened to Madeline and realized that he hadn't even thought about hiring an attorney. He'd been so caught up with readjusting to civilian life, dealing with Kevin's antics, and confronting Biggs, he hadn't thought about an attorney.

"You're right, Madeline. I hadn't thought about it," he answered as he ran his hand through her hair. "I'm sure he has one representing him."

"Can't you get one from the judge advocate general's office?"

He stared into her eyes and said, "You are one sharp lady, and a beautiful one too."

Madeline blushed and said, "You have too much to deal with alone right now. You need me, Michael, so to-morrow we're going to sit down, strategize, and get you an attorney so we can get this settled and that demon off his post and out of our lives forever. Okay?"

He kissed her lovingly on the lips and, with a smile on his face, said, "You go, girl. I'm scared of you."

She cupped his face and nibbled on his ear and said, "Don't be scurred."

Michael felt that Madeline was the answer to all his prayers. She was sweet, smart, nurturing, and extremely passionate. From this moment on, he couldn't see his life without her in it, and if he had it his way, he would try to make his dreams come true.

Chapter Nineteen

"You want to go home Super Bowl weekend?" Ramsey asked as he poured himself a cup of coffee. "That's in two weeks. I don't think we can get away, babe. It's going to be a busy weekend for us."

"I don't care," Keilah snapped at him. "I want to go home. I'm tired of not being able to come and go as we please!"

Ramsey looked over at his wife and studied her as he sat the coffeepot down. Neariah squealed to get Keilah's attention so that she would feed her more scrambled eggs. Keilah fed her daughter in silence. Ramsey realized that Keilah was clearly upset, but she knew the nature of their business, and that particular weekend was going to be extremely hectic for their agency. He didn't want to upset her any more than she already was, so he proceeded delicately.

As he poured a little cream and sugar into his coffee and stirred it, he asked, "Are you feeling okay?"

She glanced up at him and said, "I feel just fine."

Ramsey took a sip of coffee and shook his head. "I disagree. You seem a little pissed off."

"That's an understatement," she angrily replied as she stood and scraped the remainder of her daughter's eggs into the trash.

Ramsey watched her movements as she handed Neariah a cup of apple juice and then put the dirty plate into the dishwasher. He knew he was on dangerous ground, but he needed to get to the bottom of his wife's sour mood. While scanning the newspaper, he watched her make her plate with eggs, a croissant, and sausage links. He poured her a cup of coffee, and before he allowed her to touch it, he pulled her into his arms.

"Why are you so angry this morning?" he asked. "Is it just about Super Bowl weekend, or is it something else?"

She lowered her head and said, "It's everything, Ramsey. We don't spent enough time together. We don't get to see my or your family as much as we should. How many times have Xenia and Keith invited us to Tampa? We work too damn hard not to relax and enjoy life and see the people we love when we want to."

"Wow! You do have a lot on your mind. No wonder you're fired up."

"There's something else you should know, Ramsey."

"I'm almost afraid to ask, but go ahead," he said as he caressed her back.

"I'm having second thoughts about opening the office in Atlanta. I think it's taking on too much when we don't have to. I want to spend time at our new home in Florida that I haven't even seen yet. . . ."

Ramsey couldn't believe his ears. Keilah was in rare form, and since she was pregnant, he needed to calm her down as quickly as possible, before her blood pressure skyrocketed. He put his finger over her lips to silence her. As he held on to her, he could feel her body trembling as tears began to fall out of her eyes. Ramsey didn't know it if was her hormones or something else, but whatever it was, it had her extremely infuriated.

"Sweetheart, you're trembling. Calm down and take a breath. You're going to make yourself hyperventilate."

She looked up into his concerned eyes and said, "I'm sorry. I didn't mean to lash out. It's not you. It's the situation," she explained as she grabbed a napkin out of the holder and wiped her tears.

"Why have you been holding this in, babe? You should talk to me when things are bothering you."

"I've been thinking about it for a while," she revealed. "It's time for us to cut back on our responsibilities at the office now more than ever, since we're going to have another baby."

He kissed her forehead and said, "I know it's something we both want to do, but we're at a critical point right now. I don't think now is a good time."

She walked over to the sink and picked up a wet dish towel and began to clean the tray on Neariah's high chair.

"Critical time or not, I'm not interested in opening the Atlanta office anymore," she announced as she picked Neariah up and placed her on the floor. "But if you want to go ahead with it, go right ahead. I'll visit a couple of times a year, but I'm not going to be involved."

He smiled and said, "You're serious about this, aren't you?"

She picked up her coffee cup and took a sip and said, "Do I look like I'm joking?"

Neariah walked over to her father and grabbed on to his pant leg. As she stood there, looking up at him with a huge smile on her face, she held her sippy cup upside down, dripping apple juice all over his pant leg and shoe.

Feeling the coolness soaking through his sock, Ramsey finally looked down at her and said, "Neariah, you're spilling your juice."

"Daddy!" she squealed. "Juice!"

"Yeah, yeah, yeah, I see your juice," he replied as he pulled a towel out of the drawer and cleaned up the mess.

"You're going to have to mop that up, or it's going to be sticky," Keilah said as she sat down and started eating her breakfast. She felt much better after unburdening her heart with her thoughts. Talking to her brother had helped her with her decision, but it had been weighing a lot heavier on her heart lately, especially with the news of her pregnancy. She was ready to settle down and enjoy her husband and children, but Ramsey seemed clueless about her sudden change of heart about the office in Atlanta.

Ramsey let out a breath and took Neariah by the hand and led her back over to her mother. Before Ramsey could clean up the mess, Target walked over and started licking it up.

"Get away, Target!" Ramsey yelled, startling the dog and causing him to tuck in his tail and slowly disappear into the hallway.

Neariah held on to her mother's chair and sipped on what was left in her cup as they watched Ramsey mop up the floor. Keilah thought it was humorous to see her husband mopping the floor in a business suit.

"Ramsey, what are you doing?" Camille asked as she walked into the kitchen and sat some grocery bags on the counter.

"Cleaning up the rug rat's mess," he answered.

Camille tried to take the mop out his hands, but he refused to give it up.

"I got it, Camille."

She backed up and then greeted Keilah and her special little angel. Neariah ran into Camille's arms and gave her a big hug.

Camille kissed Neariah's cheek and said, "Hello, Neariah. I missed you."

Keilah stood and put her empty plate in the dishwasher and said, "She missed you too."

Camille grabbed Keilah's chin and turned her head so she could look into her eyes. "You don't look well. What's going on with you?"

"Nothing's going on," Keilah replied as she finished off her coffee.

Camille rolled her eyes and said, "You're lying. I know when something's going on. You're not getting enough rest, and I hope you're still taking your vitamins."

Keilah gave Camille a kiss on the cheek and said, "Yes, ma'am. In fact, I'm getting ready to take them now."

"Okay," Camille answered as she started unpacking the grocery bags. "Has Neariah had breakfast?"

"Yes, so she shouldn't be hungry."

Ramsey returned to the kitchen after putting away the wet mop and asked, "Can you see the juice stain on my pants?"

"Yes," they answered in unison.

"Damn," he mumbled, then headed upstairs to change his clothes.

Keilah excused herself from Camille's company and then followed her husband out into the hallway. "Ramsey, I'm going to go ahead and head out."

He gave her a kiss and said, "Okay, drive safely. We can finish talking about the business at the office if you want to."

She wrapped her arms around his waist, laid her head against his chest, and whispered, "I know you think I'm psycho."

He embraced her lovingly and said, "No, I don't think you're psycho. I think you're a fabulous mother with nothing but love for her family. Life is short, and you want to spend time with family. I get it."

She smiled and said, "Thank you."

"You're welcome. Now, get out of here before we're both late."

Keilah felt a feeling of relief as she watched her man make his way up the stairs. He was undeniably the best thing that had ever happened to her, and she loved him deeply. It was taking all her strength not to sprint up the stairs and rip his clothes off. *Then again, why fight it?* she thought.

Keilah quickly went into the hall closet and got Neariah's hat and coat. She entered the kitchen and found Camille and Neariah playing peekaboo.

"Camille, I really need to talk to Ramsey before I leave. Do you mind taking Neariah for a walk in her stroller?"

Camille stood and said, "Sure. As a matter of fact, I was just getting ready to take her to that romper room place she likes so much."

Keilah helped Neariah into her coat and hat while Camille slid into hers.

"We'll get out of your way. Call me if you need me to pick anything up while we're out."

Keilah hugged Camille and gave Neariah a loving kiss before putting Neariah's diaper bag on Camille's shoulder. "Thank you so much."

Camille opened the door and said, "You don't have to thank me, child. I know what it's like to be young and in love. Have fun."

Keilah blushed and waved to Camille as she backed out of the garage before hurrying upstairs to her husband. In the bedroom she found him sitting on the side of the bed in his shirt, tie, and briefs, watching ESPN.

He stood and started to put on his pants. "Neariah pretty much emptied her cup on my pants. I thought you were gone."

She walked over to him and grabbed the pants out of his hands and threw them in the chair. "I forgot something," she replied as she started unbuttoning her blouse.

"What are you doing?" he asked with a sly grin on his face.

In a split second she was out of her skirt and was standing in front of him in a black lace thong and bra. She fluffed her hair with a gesture she knew always turned him on.

"Are you serious?" He chuckled. "What about Camille? You know you're loud."

She pushed him back on the bed and climbed on top of him. With her lips within inches of his, she said, "Camille and Neariah have gone for a ride, so I can be as loud as I want to be. Now kiss me."

He kissed and nibbled on her lips as he ran his hands through her hair. He was seeing a softer, more sensual woman than he had earlier. Her demeanor had gone from one extreme to another, but this was the side of her that he loved most.

"You know we have a meeting with department heads in an hour, don't you?" he reminded her as he caressed her thighs.

She sighed and climbed off him momentarily. He watched her as she picked up the telephone and punched in a series of numbers.

"Cameron, it's Keilah. Ramsey and I need you to push our departmental meeting ahead to lunch. Let Sherrie know as well so she can adjust Ramsey's schedule. We're going to make the meeting a working lunch, so order lunch from one of the restaurants we normally use. We'll be in the office shortly. Call us if anything comes up."

Keilah's assistant, Cameron, noted her request and assured her he would take care of everything. She hung up the telephone and turned her attention back to her half-dressed husband, who was now sitting up on the side of bed.

"Now, back to you. We're getting ready to have our own meeting," she said as she started removing his tie. "I want you out of these clothes so I can feel your skin against mine."

He palmed her backside before lowering her thong and removing her bra. "You really know how to drive me crazy," he revealed before running his tongue across her navel, causing her to shiver.

She bit down on her lower lip as she watched him remove his shirt, T-shirt, and briefs. He pulled her into the bed and kissed her lips, neck, and breasts.

"Ramsey . . ." she panted and moaned.

He silenced her with a long, hard, wet kiss as he began to feverishly make love to her. Keilah's heart pounded in her chest as her husband's massive body plunged deeper and deeper into hers. Her body absorbed each thrust, and within minutes she began to tremble out of control. A few more thrusts sent Ramsey's body spiraling into an enormous release.

Tears rolled out of her eyes as he kissed her ear and whispered, "I love you, Keilah."

"I love you too," she answered as she held on to his muscular frame.

He caressed her face and said, "Listen, I'm okay with whatever you want to do about the business. All I want is for you to be happy. If you want to go to home Super Bowl weekend, count me in."

"Thank you, Ramsey. I'm so sorry I snapped at you this morning. If it really is a bad time for us to go home, we don't have to go."

He laughed and said, "No, we're going. This has obviously been weighing heavily on your heart."

"It has, but I don't want to burden you with all the responsibilities."

He cupped her breasts and said, "You and the children are the only responsibilities I care about. The businesses are secondary. I would never put them or anything else before you guys. Don't ever forget that."

Keilah could see the seriousness in his eyes and could hear it in his tone of voice. Even now she was amazed that she was lucky enough to have him as her husband. Then again, her brother Luke had always told her that life was not about luck. It was about being blessed.

"I feel the same way about you too."

He continued to caress her breasts in silence, and she noticed how he seemed to be in deep thought.

"Babe," she said, "what are you thinking about?"

He made eye contact with her and said, "I was thinking about the fact that I didn't make you scream."

"I wanted to, but I was being reserved," she explained.

"Not good enough," he replied as he parted her thighs and helped himself to her delicious feminine flesh.

She immediately responded with breathless moans and pleas of mercy, and within minutes she let out a high-pitched scream of satisfaction.

Ramsey laughed and said, "On that note . . . meeting adjourned."

Chapter Twenty

Michael couldn't believe that he'd received a phone call from Lieutenant Colonel Biggs's attorney requesting a meeting. He hadn't had a chance to find his own attorney, but he decided to go ahead and meet with Biggs's attorney just to see what their response was to his complaint. Before the meeting, he picked up Madeline, who was going along with him for support. They stopped by the base so he could have a brief meeting with his therapist to discuss possible outcomes to the meeting and what he wanted the end result to be. Feeling empowered, Michael thanked his therapist for the unscheduled appointment, and with Madeline by his side, he headed toward Virginia for the meeting that he hoped would give him a permanent resolution to all the anguish he'd been holding in.

On the drive there, Madeline felt a little detached from the whole thing, but she wanted Michael to know she supported him. She reached over and put her hand on his and gave it a squeeze. Michael glanced over at her and smiled.

"Thanks. I needed that. I am a little anxious about all of this. I'm curious about why they've called a meeting."

"I guess we'll find out sooner than later. I just want you to know I'm here for you. You're not alone in this, and it will be okay. We'll get through this."

"I really appreciate your support. I was a little reluctant to let you come, but I'm glad I did, and for the record, you are wearing that navy suit. Your legs are spectacular, and you're making it hard for me to concentrate on driving."

Madeline giggled and said, "Well, once we finish up here, maybe we should hop on a plane to Miami for a few days and take in some sun."

"Don't you have to work?" he asked.

"I'm my own boss, remember? Besides, I can work and play at the same time."

"That really sounds inviting, Madeline, but it all depends on how things go today. Nothing would make me happier than kicking that man's ass straight to hell."

"I hope the bastard falls down dead," she stated as she stuck a stick of gum in her mouth. "Do you want some gum, babe?"

Michael chuckled and said, "No thank you. You know, you're a hard sista."

"I'm serious, Michael. He needs to burn in hell."

"I agree with you on that one. I'm only doing this so I can get on with my life and so he can't hurt anyone else."

"You're my hero, Michael Monroe," she replied with a smile.

He leaned over and gave her a quick kiss on the cheek as he exited the expressway. "I don't feel like a hero. I just want to serve out my time and retire so I can live my life."

"It'll happen, Michael, but I don't want you to walk into this meeting unprepared. Let me act as your counsel. They'll never know."

"Babe, these men are not stupid. What makes you think you can pull something like that off?"

"That's where you're in luck. My father is an attorney, and I spent a lot of time with him at his practice."

"Yeah, but you'll be impersonating an officer of the court. It's fraud, baby."

"Sweetheart, I promise I won't say a word unless it appears that they're trying to pull one over on you, and I won't say I'm an attorney. I'll just say I'm there to represent you. That could mean a lot of things."

He pulled into the academy lot and said, "You really think you can pull this off?"

"I'm positive. I've done it before. Just trust me, babe," she answered as she winked at him. "Just introduce me, and if I have to show them a business card, I'll show them this one from my dad's law firm."

Michael shut off the engine and looked at the business card. It had SAVOI LEGAL SERVICES written on it, along with a telephone number and a fax number. He handed the card back to her and said, "Well, you sure do look the part. Okay, I'm going to go along with this, but I pray it won't come to you having to say something."

She gave him a high five and said, "I got you, babe. I'm going to send Daddy a text to let him know I'm representing a friend, and I'll ask him to let me know if they get a call to confirm my association with the firm."

In the conference room of the administration building, Michael and Madeline found Lieutenant Colonel Biggs, his attorney, and what appeared to be a legal secretary seated at the large oak table.

"Major Monroe, I'm glad you could make it on such short notice," the attorney said, greeting him. "I'm a representative from the judge advocate general's office. We thought it was best that we handle the matter as delicately and discreetly as possible."

Michael shook his hand and said, "Thank you. I just want to get this settled."

The attorney turned to Madeline and held out his hand. "And you are?"

She gave him a firm handshake, something she'd learned from her father. "Madeline Savoi. I'm here to represent Major Monroe."

The attorney's smile left his face as he glanced down at her firm grip. He hadn't expected Michael to show up with an attorney, but Michael was an academy graduate and it was a smart move. "I see. Shall we get started?"

Michael held his breath as they sat down across from Biggs and his attorney.

"The reason we called you here is to let you know that Lieutenant Colonel Biggs and I have read over your complaint and the terms that have to be met to make this matter go away. He has no plans to retire, because he still has a lot of work to do. However, he will consider seeing a therapist."

Madeline could see Michael tense up, and he was making a fist under the table. She reached over and covered his hand with hers to comfort him. Michael was stunned by Biggs's refusal to retire, and so was Madeline. Biggs's retirement was critical to Michael, and he sat there like a deer caught in the headlights, leaving Madeline no choice but to jump in to protect her lover's interests.

"That's not good enough," Madeline announced, startling Michael. "I'm sure you're aware that the state of Virginia doesn't have a statute of limitations on sexual assault."

"We are," Biggs's attorney replied.

"Refusing to retire is not an option, unless you want to take this matter to the courts."

"Of course we don't want that," the attorney replied.

"Then it would be in your best interests to get your client to agree to *all* the terms," Madeline asserted.

"Look, if you knew you were going to waste our time, you could've told us this bullshit information over the telephone and saved us some gas."

The attorney put his hands up in defense and said, "Ms. Savoi, can we all just take a breath for a moment? The last thing we want is to drag this matter into court. However, don't forget that Major Monroe's accusations can't be verified, and all we have is his word against Lieutenant Colonel Biggs's."

Madeline sat up on the edge of her seat and stared right at the lieutenant colonel, who had sat silent, along with Michael, the entire time. She pointed her finger at Biggs's attorney and said, "And don't you forget that all we need is one more victim—"

"Alleged victim," the attorney interrupted.

Madeline hesitated and then corrected herself and said, "*Alleged* victim to come forward to put this case on another level. The lieutenant colonel has had a long career here at your illustrious academy. I'm sure it won't take much to locate some of his former cadets who had encounters similar to Major Monroe's."

"Now hold on, Ms. Savoi!" Biggs yelled.

"No, you hold on, Lieutenant Colonel!" Madeline yelled as she stood.

"There's no way in hell I'm going to let this liar come here and try to destroy my reputation and take my money!" Biggs yelled.

"I don't want or need your damn money!" Michael shouted.

"Counselor, control your client, or this meeting is over before it gets started!" Madeline yelled.

"Control yours," the attorney replied, his voice slightly elevated.

"Counselor, if your client makes one more outburst, the next time you see us, you and your client will be in a courtroom, behind a defendant's table," Madeline announced.

The attorney grabbed the lieutenant colonel's arm and did his best to silence him, even though he kept on mumbling.

Madeline leaned on the table and once again stared at Biggs. "Now, what's it going to be, Counselor? Is your client going to meet the terms Major Monroe laid out or not?"

"Could you two give us a moment so I can discuss this with my client?"

Madeline looked at her watch and said, "The clock is ticking. Make it quick. We don't have all day."

Michael and Madeline walked out into the hallway and closed the door behind them. Michael exhaled and said, "You're a damn pit bull, Madeline. Hell, *I* was scared, so I know they have to be shaking in their boots. You should've been a lawyer."

She sat down and crossed her legs and said, "I told you. My dad taught me well."

"I wonder what they're talking about," Michael said as he paced the hallway.

Madeline pulled out her compact, freshened up her makeup, and said, "I guarantee you that his attorney is trying to convince the lieutenant colonel to agree to the terms. Babe, they're not going to let us leave here unhappy. They have more to lose, and they know I'm not playing with them."

He smiled at her and said, "I want to kiss you so bad right now."

She giggled. "I want more than a kiss, but you'll have to wait until we get this settled."

At that moment the door to the conference room opened, interrupting them. The secretary asked them to rejoin the meeting so they could finish the discussion.

Madeline and Michael walked back into the room, took their seats, and waited for a response.

"Thank you for allowing us a moment to discuss our options," the attorney said before shuffling some papers. "I advised my client that it would be in his best interests to agree to the terms in order to protect his reputation. This is not an admission of guilt, by any means. We thought your terms were fair, considering that you're not doing this for monetary gain. My client is prepared to retire from the academy effective immediately as long as he keeps his pension and other benefits. He also agrees not to have any other position of authority that will put him in charge of minors. Lastly, Lieutenant Colonel Biggs requests that you sign a confidentiality agreement so this won't come back to haunt him in the future and so the media doesn't get a hold of any of this information."

Madeline put her hand up and said, "My client will consider a confidentiality agreement on a couple of conditions."

Michael looked over at Madeline in disbelief. He had no idea where she was going with her request, but he had allowed her to control the direction of this meeting and he wouldn't stop her now.

"What conditions?" the attorney asked.

"First, Lieutenant Colonel Biggs has to admit to what he did to my client, and it goes on the record. If he reneges on any part of our agreement, it's a whole new ball game, and Major Monroe will file an official complaint with the local police department and sue him for punitive damages. Also, don't forget that your client must obtain and be treated by a licensed therapist outside of this establishment, with progress reports submitted to my office on a monthly schedule."

"There's a doctor-patient confidentially problem with that request," the colonel's attorney stated.

"Not in this case," she answered quickly. "You can thank your client for that."

The attorney stared at Madeline in amazement, and so did Michael.

"Third and last, we all know the lieutenant colonel is going to retire a very wealthy man with a huge pension and other fringe benefits, not to mention the money he can earn on the lecture circuit. Therefore, he will offer a full scholarship to this academy to one underprivileged youth each year for the rest of his life as the Major Michael Monroe Scholarship Fund. Major Monroe will review the candidates and will make the final selection of the scholarship winner."

Biggs's attorney looked over at the secretary and asked, "Did you get all of that?"

"Yes, sir," she answered.

Michael was in awe of Madeline and how well she knew her way around the legal arena.

Biggs shook his head and said, "This is some bullshit."

Michael and Madeline both looked at the lieutenant colonel in disbelief. Madeline held her forefinger and thumb close together and said, "I'm this close to walking my client over to the local police station so he can file a complaint. That will take this to a whole other level. If your client makes one more condescending remark, all bets are off."

"Lieutenant Colonel, please," the attorney said, pleading with his client to refrain from his outbursts. He stood and held out his hand to Madeline and said, "You have a deal."

Madeline shook the attorney's hand and said, "Great! We'll be out of here as soon as your client discloses what he did to my client."

Biggs reluctantly began to tell everyone in the room how Michael had suffered through his sexual advances off and on for two years, during which time he had blackmailed Michael, threatening him that if he told anyone about their encounters, he would ruin his life in the military and personally.

Once he finished his allocution, Madeline stood and said, "Your client disgusts me. I want the papers drawn up and faxed to me within twenty-four hours. I have to travel to another case, so I'll call you with the fax number shortly."

Lieutenant Colonel Biggs's attorney shook Madeline's hand and said, "It's been a pleasure."

"I'll have to disagree with you, but I'm glad to put this matter to rest," Madeline replied as she walked out of the conference room ahead of Michael. It was hard for the couple to contain their excitement, but they had to. At least until they got behind closed doors, where they could really express themselves.

On the elevator ride down Michael looked at Madeline and whispered, "I am so turned on by what you did in there, that it's taking all my strength not to rip your clothes of and take you right here in this elevator."

She discreetly rubbed her body against his and said, "Sounds like we need to hurry up and get to the nearest hotel, because I have to admit I'm extremely turned on myself."

The elevator doors opened, and the two of them walked out of the building and to his car. They quickly climbed in the car and pulled off the academy grounds.

Chapter Twenty-one

Super Bowl weekend came quickly for the Stones. They were packed and ready to go, except for Target, who was spending the weekend with Camille and her husband. Target was not only a protector of his family, but he was also protective of Camille. She was, after all, part of their extended family, and they loved her very much.

"Ready to go, babe?" Ramsey asked as he sat his sleeping daughter's car seat on one of the seats in their private jet.

Keilah sat down next to her daughter and buckled her car seat and said, "I can't wait. I don't want to get snowed in."

Ramsey snapped his belt in place and said, "We're good. Elliott will be taking off in a second. We'll be in Los Angeles in no time. Who's picking us up?"

"I don't know, but it'll probably be Luke or Roman," she revealed.

He put his arm around her shoulders and said, "I think it'd be a good idea to tell them about the baby while we're there. You're going to start showing soon. What do you think?"

"What about your parents and Xenia and Keith? I don't want them left out."

He put his hand over her stomach and caressed it. "Maybe we can call them and put them on speaker when we have everyone together in one room."

"Whatever you think is best," she answered as she laid her head on his shoulder. "I'm sleepy."

"Well, you have a couple of hours to sleep. I have some work to do, so I'll be awake in case Neariah wakes up."

The voice of Elliott, their pilot, came over the speaker, alerting the couple to prepare for takeoff. Within minutes they were taxiing down the runway and on their way to California.

Keilah yawned and said, "I can barely hold my eyes open."

He kissed her forehead and said, "Go to sleep, babe. Sweet dreams."

A few hours later, their jet landed just as Neariah and Keilah were waking up from their long nap. Neariah woke up crying. Ramsey gave her a cup of milk and patted her leg to calm her down, while Keilah yawned.

"Did you have a good nap?"

"I did, but I'm still sleepy," she replied as she ran her fingers through her hair and stuck a breath mint into her mouth. "Did I snore?"

He laughed and said, "No comment."

"Did I?" she asked again with a smile on her face.

"Just a little, but it was a sexy snore," he answered.

"I see you have jokes, Stone."

He tickled Neariah's feet, causing her to giggle.

The pilot pulled the jet into the area where small planes and jets boarded passengers.

He announced to the couple that they were free to exit the plane, so Ramsey unbuckled Neariah's car seat and took her out so she could stretch her legs.

Before they could gather their belongings, Luke stepped onto the plane and said, "Welcome to L.A."

Surprised, the couple turned and found Luke standing in the doorway. Keilah hugged her brother's neck in silence. He knew she was crying, because she always did when they had been apart for an extended period of time.

He hugged her tightly, kissed her on the cheek, and whispered, "I missed you too."

Ramsey gave Luke a brotherly hug and said, "Great to see you, Luke."

"Right back at you, bro," he replied.

Keilah picked up her purse and said, "I'm starving. Is Sabrinia home?"

"No, she's catering a big fund-raiser at Cedars-Sinai Hospital. She knew you guys would arrive hungry, so she made sure she had lunch waiting on you," Luke replied as he picked up his niece and gave her a kiss. "Neariah has grown since Thanksgiving."

Ramsey gathered the rest of their belongings and jokingly said, "You should see her eat."

"I bet. You guys ready to go?" Luke asked.

Ramsey nodded. "Yeah, I need to talk to Elliott first. I'll meet you at the car."

Ramsey walked over to Elliott and shook his hand. He thanked him for their safe arrival and briefly discussed their itinerary for the weekend. It wasn't uncommon for their pilot to reap the benefits of the Stones' vacations when they traveled. Elliott would be spending Super Bowl weekend with friends in the Long Beach area. The Stones provided him with an expense account, and he was paid very well for his services. After Ramsey had a brief conversation with Elliott, and once their luggage was securely loaded into Luke's car, they headed out of the terminal.

The weekend seemed to go by a lot faster than the Stones wanted it to, and before they knew it, Super Bowl

Sunday was upon them and the entire family was gathered at Roman's house to partake in all the festivities.
The family seemed to be split between the two football
teams, and everyone wore a jersey, a hat, or some other
accessory to support their team. Sabrinia had gone all
out with the menu. She took the traditional tailgate
favorites and made some of them gourmet style, while
preparing a lot of healthy alternatives. It was, after all,
what she did best, and her family loved her cooking.
Sabrinia had brought Roman's wife, Milan, into her
business. She had been an executive in a downtown
marketing firm but had decided to take a break to spend
more time with her family doing something she enjoyed.

In the kitchen Keilah helped her sisters-in-law with
the food. Sabrinia watched Keilah as she sampled several items.

As she spooned mixed fruit into a bowl, Sabrinia
said, "Luke told me he had a talk with you about quit-
ting work. Have you given it much thought?"

Keilah nodded. "I have. I hate when Luke does that
to me. It's like he's in my head."

Sabrinia laughed and said, "He worries about you.
We all do."

Milan agreed and then said, "It's past time for you
and Ramsey to retire. Neariah needs both her parents,
and neither one of you should do anything to jeopardize that."

Keilah picked up a piece of cheese and popped it in
her mouth. "I know. I kind of freaked out on Ramsey
about it."

"What do you mean, freaked out?" Milan asked.

"You know, I was venting to him about it, and it
came out like I was angry at him," she admitted. "I felt
bad that I jumped on him like that."

"You should've," Sabrinia pointed out as she spooned some hot spinach dip into a bowl. "I hope you apologized to him."

"I did. I made up with him right away."

"Good," Milan replied. "I say we get this food out there to the guys so they can get their grub on."

The three ladies carried the food out to the large table that had been set up in the family room. Everyone was mingling in the room, and the children were running through the house, laughing and playing. Keilah and Ramsey wanted to make their announcement before the kickoff, so when Luke called the family together to bless the food, it was the perfect time for them to share their wonderful news. As Roman blessed the food, he choked up as he gave thanks for having such a large and loving family. Once he finished the prayer, Ramsey made a three-way call to his parents and his sister, Xenia, and her husband. Once everyone was on the phone, he told them to put it on speaker so everyone could hear him. Then he got everyone's attention in the family room before they started digging into the delicious food.

He stood next to his wife and made their announcement. "Hey, guys, I want to talk to you for a second. I have my parents, my sister, and my brother-in-law on speaker so they can hear this as well," he said as he held his cell phone up in the air. "I just want to say how happy we are that we were able to get away from D.C. to come out here to spend time with family. In the future it's our plan to do it more often, because Keilah and I are seriously going to reduce our responsibilities at the office and possibly retire soon, especially since we're expecting another baby, who should be due sometime in late summer or early fall."

There were gasps and screams of joy. Upon hearing the news, several people starting clapping, and the couple was immediately showered with hugs and kisses of congratulations. Ramsey put the phone up to his ear and heard his mother crying. His father, his sister, and his brother-in-law congratulated them and thanked them for allowing them to be a part of the announcement.

Luke hugged his sister and said, "You're really going to have to retire now, sis."

"I know. We're working on it," Keilah admitted.

Once the excitement from the announcement subsided a bit, the family filled their plates with delicious food, poured drinks, and settled into their seats as the kickoff was made.

Later that night, as Keilah got Neariah ready or bed, she got a call on her cell. She immediately recognized the number as Michael's.

"Hello?"

"Keilah, I'm sorry to call you so late. I just wanted to let you know that I was able to settle everything with that lieutenant colonel at my academy. He won't be hurting any more boys there, and there won't be any investigators coming around to harass you. I'm so sorry about all this, and I apologize for everything I did or said to hurt you."

"I appreciate that, Michael and I hope you're able to get rid of all the things that have been troubling you."

Michael looked over to Madeline, who had dozed off on the sofa, and said, "I am. I'm off to a great start."

Keilah picked Neariah up in her arms and said, "That's wonderful, Michael."

"Thank you," he answered. "Well, I'll let you go, and I'm sorry I disturbed your evening."

"Don't worry. I wasn't in bed yet. Have a good evening."

"You too," he replied before hanging up.

Ramsey walked into the bedroom with a cup of milk for his daughter. "Who was that?"

"Michael. He was calling to let me know that everything was taken care of, and we shouldn't have any more issues."

He picked up Neariah's towel and dirty clothes and tossed them in a hamper. As he removed the lotion and powder from the bed, he said, "I hope he's telling the truth."

"I believe him," Keilah replied as she handed Neariah to her father. "Is the game over?"

"Almost," he answered as he cuddled his daughter. "Do you want me to take her back downstairs with me so you can get ready for bed?"

"No, she's almost asleep. I'm just waiting on Lucas to bring up the crib."

He passed Neariah back over to her mother and said, "I'll get it. You know he probably got distracted. After all, his girlfriend is down there."

"Ramsey, wait!" she called as she laid Neariah on the bed. "Are you serious about retiring?"

He walked over to her and said, "When I look at you and Neariah, it's not a hard decision to make, especially with the new baby coming. You're going to have to be patient with me, though, because it's not something I can do overnight."

"I know, babe. Thank you."

He patted her on the backside and said, "Thank me later. I want you in bed buck naked when I come back."

She giggled and said, "Don't take too long, because I'm a little sleepy."

He turned back to her and, with a mischievous look on his face, said, "You can go to sleep if you want to. I know how to wake you up. I'll be back in a second."

Keilah turned back to Neariah, who was staring directly at her with a smile on her face, as if she knew exactly what her parents were talking about.

"I thought you were almost asleep, young lady."

"Momma," she replied in a whisper.

"Yes, I'm Momma," Keilah answered as she crawled up on the bed next to her daughter and lay down. Minutes later Ramsey reentered with the crib, which he set up and got ready for Neariah, who was slowly drifting off to sleep.

"Thanks, babe," Keilah whispered.

He winked at his wife before scooping Neariah up into his arms and gently placing her in the crib. After covering her with a blanket, he turned his attention back to Keilah, who was yawning.

"Tired, huh?"

"Yeah, I guess I have a little jet lag, but it was worth it," she whispered. "I had a great time. I'm glad we came."

"Me too. I see how much you light up when you're around your brothers, and you should. It's all about love."

Keilah kissed him tenderly on the lips and said, "I'm so happy right now, Ramsey."

"And I plan to keep you that way," he responded before sitting down on the side of the bed. "I'm going back down to hang out a little bit. I think they're getting ready to get a poker game going. Do you want to come?"

She sat up next to him and said, "Maybe, but I want to shower first."

"You need me to hang around so I can wash your back?" he asked as he stood.

"Just my back?" she asked in a sultry tone as she wrapped her arms around his waist.

He kissed her neck and said, "Stop teasing me, woman."

She giggled and then released him. "Go play cards. I'll be down in a sec."

Ramsey returned to the family room and sat down to a game of poker, which lasted way into the early morning hours. Keilah and her sisters-in-law chatted and nibbled on appetizers until they decided to call it a night long before the poker game ended.

The next morning the women spent the day shopping, while the men headed to the gym to play a few games of basketball. On the way home the men stopped at the market, since the ladies had the night off and the men were responsible for tonight's dinner. All of them were pretty good cooks and were actually anxious to get in the kitchen to show off their skills. It was a wonderful dinner of steak and shrimp and healthy sides of mixed vegetables, baked potatoes, and salad. It was Ramsey and Keilah's last night in California; therefore, after dinner the family sat down around the pool to discuss their next family get-together. It didn't take long for them to decide upon Ramsey and Keilah's new Florida vacation home during the kids' spring break. They had decided to make sure they got together at least once every two months, but it was not to go any longer than that.

The next afternoon, the Stones were driven back to the airport by Roman and Genesis. There they exchanged hugs and kisses and said their good-byes.

While it was always good to see the family, the worst part was saying good-bye.

"Have a safe flight," Roman said as he hugged his sister one more time.

"Thanks, Roman."

Roman took his niece out of his sister's arms so he could give her a kiss. "Take care of my niece and my future niece or nephew," he said before handing Neariah back over to her mom. "Call if you need anything."

"I will," she answered before turning to Genesis. She hugged his neck and said, "I miss our talks. I'm going to call you once we get settled in."

He kissed her cheek and said, "I can't wait. I love you."

"Love you too."

Ramsey took Neariah out of Keilah's arms and said, "I'd better get Neariah buckled into her seat. We'll call when we land."

Genesis gave Neariah a kiss and Ramsey a hug and said, "Take care of our girls, bro."

"Most definitely," Ramsey replied before climbing onto the plane.

Elliott appeared in the doorway and said, "Mrs. Stone, we're cleared for takeoff."

"Thanks, Elliott," Keilah replied before giving her brothers one more hug and climbing into the plane.

Genesis and Roman waited until the plane had taxied down the runway and then lifted off and disappeared in the California sky before leaving the terminal.

Chapter Twenty-two

It had been a few days since Keilah and Ramsey returned to D.C. Keilah decided to take the day off so she could take her daughter to the National Zoo. It was a cool but beautiful day in the nation's capital and a perfect day for a walk in the zoo.

Ramsey slid into his jacket and said, "Have fun with the rug rat at the zoo."

"We will," she answered as she fed Neariah her breakfast.

He picked up his keys, gave his wife a hot kiss on the lips, and then said, "Be careful, and call me as soon as you get there. Okay?"

She nodded in agreement and said, "Okay."

Target barked to get Ramsey's attention. He walked over to the door and opened it so the dog could go out. He stared at Keilah and was unexpectedly overcome with a feeling of concern.

Keilah looked at Ramsey and asked, "What's that look for?"

"I just worry about you guys when I'm away from you. That's all."

"I worry about you too, babe," she replied as she held his hand. "We'll be fine. Have you forgotten what we do for a living?"

He embraced her and said, "Damn all that. I can't help that I'm concerned about you and Neariah."

"I understand, but we still have to try to live as normal a life as possible. Remember?"

Ramsey held Keilah in silence as Neariah drank her apple juice. He let her comment sink in as he held her in his arms until Target barked at the back door, interrupting them. She was right about living a normal life, but it would never stop him from worrying about her and Neariah. After letting his German shepherd back into the house, he kissed the top of Neariah's head and said, "I love you, rug rat. Take care of your mother."

"Daddy!" she replied loudly with a big smile on her face.

He chuckled and gave Keilah one more kiss on the lips. "Drive safely."

"You too," she answered as she put their dirty dishes in the sink. Then she picked up the telephone and made a call.

"Tori, what are you doing today?" Keilah asked.

"Not much, just looking over house listings. Kyle decided to sell his house and get a larger place for us."

"That's great, Tori."

"Thanks, sis. I'm so glad you called. What's up?"

Keilah wiped Neariah's mouth and said, "I took the day off so I could take Neariah to the zoo. We would love it if you met us there. It would give us a chance to spend some time together too, and lunch is on me."

"I'd love to," Tori answered. "I'm getting cross-eyes looking at this computer screen."

Keilah looked at her watch and said, "We'll be leaving in about fifteen minutes. Is that enough time for you?"

"Yes, it's plenty. All I have to do is change into some jeans and put on some comfortable shoes and I'll be on my way."

"Sounds good," Keilah answered. "We'll see you shortly."

The two friends hung up and prepared to meet up at the zoo.

When Keilah pulled out of her subdivision, a gold SUV fell in behind her approximately two car lengths back. Neariah sang and played with her stuffed bear as her mother sped down the expressway to their destination. It didn't take long for them to get to the zoo. As Keilah drove through the parking lot to search for a parking space, she called Tori to see if she had arrived. Tori told her that she was a couple minutes away, so Keilah decided to go ahead and get the stroller out of the car and get Neariah securely buckled in while they waited. Tori spotted Keilah's vehicle two rows away from her as she drove through the parking lot. She noticed several families with children walking through the parking lot toward the gate, but one person in particular seemed out of place.

Tori picked up her cell and dialed Keilah's number, but before the call could go through, it was too late. Tori watched as the man aimed a gun at Keilah and shot her, causing her to fall to the ground. Tori screamed and sped through the parking lot to get to her friend. When she rounded the corner, she noticed the man, who had a hood over his head, running through the parking lot with Neariah in his arms. She was crying and was in immediate danger. Tori didn't know what to do. Her best friend was on the ground, and her godchild was being kidnapped. Then she thought about what Keilah would want her to do and jumped out of the car and dialed the police as she chased after the man.

Tori was fast on her feet and had been a pretty good athlete in high school. She screamed for help as she chased after the man. She reached the gold SUV just as the driver was backing out of the parking space. Tori grabbed the door handle and frantically pulled on it, trying to open the door, but it was locked. She screamed at the man in the driver's seat as she banged on the passenger-side window with her cell phone, trying to break the window, but it was useless. As he dragged her across the parking lot, she could see Neariah on the floorboard of the vehicle, crying, and was devastated that she couldn't get the door open.

She concentrated on the features of the man behind the wheel so that later she could provide as detailed a description as possible to the police, but he had a knit mask covering his face. Tori hung on to the door, screaming for help, until the SUV rounded a corner, slamming her body into a parked car and knocking her unconscious. Within minutes, the zoo was crawling with police and paramedics. Zoo employees had run to Tori's and Keilah's aid, and by the time paramedics reached Tori, she had regained consciousness.

"Keilah! Oh my God! Where's Neariah!" Tori cried as she tried to get up off the ground. The paramedics restrained her, and the police questioned her with urgency.

"Miss Giles, we need your help," one of the officers told her. "Witnesses said that a child was taken from the scene. Can you validate that?"

She nodded to the officer as tears streamed down her face. One of the paramedics examined Tori, and she screamed out in pain when he touched her leg.

"Ma'am, I think your leg is broken. You're going to have to remain immobile," the paramedic explained.

"Miss Giles, can you give us a description of the kidnapper and the vehicle?" the police officer asked.

Tori sobbed and asked, "Is Keilah alive? I saw that man shoot her. Is she okay?"

"The young woman is alive. The perpetrator didn't shoot her. He hit her with a stun gun. What is her full name?"

"Keilah Stone. You have to call her husband, Ramsey. They own the Stone-Chance Protection Agency downtown. He's never going to forgive me for letting that man get away with his daughter."

The police officer instructed his partner to contact Ramsey, and then he turned his attention back to Tori as the paramedics put her on the stretcher. "What about you, Miss Giles? Is there someone we can contact on your behalf?"

"It's Victoria Bradford. I just got married. I haven't had a chance to change my license. You can call my husband, Kyle Bradford. He works at the Pentagon. His number is in my cell phone, but I think I dropped it."

The officer noticed Tori's cell phone on the ground in a thousand pieces. "What's your husband's number? Your cell phone is broken."

Tori recited the number to the officer, who jotted it down.

"Thank you. We'll have your husband meet you at the hospital. Mrs. Bradford, did you get a look at the license plate? Anything that you can tell us will help us locate the vehicle."

Still somewhat disoriented, through her tears she said, "I tried. I think it was D-H-three or D-eight-three. I'm not sure. Where's Keilah? I need to see her."

The officer assured Tori that Keilah was being cared for and that she could see her once they got to the hospital. At the moment it was important for the officers to get an AMBER Alert out for Neariah and the SUV.

***

Minutes later, two ambulances pulled into the emergency room entrance of the hospital, and the two women were taken to examination rooms for treatment. Keilah was clearly distraught and was crying for her missing child. Kyle arrived at the hospital first. While he spoke with officers, Ramsey ran into the emergency room in a panic.

"Where are Keilah and Neariah?" Ramsey frantically asked Kyle. "No one will tell me anything."

One of the police officers turned to Ramsey and said, "Mr. Stone, I'm sorry to have to tell you this, but your wife was attacked in the zoo parking lot. Besides some scrapes and a nasty bump on the head, she's okay, but your daughter has been kidnapped."

"Kidnapped!" Ramsey yelled. "Where's my daughter!"

Kyle tried to steady Ramsey, but Ramsey's legs gave out and he sank to the floor in tears. Neil had arrived at the hospital a moment before, and his eyes teared up as well, and the vein in his neck twitched. He'd never seen his best friend so broken, but he clearly understood why and would do everything in his power to help bring Neariah home.

"What do you have?" Neil asked the officer while Kyle consoled Ramsey.

The officer filled Neil in on the investigation. Once he had all the information, Neil rejoined Kyle and Ramsey. He knelt down at Ramsey's side and said, "We're going to find Neariah. I got your back, but you're going to have to pull yourself together. I know it's hard, but Keilah needs you right now."

Ramsey wiped away his tears and pulled himself off the floor. Once he had regained his composure, he hugged his two best friends and said, "Thanks, guys. I'm glad you're here."

A police detective approached Ramsey and said, "Mr. Stone, there's a possibility that your daughter was taken for ransom. We find that in a lot of cases involving wealthy families. Has there been any suspicious activity or incidents you can think of?"

"Nothing that I can think of," Ramsey replied.

The detective jotted the information down in his notebook. "What about enemies? Is there anyone that you or your wife may have had a recent disagreement with? A client, former employees, friends, etcetera . . ."

With his hands on his head in despair, Ramsey answered, "There's plenty, but I can't think right now. I need to see my wife."

The detective closed his notebook and said, "Okay, Mr. Stone, but it'll help if you allow us to wire your home phone, just in case someone calls with ransom demands—"

"I'll take care of it, Ramsey," Kyle said, interrupting the detective as he patted his friend's shoulder. "Go see Keilah. I have to look in on Victoria. She got hurt too, trying to save Neariah. She's messed up pretty bad, but she's going to be okay."

"Damn, Kyle. I'm so sorry. How is she?"

"She has a broken leg, a concussion, and a cracked rib, but she'll be fine. They're getting ready to take her up to surgery now. You need to go check on Keilah. I know she's scared and distraught. I'm going to look in on Victoria before they take her upstairs to surgery."

Ramsey nodded and then took a deep breath and entered the examination room, where he found his wife in a state of hysteria, which escalated when she saw his face.

"Sir, you can't be in here right now," the nurse said as she attended to Keilah.

He approached the bed and firmly said, "She's my wife. I'm not leaving. She's also pregnant. Is the baby okay?"

The nurse hooked the fetal monitor up to Keilah's abdomen and said, "So far so good, but it would help if you could get Mrs. Stone to calm down, or I'm going to have to sedate her."

"I'll try," he answered. "Could you please give us a moment?"

The nurse checked Keilah's IV and said, "I'll be back shortly."

Ramsey leaned over and kissed his wife and then stroked her cheek. With his lips against her ear, he whispered, "Sweetheart, I need you to calm down, because I'm going to have to leave and go get our daughter back. I won't be able to do that with a good conscience if you don't calm down."

"How do you expect me to calm down when some maniac has our daughter?" Keilah sobbed. "It was my job to protect her, but I didn't see him coming. He hit me from behind."

Ramsey stroked her cheek and said, "It's okay, sweetheart. Don't worry. I'm going to get her back."

"No! It's not okay! How the hell can I protect strangers and not be able to protect our own child?" she screamed.

He put his finger over her lips and said, "It's not your fault. Okay?"

She nodded and through her tears said, "Please, I won't be able to live if anything happens to her."

"Nothing's going to happen to her," he assured her as he caressed her cheek. "I need you to take care of our other baby while I go get Neariah. Can you stay strong for me?"

"We can't lose her, Ramsey," she cried.

"And we won't," he replied.

"The police told me Tori got hurt trying to save her. Is she okay?" Keilah asked.

"She has a broken leg and a minor fracture, but she's going to be okay. Kyle is going to stay here and look after you two while Neil and I go find Neariah. If you need me, just call, but I'm going to need you to calm down."

Keilah nodded. Her body was still somewhat numb from the electrical jolt of the stun gun, and she had a terrible headache.

In the hallway, Ramsey walked over to Kyle and Neil and said, "I have to go."

"Where are you going?" Neil asked.

Ramsey frowned and replied, "Where do you think? I'm going to find the bastard who took my daughter, and God help him when I do, because he's a dead man."

Neil grabbed his friend's arm and said, "Bro, I can't let you go out there vigilante style. The police are doing everything they can to find Neariah."

"It's not enough. Every second that man has my daughter pisses me off even more. I need you to find a name that goes with that gold SUV. Call me as soon as possible with any updates."

Before Neil could respond, Ramsey disappeared out the emergency room doors.

Kyle looked over at Neil and said, "He's going to kill somebody tonight. I can't say I blame him, either, because I would love to get my hands on him too. I just pray whoever took Neariah is not a pervert or murderer."

Neil shook his head and said, "I'd better get back out on the streets. I might get lucky and find the SUV. Call me when Tori gets out of surgery, and keep me posted on Keilah too."

The two friends hugged before going their separate ways.

Outside in the parking lot, Ramsey's mind was moving a thousand miles an hour. He climbed inside his vehicle and sat there, contemplating calling his parents and Keilah's family. He wanted the opportunity to get his daughter back and spare them any unnecessary heartache, but in his heart he knew they had a right to know. Unfortunately, if he informed them about what was going on, they would want to be involved, making it harder for him to find and eliminate the kidnapper. No, this needed to be handled delicately, and there was only one person close to him that he could trust to be discreet, and lethal, and to strike quickly if needed without leaving a trace of evidence.

Ramsey picked up his cell phone and dialed his brother-in-law's number. When he answered, Ramsey didn't waste any time asking for help.

"Keytone, it's Ramsey. I need your help."

"Sure, man, whatever you need."

"No, you don't understand," Ramsey replied. "I need you on the company jet en route to D.C. in thirty minutes or less."

"Whoa! Slow down, Ramsey. What's wrong? You don't sound too good."

He sighed and said, "It's bad, bro. Somebody attacked Keilah with a stun gun at the zoo and kidnapped Neariah."

Keytone was silent on the other end of the phone for several seconds, and then in a chilling voice, he answered, "Don't you worry about a goddamn thing. I'll call you when I land. Just have me a piece locked and loaded so we can turn D.C. upside down until we find my niece and bury the bastard that dared to put his hands on either one of them."

Ramsey hung up the telephone, sped out of the parking lot, and drove back to his home, where he checked his firearms and ammunition. As he sat in the family room, he noticed Neariah's favorite doll sitting on the sofa. He also noticed that Target was sitting by the door, staring at it, waiting for Keilah and Neariah to walk in.

"Come here, boy," he called out to his shepherd, who trotted over to him so he could pet him and then hurried back over to the door. Tears stung Ramsey's eyes, but he fought them back and concentrated on the task at hand.

He'd called the hospital several times to check on Keilah and Tori. Now he called Kyle, who let him talk to Keilah, who was still hysterical, causing her blood pressure to rise and therefore putting their unborn child at risk, so she was finally sedated to calm her down.

Kyle stepped out of Keilah's room into the hallway and said, "The detectives told Neil they got footage of the attack from security cameras in the parking lot. Neil said it was a little grainy, but they're going to run it on the news and hope someone comes forward with information. I told him to e-mail it to you. You should have it by now."

"Thanks, Kyle," Ramsey answered, his voice barely above a whisper.

"Ramsey, have you thought about offering a reward? You know how people are about money. People will turn in their mother for a nice chunk of change."

"What do you think is reasonable, without going overboard and without appearing cheap?"

Kyle thought for second, because he knew his best friend was dying a slow death every second Neariah wasn't home. "I say start with a hundred thousand dollars for information and capture. I know you'll pay whatever it takes to get Neariah home, but we don't want a lot of idiots coming out of the woodwork, either. All they will do is waste valuable time and personnel," he pointed out.

"Can you handle it for me and get it out to the media?" Ramsey asked as he rubbed his weary eyes.

"You bet. I'll have it on the wire in ten minutes."

"Thank you, Kyle. Give the girls my love, and let Keilah know I'm working hard to find Neariah."

"She already knows that, bro."

"I'll check back in with you a little later. Call me if anything changes."

Ramsey walked over to his laptop and powered it up. He saw the e-mail from Neil, but before watching the footage of the attack, he took a deep breath. He hit the PLAY button, and as he watched, he saw the gold SUV enter the parking lot and park down from Keilah. He also saw what looked like Tori's vehicle pull in. What happened next seemed like it was on fast-forward. He cringed when he saw Keilah fall to the ground and the man grab Neariah. Watching Tori hang on to the speeding vehicle was just as hard, especially when her small body was thrown into the parked car as the SUV exited the parking lot. The video was a little grainy, but he watched it over and over again, looking for anything that he might've missed the previous time. Then he picked up the phone and called his parents for added strength. He had thought he could handle it on his own, but he was wrong.

"Daddy?"

"Hello, son. How are you?" Marion asked.

"Not good, Daddy. Something's happened, and I want you and Mom to know about it before you see it on the news."

Concerned, Marion put his cigar down and sat up in his recliner.

"What is it, Ramsey?"

"Keilah was attacked this morning at the zoo, and Neariah was kidnapped. Keilah is at the hospital, but the doctors said she'll be okay. I can't deal with this alone, Dad. If anything happens to my daughter, I don't know what I'm going to do."

"Say no more," Marion replied as he stood. "Your mother and I will be there as soon as we can. Give me name of the hospital Keilah's in so we can be there for you."

Ramsey gave his father the name of the hospital and all the information about the video of the assault and what the police had done so far. Before hanging up, Ramsey told him that no one in Keilah's family knew except one brother, who was presently en route to D.C.

"Son, Keilah's family deserves to know what's going on."

"I don't want to worry them, and I'm trying to get Neariah back before they have to know."

Marion took a breath and said, "How would you feel if you were left out of the loop? I strongly urge you to call them. They will want to be here to help as well."

Ramsey looked at his watch and realized that Keytone would be landing shortly and said, "I'll think about it, Dad. Call me when you get to the hospital."

Marion assured him he would, and Ramsey grabbed his keys and headed out the door and to the airport.

Chapter Twenty-three

Across town, Michael and Madeline settled on her sofa to watch a little TV, but they were interrupted when a breaking news story about an AMBER Alert issued for a small child was aired. Michael handed Madeline a glass of wine and watched as a picture of the missing child appeared on the screen and then the video of the assault and kidnapping was played. Michael studied the entire video clip, and then he whispered, "Son of bitch."

"What is it, babe?" Madeline asked when she saw Michael's strong reaction to the news story.

He sat his wineglass down and said "I have to go."

She jumped up and asked, "Where are you going?"

He pulled her into his arms and gave her a loving kiss on the lips. "I have to take care of some business I forgot about," he said with a smile.

Concerned, Madeline said, "I know something's wrong. Does it involve Lieutenant Colonel Biggs?"

Michael let out a breath, walked over to the desk, and pulled out a pen, a sheet of paper, and an envelope. He wrote a short note on the paper, sealed it in the envelope, and then wrote a name and a number on the envelope. Before handing the envelope to Madeline, he said, "No, sweetheart, but if I'm not back home by dawn, contact this man at this number and give him this note."

"You're scaring me, Michael," she answered as she stroked his cheek.

He smiled and said, "Don't worry. I'll be back as soon as possible. Okay?"

"I don't know where you're going, but if you get yourself hurt, I'm going to be very upset with you."

"I know. Trust me, babe. I love you," he announced as he closed the front door behind him.

Madeline stood there in shock. He had said something she had been feeling about him since they had met. In her heart she knew Michael was her match, and she loved him as well. Praying for his safe return was all that mattered to her right now. In the meantime she would calm her nerves with the wine and hope he would be back soon.

Michael sped across town, then pulled into a quiet neighborhood he was very familiar with. He calmed himself and said a prayer before walking up to the door and ringing the doorbell. The door slowly cracked open, and Michael could see that Kevin looked disheveled.

"What are you doing here?" Kevin asked.

"Aren't you going to let me in?" Michael asked.

"Why? So you can attack me again?"

Michael hesitated and then said, "I'm not going to attack you. I'm here to apologize."

Still talking through the crack in the door, Kevin pointed out the obvious. "You could've called if you wanted to apologize. You didn't have to drive all the way over here."

"That's true, but I felt like I needed to do it face-to-face. Come on, Kevin, this is ridiculous. Are you going to let me in or not?" Michael asked.

"It's really not a good time. I'm busy."

"If you have company, it's cool. I just need a few minutes, and I'll be out of your way. I promise."

"Wait here for a second," Kevin replied as he closed the door.

Michael didn't know what Kevin was doing behind closed doors, but he would find out once he got inside the house. He'd see if his gut feeling was true. If he was wrong, no harm done. He would just make up an excuse for his unexpected visit. But if he was right, he was the best person to get close to Kevin and make things right. Getting the police involved without confirmation could bring the situation to a tragic end.

At the airport, Ramsey met Keytone as he exited the plane. He gave Ramsey a hug and asked, "How's Keilah? Is there any word on Neariah?"

"Not yet," Ramsey answered as they quickly climbed into his vehicle. Ramsey tightly gripped the steering wheel. "I saw surveillance footage from the zoo, and it looked like Keilah was targeted. He walked right up and hit her with that stun gun."

With calmness in his voice, Keytone asked, "Do you have my piece?"

"Yeah, it's in the console."

Keytone checked the weapon and asked, "Do you think it's about money?"

"I don't know what to think. I had Kyle offer a hundred-thousand-dollar reward on our behalf, so hopefully somebody will come forward with information on where to find her. My mind is going in a million different directions right now."

Keytone looked at Ramsey and saw the stress and anguish on his face. Keytone was living through his own hell, knowing his sister had been hurt and niece had been kidnapped, but all he could think about right now was the job at hand. Finding Neariah and the man who had kidnapped her was his number one priority, so he had to be his brother-in-law's strength in his time of weakness.

"Where are we going to first?" Keytone asked as he checked the clip in the nine-millimeter handgun.

"I figured we should go back out to the zoo to see if we can find any evidence the police may have overlooked. Then I want to put a plea out with the media for anyone to come forward if they know someone who has a child all of a sudden, one that they didn't have before. The police are trying to see if they can clean up the video more to make out the license plate on the perpetrator's vehicle. The police detective on the case is monitoring the Crime Stoppers tip line and our home telephone number. He said he would call if they get any calls."

"Cool. How's Keilah?"

Ramsey shook his head and said, "She's messed up. They had to sedate her."

"She's been through a lot. You both have. Once we get Neariah back, you guys really need to call it quits. Do you feel me?" Keytone asked.

Ramsey nodded and said, "Right now I can't think past getting my daughter back." At that moment Ramsey's cell phone rang. He answered quickly and prayed for good news.

"Ramsey, it's Kyle. We might have a break."

"What is it?" Ramsey asked as pulled into a gas station and put his phone on speaker so Keytone could hear the conversation.

"A call just came in at your office from a woman who said she needed to talk to you and that it was urgent."

"Who was it?" Ramsey asked.

"She wouldn't give her name or any information. She said she would only talk to you."

"Does it have anything to do with Neariah?"

"I don't know," Kyle replied. "She seemed pretty upset."

"Did she leave a number?" Ramsey asked with urgency in his voice.

"Yes, I have it."

Ramsey looked over at Keytone and said, "Get a pen and notepad out of the glove compartment."

"Who are you talking to?" Kyle asked.

"Just one of my brothers-in-law," he answered. "Okay, what's the number?"

Kyle recited the number to Ramsey and instructed him to call the woman as soon as they finished their conversation. In the meantime he would research the number to put an address and name to it.

Before hanging up, Ramsey informed Kyle that his parents were on the way to the hospital to be with Keilah, so he could concentrate solely on Tori. After disconnecting the call, he dialed the number of the unknown female caller and anxiously waited for her to answer. His wait wasn't long, because she picked up on the first ring.

"Ramsey Stone?" she asked.

"Yes. How can I help you?"

"I'm not sure, but my boyfriend gave me an envelope to give you if he wasn't home by dawn, but I'm afraid to wait that long. I think he might be in some kind of trouble, and I'm worried he might get himself killed," she explained.

"Who's your boyfriend?" Ramsey asked.

"Michael Monroe. He left my house about an hour ago, saying he had to take care of some business, after seeing a news report about a kidnapping. What's going on, Mr. Stone?"

"Get her name," Keytone whispered.

"What is your name?" Ramsey asked her.

"My name is Madeline Savoi."

Keytone jotted down her name next to her telephone number while Ramsey spoke to her.

"Madeline, Michael and I know each other. This is very important. I need you to open the envelope and tell me what it says."

With her hands trembling and tears spilling out of her eyes, Madeline opened the envelope and began to read the letter to Ramsey.

> *Ramsey,*
> *I think I know who has your daughter. If my suspicions are correct, I feel like it's my responsibility to get her back safely to you and Keilah. If for some reason I'm unsuccessful, have the police go to the following address, 742 Oak Street.*
>
> *Michael*

"That's it," Madeline said as she held the letter in her hand.

"Madeline, do you know who lives on Oak Street?" Ramsey asked.

"No, I don't. Please, Mr. Stone. What has Michael gotten himself mixed up in?"

Ramsey put his vehicle in drive as Keytone punched the address into the GPS system.

"I'm not sure, but I appreciate you calling with this information. I'll call you back as soon as I find out."

"Please make sure Michael doesn't get hurt," she pleaded with Ramsey before hanging up the phone.

"This might be the break we've been waiting on, bro," Keytone stated as Ramsey sped down the highway.

***

Kevin stood back and allowed Michael to walk inside. When he entered the living room, he noticed several suitcases near the door and boxes with items packed inside.

"Are you going somewhere?" Michael asked.

"Yeah, I need a change of scenery."

Michael sat down and asked, "Where are you going?"

Kevin nervously said, "I'm going back home for a while. I need some time to get my head together so I can decide what I want to do with my life."

Michael looked around and noticed that Kevin had even taken the pictures off the wall and that all the doors to the bedrooms were closed. "That might be a good idea. You haven't seen your parents in a while. The trip will be good for you."

Kevin walked over to the front door and put his hand on the doorknob and said, "I really have a lot of packing to do, so if you're here to apologize, thanks, but I have things to do."

"Why are you acting so weird? Are you going to get me a beer or something?"

"I would, but I'm all out and I still have a lot of packing to do."

Michael stood and said, "Okay, I'll get out of your way, but I am sorry things went down like they did. I really was confused about who I was and didn't mean to drag you into my turmoil."

Kevin opened the door and said, "Me too."

Just as Michael took a step toward the door, his suspicion swere realized, as he heard the faint cry of a baby.

"Is that a baby?" Michael asked as he turned and walked toward the bedroom.

Kevin nervously said, "Yes, I'm babysitting for a friend of mine."

"What friend?" Michael asked as he quietly entered the bedroom. Kevin had a small portable crib, diapers, and all the works for the baby set up in the spare bedroom.

"You don't know her. She's a neighbor," he answered.

Michael walked over to the crib and looked into the child's innocent eyes, playing it cool. "She's beautiful, Kevin."

"I know," he answered as he leaned against the door frame.

"Do you mind if I hold her?" Michael asked. He wanted to make sure she was unharmed and in good health.

"Yeah, but just for a second," he replied nervously. "Her mom will be picking her up shortly, and she might not want other people handling her child."

Michael held the baby close and was sure this was Keilah's daughter. Now all he had to do was get her back to her parents safely and as soon as possible. Kevin had obviously gone off the deep end to resort to kidnapping. Who knew what else he was capable of? If he let him get away with her, they Stones might not ever see their child again. He felt responsible, since adopting a child was something they had talked about when they were together.

"She's beautiful. What's her name?" Michael asked.

Stuttering, Kevin said, "A—A—Angel."

"Angel. What a pretty name for such a pretty girl."

The baby started crying as Michael held her. "I think she's hungry. Can I feed her, please?"

Kevin was reluctant, as he wanted Michael out of the house as quickly as possible. "I'll let you feed her, but after that you have to leave. Give me a second to warm her bottle."

Michael placed Neariah back into the crib and then quietly followed Kevin into the kitchen, where he found him standing at the sink with his back to the door.

"Why are you here, Michael? I thought you hated me," Kevin asked suspiciously.

"I never hated you. I just hate what you did," he said as he walked up behind Kevin.

Kevin sat the bottle of milk on the countertop and quickly turned around. He lunged at Michael with a large butcher knife.

"Damn it, Kevin!" Michael yelled as he jumped away from the sharp blade.

Kevin swung the knife at Michael again and yelled, "You're not taking that little girl from me."

"She doesn't belong to you!" Michael shouted as he tried to grab Kevin's wrist. "Put the knife down."

"You son of a bitch!" Kevin yelled as he swung the knife again, connecting with Michael's hand. Blood started seeping from the wound, but Michael was able to get a good grip on Kevin's wrist. Kevin struggled to free himself as Michael pinned him against the cabinet. He had all but cut off Kevin's circulation, but the blood running down his hand was causing him to lose his firm grip.

Kevin eventually dropped the knife and asked, "Why are you doing this to me?"

Michael put Kevin's arm behind his back and wrapped his other arm around his neck. "Oh, let me see. You sent a journalist to Keilah's office, who threatened to expose her relationship with me. You spray painted obscenities in my driveway, and you assaulted Keilah and kidnapped Keilah's daughter."

Kevin continued to struggle against the tight hold Michael had on his throat, but it was to no avail. He clawed at Michael's arm with his hand and tried to free himself; however, his air supply was quickly being cut off.

"I'm so sorry, Kevin. You're out of control and a danger to society. I can't let you hurt anyone else. Lord, please forgive me."

There was a loud cracking noise, and then Kevin went limp in Michael's arms. He let Kevin's body slide down to the floor and then grabbed a towel to wrap around his bloody hand. He quickly headed back into the bedroom, where he handed the bottle of milk to Neariah, who was still lying in the crib.

"Let's get you home," he whispered as he cuddled her in his arms and quietly exited the home. He knew he was leaving his DNA in the house, but it was more important to return Neariah to her family.

Outside, Michael looked around to see if anyone saw him leaving Kevin's town house. He put Neariah on the front seat of his vehicle and did his best to buckle her in safely since he didn't have a car seat handy. She seemed calm as he struggled to secure her in the seat while she drank her milk. He continued to speak to her in a calm, soothing tone, and when she smiled up at him, it warmed his heart and made him feel like the crime he had committed was necessary to save her life. Now all he had to do was get the baby back in the arms of her loving parents.

As he was backing out of the parking lot, Ramsey's vehicle nearly rammed his as it came to a screeching halt behind him. Keytone jumped out of the vehicle with his weapon drawn and ran over to the driver's side of Michael's car and opened the door.

"Put the goddamn car in park and get out of the car!"

With his heart beating a thousand beats per minute, Ramsey hurried over to Michael's vehicle and nervously peeked inside. He thought he would pass out when he saw the little girl lying back on the seat, quiet and content as she continued to drink her milk. As Keytone held Michael against the vehicle at gunpoint, Ramsey picked the child up, and to his shock, it wasn't Neariah.

"Is she okay?" Keytone asked.

With his voice quivering and tears in his eyes, Ramsey whispered, "She's fine, but it's not Neariah."

"What?" Keytone yelled as he walked around the vehicle to see for himself. When he looked at the child, he yelled all sorts of obscenities.

"Ramsey, I didn't have anything to do with it," Michael pleaded. "I was on my way to bring your daughter back to you."

"I believe you," Ramsey answered, then instructed Keytone to put the gun away. "But this is not my daughter."

"It's not?" Michael asked, with his voice quivering. "She looks like the picture I saw on the news."

"They have similar features, but no, this is not Neariah," Ramsey said as he cuddled the child to comfort her.

Michael slid down on the ground and mumbled, "What have I done?"

Keytone pulled the gun back out of his waistband and asked, "Whose child is this?"

With his head in his hands, Michael answered, "I don't know. I took her from the man who resides here because I thought it was Keilah's daughter."

"I need to talk to him," Keytone said as he headed toward Kevin's door, but Michael called out to him to stop him.

"He won't be answering the door. I made sure of that."

Concerned, Ramsey stared at Michael and asked, "What did you do?"

Michael ran his hand over his head and said, "He's dead on the kitchen floor."

"Shit!" Ramsey yelled when he noticed the blood on Michael's hand. "Are you shot? You're bleeding!"

"No, I'm not shot, but he did cut me pretty deep on my hand when he tried to stab me."

Keytone looked in the back of Ramsey's truck and pulled out a first-aid kit. He walked over to Michael and tended to his hand.

"What made you think he was involved?" Ramsey asked.

"I saw the video surveillance on TV and noticed the way the man walked and his build. It looked like him. I killed a man for no reason."

"Him who?" Ramsey asked.

"Kevin. The guy I used to be friends with. You remember him from the night Keilah shot me?"

"That dude?" Ramsey asked.

Michael nodded and then said, "You two need to get out of here. I'll take the heat for this. I'm sure someone's called the police by now after hearing all this commotion."

Ramsey pulled out his cell phone and said, "No way. This isn't my daughter, but you risked your life to save her, anyway."

"Who are you calling?" Keytone asked as he looked around to see it they had drawn the attention of any of the neighbors.

"I'm calling Kyle. He can get some people out here quick to help us with this situation."

"I'm sorry, Ramsey," Michael stated. "I should've handled this with more discretion."

Ramsey looked Michael in the eyes and said, "You have nothing to be sorry for. I'm the one who should be apologizing to you. You didn't have to get involved, but you did, and I appreciate it."

"Maybe we should get back in the car before people get suspicious," Keytone suggested.

All three agreed and climbed into Ramsey's vehicle and waited for instructions from Kyle. Within minutes two unmarked government cars pulled up to the complex, and four individuals exited the vehicles.

Ramsey gave the child to one of the men, who buckled her into a car seat in one of the unmarked vehicles. Then he and Michael went inside the town house with the agents to inspect the scene. When they finished, the agents put Michael in the backseat of one of their vehicles, a black sedan, and assured Ramsey that he would be taken care of. Another agent got inside Michael's vehicle and drove it away from the premises.

"Where are you taking him?" Ramsey asked, fearing that Michael might be arrested.

"Don't worry, Mr. Stone. We have to talk to Major Monroe, but he should be home before dawn, and we'll find the child's parents," said one of the agents.

Ramsey leaned down to talk to Michael. He handed him a business card and said, "Call me as soon as you get home. I appreciate everything you've tried to do for me and Keilah."

Michael took the card out of his hand and said, "It was my pleasure."

Ramsey smiled and said, "Hey, guys, make sure you get him to a doctor and get his hand stitched up, and let him call his woman on the way. I'm sure she's worried sick about him."

"We'll take care of it. Don't worry," one of the agents stressed to Ramsey. "Major Monroe's in the best hands

possible, and please know that the authorities are doing everything they can to find your daughter."

Ramsey closed the door of the black sedan and climbed
into his own car. As he and Keytone were pulling out of
the parking lot, they met a van with government license
plates pulling into the complex. They assumed it had
been called in to discreetly remove Kevin, who was lying
dead on the kitchen floor.

Keytone looked at Ramsey. "What next, bro?"

"I won't stop until I find my daughter."

Chapter Twenty-four

In an unmarked stone building downtown, Michael sat in a room while a doctor stitched the cut on his hand. One of the agents who had brought him there walked in with a notepad and a cup of coffee.

"Major, how are you feeling?" he asked.

"I'm fine. Just a little tired," Michael replied. "I'd like to get home so I can get out of these bloody clothes."

"Don't worry. We'll have you out of here in no time. Doc, are you almost done?" the agent asked.

"He's stitched up. I just need to give him tetanus shot and put a dressing on him, and he's all yours," the doctor answered.

Being in the military most of his life, Michael knew not to ask a lot of questions, but he was extremely curious about where he was and who he was with.

"Who are you, and what's going to happen to me?" Michael finally asked the man in the suit.

The agent crossed his leg over his ankle and tapped the ink pen on the table and, with a smile on his face, answered, "Oh, you don't have to worry about anything, Major. I'm a friend of a friend who didn't want to see a good man's life ruined for trying to saving a child. Your debt to this country is more than paid after your service to this country, not to mention what you suffered at the hands of those insurgents when you were imprisoned. What you did tonight for that little girl was necessary."

"All done!" the doctor announced as he removed his rubber gloves. "You're as good as new, Major."

Michael hopped down from the examination table. As he examined the dressing on his hand, he said, "Thank you."

"Have a seat, Major. I brought you some coffee. I'm sure you could use the caffeine at this late hour," said the agent.

Michael sat down across from the agent and took a sip of the hot beverage.

"Okay, Major. Let me run a few things by you. The perpetrator at the town house was an acquaintance of yours, correct?"

"Yes, sir."

The agent flipped the page over on his notepad and stated, "And you went to his town house, why?"

Michael took a breath and said, "I saw the surveillance tape of the kidnapping at the zoo this morning, and I thought I recognized the child on TV from a picture I had seen on Mrs. Stone's desk in her office."

"Don't you think it would've been safer to call the police?"

"You don't understand, sir. I felt responsible. Therefore, it was my job to make sure I got that little girl back to her family."

The agent studied Michael's body language and then asked, "Why did you feel responsible?"

With his head in his hands, Michael revealed his sordid past to the government agent. He told him about the sexual abuse by Lieutenant Colonial Biggs, which led to his confusing relationship with Kevin and their desire at one time to have a child and be a family. That was when he confessed to his plan to marry Keilah, have a child, and fight her for custody of the baby after divorcing. He explained that he couldn't go through with it. He actually loved Keilah and was very remorseful for hurting her. He felt obligated to make right all the wrongs he had committed in order to redeem himself and thus have a chance at a respectable and happy life.

"So you see, sir, Kevin always blamed Keilah Stone for ruining our relationship, and he desperately wanted a child. When I saw the person on the tape, the physical characteristics of the kidnapper looked like Kevin's. I had to do something."

"It's obvious you've had some challenges in your lifetime, Major Monroe, but I'm here to tell you that no good deed goes unrewarded. It's unfortunate that a life has been lost over this situation. Mr. Wilson is no longer here, and we have to be mindful that he probably has family who loved him."

"He has a mother in Connecticut and a sister who, I believe, still lives in Baltimore," Michael disclosed. "I didn't want things to end like this. Kevin was a friend, but he had changed and become erratic. He blamed Keilah for missing out on the best chance he had to have a child. That's why I thought he was the man on the video."

The agent jotted down some notes, and then their interview was interrupted when another gentleman entered the room and handed the agent interviewing Michael a folder.

He opened it and said, "Major, you've been most helpful in this investigation. It might ease your mind to know that we found out who the child belongs to. Her mother was a prostitute, and Mr. Wilson used to keep the child for her from time to time. Some of her friends said she sold her child to Mr. Wilson for a thousand dollars. Unfortunately, she's no longer with us, because her pimp beat her to death two nights ago."

Michael was shocked. He never thought Kevin would try to buy a child, but who best to buy one from than a prostitute?

The agent went on. "Mr. Wilson's cause of death will be described as the result of your self-defense. You have the injury to substantiate it. And the child will be put in foster care until a suitable home can be found for her. We'll notify his family of his death."

"And tell them what?" Michael asked.

The agent stood and said, "The truth."

Michael solemnly nodded, but his heart was still heavy.

"You will be listed in the investigation only as a Good Samaritan. Now, come on so we can get you out of those bloody clothes and back home."

Michael stood and asked, "What's going to happen to the child?"

The agent looked at Michael and said, "She'll be put into foster care until we have a chance to try and locate family members."

"What happens if you're unable to find her family?" Michael asked with concern.

The man looked at Michael and said, "I guess she'll stay in foster care until she can be adopted. Why?"

Michael hesitated for a second and then said, "If possible, I would like the opportunity to adopt her first."

The agent smiled and opened the door. "I'll see what I can do. Come on so we can get you some clean clothes."

Michael followed him into another section of the building, where they provided him with hospital scrubs to wear home in place of his bloodstained attire.

***

An hour later they dropped him off at Madeline's house, and before he could walk to the front door, she ran out into the yard and jumped into his open arms.

With tears in her eyes she hugged him tightly and said, "I was so worried about you. Where have you been? Are you okay?"

"I am now," he whispered in her ear as he held her tightly against his chest.

"What happened to your hand? I told that man not to let you get hurt!"

Michael chuckled and said, "It's not that bad, and Ramsey didn't have anything to do with this."

"Major Monroe," the government agent called out to him from behind the wheel.

With Madeline by his side, Michael walked over to the agent's car.

The agent reached inside his jacket and handed Michael his business card. "Call me if you need anything or have any questions."

"I will. Thank you."

He put the car in reverse and said, "No, thank you, and someone will bring your vehicle home shortly."

Once the car was gone, Madeline asked, "Who was that?"

"To be honest, I'm not sure," he answered.

"Come on inside, babe, so I can take care of you. You've been gone all night, and what happened to your clothes?"

He held up the bag with soiled clothes and said, "They're in here. They got a little dirty. I'll wash them when I get home. Right now all I care about is some breakfast and sleeping with you in my arms."

She held on to his waist and said, "That sounds wonderful. Go shower while I make you breakfast. I hope you're hungry."

"Don't worry. I am."

Michael disappeared up the stairs while Madeline took eggs and bacon out of the refrigerator.

Ramsey was pretty much running on fumes by the time the sun came up. He took comfort knowing that his parents were at the hospital with Keilah, but there was only so much he could do. He and Keytone had been to the TV station to be taped for the upcoming news segment, and they'd gone back to the zoo, but to no avail. There was still no sign of Neariah and no phone call asking for ransom. Since Tori was their best witness, they decided to go back to the hospital to check on Keilah and see if Tori remembered anything she hadn't already revealed.

Ramsey rubbed his red eyes and said, "I won't go back there without my daughter. I made her a promise, and I'm going to keep it."

"You won't be any good to Keilah if you fall asleep at the wheel. You need some sleep, and so do I. You'll be able to think more clearly once you've had some rest. Keilah knows you're doing everything you can to find Neariah, but she needs you by her side right now."

"I guess you're right," Ramsey replied as they drove toward the hospital. "I don't want her to think I've abandoned her. She feels guilty enough, but it's my fault for letting her go alone to the zoo in the first place."

"That's some bullshit! It's nobody's fault, so stop blaming yourself. All we need to focus on is finding my niece."

Ramsey pulled into the parking lot of the hospital and said, "You're right. My bad."

"Let's go. You need a few hours of sleep so you can think straight."

Keytone followed his brother-in-law into the hospital, where they joined up with Marion and Valeria in Keilah's room. They gathered around the bed, forming a circle, and they all prayed for Neariah's safe return and a quick recovery for Keilah and Tori.

Neariah continued to cry as she sat in an unfamiliar lap. The lullaby she was listening to was familiar, but the voice singing it wasn't.

"Come on. You have to eat, and then I have a nice warm bath for you."

Neariah looked into the stranger's eyes and began to cry even more.

"Shh, don't cry. I know we don't know each other, but please stop crying."

Neariah screamed even louder, and she refused to eat or drink anything put in front of her.

"Look, I have this delicious food for you. You have to eat, or you're going to be sick."

She pushed the spoon away and wiggled to get down out of the stranger's lap.

"Damn it! Sit still and let me feed you!"

At that point, Neariah screamed at the top of her lungs. Fearing that someone would hear the heart-wrenching cries, her abductor covered her tiny nose and mouth, cutting off her air supply to stifle her screams.

"This is ridiculous! I shouldn't have to do this to get you to stop crying."

Neariah gasped for air as she was finally allowed to breathe. Unfortunately, she let out another bloodcurdling scream and tears streamed down her face.

"Shut up!" Neariah's abductor yelled before leaning against the wall, clearly exhausted.

The phone rang and before answering it, the abductor left the bedroom, closing the door to drown out Neariah's crying, and went into the living room in order to talk uninterrupted.

"Hey, babe, I thought I would call you before I left on my trip."

"Trip? Where are you going this time?" the abductor asked. "Didn't you just get back from some exotic island?"

"Some island? It was Cabo San Lucas, and I asked you to go with me, but you said you had some unfinished business to take care of here," the caller answered.

"I know, but this couldn't be helped. I'll make it up to you, I promise. My unfinished business will be over soon," the abductor explained. "And then I'll be all yours. By the way, where are you going for this business trip?"

"The Dominican Republic," the caller replied. "There's money to be made, and I'm going to make it."

"I heard it's beautiful there. Listen, babe, I know we just started seeing each other, but I don't want you to think I don't care. Starting over after a bad breakup is difficult, especially after you see them happy and in love with someone else."

There was silence between the pair for a few seconds, and then the caller said, "I understand. I just hope you're over your ex and not just stringing me along."

The abductor smiled and said, "Once my business is taken care of, I'll be all yours. I'm glad we got to spend some time together before you have to leave again."

"So am I, and I like the way that sounds, babe," the caller replied as Neariah let out a wail from the other room. "Is that a baby crying?"

"No, it's the TV. Sorry," the abductor replied. "Have a safe trip and call me when you land. I can't wait to see you when you get back."

"That's a date," the caller replied before hanging up the telephone.

The abductor went back into the bedroom, where Neariah continued to cry.

At the hospital, Ramsey's peaceful nap was interrupted when Luke, Roman, Genesis, and Malachi unexpectedly arrived, and they were not happy. While the brothers greeted and consoled Keilah, Ramsey stood out in the hallway with his father to give them some privacy.

He looked him in his dad's eyes and asked, "You called them, didn't you?"

Marion folded his arms and said, "I sure did. You should've done it from the beginning. I taught you better than that."

At that moment Luke stepped out in the hallway and got in Ramsey's face. "Ramsey, I'm so angry right now, I don't know what to do. You were wrong for not calling us when this first happened. I know you thought you were doing right by bringing Keytone out here instead, but you were wrong."

Still emotional from the events of the day, Ramsey replied, "I apologize, but it was my call and I didn't want you to worry unnecessarily. My plan was to have Neariah home by now."

Luke got in Ramsey's face and said, "I love you, Ramsey, and know you're hurting just as much as we are right now, so I'm not going to beat you up about the decisions you made. Neariah's safe return is our main concern right now, but if you ever hide anything like this again—"

Ramsey lowered his head and said, "I don't want to hear that right now, Luke. I get it. I'm sorry."

Luke pulled Ramsey into a strong embrace, and with tears in his eyes he whispered, "We'll find Neariah, because we're not leaving here until we do. So what's next?"

"I'm going to kick in the door of every person I suspect could have anything to do with this."

Marion stepped in and said, "No, son, you're way too emotional for that. You need to let the police do their investigation, and I think you need to raise the reward."

"Your dad is right, Ramsey. I think a hundred-thousand-dollar reward for her safe return is too low. Raise it to five hundred thousand dollars."

Tears filled Ramsey's eyes, and he said, "I just want my daughter back. I'll pay anything."

Luke hugged him again and said, "We all do, and don't worry . . . We'll get her back. Now, go comfort your wife."

Chapter Twenty-five

Andria pulled into the parking lot of a local hotel and shut off her car. She exited the vehicle, trying not to draw attention to herself, but it was hard not to notice her tall, shapely frame and trendy clothing. She knocked on door number twenty-five and waited for an answer. Seconds later Rico Tanner, her childhood friend, cracked the door. It was clear that she had disrupted his sleep, because he could barely open his eyes.

"What's up?" he asked.

"Aren't you going to invite me in?" she asked as she pushed past him.

Andria entered the hotel room and found empty liquor bottles and food containers strewn around the room. She moved some clothing out of a chair and sat down while Rico went to the bathroom.

"This place looks like a tornado hit it. You need to clean this place up before they kick you out of here. What have you been doing?" she asked as she continued to observe the pigsty.

He lay across the bed, hung over, and mumbled, "Partying. What else? What are you doing here, Andy?"

As a kid, Andy was the nickname she inherited because she was somewhat of a tomboy, until she couldn't deny her adolescent curves and embraced her feminine side.

"Can't I come visit you?" she asked.

He laughed and said, "I know that look on your face. Are you here to talk about Ramsey some more? I don't know why you waste your energy on him."

"I was pissed off at him but didn't know you were going to do what you did."

He rolled over on his back and said, "You said you wanted him to hurt, and I helped you make it happen. Are you saying you're not happy?"

She touched his leg and said, "I'm not satisfied yet, but I will be soon."

Rico propped himself up on the bed and said, "You're becoming a pain in my ass, Andy. You're so damn wishy-washy. One minute you hate Stone, and the next you act like you're still in love with him." He lit up a cigarette.

Andria immediately snatched the cigarette out of his mouth and put it out. "I don't want to smell that nasty smoke. You need to quit, anyway, before it kills you."

"Damn! Do you know how much cigarettes cost?"

"Yes, but I'm going to get you a box of nicotine patches instead, and you need to stop thinking you have to be my knight in shining armor. I love you, Rico. You're like a brother to me."

He looked into her gorgeous face and said, "I love you too. That's why I'll do anything for you, but you need to forget about Ramsey Stone. The man doesn't want to have anything to do with you. What's up with that dude your dad introduced you to?"

With her voice cracking, she touched his face and said, "He's nice, but it's taking me a while to warm up to him."

Rico walked over to the refrigerator and pulled out a can of beer and opened it. After taking a sip, he said, "You should try harder, because I don't want to hear the name Ramsey Stone around me ever again."

"Done!" she answered.

"You full of shit, Andy. You're obsessed, but on a serious note, I need you to hook me up. I've done a lot of shit for you, and I want to get out of this hotel and into a permanent place. I also need some wheels, nothing fancy."

Andria stared at him and said, "We've been down that road before. You got evicted from your apartment for partying, and you totaled your car, not to mention that you thought it would be cool to steal that Benz."

He pointed at her and said, "I got that for you."

"I never told you to steal a car. I said I wished I had that particular model."

He looked at her, and with a big grin on his face he said, "Like I said, I got it for you."

"It's time to grow up, Rico, and you need a job."

Rico laughed and said, "Ain't you the pot calling the kettle black. I want to be my own boss. Maybe you could help me start my business."

"Maybe," she said as she stood. "Now, put on some clothes and pack your bags so we can get you out of here. Housekeeping is going to be pissed when she sees this room."

"Cleaning is what she gets paid to do," he replied.

"You know you can be an asshole sometimes," she answered as she laid a fifty-dollar bill on the nightstand to tip the housekeeper.

"Calm down, Andy. I'm just playing," Rico grunted as he headed into the bathroom to take a quick shower. He got dressed and packed his bag in record time, and within minutes they were out the door.

As they walked out the door, Andria turned to Rico and said, "I need you to do me a huge favor."

"Whose car do you want to key now?" he joked.

"I'm serious, Rico. I need you to deliver something back to Ramsey and his wife and send them a message once and for all."

"Cool. I'm in as long as I get an apartment and my own car out of the deal," he said as he buckled his seat belt.

She sighed as she climbed behind the wheel of her car and said, "Okay, but, this is the last time, Rico."

"Me too," he replied before watching her drive off.

The kidnapper felt that the Stones had gotten the message and decided it was time to return the child to her parents. A cab pulled up, and the kidnapper climbed in with Neariah covered to shield her from the cold air. The driver looked in the rearview mirror and noticed his passenger had a hat pulled down over his eyes and a scarf around his neck and mouth.

He asked, "Where to?"

"Lanham Severn Road in Bowie, Maryland."

"Right away," the driver answered as he put the car in drive and pulled away from the cottage.

It took nearly twenty minutes for the cab to reach its destination. The kidnapper paid the cabdriver and stepped out of the cab. Neariah was still asleep as she was carried into the large cathedral. When they entered the foyer, the kidnapper could see what looked like hundreds of candles burning on the altar. Scattered about the large sanctuary were approximately fifteen people. The kidnapper made a note to keep the hat and scarf in place as he moved toward the front of the cathedral. After he sat down, the large replica of Christ on the cross seem to stare down intensely at him, so he moved into a confessional for more privacy. Within seconds a priest entered and took his spot.

The kidnapper lowered his head and said, "Forgive me, Father, for I have sinned. It's been too long since my last confession. Since then, I have committed mortal sins, for which I am deeply sorry."

"What brings you here, my child?"

The kidnapper took a breath and said, "I have a child that I need to return to her parents. The child is fine and has been well taken care of, and I only took her to make a point, but I wanted to ask for forgiveness before doing so."

"Kidnapping is a serious offense, but if you honestly repent and do what's right by returning the child, there's always forgiveness in the eyes of God," the priest replied.

"Thank you, Father."

"Give thanks to the Lord for He is good," the priest recited.

"For His mercy endures forever," the kidnapper recited. "I appreciate you listening, Father, and I would be grateful if you would wait until I've left the church before you come out. You'll find the child inside the confessional. Make sure she gets back to Ramsey Stone and his wife, Keilah."

"Go with God, my son," the priest replied. "I'll continue to pray for you."

The priest did as he was asked since a child's safety was at stake. When he found Neariah, the priest cuddled her in his arms, then took her back to his office, where she woke up and began to cry. He handed her over to one of the nuns, who prepared a bottle of milk for her while the priest contacted the authorities.

Andria pulled out her cell phone and dialed Rico's number, and after three rings he answered.

"Yeah?"

"Where are you?" she asked, her voice quivering.

"In the wind, and I suggest you do the same. It won't be long before the police come knocking on your door."

Her hands were trembling as she held the phone up to her ear. With tears running down her face, she asked, "Where you are so I can pick you up? We can go up to our house on Long Island for a few days, until this thing plays out."

"I don't know, Andy. I think it would be best if we went our separate ways for a while."

With tears continuing to run down her face, she said, "Please. I'm worried about you. Tell me where you are so I can at least give you some money."

"You don't have to give me any money. I'll make do," he announced.

"That's what I'm afraid of. You're family, Rico. Let me do this for you," she pleaded until he couldn't take it anymore.

He sighed and said, "Stop crying and I'll tell you."

Andria wiped away her tears and said, "Okay."

"I'm at the IHOP on Annapolis Road in Bowie."

She pulled a tissue out of her purse and wiped her eyes. "I'll see you in twenty minutes. Do not move."

"I won't, but hurry up," he stated as the waitress sat a plate of eggs, bacon, and pancakes in front of him, along with a cup of coffee. "I'm getting ready to get my grub on, and then I'm out."

As Rico waited for Andria to arrive, he felt sorry for her and what her life had become. She had always had the perfect life, with plenty of money and status in Washington's high society. He, on the other hand, had grown up middle class, with just enough to get by, but he was able to rub elbows with D.C.'s elite by being associated with the Rockwells, even though he knew he never really fit in. What he loved about Andria was that she never made him feel inferior or beneath her. They really were like family, and he would do anything to protect her.

Chapter Twenty-six

At the hospital, Ramsey hurried into the emergency room after getting a call from Neil that a baby was being brought in that had been left at an area church. His heart was racing as he sprinted down the stairs instead of waiting for the elevator. Genesis and Malachi followed close behind, while Luke and Roman stayed with Keilah, who had been given a mild sedative and was sleeping.

"Is it her?" Ramsey asked as he rounded the corner and found Neil walking through the emergency room doors.

"I just got here. The police cruiser who picked her up is pulling in now."

Genesis patted Ramsey on the shoulders and said, "Take a breath, bro. It's going to be okay."

Tears welled up in Ramsey's eyes when the officer walked through the doors with the most beautiful baby he had ever seen in his life.

"It's her!" he yelled as he hurried over to his daughter and held her in his arms. Tears fell out of his eyes as he asked, "Is she okay? Is she injured?"

"She looks fine, but we wanted the doctors to check her out just to make sure," the officer replied.

Malachi and Genesis felt as if they were finally able to breathe as they looked into their niece's eyes. Keytone joined his brothers in the hallway, and when he saw Neariah in Ramsey's arms, a huge weight lifted off his shoulders. He was happy that his niece was back in the safe arms of her family, and if he found out who had kidnapped her, he wouldn't hesitate to take their life.

"Where did you find her?" Ramsey asked the officer.

"Someone dropped her off at a Catholic church downtown."

A doctor walked over to Ramsey and the officers and said, "We got the call that you were bringing in a kidnap victim. Is this the child?"

"Yes," Ramsey replied. "I'm her father."

"Please bring her into examination room four so we can examine her," the doctor said.

In the examination room, Ramsey held his breath as the pediatrician examined Neariah for any signs of sexual or physical abuse. Thankfully, she received a clean bill of health, but before he took her to Keilah, the police wanted to swab her mouth to compare her saliva against any trace evidence they might obtain in the future. Afterward, Ramsey wanted to give her a nice warm bath and remove the clothes she was wearing. The pediatrician instructed the nurses to accommodate Ramsey and to bring him some pajamas for Neariah to wear.

He tried to give Neariah some food, but she wasn't hungry, and it didn't take long for her to fall asleep in her father's arms. He was anxious to get her upstairs to Keilah, but his first stop was Tori's room so he could give her and Kyle the great news. When he entered the room, Kyle stood with a huge smile on his face.

Ramsey hugged his neck and said, "We got her back, bro, and I want to thank you for being here for me, bro. I couldn't have made it through this without you."

"That's what friends do. Is she okay?" Kyle said as he caressed Neariah's curly hair.

"She's perfect," he replied. "Absolutely perfect."

Ramsey handed Neariah to Kyle for a moment so he could talk to Tori. He leaned down and gave her a kiss on the cheek and said, "Thanks for loving us enough to risk your life to save our daughter. I'll be forever grateful to you."

She hugged Ramsey's neck and said, "You know you guys are like family to me. There's nothing I wouldn't do for you."

He kissed her again and said, "We feel the same way about you and Kyle."

Tori nodded. "I'm glad she's safe. Has Keilah seen her yet?"

"No, not yet. I wanted to stop by here to thank you first," he replied.

"I appreciate that, Ramsey. Now, take her to Keilah so she can see her baby."

Kyle handed Neariah back to his friend and walked him to the door, but not before giving him another brotherly hug.

Ramsey made his way down the long hallway and into his wife's room. Luke and Roman stood and gave Neariah a tender kiss on the forehead as he passed them. Tears spilled out of Valeria's eyes as she looked at her granddaughter sleeping soundly in Ramsey's arms.

"Praise the Lord," she whispered as she dropped to her knees and immediately started praying a prayer of thanks.

Marion was speechless as he hugged his wife and joined her in a prayer of thanksgiving.

Ramsey walked around to Keilah's bed and gently laid Neariah on her mother's chest and covered her with a blanket. Neariah snuggled against her sleeping mother's warm neck and grabbed a handful of Keilah's hair. Within minutes, Keilah's blood pressure started to decline.

"Ramsey, get some sleep. You've been on fast-forward ever since she went missing. I'll keep an eye on the girls," Luke promised him.

"I can't sleep right now. I don't want to take my eyes off her," Ramsey answered as he sat down in the recliner.

It was at that moment that he became very emotional and he broke down in tears. Roman covered his brother-in-law with a blanket before joining the rest of his brothers in the hallway. It had been a grueling experience for the entire family, and now all they cared about was finding the person who took her. Keytone's emotions had gone from joy to anger—anger over the fact that someone had kidnapped her in the first place and had attacked his sister. When Neil joined them in the hallway, the Chance brothers had a few questions they needed answering.

"Did the priest say who brought Neariah into the church?" Keytone asked.

Neil opened his notepad and said, "He said it was a man who entered the confessional. However, he wouldn't reveal what was said in the confessional, because of the sanctity of the confessional. He said the man asked for prayers and forgiveness and then told the priest not to come out of the confessional until he had time to leave the premises."

"Do they have cameras in the church?" Malachi asked.

"No, it's not like that at a place of worship," Neil replied.

"What about fingerprints?" Genesis asked.

Neil scratched his chin and said, "It's a confessional. Hundreds of people go in and out of those booths every day."

"So you're saying it's a dead end?" Keytone asked.

Neil put his hands up and said, "No, I'm not saying it's a dead end. The priest is being interviewed, and we have a team checking to see if they're able to lift any viable prints. The main thing is that we have Neariah back and she's safe."

"Yeah, but what's to stop this guy from coming after them again?" Luke asked. "I want everything that can be done to be done to find this person. Understood?"

Neil shook the hands of all of Ramsey's family members and said, "I understand. I'm getting ready to go over to the church to see what CSI came up with. I'll let you know what I find out."

Keytone grabbed Neil by the arm and said, "I know you'll do your best, but I need you to do more."

"Please understand that I'm working this case like it was my own child," Neil replied before shaking their hands again.

Malachi stepped up and said, "Let the priest know that once we have a chance to settle down, we want to meet him and personally give him the reward for bringing Neariah back to us."

"I'll pass the information on," Neil answered before stepping onto the elevator.

In Keilah's dimly lit hospital room, Ramsey sat with his eyes focused on his sleeping wife and daughter. There was a moment during this ordeal that he thought he would never see her again, and he sat there thanking the Lord over and over for bringing her back. He watched as Keilah wiggled and was gently awakened by Neariah softly calling out to her mother. When she opened her eyes, Keilah thought she was dreaming as she looked directly into the innocent eyes of her baby daughter.

"Neariah? Oh my God! My baby!" she yelled as she slowly cupped her baby's face and kissed her chubby cheeks. With tears running out of her eyes, she asked, "How did you find her? Is she okay?"

"She's fine," Ramsey answered as he leaned down and kissed his wife on the lips.

"How did you get her back?" she asked as she ran her hand over Neariah's curly hair.

"By the grace of God," he answered. "I'll tell you about it later. All that matters now is that she's back, and now we can concentrate on getting your blood pressure under control so we can go home."

She stared at Neariah and shook her head in disbelief. "I can't believe I'm holding her. I thought I would never see her again."

A lump formed in Ramsey's throat as he listened to his wife's voice, which was still full of agony. "I felt the same way," he admitted. "The doctor said you might get to go home tomorrow if they can regulate your blood pressure."

She nodded, and even in her joy, her concern went to her best friend, who had been injured very badly in the attack. "Did Tori come out of surgery okay?"

"She's getting there. Kyle had her moved to a private room a little while ago so you wouldn't be disturbed, since she has a lot of people in and out of her room."

"I need to see her and let her know how much I care about her."

"Of course, but wait until your blood pressure is regulated. And you still have sedation in your system."

She held Neariah tightly in her arms and asked, "Where did my brothers go?"

"They're outside. They were ready to kill me when they found out Neariah was missing and I didn't call them. It was the first time, I think, Luke came close to taking a swing at me."

"You know he's like a father to me. He loves you. They all do," she reminded him. "You just have to understand where we've come from and remember that they're very protective. They trust you, so you have to trust them."

He smiled and said, "You're right."

She looked into her daughter's smiling face and asked, "Do the police know who took her or why she was taken?"

"Not really. I'm just glad they had second thoughts and brought her back."

"Me too," she answered. "Has she eaten?"

"I tried to feed her, but she wasn't hungry. The doctor said she appeared to have been well taken care of."

"That's a blessing," she whispered.

Luke and the rest of the Chance clan reentered the room and loved on Neariah some more. While Keilah was happy that her family was there, it was getting extremely crowded.

"Hey, guys, I know you all must be tired, especially you," she said, pointing at her in-laws. "Why don't you all go back to the house and get some rest? We'll be fine here."

Ramsey stood and said, "Keilah's right. Dad, you have your keys to the house, right?"

"I do," Marion answered as he reached in his pocket and checked his key ring. "Some of you can ride with us if you like."

Ramsey handed his car keys to his father and said, "Take my truck. It has enough room for everyone."

Marion nodded and handed his son the keys to his vehicle. "Sounds like a plan. If they discharge Keilah, just bring her home in my car. Let's go family. Ramsey and Keilah need to rest and spend time with Neariah. Dinner's on me."

Once everyone was gone and the room was quiet, Ramsey made his way over to the bed and picked up his daughter. He held her high above his head. Neariah looked down at her father and giggled.

He lowered her and held her close to his heart and said, "Neariah, you don't ever have to worry about your dad not being there for you, because as of today, your mom and I are official retired. We're going on an indefinite vacation as soon as your mother is well enough to get out of here."

"Are you serious, babe?" Keilah asked.

He stroked her hair and said, "Of course I'm serious. This experience has been eye-opening, and I'll never take life for granted again."

Overcome with joy, she caressed his arm, and with tears in her eyes, she whispered, "Thank you, Ramsey."

Andria and Rico finished their meal, and after a long debate she convinced him to go with her to Long Island, to her parents' second home, to lay low until the heat from the kidnapping died down. Rico slept as she drove down I-95.

A while later Rico stirred in his seat and asked, "Are we there yet?"

"We will be in about two hours. Go back to sleep."

Rico closed his eyes and drifted back off to sleep.

The caretaker entered the cottage where the kidnapper had been staying and began to clean up the rooms. She emptied garbage cans full of dirty diapers and found a baby bottle full of milk in the refrigerator. Something was strange. She didn't remember seeing a baby when the guest checked in or out. Most of their cottages were used by tourists or for romantic getaways, but this guest didn't appear to have any luggage and didn't request any food service. Then, as she began vacuuming, she noticed something shiny sticking out from under the sofa chair. She reached down and picked it up and noticed the name Andria Rockwell engraved on the front of it. She tucked it in her pocket and called her husband on her two-way radio.

"Howard, I found a credit card belonging to an Andria Rockwell in the Cherry Blossom number two cottage. Do you have a number to contact her?"

Howard punched the name of the cottage into the computer and said, "Rockwell? I didn't have a Rockwell there," he answered. "A man named Ramsey Stone rented that cottage. He paid with cash too."

"Well, the card says Rockwell. I'll bring it to you when I finish cleaning up all these dirty diapers."

"Ramsey Stone. Where do I know that name from?"

"Did you say Ramsey Stone?" his wife asked.

Howard studied the name on the computer screen and then looked at the name he had scribbled on the piece of paper. Baffled but thankful he hadn't got stiffed with the bill, he twirled around in his chair and turned his attention back to the TV and the nightly news when a breaking story came on with an update on Neariah's kidnapping.

"The AMBER Alert issued yesterday for one-year-old Neariah Stone has been canceled as the child was found safe in a local church. A police spokesman said that the child was returned in good health. However, the child's abductor is still on the loose. Anyone with information leading to the arrest of the suspect is to call police at five-five-five-oh-one-oh-one. The family is offering a reward of one hundred thousand dollars for information that will lead to an arrest and conviction."

Howard picked up his radio and said, "Helen, get down here with that credit card. It might be related to that kidnapping case. Ramsey Stone is the father of that missing baby."

Chapter Twenty-seven

Two days later, Neil showed up at the Stones' house to notify them of a development in the kidnapping. Marion let Neil in and escorted him to the family room, where everyone except Malachi and Genesis was watching TV.

"Hello, everyone," Neil said and hugged Keilah. "It's nice to see you up and around."

Keilah smiled. "Thank you, Neil."

He picked Neariah up and gave her a kiss on the cheek and then handed her back to Keilah. "Have the detectives working the case been by to talk to you?"

Ramsey turned down the volume on the TV and said, "No. Do they have someone in custody?"

"Not yet, but they have some promising leads."

"Like what?" Keilah asked.

"They won't give me many details, because I'm too close to the case."

Luke offered Neil a seat. When he sat down, he revealed more information.

"They found the SUV used in the kidnapping. It had been set on fire, so there's no way to get any prints off it."

Neariah walked over to her father and offered him an animal cookie. He leaned down so she could feed him. Each time he ate one, she giggled loudly.

"Who was the SUV registered to?" Ramsey asked.

Neil crossed his leg and said, "A security guard at one of the museums. He has an alibi, so he was elimi-

nated as a suspect. He didn't know his vehicle was stolen until he finished his shift."

"I see," Ramsey answered with a tone of disappointment.

"There is one more thing the detectives told me that
was strange," Neil revealed. "Someone rented a cottage
under your name, Ramsey, and it may be the location
where Neariah was held captive. CSI examined the
crime scene for evidence, and they're waiting on the
results."

"My name? Who the hell would do something like
that? And how could they do it without providing iden-
tification?"

"I'm sure you've seen as many fake IDs in your lifetime as I have. Someone who's trying to cover their
tracks," Neil answered.

"That's absurd," Marion blurted out.

"The detectives don't suspect Ramsey, but they had
to show the caretaker a picture of Ramsey just to cover
all their bases. As expected, he didn't match the description of the person who rented the cottage. Ramsey
is much taller and has a lighter complexion and a larger
build."

Valeria walked in, dressed in an apron, and greeted
Neil. She handed him a bottle of water and asked him
if he was staying for dinner.

"I'd love to Mrs. V., but I have to get back out on the
streets," he answered as he stood. "Thanks for the water, though. If I'm able to get any detailed information,
I'll let you know."

Roman walked through the door with Target on a
leash and greeted Neil. "Any news?" he asked.

"Not really," Ramsey answered his brother-in-law.
"Seems like whoever did this is playing games."

Keilah stood and headed toward the hallway. She patted Neil on the shoulder as she passed him and said, "Thanks for coming by."

"Anytime."

Ramsey picked Neariah up and said, "Come on, bro. I'll walk you to the door."

"Good night, everyone," Neil said as he waved good-bye.

At the front door Ramsey thanked his friend again for updating them on the case before closing the door behind him. When he turned around, he found Keilah climbing the stairs.

"Are you okay?" he called out to her.

She stopped midway and said, "I'm fine. Just going up to take a shower."

"Need any help?" he asked. He knew she was upset that no one was under arrest yet for the kidnapping, and so was he, but they would have to be patient until the abductors made a mistake.

Keilah turned and looked down at her husband said, "Thanks, but I think I can manage. I won't be long."

"Call if you need anything," he stated before returning to the family room.

Alone with her thoughts, Keilah couldn't help but praise God one more time for answering her prayers by bringing Neariah back home safe. She stepped into the hot shower and let the water soothe her sore body. Normalcy was what she needed, and she felt like she was finally able to exhale. Things were going to be different now, and she was going to live her life with a totally different perspective. It was going to be less about business and all about family. As the suds cleansed her body, she felt like her soul was being cleansed as well, and then the unthinkable happened. She glanced down and noticed a stream of bright red blood running down her leg and through the drain. Horrified, she quickly turned off the water, grabbed a towel, and immediately yelled for her husband.

A few hours later, Keilah and Ramsey left the emergency ward with the news that she had miscarried. With a hole in her heart and tears in her eyes, she returned home, where she sat at the window in her bedroom in deep thought. Her heart was heavy over the loss of her child. She was religious and understood that God didn't make mistakes, so she knew not to question his will. Keilah realized she took a hard fall when she was assaulted and that her blood pressure had been high, but not once did she think she would lose her child.

"Hey, babe," Ramsey said softly, interrupting her thoughts. He sat a cup of hot tea on the nightstand. "Shouldn't you be in bed?"

She walked over to him and wrapped her arms around his waist. He held her close and then noticed tears running down her face.

Concerned, he asked, "Are you in pain?"

"Not really," she whispered.

"Maybe you should get into bed. I brought you some chamomile tea."

Keilah looked up into his loving eyes and said, "I'm so sorry, Ramsey."

"It's not your fault." He balled his hands into fists. He was angry that this ordeal had caused them to lose something so precious, even though they were blessed to get Neariah back.

"Thanks for the tea, but I'm tired, babe. I just want to go to bed."

He helped her out of her clothes and then into bed.

"Try to drink some, anyway. It'll help you relax."

While she drank the tea, his heart ached.

"Are you hungry?" he asked softly.

"Not really," she answered as she handed the empty cup to him.

"You have to eat something, because you have this medicine to take."

Valeria knocked on the door before entering. Target walked into the room first, and then Valeria entered, holding her granddaughter's hand. When the toddler saw her mother, she waddled over to the bed and said, "Momma."

Tears fell out of Keilah's eyes as Ramsey picked Neariah up and placed her in the bed. Neariah climbed into her mother's lap and gave her a wet baby kiss.

Valeria sat on the side of the bed and patted Keilah on the leg. "Keilah, I know you're feeling really bad right now, so if there is anything we can do to help you, let us know, okay?"

"Yes, ma'am," Keilah answered softly. "All I want to do right now is sleep."

Ramsey pulled Neariah off the bed and stood her on the floor. "You can sleep after you put something in your stomach, or this medicine will make you sick."

"Valeria, do you mind bringing me a couple pieces of toast?" Keilah said.

"Sure, sweetheart," Valeria answered as she turned and walked out of the room.

Ramsey stroked Keilah's hair and said, "We'll get through this, I promise."

She slid down under the comforter and said, "If you say so."

Target barked as he kept a close eye on Neariah, who was now trying to climb up on the window seat.

"It's okay, boy. I see her," Ramsey said to acknowledge his loyal pet. He turned back to his wife and said, "I know this might not be the right time to tell you about everything that happened, but you need to know that Michael could've lost his life trying to help get Neariah back."

"How?" she asked.

"He thought the kidnapper looked like his ex-lover, so he went to his house to verify it. When he got there, there was a baby there, who Michael thought was Neariah. When he confronted him about it, he cut him pretty deep with a knife."

"Is he okay?" she asked.

"Yeah, he had to get a few stitches. The worst part is by the time we go there, Michael had killed the guy—in self-defense, of course—and even worse, I had to tell him the child wasn't Neariah."

"How did you know to go there, and whose baby was it?" she asked.

"Michael left a note for me with his girlfriend and told her to call me if he wasn't home by a certain time, and according to Kyle, Michael's ex-lover, Kevin, bought the baby from a prostitute."

Tears formed in her eyes. "Is Michael in jail?"

"No, Kyle took care of it. He won't face any charges."

She lowered her head and whispered, "Thanks for telling me."

He kissed her forehead and said, "Me and the guys are going to step out for a minute to go over to the church where Neariah was left to give the priest the reward. Mom will be here if you need anything, and I'll be back up to check on you shortly."

Target barked at Neariah again as she continued to try and climb up on the window seat.

"Dog!" Neariah yelled as she pointed at Target. "Dog!"

"Yeah, dog," Ramsey repeated as he picked his daughter up in his arms. "Let's go so Mommy can rest."

After her husband and daughter left the room, Keilah couldn't help but wonder if she had cursed her pregnancy by expressing her misgivings about getting pregnant sooner than they had planned. Then her thoughts went to Michael and how he had risked his life for her daughter. When she felt up to it, she would call him and thank him personally.

Andria and Rico had settled into the Hamptons home and were eating lunch when her cell phone rang. When she looked at the caller ID, she frowned and said, "It's Daddy. Hello, Daddy."

"What the hell have you gotten yourself into, and where are you?"

Her heart rate accelerated. "What are you talking about?" she asked.

"Some detectives were just here, wanting to talk to you about a case they're working on."

"What case?" she asked her father.

"I don't know, Andria. That's what I'm trying to find out from you."

Andria didn't know what to say. She was speechless and afraid.

"Andria, I swear to God, if you have gotten yourself mixed up in some bullshit to embarrass this family, I am going to—"

She cut him off and said, "I haven't done anything, Daddy."

Rico noticed that Andria looked like a deer caught in headlights.

"Daddy, I wish I could tell you something, but I have no clue why they want to talk to me."

"Well, you had better figure it out and get home so we can get to the bottom of this," he yelled at his daughter. "And if those detectives find you before you get home, don't say a word until I contact our attorney."

"Yes, Daddy." She hung up the phone and covered her face with her hands.

Rico put his fork down and asked, "What's going on?"

"Daddy said some detectives came by the house to talk to me about a case they're working on."

Rico jumped out of his chair and put his empty plate in the sink. He turned to her and asked, "Do you think it's about the kidnapping?"

She stood and yelled, "I don't know. We have to get out of town."

"Are you kidding me? We *are* out of town. Besides if you run, you're really going to look guilty."

She picked up her cell phone and said, "Pack your bags, Rico. I'm taking you to New York to get you on a flight out of the country."

"I'm not going anywhere."

Andria took his hands into hers and said, "If you hang around, they'll link you to me, and I can't let that happen. You have a background, remember?"

He walked toward the door, turned back to her, and said, "I'm not leaving the country, but we do need to get out of here before T. K. Rockwell sends out an army to find you."

"I hate not knowing what those detectives want."

They made their way up the stairs. Rico stood in the doorway of his bedroom and said, "Well, it's something serious enough for the police to show up at your door."

She leaned against the door frame and said, "This has gotten way out of hand."

"What are you going to do?"

"All I can do. Face them," she answered before disappearing into her room.

He followed her into the room and said, "Well, we'd better come up with stories that match, just in case they catch us together and interrogate us."

"Like what?" she asked as she started packing her clothes in a small bag. "We don't know why they want to talk to me yet."

He picked up her bra and said, "Nice, Andy."

She snatched the bra out of his hand and tossed it in her bag and said, "I'm scared, Rico."

"I know I shouldn't say this, but that's what you get for being obsessed with that man. You keep trying to hurt him, and what is it doing for you? Nothing! I hope these little games of yours don't get your ass sent to the pen." Rico left the room, packed his bag, and he and Andria hit the Sunrise Highway out of the Hamptons.

T.K. Rockwell paced the floor after the unexpected visit from the two police detectives. He had no idea what Andria had gotten herself mixed up in, but whatever it was, he knew he would have to head it off by involving his attorney, so he picked up the telephone and got him on the line. He studied the detective's business card as he waited for his attorney to pick up.

"Steve, its T.K. I have a problem and need your help."

Andria's father went ahead and told his attorney about the detectives and asked him to contact them to find out the nature of visit and get back with him as soon as possible. His attorney agreed. After hanging up, a lightbulb went off in T.K. Rockwell's head.

"Oh damn!" he yelled. Then he picked up the phone and dialed his daughter once again.

"Hello, Daddy. I'm on my way home."

"Andria, please tell me you didn't have anything to do with the disappearance of Ramsey Stone's baby."

Her heart skipped a beat. "I'm over him," she whined.

He didn't believe her. He knew how obsessed she was with Ramsey, and could always tell when she was lying. "Where are you?"

She let out a breath and said, "I'm in New York with a friend, Daddy. Don't worry. I'll be home in a few hours."

"Our attorney is going to accompany us to the police station so we can get to the bottom of this. I'm not going to have them going on a fishing expedition and dragging our family name through the mud."

"I understand, Daddy. I'll be home soon." She hung up the phone and glanced over at Rico and said, "Daddy's pissed."

He fumbled with the radio and asked, "What now?"

"Daddy's rushing me to get back so him and his attorney can take me to the police station to see those detectives."

Rico reclined in his seat and said, "Maybe Ramsey gave you up after you went ballistic on him down in Richmond."

"Screw it! I can handle Ramsey too."

Chapter Twenty-eight

Neil couldn't believe his eyes when he saw one of the detectives working the kidnapping case escorting Andria and an unidentified man into an interrogation room. He quickly got on the phone and called Ramsey, but he made a mistake and called their house telephone, and as expected, Keilah answered the telephone.

"Keilah, it's Neil. Ramsey told me about your loss. I'm so sorry. How are you feeling?"

"I'm okay. I appreciate your concern. What can I do for you?"

He hesitated and then asked, "Is Ramsey home?"

"No, I put him and the rest of the men out of the house for the day. They've been hovering over me for the past few days, and I needed a break. They've gone to a Georgetown basketball game."

"I see," he replied as he wondered what to do next. "I'll call him on his cell."

"Can it wait? I really want him and the guys to enjoy the game. Is there anything I can help you with?" she asked.

Neil held the telephone in silence as he contemplated if he should tell Keilah the update or wait for Ramsey. With all that she'd been through, he didn't want to upset her even more, but then again, Keilah deserved to know.

Keilah sat on the sofa and said, "You can tell me."

"I don't want to worry you about this, Keilah. It would probably be best if I told Ramsey and your brothers."

Frustrated, she pounded her fist on the sofa cushion and yelled, "Goddamn it, Neil! If you don't tell me what the hell is going on, I'm going to hurt you!"

"Okay! Okay! Calm down, woman," he answered. He took a breath and said, "I saw the detectives working the case taking Andria Rockwell into an interrogation room."

"Andria? Why her?"

"I don't know. For all I know, it could be related to a different case. Listen, Keilah, I'd feel better discussing this with Ramsey. You've been through enough."

With her teeth clenched and fist balled up, she said, "Give me your best guess on why they would be talking to Andria, and don't lie to me, Neil."

Feeling the heat from his friend through the telephone, he relented and told Keilah about the altercation between Ramsey and Andria in Richmond and how they suspected that she was the one who keyed his car. Keilah couldn't believe her ears. Ramsey had kept some very important information from her, and it upset her.

"You mean to tell me that woman could've kidnapped my daughter because she was pissed at Ramsey?"

Neil said, "I don't know for sure, but I guess that's a possibility."

"I'm on my way," Keilah announced.

"You're on your way where?" he asked inquisitively.

"Down to the precinct," she announced. "Stop playing dumb."

He chuckled nervously and said, "I don't think that's a good idea. You should wait until I know what's really going on."

She walked over to the closet and pulled out her coat, ignoring his advice, and said, "That's not going to happen. I'll call you when I get there so you can meet me in the lobby. Those detectives should be keeping us informed on the case, anyway. I'll be there in fifteen minutes."

Keilah hung up the telephone and yelled for Valeria. Valeria walked into the room and noticed that her daughter-in-law was wearing a coat.

"Where are you going?"

"I have some business to take care at the police station. I'll be back shortly."

Valeria took Keilah by the hand and said, "Maybe you should wait on the guys to get back from the game. The doctor told you to take it easy."

"Valeria, this is something I have to do. This ordeal is driving me crazy, and I want justice."

"I know you do but—"

She kissed her mother-in-law on the cheek and said, "Neariah's napping right now. I won't be gone long."

Valeria watched Keilah pull out of the garage and down the long driveway.

At the police station Keilah made her way inside the building and then called Neil to meet her. Minutes later he stepped off an elevator and walked across the lobby and greeted her with a hug.

"You're going to get me in a lot of trouble for doing this," he said as they walked toward the elevators.

She waved him off and said, "If you're talking about Ramsey, he'll get over it."

"He's my best friend. I'm still going to catch hell for letting you come down here without bringing him up to speed first."

She smiled and said, "Tell him I twisted your arm."

Neil laughed out loud.

"Is that she-devil still here?" she asked as they waited for people to get off the elevator before entering.

After stepping inside the elevator, he said, "As far as I know, she is. They have her down on the major crimes floor. Her father is here too. I can call down there to see if she's still being questioned."

"It must be serious if T.K. is here. I haven't seen him in a while. Are you sure you don't know why they're here?"

They stepped off the elevator, entered the patrol room, and went into a break room area.

"I'm sure," he answered as he hung up Keilah's coat and pulled out a seat for her. "Can I get you something to drink? Coffee, Pepsi, anything?"

She sat down and said, "No, I'm good. Neil, I'm not leaving here until I know what's going on."

"Do you want me to see if I can go get one of the detectives so they can talk to you?" he asked.

"Yes, please," she answered as she fumbled with the salt and pepper shakers on the table.

Neil left the room, and a few minutes later he returned with one of the detectives. The detective shook Keilah's hand and apologized for not being in touch but assured her that they had been working hard on the case. He admitted that they were questioning Andria to see if there was a possibility that she was involved in the kidnapping because of a tip they received.

"What kind of tip?" Keilah asked.

"I can't go into details right now, but do you know Andria Rockwell?" the detective asked.

She nodded and revealed to him that Andria was an ex-lover of Ramsey's and that she had been bitter when he broke off their relationship and married her. Neil also told the detective about Ramsey's altercation with Andria in Richmond.

The detective jotted down all the information and said, "I can't reveal anything to you right now, because the investigation is ongoing, but I will tell you that Miss Rockwell has some explaining to do."

"Are you saying she could've had my daughter?"

He sighed and said, "It's possible, but we won't know until we get forensics results back from the lab."

"What kind of test?" Keilah asked.

"I can't really say, Mrs. Stone. I don't want to jeopardize the case."

Keilah ran her hands through her hair, slightly frustrated, and said, "I'll try to be patient, Detective, but you're going to have to keep us more informed with the case."

The detective shook Keilah's hand again and said, "I will, Mrs. Stone. You should go home. There's nothing for you to do here, and I promise I'll call you as soon as we have some promising information."

"I'm going to hold you to that," she replied as she stood and slid into her coat.

The detective left Keilah and Neil alone. She covered her face and said, "Neil, I feel like I'm about to explode. Get me out of here."

He took her by the arm. "Come on. I'll walk you to your car."

"I swear to God, Neil, if that woman had anything to do with my child's kidnapping, you're going to have to arrest me, because I will beat her ass down."

"I feel you," he replied as he walked her to the elevator and pushed the button.

They stepped onto the elevator, and two floors down the unthinkable happened. The doors opened, and

Andria, her father, and a man that appeared to be their attorney stepped onto the elevator, completely ignoring their presence. It took every fiber in Keilah's body for her not to lash out at Andria, and she was cool until she overheard something T.K. Rockwell said to his daughter.

"Andria, what I don't understand is how your credit card ended up in that cottage with a garbage can full of dirty diapers."

"I told you, Daddy. I didn't even know it was missing."

He shook his head and said, "You had better be telling the truth. I don't need this kind of stress right now."

Neil glanced over at Keilah and could see that her breathing had changed and that sweat had broken out on her brow. Andria glanced over her shoulder at the pair, and before she could react, Keilah punched her in the side of the head, knocking her onto the floor. She immediately jumped on Andria and started choking her as she screamed obscenities at her husband's ex-lover. It was chaos in the small quarters of the elevator.

"Keilah, no!" Neil yelled when he was finally able to pull her off Andria. "What is wrong with you?" he asked before checking to see if Andria was injured.

"How dare you attack my daughter?" T.K. Rockwell yelled as the elevator doors opened.

"Your daughter took my baby!" Keilah screamed at her former client.

They stepped off the elevator and into the lobby, causing a huge scene. Other officers started over in their direction, but Neil held his hand up to alert them that he had everything under control.

T.K. looked Keilah in the eyes and said, "That hasn't been proven. I'm sorry you and your family had to go through that unspeakable situation, but you can't go around attacking people, especially my daughter."

Keilah pointed her finger in his face and said, "Your daughter is psychotic, and I already know she's guilty, and as soon as the police get the rest of their evidence, everyone else will know too. When that happens, I'll be back and I won't be so nice."

Neil turned to Andria and asked her if she wanted to press charges against Keilah.

With her hand on her swollen jaw, Andria shook her head and whispered, "No."

Neil pushed Keilah toward the lobby doors and out into the parking lot. "What the hell were you thinking? I could be locking you up right now! Damn, Keilah! You can't do shit like that! If Andria is guilty, she'll pay, but if you don't watch yourself, you're going to be locked up before the case is solved!"

Keilah shook her head and said, "I should've snapped her damn neck."

He grabbed her arm and asked, "Are you listening to me?"

He opened the car door for her, and once she was behind the wheel, he said, "Go home to your daughter, and let these detectives do their job."

She looked Neil in the eyes and said, "I'm going home but—"

"No buts, Keilah. Stay out of this before you screw up the case. Understood?"

Keilah leaned out the window and kissed Neil on the cheek and then started her car. "Thanks for letting me come down here."

"Hell, after what you did, I regret it now," he answered. "Drive safely and go straight home, please?"

She smiled and said, "I will."

***

Back inside the precinct, Andria's attorney and her father were adamantly trying to get her to reconsider filing charges against Keilah for assaulting her, but due to circumstances unknown to them, she continued to refuse.

She made her way into the restroom, where she inspected her swollen face in the mirror. She pulled a paper towel from the dispenser and wiped the blood off the corner of her lip and whispered, "Touché, Keilah. Touché."

Instead of going home like she promised, Keilah detoured to the hospital to see Tori, who was doing much better and was scheduled to be discharged tomorrow. Convincing Kyle to go home to shower and rest was difficult, but he finally gave in and went home for some much-needed rest. Keilah updated her best friend on everything, including the loss of her child.

"I lost the baby, Tori," she announced.

"Oh no! When?" Tori asked as she hugged her best friend.

"The other day," Keilah revealed. "I really wanted this baby, Tori."

"Oh, honey, I know you did. I'm so sorry, but you'll have more children."

"I guess," Keilah answered solemnly. "Ramsey has been so sweet. He's trying to make me feel better, but there's nothing anyone can do to make me feel better about it."

Tori hugged Keilah tightly and said, "I know, sis. If there's anything I can do for you, just say the word."

Keilah wiped away her tears and said, "I should be telling you that. You're the one laid up with a broken leg."

"That's so sweet, but you need just as much care. You've been through two traumatic experiences. Don't put too much pressure on yourself right now."

"I appreciate that, Tori. I guess I'd better get back home to Neariah. After this, I don't like being away from her."

"It's understandable. Call me when you get home so I'll know you made it okay."

Keilah smiled and said, "I will. I'll see you tomorrow. Good night, Tori."

"Good night."

Keilah got home moments after Neariah woke up from her nap. She found her sitting in her grandmother's lap in the family room, but as soon as Neariah spotted her mother, she climbed out of Valeria's lap and made her way over to her.

"How long has she been up?"

Valeria stood and said, "Just a few minutes. How are you feeling? You look a little flushed. What happened down at the police station?"

Keilah picked up her daughter. Neariah laid her head against her mother's chest and started playing with her earring. "It was interesting."

"Interesting how?"

Keilah caressed her daughter's back lovingly and said, "They think Andria Rockwell might be involved."

Valeria picked up Neariah's toys and tossed them into her playpen. "You're kidding, right?"

"Nope, I'm not kidding, and when I saw her, I tried to rip her head off."

Valeria stopped picking up the toys and asked, "Are you serious?"

"As a heart attack," Keilah replied with a smirk on her face.

"Did the police arrest her?"

"Not yet," she answered. "They're waiting on some kind of test results to come in before they move forward."

At that moment she got a text message from Michael, who was checking on her well-being. She texted him back that she would call him in a second.

"Valeria, I'm going upstairs for a second to make a call. I'll be down shortly."

"Dinner's ready when you want to eat," Valeria answered as she made her way into the kitchen.

Upstairs, Keilah sat Neariah on the bed and dialed Michael's number.

"Hello?"

"Michael, it's Keilah."

It's so nice to hear from you. I was going to call you after everything settled down."

Keilah ran her hands through her hair and said, "Ramsey told me what you did to try and get Neariah back. I really appreciate your efforts."

"I wouldn't have done it any other way," he answered. "I saw the news report saying she had been found and was in good condition. Is she really okay?"

Keilah smiled and looked at her daughter, who was lying on the bed, playing with her feet. "Yeah, she's fine. We're so blessed. How are you? Ramsey told me you got stabbed."

"Cut was more like it. I'm healing nicely, though."

"That's great, Michael."

"Listen, Keilah, please tell Ramsey again how appreciative I am of the fact that he got his friend Kyle to help me with that situation. I killed a man, and while it was self-defense, I still could've been arrested for it."

"Ramsey wasn't going to let you go through that alone. Kyle is a good man, and he knows when the right thing needs to be done."

"Did Ramsey tell you about the other child?"

"Yes, he told me. Have they found out who she belongs to?"

He hesitated and said, "Yes. They found out that Kevin bought her from a prostitute who's now deceased."

"Wow, that's sad."

"It is, but unfortunately, it happens a lot. I asked the authorities to give me the first chance to adopt her. I could do it by myself, but I'm hoping my girlfriend accepts my marriage proposal. That would be the icing on the cake for me."

Keilah smiled and asked, "Girlfriend, huh?"

"Yes, girlfriend. Her name is Madeline, and she's wonderful, Keilah. I don't know what was wrong with me to be in that situation with Kevin."

"It's behind you now, right?" she asked.

He laughed and said, "Definitely! I settled my complaint against the lieutenant colonel at my academy that molested me. Life is so much better now, and I feel like for once I have a clear head and I'm truly in love."

"I'm happy for you, and I hope Madeline says yes to your proposal."

He chuckled and said, "Me too. I don't want to keep you, but I'm glad you called and that you're doing well and you have your daughter back home safe."

"I appreciate that. Let me know how everything turns out and if you get the baby."

"Will do," he answered before hanging up.

Keilah hung up the phone, sat on the bed, and then tickled her daughter. They were having so much fun together until Ramsey came in. She could tell by the look on his face that he wanted to yell at her, but seeing how happy Neariah was, he quickly changed his expression.

She glanced over at him and said, "I already know that Neil has filled you in on everything. You wouldn't have reacted any differently, so don't even go there with me."

He walked over to the bed and said, "All I was going to ask was if you're okay."

"I am now that I dented your girl's face," she replied.

Ramsey shook his head in disbelief and said, "I wish you had waited for me."

She threw a pillow at him and said, "And you should've told me about what happened in Richmond."

He caught the pillow and said, "You're right. I should have, but I didn't want to stress you out over her."

Keilah stared at her husband without responding.

He lay across the bed and said, "I'm sorry, babe."

Neariah yelled, "Daddy!" Then she crawled onto his back and bounce up and down like she was riding a horse.

"I'll admit Andria is overly dramatic, but we know it was a man who took Neariah."

Keilah said, "That don't mean she couldn't have had someone do it for her."

"True," he answered, seeing that Keilah was getting agitated. "Neil told me you swung pretty hard at her. You're lucky she didn't press charges."

"I don't want to talk about her anymore. If she had anything to do with Neariah's kidnapping, I'm going to do more than knock her on her ass."

"Not if I get to her first," he declared.

The couple smiled at each other for a second. Ramsey cupped her lovely face and kissed her. For some reason she had thought she had lost her edge. Today proved that her fierce nature was still very much intact, and even more so, since her emotions were fueled by the kidnapping of their daughter.

"How was the game?" she asked as she caressed his arm.

"It was great. The guys really enjoyed themselves."

She slid off the bed and asked, "Where are they now?"

"Everyone's downstairs, waiting on us to join them for dinner."

"Oh! Well, let's go. I'm starving."

He picked up Neariah, and they made their way downstairs to join the rest of the family for dinner.

Chapter Twenty-nine

Three weeks had passed, and the life Keilah and Ramsey knew before had changed for the better. After much thought, they decided that they would feel much better if some of the family was involved with their trusted management team in the running of their company, so they put the offer on the table for all their close family members to see who would be interested. As expected, Malachi jumped at the chance and so did Genesis. There was going to be a lot of preparation to take them through the transition from running a casino to running a personal security business, a totally different entity. The brothers didn't have to worry about a place to stay since the Stones' home would be available since they would be vacationing in Florida.

The couple held several video-conferences leading up to their departure. They said good-bye to their staff, friends, and extended families, and then packed for their open-ended trip to their Florida vacation home. As they put the last items in their suitcases, Neariah sat in her playpen, playing with a toy, while Target lay close by.

"Are you ready?" Ramsey asked as he zipped up the last of his suitcases to take downstairs.

Keilah walked out of closet, still dressed in her undergarments. "Yes, I'm ready," she joked.

He laughed and said, "You are pitiful and slow."

"I want to make sure I have everything. That's all."

Ramsey walked over to his wife and slowly traced the outline of her bra with his finger. She looked up into his eyes and said, "Careful, Stone. You know it's been a while for us.

If we're planning on hitting the road as scheduled, you had better back up."

"Seeing you half naked right now is torture."

She wrapped her arms around his neck and gave him a kiss and whispered, "Do you think you can wait until we get to the other house?"

"Didn't the doctor say we had to wait?" he asked.

She hugged him tightly and said, "It's been three weeks. We're good now."

"In that case, no, I can't," he replied as he kissed her warm neck.

"Too bad, because you're going to have to," she said as she released him and disappeared into the bathroom.

He looked over at his daughter and said, "Neariah, your mother is a comedian, but that's okay. She'll make it up to me when we get to Florida."

Neariah stood up and said, "Momma!"

He picked up her suitcases, headed for the door, and mumbled, "Yeah, Momma."

As Ramsey loaded the back of their truck, he was interrupted by a telephone call from one of the detectives in charge of the kidnapping case.

"Mr. Stone, I was calling to let you know that we're taking out an arrest warrant for Andria Rockwell. We got the DNA test results back, which verified that the diapers in the cottage where a credit card belonging to Miss Rockwell was found belonged to your daughter."

"So you're pretty sure she was involved?"

"It's circumstantial, but that's where the evidence is pointing."

"That may be the case, but it's obvious she wasn't the person on the video who attacked my wife and took my daughter. What about him?"

"We're hoping to try and use Miss Rockwell's arrest as leverage to get her to talk. It's our mission to find out who the man on the video is so we can make that arrest as well."

Ramsey gripped the phone and said, "Please keep us posted. I'm taking my family to Florida for a while."

"Enjoy your trip, and I'll contact you as soon as I have more information."

"Who was that?" Keilah asked as she appeared in the garage with the last of their luggage.

He tucked his cell phone in his pocket and said, "That was one of the detectives. They're getting ready to arrest Andria for being involved in the kidnapping."

"I knew it!" Keilah yelled. "That bitch is going to pay for putting her hands on my child!"

Ramsey pulled his wife into his arms and said, "We're not going to let this consume us, sweetheart. If Andria's guilty of this, she'll get what's coming to her one way or the other. We have our daughter back, and you're okay. That's all I care about. If you get locked up for doing something to Andria, I'll have to raise Neariah by myself, and that isn't the plan."

She stepped out of his embrace and said, "Then you'd better get me out of town with the quickness, because if I stay here much longer, I will go after her."

Andria sobbed as the detectives handcuffed her and read her, her rights.

"Daddy! Do something!" she screamed as they led her out to the police car. "I can't go to jail!"

With tears in his eyes, her father said, "I know, An-dria. I'll call the lawyer. We'll get you out as soon as we can."

"Daddy, I need to talk to Ramsey so I can tell him I didn't do this. Call him for me, please!"

"I'll try, sweetheart, but I don't know what good it'll do. I'm sure he's just as angry as his wife over this."

"Just try, Daddy, please!" she begged right before the police car pulled out of the driveway.

T.K. felt like he had been stabbed in the heart. His only daughter was in trouble, and he wasn't sure if he could help her this time. A time like this was when he needed his wife around, God rest her soul. Raising his daughter alone hadn't been easy. Andria was merely sixteen when her mother passed away, and he had cod-dled her from that moment on, which had turned her into a spoiled brat. She was right in the middle of her turbulent teenage years when her mother died, and the loss amplified Andria's delinquent behavior. She was extremely promiscuous and was constantly running up her credit cards. She had lived a privileged life and had taken advantage of it, almost feeling invincible. T.K. had bailed his daughter out of numerous situations, whether it was in school or on a job, and he knew she expected him to bail her out of this situation as well.

Maybe it was time for him to show his daughter some tough love, even though it was killing him to con-sider it. Something told him to try to help his daughter at least one more time. First, he needed to contact his lawyer and inform him of Keilah's arrest, and then he would reach out to Ramsey in hopes that he would have mercy on her. Lastly, he would try to get her into therapy so she could have a chance at a normal life.

***

Ramsey's phone rang again just as he was checking to make sure the hitch attached to the back of his truck was secure before hitting the road.

"Hello?"

"Ramsey, it's T.K. Rockwell—"

Ramsey cut him off, saying, "Mr. Rockwell, now is not a good time for me. What happened between Andria and my wife at the police station was unfortunate but warranted. If you ask me, she deserves everything that's happened to her."

"I know you're upset, and you have a right to be, but she's my daughter and at one point I thought you loved her," T.K. replied.

"Mr. Rockwell, I did care about Andria until she started acting erratically. She has a hard time accepting the word no, and she vandalized my car, not to mention that I'm aware she's a primary suspect in my daughter's kidnapping. Now, if you and Andria would do me a favor and leave me and my family alone, I would appreciate it."

"Too late," he replied. "She's already been arrested, and she's asking to see you."

Ramsey walked down their long driveway as he continued to talk to a man he honestly admired. At the end of the driveway he checked his mailbox and found a small brown package inside, as well as some other mail.

"T.K., I want you to listen to me and listen good. I understand how you feel about Andria. She's your daughter, and like most fathers, you do what you have to do to save her, just like I'm going to do what I have to do to save mine. If Andria's been arrested, I say it's about time. She took my daughter, goddamn it! What about that don't you understand?"

"That hasn't been proven yet," T.K. replied. "Please, Ramsey. I promised my daughter I would call you."

"And you have. Andria has some issues that I can't help her with. Now, if you don't mind, I'd appreciate it if you wouldn't call me again," he urged.

Don't you think you deserve to hear Andria's side of the story before you pass judgment on her?"

"I could care less what her side is. I'm sure everything will come out at her trial. Good-bye, T.K.," Ramsey said before hanging up the telephone.

"Are you ready to hit the road, babe?" Keilah asked as she brought Neariah out into the driveway with her favorite doll.

Ramsey leaned against the truck without answering.

"Babe? What's wrong? You don't look so good."

He handed his wife the mail and leaned down and picked up his daughter. "The police arrested Andria."

"Don't tell me you're surprised."

"I'm not. I'm pissed. T.K. just called me, trying to get me to go see her to hear her side of the story. He sounded like he doesn't believe she had anything to do with the kidnapping."

Keilah opened the back door to the truck and put Neariah's doll and the mail on the seat. "He's her father. What is he supposed to do? I hope you're not thinking about going."

"No," he answered as he handed Neariah over to his wife. "It's cold out here. Put Neariah in her car seat while I check the house one more time and set the alarm."

"Do you want me to go ahead and put Target in too?" she asked.

"No, I'll take him with me."

Keilah securely buckled Neariah in her seat and climbed in the front seat to wait for her husband. She couldn't wait to get to Florida to relax and visit with her sister-in-law and brother- in-law. Once they settled in, after a few weeks, she hoped that Kyle and Tori would come down for a visit. It would be a great for Tori in terms of rehab, and it would do Kyle some good to unwind as well. He hardly ever took a vacation, and this might be the perfect situation to make him take one.

"We're all set," Ramsey said as he opened the hatch so Target could climb inside the truck. Once Ramsey climbed in the driver's seat, he leaned over to his wife and gave her a firm kiss on the lips. "This is going to be great. I love you, woman."

She giggled and said, "I love you too, man."

He put the vehicle in drive and pulled down the driveway, out of their gate, and onto the road.

"Did you call the security company and let them know Malachi and Genesis were going to be living here for a while?" she asked as she checked her lipstick in the mirror.

"Yeah, I told them they should be here sometime between five and six this evening."

"Daddy!" Neariah called out to him.

He looked in the rearview mirror, and with a smile on his face, he answered, "Hey, baby. Daddy sees you back there."

Keilah glanced back at her daughter and then over at her husband and said, "You have her spoiled rotten."

"She's a daddy's girl, and I love every minute of it."

Keilah took a sip of coffee and said, "I can't wait until we get to Florida. We'll have to go grocery shopping as soon as we get there."

"That's already been taken care of," he revealed. "We have a caretaker for the property, and I sent a grocery list, as well as a list of other things we need to make that home feel like the one here."

She caressed his arm and said, "I see you have taken care of everything."

"You got that right. All we have to do is unpack."

"I love it when you take charge, Stone."

He chuckled and said, "You're a trip."

"We're spending the night in Charleston, right?" she asked.

"Yeah, it's the Palm Paradise Hotel on the coast so you can start enjoying the sound of the ocean. I sent the family our itinerary so they can keep track of us while we're traveling."

"Good. I'll check in with them from time to time so they won't blow up our phone."

Ramsey pulled out onto I-95 and headed south toward the coast. Four hours into the trip, he stopped so he could walk Target and Keilah could change Neariah's diaper. They also took this time to check in with family members and stretch their legs. After the brief stop they continued their journey, arriving in Isle of Palms, South Carolina, a little after dark. After quickly checking in and following the bellhop to the room th they were looking forward to a nice dinner and a warm bath. The view of the Atlantic Ocean from their hotel balcony was breathtaking, and it made Keilah long for the sandy beaches of Florida. She couldn't wait to get there.

After dinner in the hotel's restaurant the family returned to their room, where the couple unwound by playing with their daughter for a while before getting her ready for bed. While Keilah ran Neariah's bath, Ramsey put his jacket on and prepared to go downstairs get Neariah's playpen, which would act as her bed for the night.

Keilah laid Neariah's pajamas, lotion, and other baby items on the bed. She turned to her husband and asked, "Are you going to go ahead and walk Target while you're out?"

Target stood upon hearing his name and started wagging his tail. Ramsey patted him on the head and said, "No, I'll take him after I bring the playpen up."

"Okay. Make sure you have your key, because we'll be in the bathroom."

He kissed Neariah on her bare stomach, causing her to giggle. "Be back in a second, baby girl."

Neariah's eyes followed her dad across the room until he disappeared out the door.

Downstairs Ramsey opened the hatch and slid the baby's playpen from in between a couple of suitcases. He closed the hatch and made sure their belongings were securely locked. He returned to the room just as Keilah was bringing his wet daughter out of the bathroom.

"Daddy!" she called out to him.

He tickled her foot before setting up the playpen, padding it with blankets so his daughter would be as comfortable as possible.

Keilah laid the baby on the bed and started drying her off. Target started whining at the door.

"I don't think Target can wait any longer," Keilah observed.

Ramsey picked up his leash and said, "Come on, Target. Babe, do you need anything else while I'm out?"

She yawned and said, "Just you."

He chuckled and said, "You'll probably be asleep by the time I get back."

"No, I won't," she said as she removed a pile of mail from her purse, which she had no time to open at home and started going through it. "I'll wait until you get back before I take my shower. Hurry back."

He opened the door and said, "I will."

It was a cold night, and being on the water made it feel even colder. He hoped Target would take care of business quickly so he could get back to their warm room. They walked along the property line of the hotel and enjoyed the sound of the ocean waves. The air smelled so clean and felt so crisp. Once his loyal pet was finished doing his business, he continued to sniff around as if he was tracking. He allowed Target to sniff around a little more, until a big gust of cold ocean air blew in his face.

"Target, it's cold out here. Let's go."

Upon hearing his name, he dog started barking and jumping to try to get his owner to play.

"It's too cold out here to play," he said as he began to walk back toward the hotel. They returned to the truck so he could get Neariah's doll off the backseat.

Seconds later Target stood still and began to growl.

"What's wrong, boy?"

The hair on Target's neck was up, and he continued to growl and bark viciously.

Ramsey closed the door to the truck and looked around the parking lot to see what could have Target in defensive mode. He pulled his Glock handgun out of his pocket and unhooked Target's leash. The dog was trained to attack on command, and if there was someone lurking around the parked vehicles, he wanted to make sure Target wasn't restrained if the need arose. Ramsey peeped around the side of his truck; he didn't see anyone, but Target did, so he had to move with caution. He turned to check the other side of the vehicle, and that was when Target lunged at someone in the shadows. It was hard for Ramsey to make out who it was, and he didn't want to shoot his own dog. He saw a flash of light, and then he heard Target whimper and fall to the pavement.

"Target!" he yelled as he aimed his gun at the dark figure and fired causing him or her to fall to the ground. As Ramsey knelt down to check on Target, the figure on the ground rose out of nowhere. Ramsey was hit by the strong electrical charge of a Taser. Ramsey fought to get up on his feet, but the Taser was too much for him and he fell to the ground. The figure walked over to him and kicked the gun out of arm's reach and then leaned down into his face.

"Good shot, Stone, but I was expecting you to use deadly force."

Ramsey couldn't believe his eyes when he looked up into Trenton's eyes.

"You son of a bitch," Ramsey mumbled.

Trenton laughed. "It doesn't feel so good when someone blindsides you, huh?" He opened his jacket and showed Ramsey the bulletproof vest he was wearing.

Ramsey was paralyzed and knew that he was in extreme danger as Trenton rifled through his pockets and stole his hotel key. When he stood, he kicked Ramsey hard in the ribs and then said, "Now, this is what is going to happen. I'm going to take this doll up to your daughter, and once that fine-ass wife of yours puts the baby to bed, I'm going to make love to her whether she wants to or not. Oh, and speaking of your daughter, she's really sweet and was a good girl when we spent our little time together, even though she did cry a lot."

Ramsey's eyes widened upon hearing that revelation. He was sure Andria was behind the kidnapping. Now to find out Trenton was the kidnapper enraged him even more, but there was nothing he could do about it at the moment.

"Yeah, it was me. I had your daughter, and I set your old girl up for it," he said before laughing. "It doesn't look good for Andria, either. I heard on the news that she's been arrested, so it looks like she's going to be locked up for a while because of it too. That bougie bitch never liked me, and I didn't like her fake ass, either. She deserves to have her ass broke down a level or two. Jail is just what she needs. Besides, I had to let you know that you couldn't get away with jumping me." He picked up Ramsey's gun and aimed it at him.

"Too bad you're going to commit suicide tonight and make Keilah a widow. She's going to need consoling, and I'll be there for her, just like I used to be. After tonight you won't be jacking anybody else in the bathroom and that little girl of yours will be calling me Daddy for the rest of her life."

Ramsey fought with all his might to regain feeling in his body, but he was unsuccessful. Trenton placed his hand on the trigger, and the sound of the gunshot was deafening, causing Target to whine.

"You son of a bitch! Get away from my husband!" Keilah yelled as she pulled the trigger again, this time hitting Trenton in the head. He was dead before his body hit the pavement.

Keilah ran over to make sure the assailant was disabled, and when she looked down, she gasped when she saw that Trenton was the person who had been standing over her husband. She immediately dropped to the ground and tended to Ramsey, assuming that he had been shot.

"Baby, are you hit?" she asked as she caressed his face. She pulled out her cell and called 911 just as an employee at the hotel ran out after hearing the gunshots.

"Ma'am, are you injured?" he asked frantically.

"No, but my husband is, and so is my dog. Please, have someone check on my daughter. She's one year old, and she's upstairs sleeping in room four-twenty-four."

The employee called someone in the hotel on his two-way radio, alerted them to what was going on, and requested that they send someone to the Stones' room to check on their baby.

"Ramsey, paramedics are on the way. Stay with me, babe," Keilah said in a soothing voice as she checked his body for a bullet wound.

Another hotel employee came outside with blankets for Ramsey, his dog, and Trenton. He covered Ramsey with the blanket and asked the other hotel employee, "What happened?"

"I don't know. It looks like a possible robbery, but I'm not sure," he answered.

Seconds later, three police cars and a couple of medical vans pulled into the parking lot with lights and sirens blasting. The paramedics examined Trenton and determined that he was deceased, so they covered his body completely with the blanket. Keilah stood as the paramedics examined her husband.

She turned to one of the hotel employees and asked, "Did someone check on my baby?"

"Yes, our female desk clerk is with her now."

"Could you get her to wrap her in a blanket and bring her down? I'll also need my purse so I can go to the hospital with my husband."

"Don't worry. We'll take care of it."

A police officer approached Keilah, who was shivering in the elements, dressed only in sweatpants and a T-shirt. The officer asked her the usual questions, and then he began to ask her about the events that led up the shooting. She explained to the officer that Ramsey had gone out to walk their dog but hadn't returned. She had gotten an uneasy feeling and decided to come down to check on him and found the man, who she now realized was Trenton, standing over him with a gun. Had she been a moment longer, it would've been Ramsey's dead body lying on the cold pavement instead of Trenton's.

The coroner examined Trenton's body and relayed to the police that he had on a bulletproof vest and had a stun gun and a nine-millimeter in his jacket pocket.

"Ma'am, do you know this man?" the officer asked.

With tears in her eyes she admitted that Trenton was her ex-fiancé and that she'd had a couple of altercations with him in recent months. The paramedics put Ramsey on a stretcher, while one of the police officers put Target in the backseat of his car.

"Mrs. Stone, we're going to take your husband to the hospital to have him checked out. It appears that he was hit with the stun gun and not shot. He should be fine in a little while, but we want to make sure."

The hotel clerk brought a wide-eyed Neariah to her mother. She also brought Keilah her purse and her warm jacket.

"What about my dog?" she asked the police officer.

"It looks like he was hit with the stun gun too. I'm going to take him by the vet's office to make sure he's okay. What's his name?"

"His name is Target."

Before climbing into the back of the medical van, she walked over to the police car and stroked Target's thick fur to calm him.

"I'll be back to get you, boy. I have to go see about Daddy first."

The police officer closed the door to the police car and said, "I'll make sure he's taken care. Homicide detectives will go over to the hospital with you to further question you about everything that led up to tonight."

"Contact this detective in D.C. He can tell you everything," she said as she handed the detectives the business card belonging to one of the D.C. detectives before they all climbed in the back of the medical van.

Chapter Thirty

By the time the medical van carrying Ramsey arrived at the hospital, he had regained control of his body and mind. Keilah held his hand as the paramedic checked his vital signs.

"Mr. Stone, can you tell me what happened in the parking lot?" one of the detectives asked.

"It happened so fast. My dog started growling, so I knew he sensed somebody close, but I couldn't see anything. Target, my dog, is highly trained. He attacked the person, and that's when he was shot," Ramsey reported.

Keilah rubbed Ramsey's arm and said, "Target's going to be okay, babe. It was a stun gun, not a gun."

Ramsey closed his eyes, totally relieved that his loyal pet was not severely injured.

"Go on, Mr. Stone," the detective urged him as he jotted down the information.

Ramsey took a breath and said, "After my dog fell to the ground, I shot the attacker and he fell. When I leaned down to check on my dog, I guess that's when I got hit. I remember him telling me he had set up my ex-girlfriend for my daughter's kidnapping and he was the one who had taken her. After that, I remember staring down the barrel of the gun and not being able to do anything to defend myself. He said he was going to kill me and rape my wife. When I heard a gunshot, I thought I was dead."

The paramedics wheeled Ramsey into an examination room, where they told the doctor that Ramsey had been hit with a stun gun. As the doctor examined Ramsey, Keilah picked up the story of the attack.

"Babe, when you hadn't come back to the room, I got worried, so I put Neariah in the playpen and came looking for you. That's when I saw you on the ground and someone standing over you with a gun. I shot him, but he only stumbled backward. I saw him raise the gun again, and that's when I shot him in the head."

"Mrs. Stone, you said this was your ex-fiancé. Have you felt threatened by him before?" the detective asked.

"Not to this degree," she answered. "He has made recent sexual advances, but I never feared for my life or the lives of my family. We're headed to Florida. I had no idea he was following us."

The detective turned to the doctor and asked, "How is he?"

"He looks fine. His vitals are normal, his color is good, and his motor skills are on point. His mental state and memory seem to be accurate. I say he can be discharged, but I recommend that you rest for a day before continuing your trip to Florida."

Ramsey sat up on the side of the examination table and took Neariah in his arms. "I'm sure Charleston is a wonderful city, but I'm ready to get out of here, Doctor. My wife can drive while I rest."

The doctor nodded. "That will be okay."

Ramsey then turned to the detective and asked, "Will you need us here for anything else? I want to get my family out of here."

"I think we have everything we need for now," the detective replied. "My partner is in the process of contacting the detectives in D.C. Hopefully, they'll be able to tie up any loose ends so we can close our case. If we need you, I have your number and address to call upon you."

Ramsey stood and said, "Good. Can you give us a ride back to the vet so I can get my dog?"

The detective closed his notebook and said, "If the doctor said you can go, you can go. Sure, I'll give you a ride."

Back at the hotel Ramsey and Keilah were finally able to settle into bed. Neariah was asleep before she was placed into the playpen, and Target slept quietly at the foot of their bed.

He pulled his wife closer to him and said, "You do know you saved my life tonight."

She kissed his neck and said, "That's what I'm supposed to do. I can't believe that Trenton was the one who took Neariah. He must've gone off the deep end to do something so irrational, especially since he thought he could get away with killing you."

"I guess," Ramsey replied. "This gets Andria off the hook. She's lucky, because Trenton did a good job framing her. She could've ending up spending a long time in jail."

"I don't want to talk about it anymore. I want to get to Florida and relax and enjoy life."

"We'll get there, babe."

The couple fell asleep and set off for Clearwater the next day. Once they arrived at the house, they quickly unpacked and started enjoying the warm Florida climate. The first thing they did was take a family walk on the beach. The temperature was in the low seventies, but with the blue skies and sun beaming down on them, it felt much warmer. The couple loved watching Neariah, who was excited about the waves rolling in toward them as she rode on her dad's shoulders.

"This is paradise, babe," Keilah declared.

He put his arm around her shoulders and said, "I told you it was beautiful. I couldn't be happier right now."

She looked up into his eyes and asked, "How are you feeling? Any numbness left over?"

"I'm good. I don't ever want to get hit with a Taser again. That's a helpless feeling."

Keilah found the perfect spot and spread a blanket out on the warm sand and sat down. "You know I know how it feels. I think I was injured more from hitting the pavement than from the jolt itself."

Ramsey placed Neariah on the blanket, took a seat next to Keilah, and let out a breath. "Yeah, the baby was my concern after making sure you were okay."

She dug her toes in the cool sand in silence, reliving the pain of losing their child. "It stills hurts. You know?"

He caressed her knee and said, "I know, sweetheart, but we'll have more children."

"Listen, Ramsey, I have something to tell you that you need to know. It's about what happened in South Carolina."

"What is it?" he asked as he tickled Neariah's feet.

She hugged her knees and said, "Last night at the hotel, when you went out to walk Target, I was opening the mail. Inside one of the envelopes was a DVD. I put it in my laptop, and it was a sex video of you and Andria."

"What?" he asked, startled by her news.

"There was a note that said something like, 'No matter what you think of me, just remember that I can have him anytime I want to, just like I'm having him now.' I was shocked and pissed, and I wanted to ask you about it."

"Babe, I never made a tape with that woman!" he yelled, defending himself.

She nodded and said, "Yes, you did. You might not have known about it, but you did. Do you want to see it? I have it in my suitcase."

"Hell no, I don't want to see it."

Keilah looked over at her husband and asked, "Have you slept with Andria since we've been together?"

"No! And I can't believe you would think I have."

"I have to ask, especially since Neil said the cottage where her credit card was found was rented in your name."

He ran his hand over his head and said, "Keilah, don't let Andria's bullshit mess with your head. I stopped fooling with her when I started being intimate with you. You know neither Trenton nor Andria could accept us getting together, and as you see now, they will do anything to put a wedge between us. I love you and only you. I thought you knew that."

"I do, but I had to ask. It was hard watching you with your hands on that woman."

He pulled her into his arms and said, "That was a long time ago."

"It still hurt to see it."

Neariah picked up a seashell and handed it to her father.

"Thank you, Neariah."

She hugged his neck and gave him a big kiss. Keilah admired the loving exchange between father and daughter and was finally snapped back to reality.

"I'm sorry, Ramsey. These are the moments I live for. I should've never brought it up."

"No, I'm glad you did. There is no other woman for me, and I don't ever want you to question my love for you. Got it?" he said with a firm tone.

She smiled and said, "Got it." She paused. "I wish I had my camera on me."

Ramsey pulled his cell out of his pocket and said, "Here. Use my cell. I want a beach picture with my beautiful daughter, and then I want one with all three of us."

Keilah took a picture of the two most important people in her life, and then they took a picture of the three of them together before returning to the house for an early dinner. Once inside the house, she took the DVD in question and broke it into several pieces and tossed it in the trash.

In D.C. Andria was fuming that she had had to spend those horrible hours in jail with people she called uncivilized and ignorant. While in jail, she was accosted by a couple of women, who cornered her in the cell and basically felt her up. If her father hadn't got her out when he did, she probably would've been sexually assaulted, and for what? When she got home, she soaked in the tub for over an hour to get the stench off her body. She needed peace and serenity, and surrounding herself with scented candles and soft music while she relaxed in the tub always did the trick.

But this time instead of soothing her, the act of soaking in the tub brought out emotions that she had been holding in for a while. It was here that she broke down crying when she realized how close she had come to really going to jail because of Ramsey and how little he thought of her after they had shared such a strong intimate relationship. Maybe she did need some serious therapy to get over him, because she couldn't get him off her mind. A change of scenery was what she needed most, so maybe she should join Rico in Cabo

San Lucas and have some fun, she thought. It had been a while since she'd laughed or even felt like herself—all because she'd been obsessed over Ramsey Stone—and nothing brought that fact home more than when she got a text from Rico telling her to put her TV on CNN. Andria quickly reached for the remote and turned to CNN.

"Charleston, South Carolina, police have identified the body of the man killed at a coastal resort as that of Trenton Daniels, a university professor and a national bestselling author from the D.C. area, who has also been named as a suspect in the kidnapping of one-year-old Neariah Stone. Authorities said the shooting was the result of a domestic dispute and stalking a woman from a prior relationship. No charges have been filed against Keilah Stone, a wealthy D.C. businesswoman, since it was determined that the shooting was in self-defense."

Andria couldn't believe her ears as she sat up in the suds. She quickly dialed Rico's number and said, "Are you hearing this shit? What the hell?"

"Your nemesis bust a cap in that dude that set you up for that kidnapping," he said with a chuckle. "I would say it's poetic justice. She did you a favor."

"A man is dead, Rico. He was hurting over losing Keilah as much as I was hurting over Ramsey. People do stupid things when they're in pain."

"You can't be feeling sorry for him, Andy. He almost sent your prim and proper ass to the pen. You need to send her a thank-you card."

"The only thank-you card she's going to get from me is the one you mailed for me."

"What was in that envelope, anyway?" he asked.

"Oh, nothing much," she revealed with a giggle. "It was just a little video souvenir of me and her husband pleasuring each other."

"You're ignorant, Andy."

"I know, but that's what she gets. I had to bring her down a notch or two while she's walking around all high and mighty."

"Andy! Ramsey married the woman he wanted, and it wasn't you. Let it go!" he yelled. "Get your ass on a plane and come on down here to Cabo so you can party with me. I guarantee you'll forget about Ramsey as soon as you see this beautiful water and get a few drinks in you."

"Since it looks like the charges are going to be dropped against me, I guess I can get out of this city for a while. I'll see you as soon as I can get a flight out."

"Call me back with the details so I'll know when to meet you at the airport."

"Will do," Andria replied before climbing out of the tub.

Two days later, Andria met with her attorney and the district attorney to get the news that the kidnapping charges against her had been dismissed since Trenton had confessed to Neariah's kidnapping. She climbed into her car and headed back to her condo so she could get her suitcase and head for the airport for her flight to Cabo San Lucas. When she entered her condo, she walked into her bedroom to get a scarf out of the closet and the bedroom door slammed closed, startling her.

"What the hell are you doing here?" she yelled.

Ramsey walked over to her and grabbed her by the neck. He pushed her against the wall and held a gun to her head and said, "If you do one more thing to contact me or anyone in my family, especially my wife, I will make sure you don't see the light of another day. Do you understand me, Andria?"

Trembling she nodded in agreement.

He tightened his grip and said, "I could kill you right now and not give it a second thought, you selfish, spoiled bitch. You're going to forget we ever met, or I swear to God I will make sure you spend the next twenty years behind bars."

"Please don't," she whispered. "I can't go back to that place."

He pushed the gun harder against the side of her head and whispered, "Try me."

With tears streaming down her face, she repeated over and over that she was sorry.

Ramsey tightened his grip on her neck and said, "If you have any more DVDs with me and you in compromising positions, you'd better destroy them, because if any more come to light, I will kill you."

He released her, and she slid to the floor, trembling and crying hysterically. When she got the nerve to look up, he was gone. It was as if he was never there. She pulled herself off the floor and sat on the side of her bed to try and compose herself. She walked over to the mirror and inspected her neck. As expected, Ramsey's tight grip had left a dark bruise around her neck. Her head was tender where he had shoved the barrel of his gun against it as well. It was then that Andria realized how easily he could've killed her, and she also realized that she was trying to hold on to someone who didn't give a damn about her. She wiped the tears spilling out of her eyes and then pulled her cell phone out of her purse and confirmed her flight before gathering her belongings and walking out the door.

Several hours later, Ramsey returned home and found Keilah pulling Neariah around in the baby pool on a float in the shape of a frog. He quickly changed into his swim trunks and joined them in the pool.

"Da-dee!" Neariah yelled.

He slid down in the pool and gave both his ladies a kiss. "Sorry I'm late. I got held up longer than expected."

"I thought the trip to Atlanta was going to be a quick trip," Keilah said.

Ramsey couldn't tell his wife that after leaving Atlanta, he flew to D.C. and threatened his former lover with death if she ever contacted him or his family again. It was obvious that Andria wasn't going to allow them the luxury of peace, so he did what he needed to do to stop her, and if she didn't, he would made good on his promise of jail or death, whichever he felt was necessary. After the trauma of Neariah's kidnapping and losing the baby, he wanted his wife to relax and start enjoying their early retirement.

"It was going to be a quick trip, sweetheart, but the seller tried to convince me not to pull out of the deal. He started throwing all sorts of incentives at me. I stayed to hear him out but ultimately told him we were no longer interested," he lied as he pulled Neariah's frog float across the pool.

Neariah screamed and clapped as her father played in the water with her while Keilah snapped pictures and videos. Keilah climbed out of the pool, and Ramsey's eyes followed her over to her chair. He admired her luscious body in the lime-green bikini as she toweled off.

"You want something to drink?" she asked as she wrapped the towel around her hips.

"What I want is under that towel."

She giggled and said, "You can have it anytime you want, babe. Now, do you want a drink?"

"Yeah, you can bring me a club soda."

She walked over to their outdoor lounging area and pulled a couple of club sodas out of the refrigerator. She handed one to her husband, who continued to play with his daughter. Keilah took a sip of hers and knew this was the life she wanted with her husband. It had been a tough year personally, but it seemed like they could finally exhale and enjoy life.

Andria stepped off the plane in Cabo and gave Rico a hug. He could see that she was upset, so they went to the bar to have a few drinks before heading to the hotel. While there she told Rico about Ramsey's unexpected visit. It wasn't long before the sting of the ordeal had diminished and she started feeling more relaxed and liberated.

"*Now* are you done with him?" Rico asked.

She held up her glass and said, "Yes, I'm done."

"What about that dude your dad introduced you to? You should give him a chance."

Andria shook her head and said, "He's nice, but he's not my type."

Rico smiled and said, "Oh, I get it. You want a classy man with a little thug in him, huh?"

She held her drink up to him and, before draining it, said, "Okay? You know I need him to be a gentleman in the streets and a freak in the sheets. Now I'm ready to have some fun with my best friend. Let's get out of here so we can party."

"Now, that's what I want to hear from my homegirl," Rico stated as he took her suitcase and they exited the airport and made their way out to a waiting cab.

Epilogue

Two months later Kyle and Tori joined Ramsey and Keilah at their Florida home, along with Xenia, who by now was nearly four months pregnant, and her husband, Keith. All were in town to help celebrate Ramsey's birthday. Tori was off crutches, but when she walked, she had a slight limp, which was expected to diminish after a few more weeks of therapy. She and Kyle were planning a destination wedding in Jamaica with close family members and friends since they eloped, and everyone was looking forward to sharing in their joy. Kyle had taken family leave so he could care for his injured newlywed, and he was enjoying being out of Washington, D.C., for a while. It had been nearly two years since he had taken a real vacation, so he was enjoying becoming a beach bum with his best friend, Ramsey, and the rest of his family.

The Stones felt like they had finally arrived at their destination and couldn't be any happier than they were right now. They kept in touch with friends and family via webcam, which also came in handy when participating in meetings with their managers and brothers at their agency. The business was still flourishing, and they had received several lucrative offers to purchase their agency. The Stones were seriously considering selling, but they had to think about their loyal employees and what would happen to them if they did. They didn't want the reputation and name they had worked so hard to build to be mishandled in any way, so they were careful about which offers to take seriously.

After enjoying Ramsey's birthday celebration, Keilah received an e-mail from Michael saying that he and his fiancée had gotten married in a lavish ceremony in Washington a few weeks after they last spoke. He attached a wedding photograph to the e-mail and revealed that any day they would become parents to the orphaned child he wanted to adopt.

Andria and Rico were back in D.C., trying to get their lives on track after spending several weeks in Cabo San Lucas. She decided to invest in Rico's dream of being a business owner, so after he graduated from barber school, she became a co-owner with him of his very own barbershop. Andria was still trying to find herself and move forward. Even though she was lonely, she was sick of being defined by the men in her life, so she stepped out on faith and decided to open a designer boutique two doors down from Rico's barbershop, and both were an instant success. She seemed to have found a purpose providing quality items to shoppers who loved doing what she loved—shopping.

Three years would pass before Ramsey and Keilah would welcome the newest member to their family, and in keeping with the Chance family's tradition, they gave their son, who weighed in at nearly nine pounds, the biblical name Isaiah Christopher Stone. It was also the same year that Ramsey decided to do something he had wanted to do for a long time. He knew his hands would be full helping Keilah raise Neariah and Isaiah, but now was the perfect opportunity for him to mentor young people and coach high school football. Ramsey had been a star linebacker in high school and college, where he majored in criminal justice. Even though he could do it if he wanted to, he wasn't the kind of a person who lay around and did nothing all day.

Keilah was in love with being a mother and a wife. She was happy not to have to work long hours in risky situations. If she got bored, she would travel to visit family and friends, and if that wasn't enough, she planned to take art, flower arranging, and cake decorating classes, partaking in the simple joys of life. A slow pace of life was what they both wanted, and they were going to savor every minute enjoying their precious stones.

Notes

Notes

Notes

Notes

ORDER FORM
URBAN BOOKS, LLC
78 E. Industry Ct
Deer Park, NY 11729

Name: (please print): _____

Address: _____

City/State: _____

Zip: _____

QTY	TITLES	PRICE
	16 On The Block	$14.95
	A Girl From Flint	$14.95
	A Pimp's Life	$14.95
	Baltimore Chronicles	$14.95
	Baltimore Chronicles 2	$14.95
	Betrayal	$14.95
	Black Diamond	$14.95
	Black Diamond 2	$14.95
	Black Friday	$14.95
	Both Sides Of The Fence	$14.95
	Both Sides Of The Fence 2	$14.95
	California Connection	$14.95

Shipping and handling-add $3.50 for 1st book, then $1.75 for each additional book.
Please send a check payable to:
Urban Books, LLC
Please allow 4-6 weeks for delivery

ORDER FORM
URBAN BOOKS, LLC
78 E. Industry Ct
Deer Park, NY 11729

Name: (please print):_____

Address: _____

City/State: _____

Zip: _____

QTY	TITLES	PRICE
	California Connection 2	$14.95
	Cheesecake And Teardrops	$14.95
	Congratulations	$14.95
	Crazy In Love	$14.95
	Cyber Case	$14.95
	Denim Diaries	$14.95
	Diary Of A Mad First Lady	$14.95
	Diary Of A Stalker	$14.95
	Diary Of A Street Diva	$14.95
	Diary Of A Young Girl	$14.95
	Dirty Money	$14.95
	Dirty To The Grave	$14.95

Shipping and handling-add $3.50 for 1st book, then $1.75 for each additional book.
Please send a check payable to:
Urban Books, LLC
Please allow 4-6 weeks for delivery

ORDER FORM
URBAN BOOKS, LLC
78 E. Industry Ct
Deer Park, NY 11729

Name: (please print):_____

Address: _____

City/State: _____

Zip: _____

QTY	TITLES	PRICE
	Gunz And Roses	$14.95
	Happily Ever Now	$14.95
	Hell Has No Fury	$14.95
	Hush	$14.95
	If It Isn't love	$14.95
	Kiss Kiss Bang Bang	$14.95
	Last Breath	$14.95
	Little Black Girl Lost	$14.95
	Little Black Girl Lost 2	$14.95
	Little Black Girl Lost 3	$14.95
	Little Black Girl Lost 4	$14.95
	Little Black Girl Lost 5	$14.95

Shipping and handling-add $3.50 for 1st book, then $1.75 for each additional book.
Please send a check payable to:
Urban Books, LLC
Please allow 4-6 weeks for delivery

ORDER FORM
URBAN BOOKS, LLC
78 E. Industry Ct
Deer Park, NY 11729

Name: (please print):_____

Address: _____

City/State: _____

Zip: _____

QTY	TITLES	PRICE
	Loving Dasia	$14.95
	Material Girl	$14.95
	Moth To A Flame	$14.95
	Mr. High Maintenance	$14.95
	My Little Secret	$14.95
	Naughty	$14.95
	Naughty 2	$14.95
	Naughty 3	$14.95
	Queen Bee	$14.95
	Say It Ain't So	$14.95
	Snapped	$14.95
	Snow White	$14.95

Shipping and handling-add $3.50 for 1st book, then $1.75 for each additional book.
Please send a check payable to:
Urban Books, LLC
Please allow 4-6 weeks for delivery

ORDER FORM
URBAN BOOKS, LLC
78 E. Industry Ct
Deer Park, NY 11729

Name: (please print): _____

Address: _____

City/State: _____

Zip: _____

QTY	TITLES	PRICE
	Spoil Rotten	$14.95
	Supreme Clientele	$14.95
	The Cartel	$14.95
	The Cartel 2	$14.95
	The Cartel 3	$14.95
	The Dopefiend	$14.95
	The Dopeman Wife	$14.95
	The Prada Plan	$14.95
	The Prada Plan 2	$14.95
	Where There Is Smoke	$14.95
	Where There Is Smoke 2	$14.95

Shipping and handling-add $3.50 for 1st book, then $1.75 for each additional book.

Please send a check payable to:

Urban Books, LLC

Please allow 4-6 weeks for delivery

ORDER FORM
URBAN BOOKS, LLC
78 E. Industry Ct
Deer Park, NY 11729

Name: (please print): _____

Address: _____

City/State: _____

Zip: _____

QTY	TITLES	PRICE

Shipping and handling-add $3.50 for 1st book, then $1.75 for each additional book.
Please send a check payable to:
Urban Books, LLC
Please allow 4-6 weeks for delivery

ORDER FORM
URBAN BOOKS, LLC
78 E. Industry Ct
Deer Park, NY 11729

Name: (please print):_____

Address: _____

City/State: _____

Zip: _____

QTY	TITLES	PRICE

Shipping and handling-add $3.50 for 1st book, then $1.75 for each additional book.
Please send a check payable to:
Urban Books, LLC
Please allow 4-6 weeks for delivery